STILL CAN'T SEE NOTHIN' COMIN'

STILL CAN'T SEE NOTHIN' COMIN'

A NOVEL

DANIEL GREY MARSHALL

ReganBooks
An Imprint of HarperCollins*Publishers*

HarperCollins books may be purchased for educational, business, or sales promotional use. For information please write: Special Markets Department, HarperCollins Publishers Inc., 10 East 53rd Street, New York, NY 10022.

FIRST EDITION

Designed by Iva Hacker-Delany

Printed on acid-free paper

Library of Congress Cataloging-in-Publication Data
Marshall, Daniel Grey.
Still can't see nothin' comin' : a novel / Daniel Grey Marshall.
—1st ed.
p. cm.
ISBN 0-06-019862-1
1. Teenage boys—Fiction. I. Title.
PS3563.A72127 S75 2001
813'.6—dc21
00-045914

01 02 03 04 05 rrd/❖ 10 9 8 7 6 5 4 3 2 1

For my mother and father
and for Amma

ACKNOWLEDGMENTS

The author wishes to thank: Susan Grey, Del Marshall, Katia Marshall, Kenna Del Sol, and Tony Jarvis for their inexhaustible faith, love, and support; Alison Brooks at Barrett Books; Frank Weiman, Elise, and Bonnie at the Literary Group International; Judith Regan, Cal Morgan, Jeremie Ruby-Strauss, Jamilet Ortiz, and everyone at ReganBooks; Robert Getman for his invaluable donation of time, energy, and legal advice; Alex and Ivy Arce; Sandra Spannan; Mark Paradise; Steve Cassata; Jamie Sneider; Virva Hinnemo and George Negroponte; Stephen Spera and Sharon Johnston for their unwarranted patience, indulgence, and support; Andrew McCuaig, Julia Ziemer, and most especially Graham Lindsey and Christine Stoeffler for editorial advice; Jim Carroll and everyone else, too numerous to mention here, who read early drafts and offered encouragement; Julia Skloot, for being there; Jordan Caylor, for everything; and all those dear friends past and present who, for fear of accidental omission, will not be mentioned by name, but without whom this book, let alone the author, might not be here.

Tell it like it never really was, man,
and maybe we can see it like it is.

—Edward Leuders

AUGUST 1992

1

Leslie met me at the bus station yesterday. I was wearing these real dark glasses so most everybody just looked like shadows. Her I would have recognized in a second, even without that soft, distant voice of hers, saying my name like a far-off song.

"Jim." She looked at me then, sort of sizing me up. My face flushed a little: I was wearing these rags I picked up off some ghetto clothesline back in Jersey right before I went to the bus station. My previous outfit stunk like hell, and I didn't want everybody staring at me on the long ride home. "You okay?"

I smiled at that. "Somethin' like that, yeah."

She started cracking her knuckles as she spoke. "When I got the message that you called again I didn't know what to think but you said meet you at the bus station, so here I am." This she spit out so fast it took me a minute to figure out what the hell she said, a sure sign she was nervous, which I could already pretty much tell by looking into her pale blue eyes. Jesus, I had forgotten how beautiful she could be. Her hair was longer now, her bangs down to her nose, and darker. Sandy blond, sort of, not the almost white it had been when it was only half an inch long. "You sober?" she asked.

"Yeah." I nodded, and it was obvious she was immediately sorry she had said anything. I surprised her. Not as if it mattered. I wasn't keeping score.

I looked away then. West. The sun would be setting soon. I really wanted to watch the sun fall. I hadn't done that since I started heading back home.

"Where you been?" she asked me, almost hesitantly.

I didn't even know where I went so I couldn't exactly tell her. "I don't know."

Her lips pursed at my answer.

"The ocean," I offered, and hoped she didn't push me further.

She could tell she wasn't going to get much more out of me. "C'mon." She gestured. "Car's over here."

I kicked my shoes off, picking each up as it flew into the air and chucking them into the old army bag I always carried over my shoulder. That bag was probably the one thing I held on to the whole time I was on the run. My sister Mandy gave it to me when I was twelve, and I've kept it the last four years as if it was a security blanket or something. In some ways I feel like I'm still just a scared little kid, afraid of the dark and crying for his mother.

We didn't have to go very far. I was surprised because there were never any parking spaces this close to downtown. I guess she wasn't too much up to walking, 'cause her dark green Plymouth was parked in front of someone's driveway. Or maybe, considering the way she looked, she was just too freaked out to notice.

My breath caught in my throat. Sitting in the backseat of Leslie's rusty old car was my little brother Billy. Only six months older than the last time I'd seen him, he looked like he'd aged six years. No more preppy department-store clothes. He wore just a plain hooded sweatshirt and blue jeans. Leslie must have been giving him fashion lessons. But what really made him look so much older were his eyes. They were grayer now, like mine. They used to be baby blue. I had always been jealous. I wondered then if eyes can turn color out of grief, the way your hair can go white.

At the sight of me, he kind of half smiled and said softly, "Hey, Jimmy." I think he wanted to say more, but just sat there with his mouth open, not moving.

I smiled honestly. With all of our differences, he was my little brother and I loved him. We grew up together under the same roof; we both knew what it was to face my father's drunken raging, my mother's silent tears and helplessness. We both knew what it was to lose a sister. He was my brother, and I loved him.

The smile relaxed him quite a bit. As Leslie and I stepped into the car he blurted out, "Are you gonna go to jail if they catch you, Jimmy?" I could tell by the scared, anxious excitement in his voice that he was pleased to see me.

"Yeah, I'll go to jail. Juvie, at least. I did a lot of bad shit, Kid." I started calling him Billy the Kid when he was five or so. I think he figured he'd outgrown it by now, but it was my habit to call him that, and coming from me I don't think he minded too much.

"This kid in my class said they were gonna kill you." I could hear the question hanging in the air.

"The kids at school are full of shit, you know that," I said sharply. I was swearing too much. Billy's only eleven.

"I didn't say I believed him or anything. That's just what he told me. Anyways, you didn't have to yell at me like that." He was sniveling.

"Listen, Kid, I didn't—" I began to say, but bit my words

back. It wasn't his fault. "Hey, I'm really sorry." I looked back at him. "Cool?"

"Yeah, right, cool. Everything's cool, Jimmy."

He didn't sound so sure about that, but when I checked his face for any familiar signs of worry or fear or *anything*, there was nothing there. He wouldn't meet my eye.

Leslie was sitting behind the wheel, not saying a word, her face a mask of tension.

"Goddammit!!" I looked at them feverishly but neither said a word. I guess I would have been too scared to talk if I was one of them, but at the time I wasn't exactly thinking rationally. I didn't care that they were worried or scared. In that instant I only cared about me, my life, my world, and I wasn't planning on sparing them any rashly inflicted pain. "Here I sit, one, maybe two days left before I get locked up for God knows how long, and my little brother and my *ex*-lover—" I could see her flinch and jerk away from me. Jesus, why did I say that, what the hell's wrong with me, I'm losing it, I'm losing it. "Oh shit, I'm losing it," I gasped, and started to sob, head hung low, staring down at my hands. I could feel Leslie touch my left shoulder, Billy touch my right. Not looking up, but glad for their comforting hands, I continued in a near-whisper. "Talk, okay? Just talk to me, like I'm human, like we used to, you know?"

"Sure," Leslie spoke, and it was her voice I needed to hear most, even though I was sure I'd just broken her heart. "Where do you want to go?"

This was a question I was not prepared for. I guess I didn't really think about what the hell I was going to do once I actually got here. One day at a time, man, that's how I had to handle things when I was on the run. I didn't want to go home, that was one thing I knew for sure. I was quiet for a long time, my head completely empty of anything resembling a good idea. I knew I didn't have long. I wanted to make it count, you know?

Leslie and Billy just stayed quiet, I guess waiting for my answer. I think that they sensed what this meant to me, and wanted for me to make up my own mind.

Nothing. Dead air, dead thoughts.

Then, all of a sudden, bam, in this one millisecond, I knew exactly what I wanted to do. It was like a fuckin' lightning bolt right in the back of the head, man, and nobody could hear the thunder but me. "Let's go fishing!"

Silence. They looked at me like I was totally crazy, like that was about the looniest thing I could possibly have thought of, and I loved it. In some freaky, twisted way, I loved the brilliance, the goddam magnitude, the sheer beauty of this idea more than I had ever loved anything in my entire life.

2

It took a bit of convincing, but after a lot of mad jabbering from me and bewildered looks between the two of them—who I gathered had spent a lot of time together while I was gone—they agreed. We hatched a plan to get some fishing poles then, all of us playful and childish as hell, buzzing on the foolishness of our evening's plans, my last free night in what I figured was to be a real long time.

I loved this. It was one of my favorite things, getting all overexcited and out of breath, cooking up crazy plans and acting on them. And I'm not sure why, but this seemed to be the perfect way to spend this time. You know, quiet, mellow, bare feet in the dark green lake water, laughing, talking, just hanging, just being. Lately sometimes just the very real fact of my existence—breathing, talking, writing—seems like a blessing. It's like I think I'm supposed to be dead, you know; most everybody I knew is, dead or missing or on the street still, drowning in their own puke, and isn't that really the same thing when you come right down to it, except me, I'm here, alive, breathing, coherent. I don't know, man, maybe I'm just lucky.

Here was our plan:

We would drive back to my house, 'cause I knew there were a bunch of old poles rusting in the corner of our cluttered garage. That used to be Mandy's favorite place to hang out. All by herself, just going through all the junk and categorizing it in boxes and everything. Place reminded me of a goddam flea market. She loved it, though, just sitting in there for hours at a time, with no sounds but her own hands, sifting through all that junk. I still carry a book in my bag that she found in a box of heirlooms my mom got when her parents died. It was old as hell, like from the late 1800s, and it had all kinds of typos through the whole thing. It looked like somebody just typed it up, like that was the one copy in the whole world. Jesus, she freaked over that book. She showed it to me; she'd gone and underlined all kinds of meaningful passages in it, all kinds of crazy shit that didn't make any sense to me at the time. I remember one thing vividly, though, like I could see it in front of me today. It was a passage Mandy had underlined about a million times, just one paragraph. It went like this: "That bastard beat me till I was black and blue, and then screwed me against my will, more times than I can recall. And so I strangled him in his sleep, and I don't feel no remorse about it neither."

I asked Mom about the book, without mentioning the part I had seen, and she said it was probably my great-great-grandmother's journal. I guess old Frances always wanted it to be published, but it never was. She took it to a publisher but they turned her away; she was a woman, after all, and just a homely old widow at that. I think Mandy was pretty sure she was the greatest woman that ever lived. Even back then, when I first saw it, that book gave me goose bumps. I took it with me when I left, and I'll probably never let it go.

So I knew we had those poles in the garage, and it was only a matter of getting to them. When we got to my house, I planned on ducking down so my mom wouldn't catch sight of me. Then Billy would go in and snag the poles and a sandwich for me, telling her that he was going fishing with a couple of his buddies. I hoped that would suffice. Before Mandy offed herself it would have worked for sure, but after that and what happened to the rest of our family, I was surprised Mom even let him out of the house. At least with Dad gone, being under house arrest probably wasn't so bad. At least it wasn't a nightmare.

Actually, I didn't even know where my dad was, and I didn't feel like asking Billy. If he was anything like I was, he'd want to avoid talking about it as much as he could, and I'd be the last one to force the topic.

It wasn't too long a ride. Not for me, anyway. I just kind of zoned out and watched the old residentials and thrift stores drifting by. I was thinking of a time one winter when Mandy had me wait outside of some joke convenience store while she went inside and stole us some hot chocolate and marshmallows. She had the most riveting, innocent Irish green eyes I'd ever seen. It was really crazy, how much she could get away with, having those eyes. Her smile, too. She could get you to do anything with that smile. A lot of people thought she was extremely selfish, you know, got what she wanted, when she wanted it. The second part is true. The funny thing is, she never tried to be selfish. She would just ask for something, anything, and people would give it to her. You should have seen her spare-change sometime. She'd come back with like twenty bucks in no time at all. That time with the convenience store was no different. She popped out of the store real casual, you know, but the next thing I knew she had opened up a bag of marshmallows, the jumbo kind, and started chowing down. Somehow on the way home we ended up in this crazy, two-person snowball fight, pretending the snowballs were grenades and dying hundreds of overdramatic, exaggerated deaths by the time we finally reached home, sweating buckets in two feet of snow. And when we got inside, smothered in this gigantic army blanket sitting in front of a warm fireplace, I drank the best cup of hot chocolate I have ever had, to this day.

"Hey, Jim." Billy snapped his fingers so close to my face I could have bitten his nails. "Duck down. You live here." I looked up to find, sure enough, my old residence staring me bang in the face. I couldn't believe I was really there. After being away so long, it didn't seem real. More like one of those pictures out of *National Geographic*. Portrait of a War Zone. I just kind of sat there and stared vacantly; Billy literally had to push my head down to get me out of view. "Jeez—space cadet," he muttered, getting out of the car. A moment later I heard the front door open and shut. With my head down I couldn't tell who met him at the door, if anyone.

"Are you okay, Jim? You were in a trance the whole way over." Leslie looked down at me. I should talk to her, I knew that. But say what?

She answered the question in my head. "I still love you, Jim. I always have." This was not exactly the easiest thing in the world for her to say. Unfortunately, I couldn't make it any easier on her.

So I said the only thing I could say. "I know."

She was quiet for a minute, knowing I wouldn't return her declaration but waiting anyway, because that's what most anybody would do. Eventually I heard her swallow hard, preparing to hit back. She didn't necessarily *like* to, but she always hit back. "So if you don't love me anymore, how come I'm here? Why did you call me? You left me, remember? Why did I . . . are you still in love with me? Are you?"

I couldn't think of anything to say that I knew I wouldn't regret later, so I just kept my mouth shut.

"Answer me, goddam you Jim!" She was angry now. Too angry for me to deal with.

"I can't," was all I managed to say, and even that in a hoarse whisper.

The look she gave me was awful. My face burned, like her eyes were spitting poison. "You have a lot of nerve using me like this, after all we've been through." She looked away, into the house. "But then you always did need a crutch, didn't you?" She knew just where to hit me, and she was hitting hard. "You can't even look into my face and tell me that you need me."

I didn't think this before I said it. My lips moved, and I heard my voice, steeped in pain and frustration. "Stop! I do need you, you bitch! I called you because I care about you! You make me bleed, Leslie. You gut me. You want a confession? You stab me, you get to see my guts. I love you. Okay? Does that make you happy? Are you happy now that you're all the way inside me? I love you. I'm saying that here, now, and I know I haven't said it in a real long time. I left you 'cause I love you. I didn't want to—I *couldn't* drag you down with me. Can't you see that, Leslie? I mean, did you really want to come? Did you want this?" I looked up at her then, having said all this to the glove compartment, and turned my forearms up toward her eyes, showing her the scars like stripes up and down them. She was bawling now, real hard. Looking at her like that made me want to hold her again, and touch her face like I used to, wipe away her tears. When I spoke again I had quit yelling. "Look, I'm sorry I never explained things to you. I'm sorry I never said good-bye. Coulda saved both of us a lot of trouble. I love you, Leslie. I never ever meant to hurt you. And I love that you made me hurt enough to say all this."

I took her hand and squeezed it. She smiled a little through her tears. I was shaking. I'd torn down the last wall between us, but I knew that tomorrow there would be another, more solid one in its place. I just kept on looking at her, not even blinking, and for a while she would meet my gaze, and then look away nervously. I never took my eyes off her. I didn't have much time with her; I didn't want to waste it looking at houses and shit. There wasn't anything else in the world I felt like looking at right then.

She cracked up. "You're crazy, Jim, you know that? Absolutely certifiable." Her laughing turned into coughing, and when that was over she went quiet for a while. When she did talk again it was in a whisper. "You're crazy and I love you."

I had the feeling my body wasn't gonna quit shaking for years.

3

I heard the sound of a door opening and shutting again, and the high-pitched scraping of the fishing poles against the screen door, sending uncomfortable shivers down my spine. Billy opened the back door, sticking the three battered old poles in behind Leslie and then squeezing in to sit behind me. "C'mon, let's go before Mom changes her mind and finds a chore for me to do." He clapped his hands together in excitement. Leslie was already starting the engine.

As soon as we had rounded the corner Billy let me know the coast was clear, and I sat up, stretching my cramped muscles and rolling down the window to stick my head out. The breeze going past was very refreshing, and I took in a couple of gigantic breaths before pulling my head back inside. "Woohoo!" I yelled at some old people walking their dog, paused at this stoplight that always seemed to take forever. I saw them shake their heads, but I didn't want to leave them on a bad note so I felt the need to explain myself. Don't ask me why I gave a shit. "Don't you understand, old people? I'm free! You're walking your dog and I'm having the time of my life." I saw them shake their heads again, lips pursed. The light changed while I was yelling, and Leslie took off at about a million miles per hour. I ducked back inside to avoid having my head blown off by the wind.

Billy leaned his head forward. The wind was blowing so hard you could barely hear yourself talk. "What's with you?"

I looked over at him. "Didn't you hear what I said?" I asked. "This is beautiful!"

His face kinda twisted up and he twirled his index finger around while pointing at his head, indicating I was cuckoo.

I nodded in agreement and caught Leslie's eye.

"What's up?" she asked me loudly.

"Where the hell are we going?"

She nodded *yes*.

"Are you fucking with my head?" I asked, confused.

She nodded again, keeping her eyes on the road. I could see her lips twist up into a half smile, but it was obvious to me that she was trying her hardest not to.

"Is it a secret?" I asked, catching on.

She nodded again, and I figured that was all I was gonna get out of her, so I settled back and joined my brother in watching the scenery, which consisted of city streets, then fields and forests. The leaves were just starting to turn color. I watched the sun go down below the horizon, flooded with memories and wishes. When it got dark Leslie switched on her brights and I watched the front of the car eating up the now dashed, now solid yellow line in the middle of the road. At one point we practically skidded off the road to avoid a deer that was standing in our path, transfixed by the Plymouth's headlights. I think it eventually got the picture when we nearly crashed into it and it took off running into the woods.

Right then Leslie took a hard left into this monster of a forest we were passing, and I stayed quiet, in considerable awe of my surroundings.

I don't know if the trees were maple or oak or what—I'm not so good at distinguishing kinds of trees—but they were amazing. They must have been six feet around, easy, with roots like thick toes intertwining with each other, dancing together as they plunged into the earth. They were gigantically tall, too, real all-natural skyscrapers. I got to thinking then that nature really knows what's going on, you know? I mean these trees were so old, so wise, looking down on us humans, scampering around the world with such puny lifetimes, destroying everything in our path. Everything that the rocks and the trees and the birds had worked for millions of years to preserve, and we come along and destroy nearly everything in only a hundred years. I wondered about life expectancy, about how long these trees had, before somebody'd decide this'd be a great place for a roadside strip mall. I even felt a kind of kinship with the trees. I knew what it was to be towering and fragile at the same time. I knew danger, and time running out. Me and the forest both.

We rolled and bumped around down this old dirt path for a while, me struck dumb with the sights around me, Leslie focused on navigating the Plymouth along our tricky route, and Billy snoring quietly in the back, as he had been pretty much since we left the city and hit the monotonous fields. I didn't blame him. This had been one long motherfucking day, as far as I was concerned.

Eventually the big car rolled to a halt at an opening to a clearing in the woods. I stepped out of the car and stretched, my arms reaching toward the heavens. Looking up, I saw the trees meeting over our heads, protecting us from the outside world. Even if a plane had flown by, we wouldn't have been able to see it.

You're supposed to be scared in dark lonely forests like this, but I don't think I'd ever in my life felt so safe as I did under the branches of those ancient trees, breathing the cool night air.

Leslie killed the engine and got out, coming to stand next to me. When she was close to me I got that feeling—you know, that feeling right where they say your heart is, pain and longing and hope and desire all rolled up and stuck behind your rib cage, and wouldn't you know it'd be in a place you couldn't reach to scratch it. She was close, too, so close I could hear her breath come and go in a rhythm to match mine.

"Where the heck *are* we?" Billy mumbled, rubbing his eyes, trying to coax some life into them. Leslie smiled her playful, knowing smile. "C'mon, boys. Follow me."

She started walking across the clearing, her feet crunching over sticks and leaves. I looked at Billy; he knew about as much about this place as I did. We grabbed the fishing poles Billy had leaned up against the car and followed.

We walked down this path quite a ways. Every step there was something in my face or scraping against my bare arms, and the going was slow, especially with the fishing poles catching on branches every couple feet. My brother's asthmatic wheezing inspired me at one point to turn and ask him if he was planning on having a kid sometime soon. Leslie was always just ahead, barely in sight, never waiting up but never losing us either. I don't think she got a scratch on her the whole way.

Pretty soon I could hear running water up ahead, and our path opened up on a stream running through the forest, about ten feet across and maybe four, five feet deep. There were several rotted old tree stumps right on the bank that looked like perfect places to sit and fish. This was exactly what I wanted. Leslie had already been standing there a minute or two when we emerged from the brambles. I came up behind her, putting my arm around her waist, my other on Billy's shoulder. A little moonlight was pushing its way through the branches here, shining across the water and spilling out over us, just enough to see by and no more. I was breathless in this place, but I managed to whisper a soft, strained "thank you" in Leslie's ear. It didn't seem like enough, but she must have felt the tremble in my body and the tearstained love in my voice. She must have known that gratitude I still can't put into words without sounding shallow and empty.

Then Billy sighed loudly and said, "You guys, we forgot the bait."

I knew he was upset, but I broke out with an uncontrollable giggle. Soon I'd crescendoed into this huge bout of laughter that probably scared the piss out of rabbits and squirrels for miles. Oh boy, was I rolling. It was my first laugh, I mean real, gut-bursting guffaw, in as long as I could remember.

When I finally caught my breath Leslie helped me up, brushing some of the dirt off my back. She just looked at me, smiling at my childishness. "Well, shit," I said, coughing and looking over at Billy. He was pretty frustrated, I could tell, sitting on one of the old stumps with his feet dangling in the murky water, arms crossed, chin resting on his chest. "C'mon, cheer up, Kid," I said, walking over and plunking down next to him. "It ain't all bad. Check this place out, man. It's amazing. Really fucking amazing. Hey, listen." There was an owl hooting nearby, practically right in our eardrums.

I saw a flicker of interest spread across Billy's face. "Wonder what kind of owl that was," he said quietly, with a hint of enthusiasm. "Probably a fucking great horned, I bet."

"Hey, watch that mouth, Kid," I reprimanded him, more out of reflex than real concern.

"It's magic, isn't it?" Leslie mused, more to herself than anything else. "It's really magic here. You can feel it."

"Yeah."

She looked at me then, with genuine sadness if I've ever seen such a thing. "Your sister would have loved this place, you guys. At least as much as the three of us, probably more. She would have run around in her bare feet, jumping in the stream no matter how dirty it was. Whenever I come here I think of her. Of how much she'd love this place. It reminds me of her, every time."

Talk like that about Mandy hit me like a fucking brick, right in the face. My knees gave out entirely. The sounds of the forest were gone. Anything outside my own body was out of range. Over and over, those words swam through my mind. The silence outside my head was broken only by the squeaks and cries of Billy's muffled sobbing. Leslie broke out crying then too, and the three of us, the three of us who were incapable of feeling what my dead sister could feel, the way my dead sister could love something, sank together, clinging to each other like there was no tomorrow, each of us desperately trying to hold on to the fragments of sanity we still had. And Leslie's words relentlessly tormented my mind, my heart, even my soul, if there is such a thing.

FEBRUARY 1991

4

"C'mon, Jim, jump on!"

I looked down, way the hell down.

"I dunno, Mandy, this is one big hill. You know, maybe they call this Suicide Hill for a reason. I mean, maybe we could kind of look around for, like, a little hill."

Mandy was pestering me to join her in attempting to brave the terrors of Suicide Hill, the hill that everybody talked about but nobody would even think of daring to sled down.

"C'mon, Jim, this is history in the making. We'll be heroes!"

I was unconvinced. "It's straight down, sis. Ninety degrees. Hell, why use a sled at all? We could just fall, save a perfectly good piece of colored plastic."

Mandy rolled her eyes. "Oh, man, the sled won't break—"

"*We* might," I protested.

"Just think, Jimmy." She was giving me her puppy-dog eyes now, knowing what a sucker I was for that look. Almost everyone was. "Every time someone comes here from now on, they'll think, 'Remember the Great Amanda and James Drake Duo? The first—'"

That was enough sap for me. "The first idiots to die while sledding. I can see the headline: 'Stupid Brother and Sister Die on Sled. Must Run in Family.' Maybe we'll even get a plaque. They'll put it right between our graves at the bottom of the hill."

She stood up, and I could tell by the smile fighting its way onto her face (although obviously she was trying to hide it) that she was up to something funny. But I had always been kind of weak, and Mandy the total opposite, so that by the time I realized what she was planning it was way too late—there was no escape.

"Hold on to your hat." She laughed, wrestling me into the front of the sled and sliding in behind me. Then, still in the same graceful, fluid motion, she kicked off, and my mouth opened in an eardrum-shattering scream.

We weren't sledding. We were flying. Maybe plummeting is the better word, come to think of it. I had never moved that fast in my entire life. Snow and ice flew into my face. I guess that was why Mandy sat in back; I had involuntarily signed up to be her human face mask.

I can't even begin to really describe the feeling of flying through the air that day, with my still-living, breathing sister clutching my sides. Not and really do justice to it. Looking back on it, I realize it can't have been more than ten seconds down that hill. But at the time, that ride defined infinity. It was the craziest rush, shooting through the icy debris like a snow-pants-and-plastic bullet, one set of speeding siblings with absolutely no control over their immediate future.

Suddenly—so suddenly I didn't even have time to scream in terror—we launched ourselves off a well-camouflaged bump, flying a good fifteen feet before landing hard and dumping over on our trembling sides: mine with post-traumatic shock, Mandy's with wild, insane laughter.

"Jim! Jim, that was fucking fantastic! I mean, seriously," she said, rolling over and getting right up in my face (something Mandy tended to do, having no real personal space of her own), "have you ever, ever felt like that before? Oh man," she said, looking to the sky as if in reverence. "We did it. We fucking took Suicide on a sled. A motherfucking sled!" She jumped up, beating her chest like an ape, and howled at the top of her lungs, "We did it! Hey world! Jim and Mandy Drake aren't afraid of anything! We're invincible!" She collapsed down next to me again, out of breath and out of her mind. Her maroon-dyed bangs fell down in front of her eyes. She brushed them back and held them there as she looked at me. And maybe I'm only imagining it, but I remember it as if she were setting aside this moment, holding it high above the rest. "Me and you, Jim," she declared magnificently. "Me and you."

Maybe I'm the one that preserved it. Later, in the weeks, months, years after she died, I would remember this moment more than any other we shared together. It was happiness, and innocence, and warmth. It was the one I could never forget, the one that still haunts me, permanently latched onto my heart.

It was the day I met Leslie.

"Hey, let's go," Mandy said, taking her hand away from her own head and touching mine. Moving. Sealing the moment. She scrambled to her feet again, then helped me up gently. She was always gentle with me. Even when she'd forced me into the sled at the top of the hill, she had done it in her own soft way. I loved that. It just made me feel cared for, you know? Like I had a protector. Someone that really, really loved me. And she did, too. In an almost fierce way, I thought sometimes.

I think that if she had lived, she wouldn't have let any of the crazy, terrible shit happen to me that did. Truth was, she always had one eye looking after me, wherever she was and whatever she was doing.

5

Our sled had a rope rigged up to it, and I knotted the free end around my wrist so I could drag it easily on the short walk home. Suicide Hill was only a few blocks from my house, just a couple of newly paved, upper-middle-class roads.

"This, Jim," Mandy broke out suddenly, in the funny way she had of announcing some earth-shaking revelation, "is White Bread Land. Really. I mean, do you think any of these people know what it's like not to take everything for granted? No, they don't, and neither do we. We're supposed to feel lucky, I guess. This is suburbia. Civilization at its finest. All the houses built the same exact way, color-coded and shit . . . no variety, no imagination. This is a neighborhood of clones, of normal people that are just like everyone else in all the other stupid suburbs. It makes me sick."

I just nodded silently. I mostly didn't reply when Mandy got started like this. It usually got me to thinking, too, and I was too busy mulling over what she'd been saying to contribute to it.

"We're missing so much by growing up here." She'd been walking slowly, her eyes watching her feet and the ground underneath them, which was the way she thought best. But then she looked up at me, one of her famous smiles inching its way across her face. I brightened at this,'cause there was nothing I liked better than seeing my sister happy. That was getting rarer and rarer.

"Hey, Jim," she said, "I got somebody I want you to meet."

She took off running then, in the opposite direction. Left standing there in the middle of the desolate, snow-covered road, watching my sister cruising off to God knew where, all I could think of to do was follow her. This wasn't exactly easy, trying to keep up with her in my snow pants, with a sled trailing behind me and getting caught on nearly every car on the street, as Mandy barreled at warp speed toward the closest bus stop. Eventually I caught up with her, sprawled out on the sidewalk next to a bus shelter on Sherman Avenue with all the windows broken out of it, looking up at the cloudy sky and making a halfhearted attempt at catching her breath. I collapsed down next to her, sitting on the curb with my feet sticking out into the street, even though I knew there was a lot of traffic this time of day. I did careless things like that pretty often. Mandy always jibed at me for being absentminded. Me, I think most of the time I just didn't give enough of a damn to watch out for myself.

"Where the *fuck* are we going? It better be worth getting our asses kicked. You know we're gonna be in deep shit if we miss dinner." I managed to choke all this out between coughs; I had asthma pretty bad back then, and it really got me when I ran long distances like that. Plus like a genius I never remembered to carry around an inhaler.

"Don't worry about it, it's close by," Mandy assured me, patting me on the back through my thick red coat. "This really amazing chick. You just have to come see her. It's very important, she's really dying to meet you."

"Dying to meet *me*? How the hell does she even know who I am?"

"Oh yeah, I told her all about you." If Mandy was anybody else, I probably would have been really annoyed about something like that, somebody going off and telling someone else all about me. But with Mandy, there was nothing I could really do but laugh. Being around her all the time, either you learned to take things in stride or you went nuts.

Besides, if you ask me, shit like suspense and not knowing are about the worst things on the planet. So I sat there on the curb, shoulders hunched over and my coat zipped up all the way over my mouth—anything to keep out the cold—and waited, the whole time tasting my zipper.

By the time I finally heard the roar of the bus engine off in the distance, I was about frozen to death. My nose felt like it was about ready to shrivel up and fall off, and I thought my toes had checked out of the existence hotel. Mandy was doing a pretty good impression of an icicle, and I think even she would have been starting to have second thoughts if she hadn't been so hyped up about seeing this fantastic person. I was beginning to think this girl was some kind of a saint or something.

Funny—that turned out to be pretty close to the truth, in a twisted sort of way.

I sat right next to a heating vent on the bus and got thawed out in no time. Even a bus can be cozy if you've been out in the cold long enough. Mandy cuddled up next to me and we settled in for the ride. I didn't know how far we were going but I didn't bother to ask. I was pretty wrapped up in being warm.

Mandy sang while we rode. My sister was always singing. With anyone else that would probably get on my nerves, but I swear she had the most beautiful singing voice in the world. It was like it was from another world, smooth and feminine and strong and soothing. I was always telling her she could be famous. We used to joke about her being a star singer, only in our fantasy it was the 1920s, and we would picture her performing in these classy lounges filled with gangsters, dressed in a pearl white velvet dress. Mandy in a dress was the real joke, though. I'd never seen her wear anything but blue jeans. She said she never felt right wearing a dress. I think maybe she was afraid she wouldn't look so hot in one. This was also a laugh in my opinion though, as my sister was very pretty, actually. Not that I'm bragging like our whole family is models or anything. I mean, I've always thought I was also a little on the pretty side, as opposed to being handsome or manly in any way. It sounds corny, but I always wished I was more of a tough-guy type. Any time my hair was the least bit long, people were always calling me miss, stuff like that. It got to be a little embarrassing, which is why I usually cut my hair pretty short. Anyway, what I am trying to tell you is my sister really was a fabulous singer.

6

I guess I must have nodded off, exhausted and warm and close to Mandy and her songs,'cause the next thing I knew she was elbowing me gently in my gut, trying to roust me and telling me we had to get off at the next block. Rubbing my eyes, I looked out the tinted window, trying to guess where we'd ended up.

"We're over on Mary Street," Mandy told me, pulling the cord to let the bus driver know this was our stop.

"Okay," I acknowledged, still a bit sleepy as Mandy helped me up and we stepped off the bus. I neglected to obey the WATCH YOUR STEP sign above me and almost ended up face first in the gray slush blanketing the road. We hit the sidewalk and went right, the bus speeding noisily off into the distance behind us.

"It's that building, fourth from the corner across the street," Mandy gestured. "Wait till you see the apartment she lives in. I love it."

"An apartment?" All my friends lived in the two- or three-story houses that were typical of my neighborhood.

"Yeah, the one with the tower on the corner like it's a castle," she said, skipping ahead quickly and spinning around, beckoning for me to hurry up.

Mandy ran across the street in no time, splashing carelessly through the slush. I stayed a ways behind her to avoid getting sprayed. "C'mon, slowpoke," she said, taking my hand and galloping forward.

Standing on the porch of the building, it was less impressive than from a shadowy distance. The paint was peeling everywhere, and one of the steps was rotted all the way through in places. The mailboxes were also in pretty sad condition, two of the three hanging cockeyed from a single nail. Mandy pulled the windowless front door open; it looked like it had been ripped off most of its hinges, and after you passed through the doorway you had to just pick it up and put it back in place.

"Jeez," I whispered. "This is one sorry castle."

Mandy looked back at me somberly. "All the houses around here are like this. The city doesn't care enough to fix them up, and the people that live here can't afford it. Leslie likes it here, though. She says this place has soul."

"Leslie?"

"That's her name, silly. C'mon, she lives at the top of the stairs."

And she was off, clambering up the three flights in the dark, with me right on her heels. The stairway was terribly narrow; there was barely any room to move, and no light at all after we were out of range of the flickering EXIT light above the doorway at the bottom.

The noise of cartoons was blasting frantically out at us, so loud it was impossible to imagine anyone was able to think on the other side of the door. Mandy stepped up and knocked. The noise of the cartoons died down abruptly, and I heard the voice of an old woman say, "Who is it?"

Then the voice of a younger girl: "Don't worry, Gramma, stay where you are, I'll get it. Who is it?" I don't know what it was about that voice, but every word she said echoed in my heart. It sounds corny, I know, but that's just the way it happened.

"It's Mandy."

Behind the door I heard a gasp of excitement and the door was flung open.

Just an hour earlier I had been wondering what kind of saint Leslie must have been for Mandy to get this worked up over her. Now that thought came flying back; there was no other way to describe how Leslie appeared to me that night. Her head was completely shaved, she was wearing a white dress, and the blue light cast by the television behind her gave her an appearance no less than ghostly, angelic. She looked nothing like the other girls I knew. I was dumbstruck. It was the vision of a girl with no hair. It was the cigarette she held in her hand like it was just an extension of her, not like she was trying to show off. It was her beautiful smile, her pale, spiritlike face, her sad, knowing eyes. That was the way I saw Leslie, and would continue to see her. It was what made me love her, that she could just as easily run me over as caress my cheek. And that she didn't.

For all the times I forgot it over the next couple of years, I knew that night that if I just stuck with this strange, wonderful soul who stood facing us in the doorway, enveloped in this luminous blue light that for that moment had nothing to do with the television—if I just stayed close to Leslie, everything would be all right.

The first time I saw her lips move, she said my sister's name. "Mandy! Wonderful! Where have you been? I thought you didn't love me anymore." She embraced my sister, her eyes shut tight while she held her. "C'mon in. I remodeled my room. You have to see it."

Mandy laughed. "Your room's different every time I come over."

"Of course. I have to rearrange it at least once a week. Who's this? Your brother, I presume?" She said this last in a very uppity mock British accent, staring down her nose at me.

Mandy looked at me, but I was pretty speechless still, so she spoke for me. I kind of tended to close up around people I didn't know, even if they were the greatest people in the world, and Mandy knew it. She was used to bailing me out like this.

"Yeah, this is Jim. Jim, Leslie."

"Hi," I mumbled.

"Good to meet you, Jim. I already know you, though." She smiled mischievously. "Mandy told me everything about you. Even your deepest darkest secrets. Just kidding. She didn't tell me what a cutie-pie you were, though." I blushed and sort of shuffled my feet around, trying to change the subject without opening my mouth. "Oops. How rude of me. I'm so absent-minded. Come in, come in." We followed her in and she shut the door behind us. We were in the tower room that you could see from outside. An old woman was sitting on a brown, decrepit-looking couch, knitting a sweater or a blanket. I could see the cartoons on the TV now. It kind of took away from the magic of the whole thing, but maybe it was better that way. "This is my gramma. She's neato." Her grandmother turned to look at us, pretty blankly. "Gramma, this is Jim, and this is Mandy. You remember Mandy, don't you?"

It sure didn't look to me like Gramma knew what the hell Leslie was talking about. "Hmm. You have to get some rest tonight, Leslie. Your mom told me to make sure you get lots of sleep."

"I know. I'm going to go to sleep just as soon as my friends leave, okay?" Leslie was talking to her the way you would talk to a little kid, but I got the feeling that Leslie had no intention of bullshitting her grandma, like you do with kids. Actually, I had a hard time picturing Leslie lying to anyone. "C'mon, guys, come see my room." She skipped down the short hallway and took a sharp turn into her room. Again we followed quietly behind her.

It was much warmer here than in the living room. A huge white radiator in the corner was letting off almost stifling waves of heat. The walls of her room were white stucco, decorated with paintings, photographs, posters, and various colors of dried chewing gum. The floor, not to mention her bed, was drowning in clothes, notebooks, tapes, a clay statue of a woman's head, a dismantled record player, what looked like a treasure chest, and about a hundred drawings and papers with writing scribbled all over them in weird patterns and shapes. Under the bed there was a semi-hidden little alcove that was obviously her sleeping space, protected from the outside world. There was a single window with a writing desk in front of it. Looking out of it, you could see why Leslie liked to write in front of it. The ancient rickety buildings, casting their elongated shadows across each other, made for a pretty impressive view. "Do you like it?" she asked us hopefully.

"Um . . . yeah. It's real, uh . . . nice."

"Yeah," Mandy broke out. "It's really wonderful." She was as in love with Leslie as I was, I could tell.

"Have a seat," Leslie said, clearing a space on the floor by kicking everything off to one side, sitting herself down on a black stool in the corner next to a gigantic ashtray, a mirror broken and rearranged to form a kind of rough circle, and a piece of stretched canvas. "I'm going to finish my painting while we talk, okay?"

Mandy said that would be cool, and I nodded my head.

"You don't talk too much, do you?" Leslie asked me, sounding a little disappointed.

That was the last thing I wanted, so I did my best to talk to her. "Not too much around new people, no. But—"

"Oh, don't be silly," she said, leaning down toward me gracefully, but very quickly, too, and I pulled my head back more out of reflex than fright. "I won't bite," she whispered into my ear and gave me a kiss right next to my lips. This was pretty startling; even though I had just turned fifteen and all, I had never kissed a girl, not even on the cheek.

I grinned despite myself. Her lips were the softest thing I'd ever felt. I mean, I know it wasn't a *kiss* kiss, on the lips and all, but it was sort of halfway between a cheek kiss and a lip kiss, and that certainly counted for something. I know I'm sounding corny again, and it was just one kiss, but somehow I knew that this was the beginning of something great, something beautiful. The way she turned my insides upside down, the way I fell in love with everything she did, the way she moved, the way she talked, the way she smiled with her eyes and her shoulders as well as her lips. And Jesus, her lips. I just couldn't keep my eyes off them. If it was anybody else, I would have thought this whole thing was pathetic and forced myself to turn the other way, but with her I was shameless. I wasn't afraid to stare at her. For the first time in my life, I wasn't afraid to be immediately, desperately, hopelessly, senselessly *in love.* I felt this in my heart, without wondering about or doubting it, and I knew that no matter how long it took me to say it to her, it would always be unwaveringly true. And I knew that she didn't bite.

"Okay," I said, gathering courage. "I'm just kind of shy around strangers. But, um . . . it doesn't mean I don't like you."

Leslie clapped her hands to her mouth gleefully. "You guys are so wonderful! Come see me any time you want. I get lonely up here, and I'm pretty much grounded. Gramma lets me go out once in a while, 'cause sometimes she forgets I'm grounded. She's a sweetie. When my mom's around, I never even get to go out for fresh air. Which is bad 'cause she works at night, so she's home all day. I'd rather get to go out when it's sunny. But I've always got my window. Windows are good." She jumped up and pushed her window up, sticking her head out and inhaling deeply. Then she sat back down on her stool, leaving the window open. It let in a pretty cold draft, but to me it was welcome in the overheated room.

"Why are you grounded?" I asked her.

"My dad was getting married to a mean ol' lady and he made me shave my legs the day before, and I shaved my head, too. He was really pissed, and my mom grounded me till it was an inch long."

"Way to go," Mandy said admiringly, laughing.

"Oh, I didn't do it 'cause my dad was getting married; I was just bored."

"Oh," Mandy said, a little let down.

But Leslie just breezed on through, oblivious to Mandy's disappointment, or if she noticed she didn't care. Leslie was so unpredictable, at least in those days, when she was still young. Eventually, she had to grow up faster than any of us.

She told me once, much later, what she did after Mandy died. She told me she went home and showered for the rest of the day, using up all the hot water and staying in even after it was gone, freezing, for hours. Bathing, for hours. Soaping up her entire body, over and over. She told me that even after that she could still smell Mandy on her. She could still *feel* Mandy on her. I think she still does.

Back then, though, you never knew how she was going to react to anything. It was a little maddening, but at least she kept you on your toes. She picked up the painting next to her, looking at it critically. "Do you guys like this background?" She showed it to us. It was a mixture of grays and blues smeared together so it was hard to tell one color from the other. We told her it looked good, which I meant and I knew Mandy did, too. If Mandy thought it was bad, she would have said so. She could be brutally honest. At least about other people.

"I haven't finished it yet," Leslie said matter-of-factly, putting the painting back on her lap and taking a bright yellow paintbrush dripping with red paint to it, moving it in quick, sharp strokes like she knew just what she wanted and there was no question about what was going on in the picture. "I was waiting for you to get here."

"How come?" I asked her.

"It's my Drake portrait. I can't work on it any more without you guys in front of me. Hey, Jim, was I in your dream last night?"

What a strange question. Not something people asked you in everyday life. Cue up the internal sigh of desperate longing. "No, why?"

"People usually dream about me before they meet me. Mandy did."

I looked at my sister questioningly. I couldn't believe I was really taking this seriously. And here I was asking Mandy if she dreamed about Leslie before she met her. Mandy nodded, whether to let me know that she thought it was a loony question, too, or to tell me it was true, I wasn't sure, but I think it was the latter. "Well, maybe I did dream it and just forgot. I'm not too good about remembering dreams."

"Oh, that must be it," Leslie said as if that were the only explanation; then she moved on to something else that captured her short but devoted attention span.

She went on like this for hours, switching from one thing to another, the crazy to the tragic, anything and everything worth talking about. And there were so many things that weren't, she insisted feverishly, so many things that were just nothing in the big scheme of things, and it wasted precious time to worry and fret about them. That was the word she used, fret. But she was so excited about everything, so in love with life, it was mystifying. And I was catching the bug, agreeing intensely with nearly every word she spit out, and I could tell that she was frustrated because her mouth wouldn't form the words fast enough to keep up with her endlessly twisting train of thought. It was like we started reading each other's minds, and the only reason we spoke out loud was just to separate one thought from another so it didn't get all boggled up. She reminded me of my sister, and how I had always been with her, before she had started acting so funny and sad all the time. Maybe that's why Mandy liked her so much.

I told her so, and she blushed and looked away.

She looked at my hands then and told me they were beautiful, even the dirt under the fingernails.

We were quiet awhile after that, content to lie in each other's presence, our bodies touching only at our fingertips. It was after midnight, easy. Mandy had long since passed out, whether from our nonstop chatter or from sheer exhaustion, I didn't know.

7

I glanced tiredly in the direction of the clock radio that was sitting cockeyed on a pile of dirty T-shirts and skirts. It was 2:33 A.M. Way past time to split. We were gonna catch hell for sure. Leslie phoned for a cab, and after a few halfhearted tries I rousted Mandy and dragged her to the door, Leslie trailing along behind us.

I turned to her. She smiled a nice, warm, secret smile. I smiled back and embraced her, both of us holding on tight yet pulling away easily. I think we both knew there was more where that came from. Leslie shut the door softly, wordlessly. I hauled Mandy down the steps, feeling tremendously high.

The cab must not have been far away because we weren't waiting more than a minute or two when he pulled up. It was a good thing, too, 'cause boy, was it freezing out there. The two of us squeezed into the smoky, vinyl-covered backseat. Mandy immediately zonked out again. Not me, though. I couldn't have passed out if I tried. The cabbie, a greasy-looking long-haired kid, about twenty probably, kept shooting questions over his shoulder at me, but after I fed him our address I didn't say anything back. I didn't even really register anything he said. I was only half conscious of a deep, mellow monotone voice in the background, more hypnotic than conversational.

We came to the end of our ride about fifteen minutes later. He must have taken a roundabout route, but I was too out of it to care. I even tipped him a couple of bucks. I don't think he minded that I had ignored him the whole way over. What else could you expect at three in the morning? He said good-bye cheerfully and squealed out of the driveway and around the corner.

I stood in the driveway for a minute, and just as if it had been waiting up for me, a shadow of fear crept up on me. I was thinking about what Dad was going to say about us being nine hours late for dinner. Maybe they would be asleep. Best not to wake them up, try to convince them tomorrow that we got home earlier, like right after they went to bed. That would be tough to guess at, but Billy would help us out; he liked to stay up late and read, so he'd know when they crashed.

I guided Mandy around to the back, trying to make as little noise as possible tromping through the snow next to our parents' bedroom. The light was off, that was something. This was starting to look like it wouldn't be so bad.

The back porch had a sliding door on it, and I knew it would make less racket than creaky hinges. We tiptoed into the living room where the monstrous television lived, along with hundreds of sophisticated-looking books that neither of my parents ever took off the shelf. They were just there for show, to impress guests and shit. There were also a couple of family portrait pictures hanging on the wall. Your average "family" room. It was pretty disgusting, if you bothered to think about it.

Suddenly the light flipped on. I looked over to the doorway, about to whisper to Mandy to turn the light back off. But Mandy was right behind me. I froze. It was my mom who had turned on the light.

She was standing in the doorway, still wearing her gold realtor's jacket from work. She looked more afraid than mad. She'd been crying. When I saw my father next to her, I could see why. There he stood, all six and a half feet of him, a shot glass in one hand and the other holding him up, grasping the side of a shelf. He was a pretty normal-looking man most of the time, slightly balding, with a bad slouch and a sagging beer gut that was usually disguised by a business suit. But at night, after he'd been drinking, he was terrifying. I remember as a little kid being more frightened of him than of any nightmare. He stood toweringly tall and shouted and swore at us, his deep, commanding voice softened only by the slur of drunkenness. He had these dark piercing eyes that turned bloodshot and crazy with booze. All of this made him incredibly scary and at the same time sorry and pathetic, a horrible nonsensical violent weakling. You didn't know whether to run or cry. But at times like this, when his face was twisted by anger, you wanted to run.

I couldn't run, though. I was petrified. Even when I saw him wordlessly put down his drink and raise his hand to hit me, I couldn't make myself flinch.

But you can bet I moved after he hit me. His big burly fist connected with the bottom of my jaw, and the crunch I heard let me know I was going to be sore a long while. I figured that out later, though. The second he hit me I was on the ground, staring up at the ceiling and seeing funny-colored spots, focusing all my willpower into not crying, not making a sound.

I lay there silently, gritting my teeth against the pain, clenching my eyes shut against the tears that were fighting to break out of my eyes, to slide down my cheeks and betray me. I heard Dad's open hand connect with the back of my sister's head. He never hit her in the face. He always said he didn't want to ruin such a pretty face. I heard my sister hit the floor, hard. I heard him scream at us. I heard him tell us we were shit. We were nothing, he ought to throw us out on the street, the only one of us worth anything at all was our brother Billy. I heard my mom whisper softly to him that that was enough, that it was time to stop. I heard him tell her to shut up, that this was good for us, we shouldn't have come home this late and made her worry so much. I heard Billy wander into the room and ask what was going on. I heard Dad tell him almost gently to go back to bed. I heard heavy footsteps, coming close. I heard my father tell me to get up, with none of the affection that he had shown my brother. And I was suddenly sure that it could not possibly get any worse. So I opened my eyes, slowly stood myself up, and, leaning against a shelf the way he had done just a few minutes earlier, I looked at him straight in the eyes. There was nothing he could do to me that he hadn't already done. I summoned all the hate in me, all the hate and anger from the core of my being, and I got right up in his face and spit. Spit right in his sorry bloodshot eyes.

He was still for a moment. He didn't say or do anything. He just stared at me with shocked disbelief. And I started to laugh. It was not a nice laugh. It was loaded, and harsh. It was almost silent at first, but then gradually crescendoed, louder, harder, angrier, crazier, until I was roaring at the top of my lungs. I must have woken up the whole world. There was nothing but laughter, pouring into and out of every part of my being, laughter at this sad excuse for a father, this sad excuse for a *man*.

When he hit me it didn't make any difference.

And that was it. I fell down, he stormed off, taking my mother with him. Hell went back underground for a while. Mandy helped me up and carried me into my room and onto my bed. She was strong and I was small. It wasn't the first time she had done that. It had become a ritual for us. Whoever was hurt worse put the other to bed.

I didn't say anything as she tucked me in. I don't know why, but I didn't want her to know I was awake. Unlikely as it was, I was content just to pretend to be asleep or knocked out, to let her finish covering me and then kiss me good night, leaving the door open a crack the way I liked it. I almost smiled. Almost, but not quite. My jaw hurt like hell. I tried touching it, then decided it wasn't worth it. Better to wait until morning when the pain would have gone down some.

I couldn't sleep. I was thinking about Leslie, and wishing my father would have granted me a peaceful night. It was too much for me, going from a kiss to a fist in less than an hour. Ten to one by morning I'd be a complete loon. They'd have to suit me up with a straitjacket.

I heard the door to my sister's room creak open and shut again. Then her voice and one much lower: my dad's. They didn't say much. That's all I could tell. The closed door made it impossible to hear exactly what they were saying. Then it was quiet and I forgot all about them until I heard the door open again a while later. There was the sound of water running in the bathroom, and then nothing.

A minute or two after the water stopped, Mandy knocked

on my window. Our rooms shared a wall and our windows were on either side of it. When we were both grounded to our rooms and wanted to talk, we would stick our heads out of our windows. We could even give each other hugs, with a little effort.

I slid my window open and stuck out my head. She was waiting for me.

"Hey, Jim?"

"Yeah?" I said, rubbing my eyes. It was very dark out.

"You love me, don't you Jim?" She'd been crying, I could tell.

"Sure I love you. More than anyone else in the world." I meant it.

"Really?" She sounded hopeful, but not confident.

"Mandy, listen to me. You're wonderful. I love you tons, and I always will. Nothing can change that. Besides, you're my favorite sister."

She laughed. "Thanks. You'll never leave me, will you?"

Now I was the one who laughed, despite the pain. "Of course not. We'll always be together."

"Good." She sounded relieved. We were quiet for a while, looking up at the sky. There wasn't a whole lot to see. Even the moon was missing, hiding behind clouds that were almost too black to make out themselves. "Jim?"

"Yeah?"

"Take care of Billy, all right?"

"What?" I didn't understand. "Are you taking off, Mandy?"

"No. Just . . . don't let Dad fuck him up, okay?"

I looked at her. Her eyes were pleading.

"Okay."

"Good." She leaned over and kissed me again, and then she was gone. Her window slid shut a couple seconds later. A carful of jocks pulled up and the kid that lives across the street got dropped off. The jocks were shouting their heads off, the kid trying unsuccessfully to shut them up. I don't know why he bothered. I guess he didn't want his parents to wake up. I wondered how much was at stake. I wondered if his life was like mine. I figured not. I hoped not. The car waited until he was inside and the door was shut, and then drove off down the street, picking up speed till it must have been going at least forty-five. I stayed out there for a minute, I guess waiting for something to happen. Nothing did. I pulled my head back inside and went to sleep.

APRIL 1991

8

I got a letter from Leslie today. I could tell when I saw it because she wrote my name in this real fancy writing, like we were royalty or something. Also, there were ink spots dripped all over the envelope. Leslie loved using the fountain pen Mandy got her for her birthday, but she wasn't too good at it. I tore open the envelope as gently as I could. She always used this ancient-looking brown paper to write on. She thought it added more spirit to what she wrote. The only thing was, it was incredibly fragile and you really had to be extra careful not to tear it.

I flattened it out gently, smoothing over the creases with my hand. My heart was pounding like crazy. It felt like it was going to break right out of my chest. Leslie was out of town visiting her aunt with her mother, and I hadn't talked to her in a week, but that didn't stop me from thinking about her constantly, as hard as I tried not to.

I closed my eyes for a minute before I started to read the letter, picturing Leslie writing it in faraway Nevada, where she was staying in a trailer with her aunt for three weeks. I liked to get a photograph in my mind of someone whose letter I was reading. It made it seem more like they were close to me, like I could touch them.

Then, after I had conjured up a good picture of her, I began to read, slowly, savoring each word, tasting it on my tongue and breathing it in.

Dear Jim, my loverly friend,

A million wet kisses from the magnificent desert of Nevada. There are four of us in a trailer here that I think was meant for one person, and that person would have to be a midget. I bet it was a dressing room for one of the munchkins in the Wizard of Oz. *My aunt Maggie has a seven-year-old daughter named Yasmine. She is super spoiled and expects me to be her maid or something. I think I am going to murder her. Well, maybe not, but sometimes I think I could. Her mom is bad too. She's always asking me to run errands for her. Bitch. I have been designated Official Baby-sitter so Maggie and my mom can drive into town and party while I make sure Yasmine doesn't die. I don't know why. I think I am more of a threat than a protector. Ha ha. It is very cramped here, and I try to spend as much time outside as possible. I like to walk around and take pictures of the land. The sunrise especially is beautiful. I will take you back here sometime, just the two of us. Ooh, how womantic!*

I met a real live cowboy today. I wandered a couple miles from the trailer and found an old shack where he lived. He is oooold. He told me all kinds of stories about when he used to be a cattle herder, and he would ride across the country. Now he is a painter and a wood carver, and he has a little shop where he sells his art. He was a splendid man, and I sat and talked to him for two hours. He was very nice, and he gave me some pie and let me refill my canteen in his sink. I took tons of pictures of him. I have lots of film. I took two rolls from my mom and told her I only took one. Oh well.

I'll pay her back if she finds out. With her money. It is very late now and I think I am going to go. I miss you bunches. I'll write you later. I love you.

Leslie

P.S. I got you something. Woo-ee.

I read the letter over and over. I got a hard-on just looking at the handwriting. Leslie turned me on more than any other girl ever had. I ripped a few sheets off a roll of toilet paper I kept under my bed for this express purpose, folded them over a couple times, and set them on my pillow, which I took from the head of the bed and positioned in the middle so that I could comfortably lie on top of it and thrust into it with my cock shooting directly into the tissue paper. I know this is a pretty complex procedure for simple whacking off, but I had transformed whacking off into an art, simulating real sex as much as possible. Of course I had never had real sex, or anything close to it, so it was all guesswork, but I had it figured I was doing a pretty good job, considering my resources.

I took my time, leisurely thrusting away, picturing every detail of Leslie's naked body under mine, imagining her hands caressing my back, her lips dancing over my neck, her hips thrusting to meet mine. After about ten minutes of this, I hit that limbo hang time, the point of no return, and I held myself there as long as I could, all my muscles tensed up, shuddering with pleasure, and then I went wild, thrusting my little heart out before I shot ecstatically into the tissue.

There was something very cozy, very comforting about the whole affair. Familiarity. Privacy. I liked that pillow. It saw parts of me nobody else did. When I was done, spent, I usually liked to lie on top of it a while longer, sopping wet cock and all, just to think for a while. Just to be quiet, and alone.

I could never tell whether Leslie wanted me as a friend or as something more. She drove me crazy giving me so many mixed messages. I knew one thing for sure: I had never in my life wanted anything so much as I wanted her.

"You ready, Jim?" Mandy's quiet voice outside my door broke my thought train.

"Oh, yeah. Sure." I cleaned up in a hurry, stowing the letter in the pocket of my hooded sweatshirt and following my sister through the living room and out the front door. Which was as far as we got before I heard my father's voice shouting at my sister.

"Mandy! Where are you going?" He had been in the backyard, planting seeds in the garden, but now he was standing between the corner of the house and Mandy's car, almost daring her to get in and drive off. He was looking only at her. He had barely spoken to me since I spit in his face.

"I'm just taking Jim over to Philly's house," she answered him in a near whisper. Mandy was getting worse. She didn't go out much, and pretty much did as my father wished. My mother worked all the time, so the task fell upon my sister to cook dinner, clean up, watch Billy, and play fetch-the-beer for my dad. I felt horrible about it, but every time I brought up her leaving or me helping her out or *anything* to bring her spirits up, she just asked me not to talk about it, saying she didn't mind doing all that. I knew different, though. Mandy had changed. She never talked to me in the middle of the night. She never kidded around anymore and played funny dress-up games with me and Billy. Every day she got a little thinner, a little weaker. Every night I heard her crying, wailing hopelessly into her pillow, but whenever I confronted her about it she just denied it, said maybe it was the wind or something.

"All right," he said. "But be back in time to make dinner. Your mother isn't going to be home until late."

"Okay," she said, and I heard her choke on her tears, holding them back. I looked at her, but her face was blank, her eyes empty. It was amazing that she was even standing. If I'd been anyone else, I wouldn't even have been able to tell she was almost crying. But I could see she was on the verge of breaking down.

Still, I said nothing as we got into her car and drove away, under the crushing glare of my father's eyes until we were completely out of sight. You could feel it, him staring at you. Like heat. Like weight.

I looked at her, watching her drive. She was quiet, and I didn't think she wanted to talk, so I didn't. The silence was heavy, and I was acutely aware of her every breath. I glanced at her hands, and saw that they were clenched white, one against the steering wheel and the other against a bottle of vodka she had taken out of her jacket. She drank all the time now, like it was water or something. I didn't know what to do. I couldn't touch her, for fear that she would be startled or angry. I was helpless. I felt like screaming. I looked at her again, opening my mouth to say something. I didn't know what. Anything would do, just so I could feel like I was *doing* something.

But I stopped, closing my mouth abruptly. A tear was making its way down her cheek. It was the first tear I had seen out of her in months. And I know it's crazy, but I was glad. I was relieved just to see some sign of emotion out of her. She had let the bottle hand fall to her lap, and I took hold of it, lacing my cool fingers through her sweaty ones, and she was grateful, I think, holding on as tight as she was.

She pulled into my friend Philly's driveway then, but I didn't get out. I stayed there with my sister, and before long she had collapsed. She was crying and screaming at the top of her lungs, rocking back and forth, head buried in my chest, crying for her mother, crying for me. "I'm here," I whispered. "I'm here, honey. Don't you worry. I'm here." I went on like this trying to soothe her for what seemed like forever, praying to some unknown god to save my sister, to swoop down and make it all better, shooting silent cries for help out into the open air, desperately hoping that something would hear me, would help my sister. Nothing did, though, and much of my desperation came from knowing nothing would. Eventually she stopped crying, but even then she didn't move, protected within my arms, afraid of the outside world and all of its monsters.

And you know, holding her, I began to really understand what my father had done. He had made my big sister small, and now I was the protector. It hurt, knowing that, but I didn't fight it. It was what it was. It was my turn.

I nudged her off of me, trying to get her to look up by herself, whispering for her to look out the window. "Hey," I said. "I'll take care of you, kid."

She looked at me and smiled sadly. "Shouldn't I be the one saying that to you?"

I forced a smile, so faint I wasn't even sure it showed. It was all I had. "Nonsense. Nobody's invincible." I kissed her and stepped out of the car. "I'll see you soon. Thanks for the ride," I said, closing the door. I stood there, seeing her off, and then went to the door, closing my eyes for a minute before I knocked.

I would have made a wish if I thought it would have done any good.

9

Philly's house used to be a fire station like a hundred years ago. The poles and everything were gone now, but it still looked the same from the outside. Sitting on the lawn there, you just kept expecting a great old fire engine to come roaring out of the garage, sirens blasting away. When we were younger, Philly and I had made a pact that as soon as we got our licenses, we'd go off and buy our own truck and turn the place back into a fire station. Of course we never did. It was one of those promises you make when you're little that nobody ever keeps.

I pounded on the door as hard as I could. Usually everyone was on the second floor and if you just knocked normally nobody would hear you.

I heard someone come tromping loudly down the stairs, and when the door flew open, I was greeted by a picture of a naked woman with her legs spread wide open. Philly's tongue was sticking out through a hole where her pussy should have been. "Jim! My friend! Come on in!"

Philly pulled me inside and slammed the door shut behind me, traipsing up the stairs and shouting for me to follow.

He was three months older than me, but he acted younger. His real name was Terence Watters. I called him Philly because when I first met him five years ago, just after he moved to Madison from Philadelphia, everything he said started off "Back in Philly . . ." I started calling him that sort of as a joke, but it turned out he'd always hated his real name, so it stuck.

We had decorated the walls of his bedroom by splashing different cans of colored paint all over them till you couldn't see any of the original gray tile. It was fun doing it, and Philly loved it, but I found it kind of hard to sit in there for long.

"Hey, Jim." I was surprised to see my friend Jeremy Thayer there, too. He was stretched out on the bed, flipping through another one of Philly's numerous porno mags with a bored look on his face.

"Whatup, Jeremy," I said. He glanced up at me and nodded. If he was glad to see me, it didn't show on his face. I was used to that. He never showed a whole lot of anything on his face.

Jeremy was a year older than Philly. He didn't fit in too well at school, partly because his hair, which would have been blond if it wasn't so dirty, was about two feet long. Also, he was always failing his classes or just barely scraping by. That was why he was in the same grade as I was, even though he was over a year older. It wasn't that he didn't get it, though. He was a real genius, in his own way. He just wasn't interested. The stuff you learn at school was too shallow for him. I mean, the guy flunked kindergarten for refusing to learn to write his name. He said he had more important things to worry about. At five.

I pushed the magazine aside and sat down next to him. "So, Jim," Philly said, kneeling down so he was at eye level with me, "what kind of trouble should we cause today?" He had blue-green eyes that lit up like stars when he smiled, and a big, messy shock of curly red hair on top of his head.

"I want to do some shopping today," Jeremy piped up, grinning kind of wickedly. What he meant was shop*lifting*. He might have been a genius, but he was no goodie-goodie. We all stole a little, but Jeremy stole a *lot*. He said he wanted to get caught, just for the hell of it. He wanted to get arrested and then totally spook the cops at the station by like drooling and screaming and hitting the cops' headrests and shit, and then get put in a rubber room, and once he was in there just act completely normal and deny that anything funny ever happened, like he had been perfectly quiet the whole way over. He was always thinking up crazy schemes like that. Sometimes I thought he was about as bored with living as a person could get.

"Where do you wanna go?" I asked him.

"Who cares?" Jeremy said. That was another thing. He barely ever took something 'cause he needed it, like I did. He would steal just to see if he could get away with it.

"Let's go," Philly said, punching my arm playfully and

hoisting me. He was always horsing around, acting childish. Innocent, even. Maybe it was from all those years going to church, sheltered from the world by books of God and stained-glass windows. He still went, every Sunday with his mother. He wasn't devoutly religous or anything. He always said he liked the idea of it, though, of living like Jesus. Nobody did, of course, least of all him, but I got the feeling he was sorry for that. He would try to do things, maybe to sort of make up for all the hell we raised. Like walk an old lady across the street while we're trying to ditch the cops. Or we'd just be leaving some deli and he'd still have half a sandwich in his hand, and he wouldn't eat it. He'd just hold on to it until he found a hungry-looking bum to give it away to. Real Good Samaritan–type stuff that Jeremy and I never bothered with. We respected it, though, and we never interrupted it or gave him a hard time about it. As much as I think we both wished we could be like Philly, we weren't. He really loved us both, though. We were his first friends when he came to town, and we were still his best. "Time to move. We gotta go to Walgreen's sometime. I want to get some booze." The downtown Walgreen's drugstore was gigantic, and had just about anything you would ever want. The security there was horrible, so we went there all the time. Philly said it was especially okay to steal from them since they were so stupid. When you steal a lot you start to make up excuses to justify it. None of them were ever any good, but we went along with them because it made us feel less guilty.

Personally I was frequently plagued with pangs of guilt, and it tended to keep my theft to a minimum, except when I was depressed, and then I didn't care so much.

We caught a bus headed downtown, where most of the shops and real city life was concentrated. Jeremy listened to me and Philly shoot the bull back and forth about our various exploits at school, an amused smile playing across his lips. We were always wreaking havoc there, just to make it halfway endurable. Jeremy mostly just slept through school as much as possible, leaving the rebellion to us. He did like to hear about it, though. "Whatever happened to Bore?" he asked after the bragging had died down. Philly and I exchanged looks and agreed to tell him. It was a long bus ride and we had time to kill. Besides, in those days we kept nothing from each other.

We were both in a journalism class that we'd taken for easy English credit, but it turned out to be the most heartrendingly boring class either of us had ever signed up for. One day Bore, as we called our horrible old lady teacher, made the mistake of assigning us to work together on a project. We were sitting in a back corner of the room, completely ignoring our assignment because we had come to the decision that it hurt to look at it, so we'd therefore be justified in throwing it away. I was hanging my head over my desk, trying to create a pond on the floor through a steady stream of drool I was working very hard to keep up. It's really an art to keep it going continuously.

Suddenly Philly tapped my shoulder vigorously.

I ignored him, meditating on my drool.

"Jim!" he whispered urgently.

"What?" I asked, annoyed.

"Lift your head up."

"Why?" It was taking a great deal of unnecessary effort to keep my stream going and talk at the same time. I wished he would shut up.

"Quit drooling and lift your head up. I want to show you something."

I sighed. With Philly there was no way to get him to leave me alone except to humor him. So much for my pond. "So long, pond," I said, breaking off my stream and wiping the strand that was hanging forlornly from my mouth on my sleeve, picking my head up, and looking at my friend. "Yes?"

"Why do you do that shit? It's really disgusting."

I ignored him. I happened to think drooling passed the time at school very well, but we had had this conversation before and I didn't feel up to trying to make a convert of him today. "What do you want?"

"Listen to Bore talk," he said, pointing at our teacher.

"Aw, Philly, c'mon." I listened to her drone enough as it was.

"No, really. Just listen. She keeps saying it."

"What?"

"I'm telling you. Listen."

I sighed again. Philly tended to do that to me. I listened to her talk for a while, and then I burst out laughing, just for a second before I managed to stifle most of it and keep us out of trouble. What Philly was talking about was that Bore slipped a "shh" in like every third word or so. It was the funniest thing ever. She would be right in the middle of a sentence, and she would just say "shh." Like "Maybe you need to shh think about doing shh your tardy home shh work before you work shh on your newer assignments shh."

Pretty soon we came up with the idea of the Shh-ometer. I can't remember which of us thought up the name. What it was was, we would make a tally mark on a piece of paper every time she said "shh," and then we would count 'em up at the end of the hour. We were planning on doing it for a month, keeping it real quiet and then averaging the results at the end of the month and posting them. It would have been one of our greatest gags ever. Unfortunately it didn't get that far.

The day after we came up with it, a kid that sat next to Philly saw him marking off the "shhs" and caught on to what he was doing. No matter how hard Philly tried, he couldn't get this loudmouth to shut up, and soon a good chunk of the class knew what was up, and most of them were keeping track. Since Philly and I were looked upon as the experts, every once in a while people would whisper over to us and check their scores against ours. Everyone except the oblivious Bore wondered what was going on, and by the seventh day it had leaked to the entire class. Not exactly what we had planned, but it was plenty of fun this way, too. There were only a couple of kids that weren't at least somewhat interested in the current tally, and those in the right places were marking it on the front and back chalkboards. It was getting out of hand. With the whole class into it, kids were braver and they started shouting across the room to us experts and asking for the count. This only made Bore have to insert even more "shhs" into her speech, and on the ninth day we got to a hundred. One hundred "shhs" in under fifty minutes. When she finally hit the magic number, kids went wild. People were hurling their book bags into the air and standing on desks, hollering and cheering as loud as they could.

Me and Philly didn't get into that. We just sat in the corner, threw our heads back, and laughed innocently. There was no way Bore would figure out who had started this mess. Everybody was having too much fun to rat on us. We had never stirred up a greater ruckus. The chaos was wonderful.

Even at the height of the glory of the great Shh-ometer, it was almost over. On the tenth and final day, things were looking pretty good. Everyone was set for the biggest day of all. There was talk of shooting for two hundred. Bore walked into the classroom a little late, and immediately began her lecture.

There was something wrong. It took me a couple minutes to notice, but there was definitely something wrong. Bore had gone two entire minutes without uttering a single "shh." At this rate we wouldn't even clear ten. In another couple minutes the rest of the class, one at a time, started turning to us for answers, asking us what was going on, and how we could get her going again. Like *we* knew. All we did was start counting 'em. We had no clue how to instigate her. After a while the demands got really loud. People were upset. They were trying everything. Paper airplanes, dirty jokes, outright screams. Nothing was working, and people were getting pissed. I looked at Philly helplessly. He shrugged, but I could tell by the look in his eyes that he felt the same way I did. We felt *bad* for her. The kids were tormenting her.

Then, when nearly everyone in the room but me and Philly was screaming at the top of their lungs, and I couldn't even hear myself think and suddenly it wasn't funny anymore—I mean, God, how awful Bore must have felt—suddenly she lost it. I had never seen anything like it. Her eyes bugged out, her face turned beet red, and she roared, "SHUSHUSHUSHUSHUSH!!"

And then everything was quiet, and Bore slumped onto her desk. I could hear her sobbing, and I was completely ashamed. I couldn't even look at Philly, but I was sure he felt the same way. A couple of kids tried some jokes about it, but they fell on deaf ears. It was like we'd released all the aggression that had been bottled up over ten years chock full of tyrants and idiots forcing us to get up too early morning after morning to go somewhere we didn't want to go on this one defenseless old lady who was probably too old to be teaching at all.

After a while I stood up, and even the worst of the comedians shut up, waiting to see what one of the geniuses behind this master plan was going to do. They were expecting something spectacular. A real gut-burster. And that's why they were paying attention. But I couldn't give them that. All I could give them, for once, was me. All I could give them was my sorry self walking silently out of the room. The door shut loudly behind me. I kept walking, down the hall. I didn't know where I was going. I just wanted out. Out of this school, this awful mess of shame and hate. I heard the door open and close again, and I didn't need to hear his voice to know it was Philly. I waited up for him.

"What do you want to do, Jim?" he asked me quietly.

"I don't know," I said. I felt like curling up in a ball and crying. I looked at my friend. It was one of the only times since I'd met him that I'd seen him without some kind of smile spread across his face. "Let's get outta here, at least."

We did. We walked around for a long time, not saying much. Eventually we parted ways and I went home.

I never went back to my journalism class. I failed the class, and so did Philly, but at least we never had to face Bore again. I felt like by failing the class I had sort of atoned for my sins, at least as much as I could without actually apologizing to her. And I couldn't do that. I didn't have the guts. Failing would have to be good enough. For me and for Bore.

10

We had never mentioned that to Jeremy before, just 'cause it freaked us out so bad. Nobody said anything after we explained it. Even more than us, maybe, Jeremy understood why Bore losing it had bothered us so much. He was always going on about the poetic tragedy of everything. There was a depth to Jeremy that most people didn't have, or if they did they didn't show it. Most people were scared of it. Philly and I took shelter under it.

The silence didn't last long. After a minute or so Philly let fly with this incredibly loud, raunchy fart that had all of us in instant laughing fits. We almost missed our stop because of that, but Jeremy by chance glanced up at the last second and managed to pull the cord in time. We got off the bus right outside of an old convenience store called Sunshine, stumbling and coughing all over each other. I guess things like that are even funnier right in the middle of a bunch of dead seriousness.

The air inside the store was hotter and muggier than it was outside. The Mexican family that owned it was too poor to install air conditioning. Philly went up to the counter to buy cigarettes while me and Jeremy got Cokes. We wouldn't steal from Sunshine, seeing as how it wasn't a chain or anything, just a family-owned store. When we got up to the counter Philly was packing the cigarettes down and shooting the bull with this kid that worked the register, Charlie. Actually his name was Carlos, but once Philly called him Charles as a joke and he dug it, so now we all called him Charles or Charlie. Jeremy and I probably never would have talked to him at all if it weren't for the fact that he and Philly were sort of friends. Charlie really looked up to Philly. He was sort of a hero for him. Philly was real good about it, too, always stopping in and checking up on him, never giving him a hard time about anything or teasing him like we sometimes did to other young kids. He was quite a bit younger than we were, probably twelve. He was a really nice kid, very shy and polite and all. He always wore this raggedy black-and-red Harley-Davidson shirt. He told us one day that his dream was to get a brand-new Harley and bike straight down, all the way down to Méhico, find some Hispanic babe to marry and raise a family proper, in their own country. He was a good kid. Still innocent. I liked that about him.

We all said so long to Charlie and took off. I passed out the Cokes, and then a little later, when we had rounded the corner and we were pretty sure no one was looking, we split up the cigarettes, too. We were on our way to a good day, that was for sure.

We walked along some railroad tracks that gave us a straight shot from Sunshine to Walgreen's. There's something about walking on the tracks that's very different from a regular old sidewalk. We never really thought about it, but whenever we could we always chose the tracks over walking along the side of some road. On the tracks it was like we were walking on something alive, something magical. I liked picturing them piercing the land like some kind of iron bloodline, trains lurching and speeding over them across America, being swallowed up by the magnificent countryside.

And that was a great, almost beautiful thing, on our way to a shoplifting spree with cold Cokes in our hands and cigarettes all our parents would have killed us for having in our mouths, blue sky and train tracks as far as we could see. The hot, lively sun of spring shone down on us, lighting up the day and our lonely desperate hearts that we all tried so hard to open up and succeeded only in keeping them beating.

Walgreen's was a walk in the park: I lifted a pair of red-lensed sunglasses that made the world look like a stained-glass window and a notebook and some pens 'cause I was running low. I was always writing things down: poems, stories, random thoughts. I had a diary, but it wasn't all kept neatly together in one book. The story of my life is scrawled out on old napkins, walls, jeans, in the margins of library books that never got returned, toilet stalls, anything that ink shows up on.

Jeremy stuffed his pockets with packages of black dye. He wore only black and his mom was always buying him brightly colored clothing that was supposed to "lift him out of his depression," but Jeremy just dyed everything she gave him black. It wasn't like he was trying to be scary or morbid or anything, it's just the only color he felt comfortable in.

Philly filled up his backpack with a pack of batteries for his Walkman, enough candy bars to last him the rest of his life, a couple bottles of hard liquor, and an aluminum camping spork. I didn't even bother to ask why. He was like a goddam bird, always chasing after shiny things. Also he had a pretty nasty scrape on his elbow, so he opened up a package of bandages and put one on it. I was getting antsy by this time and really wanted to get the hell out of there, you know, the usual paranoia bit, but Philly, cocky as all hell, goes and borrows the manager's pen, which he uses to cross out the number *10* next to the word *BANDAGES* on the package he opened and write a number *9* over it. He gave the pen back to the manager, me biting my sleeve to keep from laughing out loud. After we're all clear and around the corner, I can't hold back any longer. Neither can the other guys, as it turns out, and we end up falling all over each other, collapsing in the shadow of a Dumpster in the alley behind Walgreen's. Then we stupidly emptied our pockets, showing off our loot and trying to calculate how much it was all worth. Jeremy was working it through in his head, and he was on the verge of spitting out the answer when the alley door flew open and out comes the manager Philly had bummed the pen off of, two giant trash bags in each hand. Seeing us huddled together around a pile of his store's merchandise, it took him just under three seconds to put it together. He got the picture and dropped the bags, lunging at us. We knew we were in hot water the second he came out the door, so by the time he had gotten past his enormous bags we had already been through a panicky scramble, grabbing our shit and getting on our feet.

Then it was a mad dash across a traffic-ridden street, cars honking and middle fingers flying up all over, as we plunged through a row of prickly evergreens that marked the beginning of a massive park. After that we each had our own ideas and we split up, sailing off in different directions. My feet were barely scraping the ground, and even then only every few feet.

The manager guy was really very old—I was surprised he even worked there at all—and I doubt if he even made it past the bushes, but I could hear his voice a long way off, yammering about calling the police and calling us little whippersnappers. It would have been funnier if I didn't feel kind of sorry for him, the way I did for Bore.

A few weeks earlier, the three of us had decided on the little pond that was roughly in the center of the park as a meeting place if we ever got split up when something like this happened. Not that we ever actually believed it would, but Jeremy had insisted on a plan. Good thing, too, or we would have never found each other. The park was huge, and we'd gotten completely separated. Five minutes later, though, I reached the pond, panting and wheezing my way over to a towering maple tree where I figured the shade would be a relief.

I was slouched in that shade, rowing through my pockets for the inhaler I needed badly, when I heard pounding footsteps and my friends' maniacal laughter. A couple seconds later they appeared through the thicket of trees on the other side of the pond. They saw me and grinned, making their way over to me and clapping me on the back, relieved that we had all made it. I felt the same, but it wasn't until I finally found my inhaler and used it that it started to show on my face.

We rested there for only a few minutes before we started to get a little worried that the old manager actually would tattle to the cops and we decided to get moving.

Then we were on our way back to Philly's house, traipsing back along the train tracks, on a high from all the shit we'd taken. We were still working on that same pack of cigarettes. With one in each of our mouths there were still ten or eleven in the pack. None of us were real smokers, and three a day was about the limit of what we could handle.

All we could talk about was that crazy manager, and how

fast we ran, and how great we were. God, we felt good, buzzing on nicotine and adrenaline, and the sheer weight of all the loot in our pockets. The more we got, the better we felt about ourselves. Some backwater part of my mind realized this, and realized how fucked up this was, but it was smothered by the majority of me that would do anything to feel good, to get ahold of some kind of happiness. We did what we had to do.

Too bad I didn't listen to that pipsqueak little backwater voice all the way back then. Sometimes I wonder how much would have been different if I had.

11

On the way back we stopped off at this Italian restaurant that was near the tracks, right next to a bunch of old abandoned warehouses. We got a huge kick out of that place. There were all kinds of rumors floating around about how it was just a front for the Mafia and how all the "empty" warehouses were really chock full of stolen bikes, cars, stereos, anything they could get their hands on. Plus, all the workers there looked like these incredibly mobby characters, like hit men and bosses, guys named Guido, the whole bit. There was almost never anyone in there, and we had it figured that the only way the place could stay open was if the rumors were true. We never ate there, but sometimes when we were heading back to Philly's we would stop in there to go to the bathroom, even though Philly's was so close. The back hallway leading to the bathroom at the place was straight out of a James Bond movie, and we loved to go back there and goof around, eavesdropping on the conversations of the guys in the kitchen and trying to figure out what went on behind this one unmarked door that was always kept locked. We never saw anybody go in or out, but you could almost always hear muffled talking behind it. This time we couldn't catch any conversations so we set about trying to open it, when Jeremy got this wise smirk on his face and said he had to use the bathroom. The break-in idea was probably not too brilliant in the first place, so we went in there with him. While he was squatting in the stall for what seemed like forever, we were messing around like morons, turning the lights on and off and throwing soap and wet towels over the stall, laughing our heads off. The weird part was Jeremy never yelled at us about anything we threw, in fact he never made a sound, except when we turned the lights and the noisy fan off, too, and we could just barely hear a faint, occasional giggle. Eventually, after five minutes or so, me and Philly started ignoring him, making faces in the mirror, and when that got old we started swigging off the bottle of whiskey that Philly ripped off. This only made everything funnier, even with the stuff burning its way down my throat. By the time Jeremy came out after about fifteen minutes of silent stall time, I was slouched in the corner with the bottle in my hand, wearing this sloppy half grin I always get when I drink. I wasn't drunk yet by any means, but even the prospect of it happening soon got me giddy as hell. So right then Jeremy came flying out of the stall, slamming Philly against the wall with the door he was about to start knocking on, and fell to his knees right on the outside of the stall. I was about to ask Jeremy what the fuck he was doing when he gestured me and Philly over. He backed up so we could get in on what he was looking at. He was watching the bottom end of the stall wall like it was about to blow up or something. He had this crazy smirk spread across his face, like he was waiting for something, and just as I started getting bored and thinking about turning back to my bottle, what Jeremy was waiting for finally happened. This white gunk that even in my slightly tipsy state I immediately recognized as come just sort of gooped off the inside of the stall and plopped down onto the floor.

As soon as it happened Jeremy leaped into the air, roaring with laughter. Philly jumped, too, because when Jeremy's jism dripped off the stall his face was so close it almost fell on his nose. He'd also been hitting off the bottle, and even though he'd only had as much as I had, he always liked to make a big exaggerated show of things, and he immediately fell backward against the wall.

It was pretty disgusting, but I have to admit we were all laughing like idiots again. Then it hit me that if one of the mob heavies came back to check on the noise and saw Jeremy's mess, we'd all be in for it. I mentioned this to the other guys and they agreed that the best move was to take off—quick.

We thanked the cashier on our way out. He just nodded, and gave us a look like, If you're not gonna buy anything then get the fuck out, yunnerstand? We didn't waste any time.

The bus ride back consisted of falling all over ourselves, bugging our eyes out at fuzzy-looking strangers, making a lot of sick jokes, watching the sun on its way out, and freaking on the blue lights of the bus when they switched on, which combined with the bumpy ride and the noise of the engine made me pretty dizzy and nauseous. All in all I was in a very good mood.

Getting up to Philly's room was kind of tricky; with all those steps I found out I was a little drunker than I'd thought. Jeremy was itching for the bottle like crazy. He was still trying to catch up to us since we started before him in the bathroom. We gave him the half-empty bottle while Philly and I started working on the two bottles of ninety-proof vodka he had lifted.

After a while the crazy paint on Philly's wall started to give me a headache, and for some reason this struck me as quite funny. I wasn't really too sure what was going on, but I tried to stand up to tell the colors to go away, or at least agree on what color they were going to be, and suddenly I was staring up at the ceiling, flat on my back. Jeremy thought this was hilarious and spit whiskey all over me. I was all wet, but there was really nothing I could do about it, seeing as how I couldn't even crawl. I kept saying "Guys, I can't get up," over and over, and every time I said it Philly and Jeremy cracked up like that was the funniest thing ever. Then Philly started yelling about curing me with cough syrup, and he took off for a couple minutes while I lay there wondering how cough medicine is gonna help and telling Jeremy over and over how paralyzed I am—which only made him laugh even harder, instead of trying to help me up.

Philly came back in then with a bottle of Robitussin in his hand. He picked my head up and rested it on his lap and was bitching about childproof caps when I asked him why he was doing this. He said it would make me feel better for sure, and by this time he had the cap loose and he opened my mouth and started pouring. It tasted like shit but I really wanted to get up and I figured Philly ought to know what he was talking about, so I gagged it down the best I could. Some of it ended up on my shirt, but I swallowed most of it and when he was done pouring I found out he'd just given me eight ounces of the stuff: the whole fuckin' bottle. I started yelling at Philly, but he just told me to chill out and let the medicine take its effect. I was so scared I was crying a little, but after a while I quieted down, listening to the other guys talking about superheroes. My head started to pound real bad, and when Philly turned on a Batman cartoon I decided to watch, hoping it would take my mind off my headache.

This turned out to be a bad decision because about ten minutes later the Robitussin kicked in all the way. At least I'm pretty sure that was what was making the show 3D. Batman got right up in my face, and I was trying to dodge his punches as best as I could, but I decided this was way too weird for me, and I rolled over and started puking. It got all over my shirt and Philly's carpet, and Jeremy was cracking up again but then Philly said something that really wigged me.

"Oh shit man, don't puke, it gets way worse when you puke."

Too late for me. I turned around to look at Philly but I had to close my eyes right away because his head was starting to inflate like a balloon, but oh God when I closed my eyes I saw the most fucked-up shit, man, no kidding, it scared the piss out of me, all the monsters coming at me and my head hurt so goddam bad.

I started to cry really hard then, curled up in the corner and bawling my eyes out, and before I knew it I was so tired, so heavy I felt like a thousand pounds, and I had no trouble drifting off.

That's the trouble with Robitussin, I figured out after a few more trips. Eventually it always puts me to sleep.

JUNE 1991

12

"James Evan Drake, come in please. Earth to Drake. Come in please."

I woke up to Mandy leaning right over my head, whispering into my ear. "Mmmmmm," I said, rolling onto my back from the fetal position on my left side that I always sleep in.

She giggled. "The creature stirs," Mandy said, playfully tickling my armpits. I didn't move. There are times when I can be extremely ticklish, but right after waking up isn't one of them. She hugged me and kissed me on my cheek. "Mmmmmm," I said again, thoroughly content.

"Get up, mmm-head," Mandy said, abruptly jumping off my bed and heading out the door. "I made you breakfast. Paaaaaaaancaaaaaaakes," she sang, traipsing out the door.

It took me longer than I would have liked to accomplish the task of getting up. Those pancakes sounded damn good, but my head felt like it was on the verge of exploding and my arms and legs were cemented to the bed. Mandy and I had gotten stinking drunk the night before, and it was a fucking blast then, but now I was paying for it. I always got hung over really easily.

Summoning every bit of physical strength I had, I forced myself out of bed. Miraculously, I actually made it without falling on my face. I congratulated myself. Luckily I was still wearing my clothes, sneakers and all, from last night, so I didn't have to tackle the task of dressing.

My success was short-lived. There's a place in the hallway leading from the bedrooms to the living room and kitchen where the ceiling dips down real low to accommodate a water pipe. Bad design, I guess, but every time you walked under it you had to duck a little bit, and in my gleefully groggy stupor I forgot all about that dip and bashed my forehead right into it. Suddenly I was staring at the ceiling, moaning. Mom was gonna be real delighted when she noticed the missing chunk of plaster which at that very moment was pasted to my face.

Mandy heard me moaning and came back from the kitchen. At first she starting laughing hysterically, but as she got closer and noticed the blood leaking out of my head she got serious. "Ohh, Jimmy, look what happened," she said, kneeling next to me.

I grinned through my pain. She was treating me like a baby but part of me enjoyed the whole maternal bit, probably 'cause I didn't experience much of it when I was younger. "I'm okay," I mumbled, which was really a silly bit of macho acting if you think about it.

"Don't be ridiculous, Jim. We have to take care of this." Mandy shushed me, picking up my head and then my shoulders so I was in an almost sitting position.

"Fine with me," I said.

"Can you stand?" she asked, helping me up.

"Yeah." I laughed. "Sure thing."

"Jim, this really isn't funny," Mandy said.

For her sake, I tried to put on a straight face. The thing was, though, that as I plodded heavily down the hallway to the bathroom with her help, each step meant blood dripping onto the floor and onto Mandy, and the whole thing just struck me as really funny, a real gag, and by the time I was sitting on the toilet and Mandy was scrambling around looking for first aid stuff, I was laughing my head off. I'm really quite accident-prone, have been my whole life, and you either acquire a sense of humor about stuff like this or you spend your whole life crying like a baby. Mandy found a gauze patch and pressed it onto my forehead, trying to wipe away the blood and get a look at the actual cut. When she saw it, her face brightened. "It's really not that bad."

The next fifteen minutes consisted of my sister stopping the blood, cleaning it up with peroxide—no big deal as the stuff stings only when it's infected—bandaging my head and making jokes about how I looked like I should be on *M*A*S*H*. This was all fine and dandy except for the jokes. I really did look like a fucking idiot; head wounds are not for the ultra-cool. I tried to position the bandages into a headband so I looked more like Rambo or some kind of Indian warrior, which was another big laugh. I ended up stealing one of Billy's baseball caps.

When I was all taken care of we went into the kitchen—a real blast from the past, with lime green Formica counters and this orange pyramid-style floor tile that had entertained me on more than one Robitussin kick. The table was already set, with orange juice and a beer for both of us and some very delicious-looking pancakes. I ate my share in about five seconds. I was famous for being a lightning-fast eater. Philly and Jeremy were always teasing me about that. Philly liked to go on about how for the first six months he knew me, he never saw me eat a meal. He would eat with me all the time, and he'd see me take the first bite, but after that it was all over. He was convinced I inhaled my food. This morning was no different, and like usual I finished way before Mandy and then just sat at the table, eyeing her food, practically drooling. No one I knew of had a bigger appetite. It's funny, too, 'cause I was always a skinny kid.

"What are you up to today?" she asked, mouth full of pancakes. She loved talking with her mouth full, showing off her half-chewed food. She got a huge kick out of it. I thought it was sort of disgusting.

"I was going to hang out with Jeremy and Philly," I said.

"Oh," she said, looking down.

"You're welcome to come," I offered, in an effort to cheer her up. It was actually kind of strange that I had never invited her before, what with how close to her I was and everything. I guess Philly and Jeremy and I were so used to ditching our familes and only depending on each other, I'd never thought of bringing Mandy into our circle. But if anyone deserved to be there, it was her.

"Sure," she said casually, but I could tell she was glad I invited her.

Although I had never brought it up with her, I suspected that she was soft on Jeremy, and I figured that was why she was so hot to come with me. I'd never known my sister to go out with anybody or anything, but it didn't bother me too much. Better Jeremy than just about anybody else.

Just as we were heading out the door my mom pulled up in her tiny white hatchback, which foiled my plan to escape before she showed up. She's always ready to nag me about whatever I'm not doing right on any given day, but today was a doozy. She was gonna lose her mind when she saw the blood on the carpet. Luckily my dad was out of town on business for two weeks, so at least for now I'd skip the beating.

Dad's absence was a good thing for my sister, too, who had cheered up enormously while he was away. At the time, I thought everything was really getting better.

Mom briefly greeted us on our way to the blue car, which

Mandy got to use whenever Dad didn't need it. She was wearing high heels and her gold jacket outfit. Her hair looked like it was newly blondified. Dad had told her once that it took ten years off her life, and now she was a hair dye addict. Personally, I thought it made her look like a forty-five-year-old Barbie doll.

If she noticed my bandage, she didn't say anything. She probably didn't want to know how I got it. I think she had gotten the impression that I'd become this big thug just 'cause I stayed out late with Philly and Jeremy a lot. Although she'd never come out and say it like Dad did, I really don't think she liked them much. She really viewed them as a negative influence on me, and later on my sister, as if we would have been perfect angels if they weren't around. They were easy scapegoats at a time when she needed to point the finger at somebody; she chose them, and probably always will. They're not around to convince her otherwise, and I don't think they would bother if they were. And knowing that, neither do I. Anyway, when they *were* around, she pretty much stayed out of the way, being distantly hospitable but secretly blaming them for everything. You shoulda seen the funeral. She was exactly like that.

Mandy was just starting the engine when I heard Mom start screaming. "JAMES EVAN YOU GET BACK IN HERE!" Boy, was I gonna get it.

Mandy started backing out of the driveway. She was giggling. "I'll see ya later, Mom!" I called out, pretending not to hear her, even though I could have heard her from Canada.

Mandy threw the car into first and stepped on the accelerator. Mom was still screaming as we rounded the corner. I could see her out on the curb waving her hands with her mouth open wide enough to catch a baseball. I was screwed, I knew it, but I figured I might as well have my kicks all day and then come home and catch hell, instead of getting yelled at now and then being grounded all day. I could be a professional procrastinator.

13

I was pretty excited because today I was going to smoke marijuana for the first time. Philly and Jeremy already had like a month before and they'd been giving me all kinds of shit, calling me "Virjim" constantly. Very hilarious, let me tell you, and they were both acting like they were suddenly the world's biggest big shots. That was fine by me, though, since I could outdrink the fuck out of either of those guys and they knew it as well as I did. It would be nice to get high anyhow. At least I could figure out what the big goddam deal about it was.

We swung by Philly's house first to pick him up. He didn't know I had a car and he was planning on catching a bus over to Jeremy's house where we'd all agreed to converge, but I figured I could surprise him with a ride.

He didn't answer the door, even after I practically broke my knuckles pounding on it. He was probably in the shower. He took two showers a day, every day. He said one was for him, and the other was to make up for Jeremy's dirty ass, who bathed about as often as Philly went a day without.

I tried the door. It was open, as usual. Philly's ma never locked it. She said true Christians never do. I guess she never heard the expression "Trust in God, but lock your door." That one never made a whole lot of sense to me, anyway.

Mandy followed me inside. The shower wasn't on, but we went upstairs anyway, calling his name.

The bathroom was empty, but Bob Marley was singing softly about three little birds on the other side of the door to his room. I put my hand on the doorknob, but decided against turning it, instead cupping my ear against the door. Almost immediately I had to clamp my free hand over my mouth, stifling a laugh that was just dying to pour out.

He was getting laid. I caught the tail end, to my great amusement. The girl was quietly going wild, and I'd never heard old Philly whimper before. I managed to keep quiet while they wrapped up, banging their hearts out then slower and slower creak-pause-creak-pause-final . . . moans-pause-one . . . cree*eek*-sigh. This was almost too much for me, but what I heard next—

Philly: "Hey, check this out!" Thump, tha-thump. "Betcha never seen this before!"

Girl: "Oh, Philly. Oh God. Oh my . . . they're *firm*."

—pushed me over the edge.

I fell hard against the door, laughing uproariously as it gave in to my weight and burst open, swinging out and away from me. I wasn't expecting it to do that and I kept moving, flying on the wings of my hysterical momentum, clutching my sides too hard to even break my fall, landing in a heap at Philly's naked feet, still howling.

"Oh man, Jim, ah—fucking A, man, don't . . ." Philly's face was beet-red by the time I finally managed to twist around and gaze up at him. He was choking on his words on their way out, trying to calm me down, trying to defuse the situation. The girl, who I recognized from school as Lucy Stern, could have used a little defusing herself. She'd been naked as the day she was born when I burst in, and by that point she was futilely trying to recover from her instant freak-out, which had consisted of a series of earsplitting shrieks crescendoing into an outright death cry (she was a screamer, I had on good information from sex maestro Philly) and simultaneously scrambling around searching for her clothes, half clad in a sheet I was very glad I could see through.

I stared unabashedly: I was fifteen years old and it was the closest thing to a good look at a naked girl I'd gotten in all those years. No way was I going to pass it up.

Philly looked sick. I'd blown his whole scene. He glanced back and forth between Lucy and me a couple times, muttered "I have to piss," and stumbled out of his room. He had to squeeze by Mandy, who was standing tentatively in his doorway. She hardly knew Philly, and you don't just pounce in on strangers giving butt-flexing shows. Not even Mandy did that. She did giggle a little bit as Philly brushed against her, though, hard as I could see she was trying not to. He was still entirely naked. I guess he figured the jig was up and there was no point in pretending otherwise. See Exhibit Lucy. She came off as a total floozy, falling all over herself trying to get clothed without our witnessing her I have to say very fine birthday suit. Philly at least retained a few ounces of cool.

Lucy was dressed and gone by the time Philly made it back into his room, which I guess was the way he wanted it. Not a bad play, either, in my opinion. Sometimes there's just no saving a thing, especially when that thing is as far gone as this one was. Times like that you just gotta fold, or hide in the bathroom, as the case may be. No, Philly would never again make passionate love to Lucy Stern. In fact, Philly would probably never again get to *talk* to Lucy Stern. That was fine by me. I didn't like her anyway. She hadn't said a single word to Mandy or me on her way out. Of course, I'd had my eyes closed and my head in my hands, giving it everything I had to preserve Lucy's half-naked image in my mind forever more. Mandy at least had tried to make pleasant conversation, saying she was sorry we'd come at such a bad time and all. Lucy hadn't even looked at her. Good riddance, I figured.

I could tell from the look in his eyes and the tone in his voice, though, that Philly couldn't have agreed less with me.

He was trying to be civil in front of Mandy, but it was pretty obvious he would have throttled me in cold blood if I wasn't one of his best friends. As it was, I was lucky he was talking to me. I didn't worry too much about it, though. I figured he'd be over it soon.

He was, too, by the time we were in the car and on the way to Jeremy's house. He wasn't one to hold a grudge, especially against me or Jeremy. And besides, for Philly there were always more girls.

Five minutes later we were in front of Jeremy's garage. Almost *in* Jeremy's garage, actually. He lives in an area of twisty backroads that Mandy always took like a roller coaster and slammed on the brakes at the last second. I swear we were going forty when we hit the sidewalk in front of his house, and my lungs were about to explode. I get asthma sometimes when I'm nervous, and cars scare the piss out of me. Riding in them always makes me think I'm on the verge of death.

Mandy skipped up to the front step of Jeremy's lima bean–colored house while I fumbled with my inhaler. Philly waited up for me. After a couple desperate puffs of the vile-tasting medication I was okay, and we walked across the lawn, slaloming between the Chemlawn signs. Jeremy's family was kicks. His dad was a neat freak who wanted to have the nicest-looking lawn on the planet, so he doused it with every weed and bug killer he could lay his hands on. Jeremy's mom always freaked out about this because she was an obsessive cat lover. She was afraid the Chemlawn would kill the neighborhood cats. Her solution to this national crisis was to put a DANGER KEEP OFF sign on every square foot of the lawn. The problem with this was that, as far as I could tell, neighborhood cats were allowed to run loose, and as far as I know cats can't read. I remember one time bringing this up to her but she broke down crying and asked me if I had a better idea. I didn't, so I quickly shut up, sorry I'd said anything.

Maryann let us in. She didn't seem exactly overjoyed to see us, but she did manage to mutter a quick "He's in his room," before going back to the *Mademoiselle* she was reading. Dick, the lawn lover, sat next to her on the brown loveseat, flipping through a magazine of his own and puffing on a cigar as long as my arm. The man breathed more smoke than air.

"Hi, Dick," I said in a mock friendly way, more to antagonize him than anything else. He really wasn't fond of me, and he didn't try to make a big secret out of it. Knowing this, though, I couldn't help but be super nice to him.

He looked up and grunted disapprovingly. How anyone can convey so much just by grunting is beyond me, but Dick did it all the time. It was practically his primary means of communication.

Mandy didn't know Jeremy's parents at all, so she didn't say hello and his parents ignored her.

We walked down the hall to the stairway that led to Jeremy's room, watched from all sides by framed felines. Opening the door to the basement, though, we entered a different world. It was obvious who was king of the basement. The stairs were lit by a red bulb hanging in the corner at the bottom, and the room itself was painted black and lit by Christmas lights and an ultraviolet tube glowing above his bed that he used to read by.

Jeremy was lying across his bed, which hung on chains attached to the ceiling. He was wearing sunglasses and strumming his guitar, the same two chords over and over. The strings were about five years old, and it wasn't a pretty sound, but he said it relaxed him. Any time you walked in on him unannounced, it was a good bet you would find him doing exactly this.

When Jeremy saw us he gently set down his guitar and jumped off the bed to greet us. It swung wildly behind him, smacking loudly against the wall repeatedly before losing its momentum. Jeremy grinned as we winced. He loved his bed, and not just because it rocked him to sleep at night, although I'm sure that was precious to him. It was just like him to have a bed that scared people and annoyed the hell out of his parents upstairs every time he got on or off of it. He took our flinching as a compliment.

Embraces went all around. In those days we were very physically close to each other. With the kind of parents we had, it was pretty understandable, even necessary. We never talked about it or anything, it was just part of life. Part of surviving.

The guys even hugged Mandy.

She and Jeremy hugged last, and they stayed together the longest. This was quite fishy as far as I was concerned, especially the way their hands were still touching even after they let go. And they were looking at each other almost excitedly. As if they were challenging each other, testing each other. As if they were *flirting*. I mean, maybe I was jumping the gun on all this, maybe thinking about it even before they were, but I saw their eyes shine, lighting up their faces, and I saw them smile the way they did, I saw them wanting to stand there holding hands all day, and I *knew*. Maybe even before they did, I knew. She was my sister, and he was one of my best friends in the whole world.

Naturally I stayed close to Philly. People always do that. If it's an even number you always end up splitting up into smaller groups. Most of the time it didn't bother me too much, but right then I was irritated, mostly 'cause I was looking forward to seeing Jeremy, and it didn't look like I would have a chance today with him glued to my sister like he was.

I turned my attention to Philly. "So whatup, man?"

He shrugged. His eyes were glazed over, and he seemed a little tipsy. I looked down by his feet and noticed an empty bottle of Robitussin, which he must have consumed while I was observing the love connection. Good old Philly. He was addicted to the shit. Like I said before, I didn't like it 'cause I was always falling asleep. Cool dreams, true, but I much preferred booze, because I could function so much better. Maybe after today I'd get into dope as well. That on top of a serious alcohol-induced stupor might prove highly valuable.

Needless to say I was all set on breaking out the marijuana right off the bat, but right then Jeremy's mom opened the door at the top of the stairs and said that Jeremy had too many people over and we'd have to leave very soon. Jeremy said there was no point in arguing and we should just bail. I was bummed at first, but Mandy sprung the idea of going to get Leslie and of course I was all for that. Philly and Jeremy were game, so we took off, filing out through the living room where we were subjected to more grunts while Jeremy asked for his allowance. After he'd pocketed it, we piled into the car and sped over to Leslie's.

14

Standing in the alley that ran alongside Leslie's house, I threw a handful of pebbles up to her window. Me and Mandy sang out "Lesleeeeee!" in the way we always did to get her to come out, in this ridiculously high, cheeseball falsetto. Philly and Jeremy looked at us like we were lunatics.

It never failed. The window slid open and Leslie's head,

now sporting the inch-long hair that was her ticket to freedom, poked out the window, smiling down at us from three stories up. She was there just long enough to screech in gleeful surprise, and call out "Hi you guys! I'll be right down!" We walked around to the front of the house just in time to see her skipping out the front door and down the steps of her rickety old porch, sailing first into Mandy's arms and then into mine, her touch as always leaving me a little out of breath.

"Ooh, it's so warm out." She sighed, and for the first time I noticed what a really great day it actually was. I mean, the sun was shining and the temperature was perfect, just warm enough to keep the chill outta your bones but cool enough so you don't have to sweat all over the place and look for a water fountain every five seconds. Leslie always noticed things like that right off, but sometimes I was so lost in my own head it could be the nicest day ever and I wouldn't even pay attention.

Leslie was dancing around her front yard like a ballerina. She was wearing this white skirt with little green frogs all over it, and it kept twirling out like crazy every time she spun around, which was quite a bit when she was this happy. Even though I was basically sober, except for a beer at breakfast, I was really flying. Even my sister had a smile on her face for once. According to her, the anticipation of getting stoned was almost as good as the actual thing, enough to cheer up anyone in their right mind.

Recently Leslie and I had agreed that we wanted to "go out," instead of just being friends—mostly on her initiative, seeing as how I don't have the balls to bring up things like that, and even when I do I just stutter like crazy and choke on my words. Anyway, I had never been happier in my life. I still couldn't believe that a girl like her would want a guy like me, but hey, I wasn't gonna argue about it. Still, though, we hadn't kissed or anything yet, or even talked about what the deal with us was since that one conversation. In case you're interested, it actually went like this:

Leslie: "Hey, Jim, will you be my boyfriend?"

Me: "Um, okay. Yeah, I mean."

Leslie: "Okay. That's good."

Me: "Yeah."

So it wasn't even a huge deal, really. We were both so shy about it and all. It seemed pretty childish even, her asking me like that. Leslie was that way though. Sometimes she went around acting like a wise old woman and the next second she was a little girl.

She turned back to us and her eyes lit up like little blue light bulbs. "Let's go swimming!" There was no arguing with her about that, and she started skipping off down the street. We caught up with her quickly enough. "Do you guys like my green frog skirt? I got it from the free clothing store yesterday. I felt a little bad because I don't need it and somebody else could have gotten it, but I just had to have it. It's the best skirt in the world." I exchanged sidelong looks with Philly, who also had a huge crush on Leslie, although he would never have done anything about it, knowing how in love with her I was.

It was a short walk to get where we were going. None of us knew where that happened to be, and asking Leslie on the way didn't do any good, since besides her skirt, keeping secrets was probably her favorite thing in the world. It turned out to be this huge rusted railroad bridge that ran over a little ten-foot-deep river that was so clear you could see all the way down to the bottom. Leslie ran right up onto the bridge, and with an excited scream dove straight down into the water. She came up gasping for air, telling us how warm it was and how we should all jump right in. That's exactly what we did, Jeremy first making sure to hide the pot under some scraggly bushes that ran along the shore so it didn't get all soaking wet. I also ditched Billy's cap and the *M*A*S*H.* bandage. The cut was closed up pretty good by now. I waited for the other three up on the bridge and we jumped in at the exact same time, Mandy just swinging her arms and legs around all over the place and me rolling up into a cannonball that completely soaked Leslie on impact and got us started on a five-minute splashing war, me against both Leslie and Mandy. Philly and Jeremy loved the jumping rush and as soon as they hit the water they would run up and do it again, alternating daring dives with trying for the most devastating cannonballs.

"Don't fuck with the Splash Master!" I howled, and ended up pretty much winning the battle with my special sweep-of-the-arm splash that practically scooped up the entire river and dumped it on their heads.

After another half hour or so of lazy swimming, Leslie trying unsuccessfully to teach me to back-float while Mandy swam around a good ways away with Jeremy, Philly grumbling nonstop about how he wished he had one of his many girlfriends with him, we all crawled up out of the water and onto the shore, drying off quickly in the exquisitely warm sun. Except for us the place was deserted, and Jeremy retrieved the pot from under the bush where he had stashed it. While we sat waiting he fumbled around trying to roll a joint, obviously no expert. After various jeers from me and Philly, he retorted, "Shut up Virjim," and Mandy offered to show him how. She placed just enough green in the middle to leave room for rolling space, then licked it and sealed it up, not making fun of Jeremy in the slightest but patiently explaining exactly how to do it. When she was finished, she leaned over and kissed him gently on the lips before lighting up.

My face flushed hotly. It wasn't that *I* wanted to kiss Jeremy and of course not my sister; I was just used to both of them paying a whole lot of attention to me. Today, since they'd gotten close to each other, neither of them had so much as glanced at me. Not that I blame them. They were fucked-up kids, like I was, maybe even more so. And they fell in love. I was just jealous, is all. I missed them already.

Mandy inhaled deeply on the joint, then passed it to Leslie, holding her breath till her face was red. She didn't exhale until Leslie was done and it was my turn. From carefully watching the girls, I figured this would be no problem. I was pretty sure Leslie didn't know this was a first for me, and I was going to make out like I was an ace at this. This was pretty stupid thinking on my part, 'cause of course Leslie wouldn't think any less of me for something as dumb as that. Not to mention the fact that there's more to toking up than meets the eye.

My plan was foiled right away; the first hit I took in I coughed right back out, wasting good weed and making a total fool of myself. Philly was quick to turn around and snicker at me, and Jeremy took the opportunity to repay me further for jibing at him about his rolling capabilities. Luckily Mandy and Leslie were both totally cool about it; they were patient with me while I fucked it up a couple more times before I finally managed to keep a hit in, and passed it over to Philly. It burned like hell on the back of my throat, and I still couldn't hold it in nearly as long as the girls could. Leslie understood the problems I was having and patted a reassuring hand on my back. I shuddered a little; her touch sent tingly slivers of nervous pleasure up my spine.

My throat was smoked raw by the time we finished off the joint, but that didn't bother me at all. I just lay there sprawled out in the sun, listening to everybody laughing and playing around, doing somersaults in the dandelions next to me, feeling nothing but giddy. When a few minutes later they all got tired out and came back over and Leslie lay down with her head on my chest, I had this nice three-quarters hard-on I was pretty sure she could feel. But that was just fine, everything was just fine, and who cared about what happened next or the hidden meanings I was always looking for behind everything Leslie did? Of course she was into me, you know, she wants to lie on me, that's cool, I'm down, and I was thinking goddam, I love this shit, this stuff is fucking great. Like I just drank from the goddam Fountain of Happiness or something. Things were pretty funny, too, I mean like the water kept trying to whisper knock-knock jokes in my ear, amusing shit like that.

I didn't really exactly hallucinate, not like on Robitussin or anything, not that day. Everything just looked kind of different. Like it was glowing or something. It's really hard to describe the visual side of a mild pot high. It's different if you get high out of your gourd. But if you don't smoke too much . . . it's just like everything fits together so much better, like suddenly no pieces are missing from any of the puzzles that we're always surrounded by.

We lay there a while longer, pointing at recognizable shapes in the clouds, tickling each other lazily and giggling like madmen. After the high had settled in we started playing on the bridge again, balancing on the railings. At one point Philly and I were trying to go in opposite directions on the same railing, and neither of us would get down, so we attempted to walk around each other on an area narrower than one foot across. Of course we failed miserably and plunged headlong into the water, but we were all getting hot again anyway. It became a game before long, first all of us trying to get around each other, then someone started pushing—I think Mandy—and it escalated into a game of chicken. Clumsy as I am, I'd probably fallen by far the most times when the cop car pulled up. Suddenly I was really nervous and got on this whole paranoid kick, like *They're really going to bust us hard, they're going to throw us all in jail* and everything. Dope can do that to you, too. One second you'll feel great and the next everyone's out to get you.

Well, *they* turned out to be just one old-man cop, who got out of his car like it was the last thing he wanted to do and sort of hobbled over to the bridge. I was the only one in the water at that point, and he walked up to the majority of the group who were up on the bridge. I walked up and around as soon as he started talking to them, and I was on the bridge by the time he finished his first couple of sentences. I figured we were all in deep shit, and I might as well face the music with the rest of them.

"How you kids doin' today?" He had a real over-the-top Grizzly Adams–type voice, if I wasn't just imagining things in my euphoric stupor.

"Fine."

"Fine."

"Great."

"Good."

"Pretty good."

We were all staring down at the tracks, saying the first thing that came to our heads. We wanted to get this over with as quickly as possible, hopefully without getting busted for the weed. I crossed my fingers and silently prayed that Jeremy would not choose now to do his spasmo act with the cop.

"Y'all know it's highly illegal, not to mention dangerous, to be up playing on this bridge?"

"No."

"No we didn't, sir."

"*I* wasn't aware of that."

"Me either."

"Gosh, we're sorry, Officer."

We were all shaking our heads like mad, trying to gloss over the situation and have him let us off the hook.

"Big tickets get issued for this kind of thing, guys," he said, shaking his head. He might as well have been wagging his finger. Besides that, his voice was really getting to me. I was having a hard time remembering he was a cop and not a lumberjack. I just kept on nodding my head at him and gritting my teeth so as not to burst out laughing uproariously. "You kids wait here," he said disapprovingly and walked back over to his car, getting on the CB to say God knew what. Maybe he thought we were too much for him to handle and he was radioing in for assistance.

He gave us our chance, and we jumped at it.

"Should we run?" Philly asked.

"Whaddaya mean!" Mandy exclaimed. "Fuckin' of course we run!" She took off then, leading the whole pack of us down the tracks, away from Officer Grizzly. I was at the rear end of the line because after everybody was long gone, I was still standing there staring at the old cop, picturing him wearing a flannel and carrying an axe. It didn't occur to me that it was time to follow my friends until I witnessed the grizzly geezer rushing toward me for all he was worth, his heart set on making the big bust. Well no sir, pal, not me. I dashed off in the direction of my already fleeing flock of best friends and loved ones.

The guy put up a good fight, but his legs were over half a century old, and mine less than a sixth; I left him to choke on my dust.

That was twice now in the past couple months that me and mine had led a senior citizen on a wild chase. I was starting to feel guilty. It was nobody's fault but theirs, though. I mean, they shouldn't have a job where they have to nab teenagers at high speeds if they can't hack it, right? I was holding up my end of the deal, fulfilling my self-assigned role as juvenile offender, putting up a good fight. I would have been a worthy challenge for the right candidate. Maybe it was hard to get good help in law enforcement around here.

By the time I was done justifying my abuse of Officer Grizzly and the previous offense of running away from the elderly manager at the drugstore, I had caught up with my friends, who were by then proceeding at a leisurely pace.

We wandered down the bank of the river for a while, still mighty stoned actually, and Philly passed out stolen smokes. I took one and smoked it leisurely. Just as I was wondering what happened to Leslie, she snuck up behind me and slipped her hand into mine, kissing me lightly on the neck. I leaned my head against hers, and we were stuck to each other for a while, Siamese twins trying to keep up with the others. My knees and heart were melting.

Eventually we got hungry and decided to go over to my house and raid the fridge. We started walking back to Leslie's to get the car, taking forever because every ten feet or so one of us would stop to look at something or fall over laughing or just trip and fall on their face. Philly and Jeremy repeatedly slowed us up, lying down in the middle of the road and pretending they were cars. I wasn't convinced, but Jeremy was churning out some pretty nice engine-revving sound effects.

We walked by Sunshine, and Philly insisted on going in to say hi to Charlie. I went in with him.

"Charles!" Philly shouted at Charlie, who was standing behind the counter as we walked in the door. "Charles in Charge! What's happening, my man?"

Charlie's face lit up the moment he saw Philly. "Oh, not much, Philly, just working, you know. What's up with you?"

"Not much here either," Philly said, waltzing up to the counter and clapping his hand on Charlie's shoulder. "We's just hanging out, brother."

When you listened to the two of them chat back and forth,

you'd have no idea that anything more than small talk was crossing between them. There was, though. Philly had this deal worked out with me and Jeremy, an agreement that we would never swear or talk about stealing or drinking or fucking or anything in front of Charlie. He wanted us to be heroes in front of Charlie. All Charlie's older brothers were thugs, and Philly knew how important it was for him to have some genuinely good older kids to look up to, and if we weren't those kids, we goddam well better pretend we were. So we did. We tried our best to be the picture of perfection. We pretended, and did a pretty good job of it, too, for as long as we possibly could, well after it was very clearly only an image.

When we finally did get to Leslie's, me and Mandy and the guys sat down in the front yard having dandelion wars while Leslie went inside for a minute. The second she was out of sight my sister and I forgot all about the dandelions and started singing out "Lesleeee!," which struck us both as so hilarious that when Leslie finally did come out we were still rolling around on the ground laughing idiotically. Philly and Jeremy weren't paying any attention to us. Philly had gotten into the driver's seat of Mandy's car, and Jeremy was sprawled face-down on the windshield, making funny faces at Philly. Philly pulled the windshield wiper fluid lever, and the stuff sprayed directly into Jeremy's eye; the wipers started swinging, smacking poor Jeremy in the face as he slid down off the windshield and onto the hood, holding his eye and his jaw. I just about pissed my pants. Mandy was still writhing around, clutching her ribs and turning blue. Philly was in the same condition, unwittingly honking the horn over and over as he pounded his head against the steering wheel. The whole situation was crazy. It was time to split before somebody called the cops again.

When we could stand up we all piled into Mandy's car. The three of us scrunched into the backseat, our elbows practically punching holes in each other's guts. Leslie sat up front next to Mandy. She had this big block of cheddar cheese and a knife she had brought along from her house and we munched on that on the ride to my house.

When nobody wanted any more I took the last wedge of it and slid it down the knife so it was resting at the top of the handle. It made the knife look to our stoned eyes a lot like a sword, and I started swinging it around and jabbering in an English accent like I was a knight or something.

15

Neither car was in the driveway when we got home. This was a plus, 'cause it meant that we wouldn't have to go through the usual routine, putting on this giant sober act and getting the hell out of the kitchen and into one of our bedrooms as quickly as possible without raising suspicion. It always ended up being this huge hassle, and ruined half the fun of getting fucked up in the first place.

We walked inside, and Mandy and Jeremy (who had made a full recovery: his wounds were a lot more humorous than they were painful) collapsed together on the old orange couch that had lived here longer than I had. It was starting to get pretty threadbare in places, but the fancy mahogany legs were still pretty impressive, except for where me and Mandy had carved our initials into it with a penknife I got for Christmas when I was six. She kept her feet dangling off the edge—a casual gesture, but in a house like ours you do what you can to stay out of trouble. Leslie had never been over before, and she skipped around the house happily, humming tuneless ditties to herself and exploring every room like she was looking for hidden treasure. I guess that's what life was like to her, most of the time. She was always looking for the treasure in life, the little bits of poetry that are there for all of us if we look hard enough.

I showed her the door to the basement and then left her to check that out on her own. I walked back through the kitchen and the living room, where Mandy and Jeremy were lying on the couch tickling each other half to death, and down the hallway that led to everybody's bedrooms. The white stucco walls were still stained from when me and Mandy used to track mud all over them by planting one hand and one foot firmly on each wall, and then literally walking on the walls. This was always great fun and laughs for us until Mandy fell and broke her arm, and neither of us had done it since.

My brother's door was the first one on the left. It had this big black-and-white sticker, right at eye level, that said, IT'S NOT HOW YOU PICK YOUR NOSE BUT WHERE YOU PUT THE BOOGERS. The sticker wasn't so white anymore, though, because whenever one of Billy's friends had a booger they stuck it right on the sticker, usually when Billy wasn't looking, so by the time he found it it was all dried and caked on. He would actually scrape them off, but the stains couldn't be helped.

I knocked, careful to avoid the boogerfest. My little bro opened the door almost immediately. "Hey Jim," he said cheerfully, opening his door wide. His room was practically spotless, as usual. The walls were covered with *Star Wars* and *Star Trek* posters. Billy loved both; I don't think he really even distinguished between the two. Philly was already in there, playing with a half-finished model of some kind of spaceship on his bed.

"What's that?" I asked him.

He looked at me like I was hopeless. "The *Millennium Falcon,* silly." He might have worshipped me, but he sure didn't act much like me. I guess in the end that was a pretty good thing.

"Jeez Louise, Jim, even I knew that," Philly said, rolling his eyes.

"Yeah, well . . ."

"What's going on?" Billy asked me.

"Ah, we all just came over to grab some food. We might go out again. I'm sure it'd be cool if you came." I hadn't seen much of him lately and I felt guilty, like I was neglecting him, so I was sort of trying to make things up to him by inviting him along with me *and* my friends, which I wouldn't normally do. My brother was a cool little guy, really very openhearted. Sometimes I would try to play a trick on him or be sarcastic with him, and he wouldn't get it at all. He couldn't even conceive of the notion that I would be a jerk to him.

"Sure, yeah," he said. He liked the idea of coming with us, I could tell. Philly and Jeremy got a big kick out of him, and whenever they were over they'd hang out and shoot the bull around with him, I mean without being the least bit condescending or anything, and Billy loved getting that much respect. My parents sure didn't give him any.

Billy started talking to Philly about the model he was making, showing him the detailed blueprints, which I guessed was the conversation I interrupted when I walked in. Stuff like that bores me to tears so I said good-bye and left them alone. I don't think they even noticed.

Mandy and Jeremy were still in the living room, lying on the couch together. It looked like she'd passed out on top of him. He asked me if he should wake her up. I told him good luck. Usually it was practically impossible to get her up once she was out. Once, for a joke, when I was trying to get her up to go to school and she just wouldn't lift an eyelid, I called 911 and told them I thought my sister was dead. An ambulance came and everything. It was pretty funny until I got the lecture from my mom about how there could have been someone that really needed that ambulance but couldn't get it because of my immature little prank, and now someone was probably dead because of me. She had me convinced I was going to jail for murder. I was terrified. The ambulance guys were pretty cool about it, seeing as how I was only eight, but they explained to me how I could have gotten in a lot more trouble. Basically the same spiel as my mom's, only a lot nicer. This one guy, the one who did most of the talking, I could have sworn he was one of the same guys who picked me up by the railroad bridge eight years later right after that bullet took a chunk out of my back.

Jeremy shook her a little bit, and by some stroke of good fortune she opened her eyes immediately.

"Where's Leslie?" Mandy asked me, rubbing her eyes and letting loose with a terrific yawn. Nobody could yawn like her. Her jaws opened incredibly wide. One time I saw her fit a whole grapefruit between them.

"I dunno. I was just about to go find her," I said, grateful for the opportunity to leave them. I headed off in the direction of the basement, which is where I'd last seen Leslie going. At least she'd be glad to see me.

Our basement is furnished, with a nice carpet and a couch, a couple of recliners, some very so-called chic, high-class razzle-dazzle prints by famous artists, and, of course, a television, which the couch and the chairs all pointed at, like the TV was some great ruler. But no sign of Leslie. I glanced out the window in the door to the garage, about to head back upstairs.

There she was, sitting in the middle of a circle of boxes, like a saint surrounded by her disciples. She was going through those old boxes that Mandy loved so much, full of trinkets, photographs, wedding gifts, letters. God, I wished I could have known my parents when they were happy. When I was born they'd already been married for six years, and things started going downhill when I was three and my dad started drinking again. I never liked looking through those boxes. It always depressed me. Mandy sure did, though. She holed up in there most every day for at least an hour or so. She remembered that time. She had happy, loving parents until she was almost six, whereas I was too young to remember. Sometimes, after me and Mandy got in trouble with Dad or something, she would hold me in her arms and tell me stories, stories about when our parents were good to us. Sometimes even little Billy would listen, 'cause even though my mom babied him a lot and all, he was still deathly afraid of my father. My dad never hit Billy, but he tasted the abuse and the hatred of my father in other ways. It came through, believe me. It came through.

I opened the door to the garage as quietly as I could, but Leslie looked up anyway, her face solemn in a way I had never seen it before. "Come here," she said, scooting over and making room for me.

I shook my head. "Oh, I don't—"

"No, really," she said, her eyes pleading with me. "I want you to see something."

Something in her voice convinced me, and reluctantly I joined her amid the boxes.

"Look at this." It was a black-and-white picture, frayed at the edges, of a little boy in a black suit standing in front of a white house with a white picket fence around it. The boy's face was blank, but his eyes looked very sad, on the verge of tears. "So, so sad," Leslie said quietly, echoing my thoughts.

"Who's this?" I asked, looking up at her.

Her eyes met mine, and didn't look away. "Your dad. Look on the back."

I turned the picture over. In the lower left-hand corner was written, *"Steven, after Mom's funeral, '55."*

My jaw dropped. In 1955 my dad was five years old. I never knew his mom had died. Abruptly, I handed the picture back to Leslie and stood up, looking away.

"What a sad, sad man," I heard Leslie whisper from a long way away. I was too lost in shock to respond right away. She spoke again. "Don't you get it, Jim?" She was standing next to me now.

"Huh?"

She took my arm, trying to force me to look at her. I wouldn't. "He hasn't changed, Jim. He's still that sad little boy. Don't you get that?"

"No," I said, irresolute. "I don't." My voice faltered. I'd always considered my dad evil, or close to it, but I was so busy hating him I never thought to ask why. That photograph was like a secret window in the house of scarred oblivion I had been raised in; looking out of it, I could see my father not as a terrible, evil man, but as a sad man, scared to death himself, at least as confused as I was. For once I understood him. I keep trying to hold on to that, even now.

The door swung open then, and Mandy walked into the garage. She looked funny—one side of her face was plaid from sleeping pressed against the couch—but she didn't look like she was feeling very funny. "You found the picture," she said.

"Yeah," I said, glancing down at it.

"I found it a couple of years ago. It's the only picture of him as a kid I've ever seen."

"Me, too."

"It's the only reason I don't murder him," she said softly.

"Yeah," was all I could think of to say. Then, "Why didn't you show me?"

She shrugged, I think not wanting to answer. When she did speak, what she said would stick with me forever. "I didn't want you to be trapped into feeling sorry for him. I was hoping . . . I was hoping maybe you would kill him."

I looked at her, almost blankly. I opened my mouth to speak, then shut it. I felt suddenly tight inside. What was I supposed to say?

At the time, I thought she needed a saint, the saint I wanted so badly to be. To once and for all lift her spirits, to somehow, anyhow, make things well again. Later, when I finally, suddenly, realized how much she meant what she said to me that day, I wanted to be a killer. But I was neither. I wanted, more than anything, to be the kind of person who could save my sister's life. I should have been wiser. Tougher. Older. That was my real sin, dumb as it sounds. I was just a fucking kid. I'm still just a fucking kid.

It was Mandy that finally spoke. "Mom's home. She says we can't go out 'cause we're all eating here tonight. It's a family bonding thing, I guess. Oh yeah, Jim, Mom wants to talk to you about the floor."

I'd forgotten all about the bloody floor upstairs. I didn't even mind knowing Mom was gonna let loose on me about it. I was grateful for the distraction.

Leslie stood up then. "I better go," she said awkwardly.

"You can stay," Mandy said, smiling wanly. "Jeremy and Philly are already sticking around, and I don't think you being here will make her flip out more than she already is."

"Yeah, it's cool," I said, trying to sound all casual. Truth was, I wanted her to stay badly.

"I know, but my mom gets lonely, all by herself with Grandma all the time. I've already been gone all day. We fight a lot, but I know she really needs me around."

We walked her upstairs to the front door. She hugged everybody good-bye and said it was nice to meet my brother. I was about to walk her to the bus stop when my mom came in from the kitchen, looking like she was ready to tear my head off, but still pleasant in front of all the "guests." She was great that way.

"Jim, could I see you in the kitchen for a minute?"

"I'm just gonna walk Leslie to the bus stop, I'll be right—"

"Jim, *now.*"

"Okay." I was still trying to play it off like it was no big deal. I glanced around at everybody as I followed her half solemnly, half still grinning into the kitchen. Philly and Jeremy were smirking and whispering to each other. The others gave me sympathetic looks. I didn't know which was worse.

In the kitchen it was all serious. "*What* did you *do* to the *floor*?" Mom talked like that when she was majorly pissed off, accenting words, really laying it on.

"Well, uh, you know, I, uh, see there was this . . ." That's what I did when she got like that. Pure bullshitting, actually, but, sometimes it got me off the hook. This time I couldn't even come up with the lamest excuse. I was drawing a complete blank.

"*Why* did you—*how* could you *do* such a thing, Jim?"

"What?" Play dumb, that's a good one. I felt like an idiot, trying to cop out of this.

"Jim, there's *blood* all over the *carpeting*. How do you expect me to get that out?" She was practically crying. Very panicky, let me tell you.

I couldn't stand it anymore. I hated seeing Mom cry. "Listen, Mom, don't worry, I'll pay for it. Don't give me any allowance for the next twelve years. Okay?"

She was really bawling now. This is where she falls all over herself apologizing, hugging me and telling me how much she loves me but how hard I make things for her sometimes.

"I know, I know, it won't happen again," I always say.

So that's how it ends. I agree to take care of everything, seeing as how it's all my fault, and let my mom know I know what a good mother she is; she stops bawling and smiles real big for the next hour, like she wasn't just screaming at me. Even if I yell back, call her names, even after Dad beats me, she's always grinning from ear to ear afterward like we have this *Leave It to Beaver* family where everything works out. God, I get sick of that. Just for once I want her to acknowledge that everything sucks and there's nothing she can do about it.

When she finished hugging me the routine was over, and we both went back into the living room, Mom making sure everybody saw how happy she was. I made a beeline for the door, where Leslie was still standing. As we left I heard Mom making small talk with Philly and Jeremy, asking if they were enjoying their summer and all that, offering them sodas like a perfect host. Nauseating, man. I could puke.

16

Outside it was getting dark, and the air was cooling off a little, but it was still pretty warm. I love nights like that, when you can stay out all night in a short-sleeve shirt.

Leslie took off her shoes and started walking in the grass by the sidewalk, as she almost always did.

I walked along next to her, feeling awkward and clumsy beside her graceful steps. Still, she took my hand in hers and squeezed it gently, so at least I knew she forgave me my feet being twice as big as they were supposed to be.

We walked together quietly for a while. It was more a nervous silence than a peaceful one; I was biting my tongue trying not to say the wrong thing while Leslie waited patiently for me to say something. I kept making little goals for myself—by the time we get to that tree I'm gonna say something, or by the time we get to that stop sign—but every time I hit the mark I would choke, and when we got to the bus stop I still hadn't said a word. Knowing I didn't have much more time—and that I would feel like a total idiot if this girl got on the bus and I hadn't said something or kissed her or hardly even looked at her—I finally managed to stammer out, "I don't know what to say." Boy, what a great line. Now I could just flash her my winning smile and everything would be marvelous.

Leslie looked up at the sky for a minute and then closed her eyes tight, as if she were making a wish. "I know something you could say," she said softly, almost hesitantly, which was weird for her.

"What?" I asked anxiously, deeply anxiously, like in the farthest, itchiest, saddest, most painful and childish and jittery part of my soul, I needed to know what she was looking at behind those scrunched-shut eyes.

"You could say you are madly in love with me and you never want to leave me."

My jaw dropped. Actually, it felt like my heart dropped right onto the sidewalk. Slowly, shyly, a smile spread across my face, until I was grinning as widely as I ever had. After I convinced myself she had actually said what I heard her say, I returned her gaze, which was now on me. "Well, yeah, I could definitely say that."

"Really?" Leslie asked me hopefully, earnestly, and I realized she had been as unsure about how I felt as I had been of her. I liked that. It reminded me she was human. I kept forgetting that.

I opened my mouth to say it, to swear my undying love for her, but when I opened my mouth it was like all my oxygen was cut off, and what came out just sounded like a big gulp.

Right then the bus came around the corner, and Leslie looked over at it and at me and back and forth again, and I just kept on gulping for air like I was in outer space or something. I knew I only had a couple of seconds but I couldn't say it, I really couldn't, not right then when I needed to, so I did what I figured was the next best thing. This I thought would be really harder than talking, but I was going to explode if I didn't do something, something really drastic, so just as the bus pulled up to the curb I leaned toward her and put my arms around her neck, gently but urgently, desperately, and I pressed my lips against hers, and our tongues were dancing and my heart was only inches from hers, and it was fantastically beautiful.

It lasted about ten seconds or eternity, depending on who you're asking.

When her lips left mine I could breathe again, or at least enough so I didn't feel like I was getting strangled. I wasn't sure how she was going to react, in fact I hadn't even thought about it until right then, but she was smiling and her eyes were glowing and I knew for sure that it had been something good. She got on the bus then, without looking back.

I brought my hand to touch my lips, running my fingers over them almost disbelievingly. Then, when the bus was small and far away, I yelled, knowing she couldn't hear me but needing to say it anyway. "Hey Leslie! I'm madly in love with you and I never want to leave you!"

Then, with a whoop and a holler of wild, unconstrained joy, I took off running down the street back toward my house. My feet touched the ground only every six feet or so, and I felt like I was flying. I collapsed in a heap on my front doorstep. I had asthma but I didn't care.

Philly and Jeremy had been hanging out by the picture window in the living room, waiting for me to get back. As soon as they saw me, they opened the front door, tripping over each other to get to me, both of them playfully socking me in the arms and asking me a million questions.

"What happened?"

"Did you kiss her?"

"What'd she say?"

"You hit on her?"

"When are you gonna kiss her?"

"Didja fuck her?"

"No, I didn't—what kind of a question—we just went to to the *bus* stop, for God's sake."

"All right." Philly backed off, I guessed not wanting to rile me up.

I was wrong. He always did get a rise out of messing with me, and as we walked together into the living room on our way to the dining room where everybody else was already sitting at the table, Philly muttered, "I still think you coulda done it. That bus shelter's got a bench—"

That was as far as he got before I roared playfully and tackled him to the floor. We rolled around on the carpet, taking turns pinning each other, more him on top of me than me on him, as he was actually a lot stronger than me. I'm sort of a weakling, if you want to know the truth.

Jeremy joined in, jumping on top of us, but his wrestling was halfhearted and almost as quickly as he started he got up and joined everybody in the dining room. I looked up at him, concerned. I didn't want to leave him out of things. He acted like that sometimes, though. He told me once that he always felt alone, even with Philly and me. I worried about it sometimes, but right then Philly pounced on me, and I didn't have time to think about it.

My mom tolerated our antics for about a minute—until I accidentally slammed my foot into the couch, making a much louder bang than you'd think it would. "Jim, it's time for dinner."

She liked to talk with her teeth clenched shut to let me know she was annoyed.

"Beat ya again." Philly grinned as he helped me up, combing his bright orange mop of hair out of his eyes with his other hand.

"Yeah, yeah, you're a wimp," I muttered as we walked into the dining room, even though we both knew he was right.

We sat down in the two empty chairs, me next to my mom and Philly on my other side. My mom looked impatient. Jeremy and Mandy were pretty occupied with each other, holding hands and lost in each other's eyes. Billy was lost in his food, staring at it longingly like he hadn't eaten in a year. As soon as we sat down my mom started eating, which gave everyone else the signal that it was okay to do the same. Mom was the queen of manners when guests were around. Sometimes we even said grace, but I think she was probably too irritated tonight. The whole thing, waiting for us to sit down to start eating and all, was a joke anyway. When there were no guests over we didn't even usually eat at the table together. Dad usually ate in front of the TV, my mom and Billy at the table, and me and Mandy together in one of our rooms. Sometimes Billy ate with us, if Mom was having one of her crying fits. It didn't surprise me, though. I was used to pretending we had a normal family any time we had visitors. It was kind of amusing actually, in a sick way. Especially when my dad was around. It was a real trip watching him trying to be sociable. At least then he treated Mandy and me like normal human beings. Still, the fakeness of the whole thing always made me lose my appetite, and I only ate about two bites and then just sat there waiting to be excused.

17

After dinner Philly and I went into my bedroom and Mandy and Jeremy went into hers. I felt another little pang of jealousy as I watched him walk past my room and into hers; I'd been expecting him to hang out with me and Philly, but he didn't even consider it.

Philly and I were planning to get drunk on a bottle of vodka I had lifted from my dad's liquor cabinet. It was pretty harsh stuff, but we had some soda to wash it down with. We just kinda kicked back in my bed with the light turned low, listening to Pink Floyd and every now and then downing a shot and chasing it with soda. It wasn't so bad that way.

After a couple hours of that we were pretty plastered and trying to think of something to do. I wanted to call Leslie. Luckily the phone was next to my bed because I wasn't too sure I would be able to walk anywhere. I dialed the wrong number about a million times, including a pizza place, which I accidentally ordered from.

"Hello, Pizza Supremo." The guy had this really nasal, squeaky voice. If he was right in front of me I probably would have punched his lights out. That's how I get when I'm drunk.

"Leshlie?" I answered. I would have done drunks proud all over the world.

"This is Pizza Supremo," he repeated.

"You have pizzha at Leshlie's houshe?" I was wishing he'd just hand the phone to Leslie, but he seemed like he really wanted to talk.

"Look, buddy, are you gonna order a pizza?" The sound of his voice was hurting my ears. He was breathing loud and heavy, like he'd just got done running the goddam Boston Marathon. My fifth grade teacher, Mr. Cassetti, almost won it one year. He was this tall thin guy with a little wispy brown mustache, and he was always running between classes. He was my favorite teacher all through school. He was always smiling at me and telling me to keep writing and all. I wondered what Mr. Cassetti would think if he saw me drunk out of my mind like that.

"Do you want a pizza there or not, buddy?"

"Okay, a large cheeshe." Maybe if I ordered a pizza he would let me talk to Leslie.

"Where to?"

"Leshlie," I said. Boy, I was really a goner. Philly was laughing like a madman and trying to get me to drink more, but I was trying to talk at the same time, and I ended up just spitting it all over my chin and shirt.

"Where's Leslie?" He was practically yelling in my ear, like that would make me understand better or something.

"Ish thish a tesht?"

"What?"

I figured I'd just give him Leslie's address and then he'd shut up. "Sixteen twenty-one Mary Street."

"Okay, buddy. Nine ninety-five, be about forty-five minutes."

"Now can I pleashe talk to Leshlie?" I was begging him, but I was talking to a dial tone.

I looked at Philly. "He hung up on me."

"That wasn't Leslie's house, you dummy. Gimme the phone. Here, have a drink." Philly grabbed the phone from me and was in the process of dialing when Billy barged into the room. He was holding the *Millennium Falcon* model in his hand. I guess he had just finished it.

"Hey, guys, check this—" He looked up and saw me holding

the bottle of vodka. He was old enough to know what it was. He'd seen Dad drinking enough times to know, anyway. He didn't say anything to me about it, but he'd never seen me drink before and I could see the shock spread across his face.

"Get outta here, Billy," I said, setting the bottle down and standing up off the bed and moving closer to him, firm even in my drunkenness. The last thing I wanted was for my little brother to see me drinking. I felt terrible that he'd seen as much as he had already. I wanted to be more than that to him, you know?

He was practically tugging on my shirt. "Aw, c'mon, Jimmy, I won't *bother* ya. I just want to hang—"

"I said *no*, Billy. Now scram, okay?" I'd raised my voice, which I'd never done with him before. Even as something inside me was telling me to stop, to back off and leave him alone, I moved ominously closer to him.

"*Philly* doesn't mind, do you, Philly?"

He shrugged his shoulders. "I don't care. Jim, why don't ya—"

"Yeah, Jimmy, *please*—" Billy was right in my face, or as much as he could be being a head shorter than I was.

"I said NO!" I pushed him out the door, I guess a lot harder than I meant to. He slammed against the wall of the hallway. His head snapped backward, making a loud crack as it smacked against the wall. He fell to the floor, doubled over and crying.

I rushed over and knelt next to him, suddenly feeling a lot more sober. I wasn't angry at all anymore; I just wanted to make sure he was okay. "Are you all right, Billy? Are you okay?" My heart was beating about a million times a minute, and I could barely breathe. "I'm sorry Billy, I'm sorry, I'm sorry . . ."

He was really bawling, calling for his mother. He wouldn't say anything to me or even look at me. I did manage to feel where he hit his head; there was a big bump, but he wasn't bleeding or anything. It wasn't even as bad as the cut I had gotten on my own head that morning, walking into the low ceiling. Still, I felt horrible. I knew he was mostly crying because I had hit him, not because of the pain. I just kept telling him I was sorry, over and over again, not knowing what else to do. He wouldn't let me hold him.

My mom came running into the hallway, wearing her bathrobe. Her hair was all wet, and it looked like she had just gotten out of the shower. That was why she hadn't come right away when Billy started calling for her. Usually if one us started crying she was there immediately.

She shoved me out of the way and wrapped her arms around him, standing up with him and asking him where it hurt. All he would say is that I hit him. He just kept saying that over and over. Mom moved him farther away from me, as if there was a chance I would hit him again. I wondered briefly who she thought I was. I wondered who I thought I was. Suddenly I got too depressed to move. Mom was yelling at me about how my father would hear about this. Philly was standing in my doorway, looking worried and confused. He was holding the cap to the bottle of vodka we had been drinking. I don't know why I noticed that. Everything in my vision had become real sharp, crystal clear. If I had to pick one moment over the past couple years, one instance when everything slipped, when suddenly nothing was okay anymore, that would have been it.

I noticed then that the door to my sister's room was open and she stood in the doorway, Jeremy behind her. They had been making out, I could tell. Mandy's maroon hair was all messed up, and her shirt was on backward with the tag out. Jeremy was wrapped in a green blanket, the one that usually covered Mandy's bed. I was too sick and depressed to care. Jeremy was looking at me with these sad eyes that just made me feel worse. I looked into Mandy's eyes, hoping for some kind of redemption. Forgiveness, maybe. I wanted her to tell me it would be okay. Her eyes were cold. She was staring at me, her mouth slightly open. I wanted to speak, to tell her I didn't mean it, that it was an accident, but I couldn't make myself say anything at all. I wanted her lips to move. Out of place as it would have been, I wanted desperately for her to smile. After what seemed like a very long time her lips did move and I heard her voice, as if from very far away, form three words, softly, weakly.

"How could you?" she said, and my world shattered.

I never saw her smile again.

AUGUST 1991

18

The day my sister died was a beautiful one. Don't think I've seen a bluer sky or a brighter sun before or since. Sometimes I think it was the sky's way of saying good-bye.

Leslie had shown up at my house early in the morning, around nine or so, which was way earlier than I was used to getting up during the summer, especially as hung over as I was. I had spent the night alone in my room, getting high on pot and whiskey and listening to Mandy cry. Getting high alone is about the most depressing thing in the world, so I was glad to see her. I was always happier around Leslie, at least back then.

I woke to her knocking on my window. I sat up in bed quickly, startled. Everything was pretty blurry. I had been dreaming I was at a circus and somebody let the lions out and they were chasing me around. At first, I wasn't quite sure which was real, Leslie or the circus, and I rubbed my eyes to get them to start seeing right. I saw Leslie standing outside, looking at me expectantly. I opened the window and stuck my head out.

She kissed me tenderly on the lips. I grinned. Not a bad way to wake up. "Get up, silly. It's practically noon."

I glanced at my clock next to bed. "It's *nine-thirteen*, Leslie."

"Were you sleeping?" she asked innocently.

"Sure I was sleeping. Why aren't you?" I said it curious, not mean.

"Because we have an important mission today, and we can't waste any time. Get dressed. I'll wake up Mandy."

A sliver of pain hit me in the gut when she mentioned my sister. Things had really changed after what happened with my brother. Mandy didn't go out much anymore, and when she did it wasn't with me. Leslie saw her sometimes, but mostly she hung out with Jeremy. Sometimes I would hear her in Billy's room, talking to him. Not much, though. She barely talked to me anymore. Mostly she stayed in her room. She drank even more than I did, and most every night I heard her cry herself to sleep. Every day I tried to talk to her, but she would just kind of look at me for a while and then go back into her room and lock the door, which she never used to do.

I tried to tell Leslie it wouldn't work but she wouldn't listen.

"Nonsense. This nonassociatin' business between you two has gone far enough. Now get dressed. Philly and Jeremy are going to meet us down at the railroad bridge. Hurry up."

Then she was gone, moving away from my window. As I closed it, I heard her rousting Mandy. I started sifting through clothes on my floor, trying to find the least dirty ones and pulling them on. If anyone could make this work, it was Leslie.

I stepped out into the hallway at the same time as my sister did. We looked at each other tentatively. Her eyes were red, her cheeks streaked with tears. My heart ached, but all I said was "Hi." It sounded weak and useless between us.

"Hi," she said, and walked past me. She brushed against me,

and her hand touched mine in passing, and I could have imagined it but I would swear she sort of took hold of my hand for a second. But it was only a second, and then she went into the kitchen. I followed a moment later, and we quietly poured ourselves bowls of cereal and sat down at the dining room table across from each other. I wanted badly to look up at her, but I could only stare into the bowl.

I heard Leslie come in the front door and walk through the living room. She didn't come into the kitchen. I heard her walk down the hall, speaking quietly to my little brother. Leslie loved to fix things, but I was afraid this time she was taking on more than she could handle. Billy still talked to me a lot more than Mandy did, but I noticed lots of little things different now between us. Everything would seem fine if we were in the living room together or something, but he wasn't exactly busting down the door to talk to me when I was in my room. And every now and then when I was around him I would make some kind of a sudden motion, you know, just to grab something or whatever, and he would jerk away like he was afraid I was gonna hit him. I didn't know how to make him trust me again. I was afraid he never would.

By the time I'd washed my dish and come back into the dining room, Billy was standing there in the doorway, looking at me. Leslie was behind him.

"Go ahead," she said, gently nudging him forward a little and smiling at me.

"Jimmy?" he said, like he was making sure I was really there in front of him, listening.

"Yeah?"

"Could I . . . can I come with you guys?"

"Sure, Billy." I walked over to him, ruffling his hair, but making sure I moved my hand slow enough so as not to freak him out. "Sure you can." I smiled at him. After a moment, he smiled back.

A few minutes later Leslie ushered us all out, saying we had to catch the bus. I guess she was probably in a hurry to get us out of there before one of us decided this was all a bad idea.

Outside there wasn't a cloud in the sky. It was really warm out, especially for so early in the morning. We walked to the bus stop slowly. Leslie and I paired up in front, Mandy and Billy behind us. Leslie looked especially beautiful that day. She was wearing this blue-and-white checkered dress I'd never seen before. I smiled when I looked at her knees, all scraped up.

The bus showed up just as we were meandering up to the stop. Billy didn't have any money, so I paid his fare. The ride over to the railroad bridge was a long one, and Leslie took a catnap, resting her head on my shoulder. Mandy sat next to me, with Billy on her other side. She still wasn't talking much, and when I glanced at her eyes they were all watery, like if you'd so much as bumped her the tears would have spilled over onto her face. After a while I shut my eyes, to rest them and also because right then I couldn't bear to watch Mandy the way she was anymore.

I leaned my head against Leslie's. Just touching her soothed me. I don't think she knew how much I needed her, as I didn't exactly let it show on my face too often, but her presence kept me breathing. I was terrified of her leaving me. I was afraid if she did, my heart would stop. And in a way, I was right. In a way, when she disappeared after Mandy died, it did.

Billy pulled the cord as we approached our stop. Without him, I don't know where we would have ended up. He was the only one looking.

19

Philly and Jeremy were waiting for us, sitting on the ledge of the railroad bridge, swinging their legs back and forth in time with each other. As we walked up the hill to the bridge Jeremy jumped down to greet us, and Philly casually fell over backward, laughing as he took the ten-foot plunge backward into the water. Jeremy slapped my little brother five and gave Leslie and Mandy hugs, lingering close to Mandy. I extended my hand to him awkwardly. He had become much more Mandy's than mine.

He pushed my hand aside and gave me a quick hug. I was grateful for his affection. At least some things were still the same.

Philly came scampering up the hill then, soaking wet in all his clothes. Everybody but me and Leslie shied away from him. Neither of us really cared about getting wet and we both hugged him. After I did, though, I sort of changed my mind. Even in the heat it gave me goose bumps, especially as water ran down my pants.

We all sat down in a circle, without a word, just looking at one another. Maybe it was because we were all used to doing joints together. All of us except for Billy, anyway, who just followed suit.

"So what's the plan, man?" Philly piped up, never one to sit around doing nothing.

"I know!" Leslie said, her eyes lighting up. "Let's play hide and go seek!"

Everybody kind of groaned at that. Leslie was like that, though. She really got kicks out of playing childish games, and it didn't take long for her to talk us into it. Still, Mandy didn't look too excited. I wasn't even sure she heard the idea, actually. She kept staring off into the distance, into the horizon, like she was looking at something nobody else could see.

"Will you play, Mandy?" Leslie asked her, putting her hand on my sister's shoulder.

Mandy closed her eyes then, swallowing hard. "What the hell's the point?"

"The point?" Leslie asked, looking hurt.

Mandy began to rock back and forth on her heels, slightly, hugging her knees. "Why bother? It's just a stupid game." Her eyes were still closed, like she was afraid to look at any of us while she said this.

"Fun," Leslie said, smiling tentatively, as if she could get Mandy to notice even though her eyes were closed. "You know, playing? Laughing, remember? Remember laughing?" She meant well, but I could see she was probably doing more harm than good.

"Leslie, I don't—" I was going to cut in on her, but Mandy opened her eyes and started talking again and I shut up.

"No, Leslie, I hardly do remember, it's been so fucking long. I don't remember smiling, I don't remember laughing, and I don't remember fun. Nothing is fun anymore, and there is no *point* to your stupid game. Play without me." She was crying freely now. She stood up, turning away from us. "I'm sure it won't make a difference. Fuck it, do everything without me. I don't owe you anything, not any of you." She was walking away from us then, up the hill and toward the bridge.

I was thinking about how wrong she was. I kept thinking, "You're so wrong," over and over. Once I even said it out loud. She didn't turn around.

Leslie stood up and started walking after her. I was getting up to follow, but Jeremy grabbed hold of my arm and pulled me back. I was about to yank my arm free when he spoke, quietly, but with such certainty in his voice that I listened. "You can't do anything, man." I looked at him. His soft, sad brown eyes were looking right into mine. "It hurts her to even look at you."

"Why?" I asked him lamely, knowing the answer by heart but needing to hear it anyway. And I knew that if anyone could tell me, it would be Jeremy.

"You let her down, man. At least she feels like you did."

"But I didn't mean—"

"I know you didn't, Jim," he said, putting his arm around me. "I know you didn't. Let Leslie handle this. It'll be okay."

He was wrong about that, about it being okay, but he sure sounded right at the time, and hearing it calmed me down quite a bit. Sometimes I think he knew that it wasn't okay, but he also knew there was nothing he could do about it. I remember a conversation I once had with him when we were coming down off a Robitussin trip. We were talking about suicide, and what we would do if a friend of ours was going to kill himself. I said that I would do whatever it took to keep that person alive, hold them back, call the cops, tie them up even, anything. I remember now that he said that he would tell them he didn't think it was a good idea, but the final choice would be up to the person, and if they decided to do it he wouldn't try to stop them. I remember because we disagreed about it so intensely. Jeremy and I almost never disagreed like that.

So I think he might have known, with a deep sorrow in his heart, what was going to happen that day. Sometimes I feel like I'll never forgive him for that. Other times I remember his words to me that day and I believe what he said, that there was nothing I could have done. I never asked him if he knew, and I'll never know. I only wish I could stop guessing.

"C'mon guys, let's go swimming." Philly spoke, breaking

the awkward silence that had fallen upon the four of us. Billy jumped up right away, eager to play, maybe just to get his mind off his sister. He was young, but he wasn't dumb, and I could tell he was worried about her. He and Philly pulled their clothes off down to their shorts in about ten seconds flat, and they were already jumping off the bridge for the third time by the time Jeremy and I made it down to the shore. Neither of us was really in the mood for crazy jumping, and we just sort of slid into the water and dog-paddled around, a good ways away from Philly and my brother. We were quiet awhile, letting the warm water wash over our skin and hair, hanging out under the surface until we ran out of breath and then coming up just long enough to get a few gulps of air before going down again.

"I wish I had plugs," Jeremy said as we floated on the surface.

"What?"

"When I was a little kid I used to have these noseplugs and earplugs and I would float under water in my bathtub for as long as I could. Back then I could stay under for a whole minute. With the plugs in it was like being in the womb." Jeremy was always talking about being in the womb. "I never wanted to come out, you know that?"

"Of the womb, you mean?"

"Yeah. I was like two weeks late, and even then they really had to coax me out. I was bawling my head off and all."

I laughed. "Everybody cries when they're born, Jeremy."

"I know," he said, "but it's like I remember it. And I remember why I was crying. All I wanted was to stay in my mom's womb forever. It was warm, safe. Not like this world. Not like this."

"Hey, Jim!" I heard Billy call, and Jeremy and I swam over to where he and Philly were splashing around. I had this thing against yelling like a madman just to talk to people if they were far away or something.

"Yeah, Billy?" I responded when I was right up next to him in the water. Your feet could touch the ground where we were, right up next to the shore, and I quit dog-paddling and just sort of squatted there, not wanting to stand up out of the water and freeze my ass off with the wind on my wet skin.

"Wanna have a race?" Billy was crazy about racing in the water. He was like the star of the swim team at his school, and he got a real rise out of the fact that he could beat the pants off me.

There was a freight train coming down the tracks, a little ways off yet, but it was already loud as hell and the engineer was blowing the horn like crazy. I wondered why the hell he was doing that.

"Sure," I said. I was never mad about racing, really, but I did want to get the hell away from that train before it ruptured my eardrums.

"Last one out to the point's an ugly geek!" he hollered as he took off, swimming underwater out toward this spot where the land on our left came to a long narrow point out in the water. Only thing was, from where we were all the way to the point the shore was covered with brambles and rocks, and you had to swim practically all the way back in order to get on land. It was a good half mile out there and back and you had to be a pretty good swimmer to make it. I could hold my own in the water, though, so with a shrug and a grin at Philly and Jeremy I took off after my brother.

I always used to wonder if it was possible, I mean if you were really paying attention, if you could sort of tell when a disaster was about to happen. You know—maybe things would sound different, or the air would be really still or something. I thought maybe you would just be able to *tell.* You can't, though. You can't tell. Like when I looked at Philly and Jeremy for a moment and then took off swimming after my brother, or even when I saw my sister walking away with Leslie behind her, there was nothing different that would let me know something awful was about to happen. There should have been, but there wasn't.

My brother was waiting for me at the point, holding on to a log that was jutting off the shore. I grabbed hold, too, glad to rest my tired limbs, and glanced back to see the train crossing the bridge. That was when it really started to lay on the brakes, and even from a quarter mile away it made this terrifically loud screeching noise, like a huge set of fingernails on a hundred-foot-high blackboard. I saw Philly and Jeremy climb out of the water and run like maniacs off in the direction the train had gone, just around the bend. At first I thought they were just checking out the train, but when it finally did come to a halt, not far away but out of view behind the brambles, that's when the screaming started.

20

"Maaaandeeeeeeee!" It was Leslie's voice; I knew it even though I'd never heard anyone make a sound like that. It was an awful sound, filled with pain and horror. Real, immediate, immense, soul-jerking, heart-wrenching horror. I dove underwater then, and started swimming faster than I ever had in my life back toward the bridge where I could get back up on shore. Even under the surface I could hear the screams, and every time I came up for air there were more to refresh my memory, as if I needed it. I can still hear Leslie screaming, even now. Every time I hear someone shout or yell on the street, for one terrible, dreadful moment, before I realize it's just a stranger, some mother calling her kids in for dinner, it is Leslie screaming my sister's name.

As I got closer I saw Philly come back down the hill, walking slowly, taking each step like he wasn't sure he'd be able to take another. By the time I made it to the shore he was standing there, waiting for me. Leslie was still screaming.

I hit the ground running, trying to dash past him, but Philly grabbed me hard by my shoulders, stopping me dead. "Don't go up there, man," he said quietly, and there was terror in his voice and in his eyes. Terror of what was up on the hill, maybe, but I think maybe not. I think he was terrified of what would happen to me if I saw it.

"Lemme *go!*" I said, fighting him, swinging my arms like crazy trying to get loose.

"No, Jim." His grip on my shoulders only got tighter.

"LEMME GO!" I had really lost it. I watched drops of my saliva fly into his face as I shouted desperately at him, still struggling.

He winced at the spit in his eye, but he didn't let go. His teeth were clenched shut, his face bright red. He looked determined in a way I'd never seen him before, but even Philly couldn't hold me back. One of my wild arm swings caught him in the jaw, and before I knew it my other fist had smashed into his right eye. He let go of me, covering his face with his hands as his knees buckled to the ground. He tried to get up to chase me, but I was long gone.

I got up over the hill and ran toward Leslie's voice. The brush and woods from the point continued up to a few feet off the tracks, so even as close as I was I still couldn't see her.

I came around one more bend and skidded to a halt, sure as if Philly had grabbed me again, but he was nowhere in sight. What was in sight was a scene burned into my memory even now, clear as a photograph. Pretty as a picture.

The train was stopped just a few feet ahead of me. The sky was perfectly blue behind it, looking down impassively, framing everything. The man who had tried not to kill my sister was sitting on the ground, his back against the train, looking stunned. He was a younger man, maybe in his late twenties, wearing a dark blue engineer's jumpsuit. There was another man, older, gray-haired, in a suit, standing next to him. He was radioed ahead, looking a little panicky, but still subdued.

I heard sirens in the distance.

Jeremy was standing sort of off to the side of things, his eyes wide open, unblinking. His face was the color of ashes, striped with tears. His nose was running freely. He was biting the hell out of his lip, a habit he picked up that day and never broke.

Leslie was on the ground, on her knees. Her beautiful blue-and-white checkered dress was drenched with blood. It made the white squares red and the blue ones closer to black, so it looked almost like a real checkerboard. She was crying, hard, the tears rushing down her face to make room for more. Her face was bright pink. Her mouth was wide open, and she was still screaming. I didn't know if she'd ever stop. She was cradling Mandy, who was laying on the ground a ways off the tracks, where I guess she must have been thrown by the force of the train .

Oh, God, Mandy. Her whole body was soaked in blood. Her legs looked like they were just barely hanging on to her body, and her right arm was twisted around all cockeyed. Was it her right arm? My left side equals her right—yeah, her right arm. And her face. Her beautiful, beautiful face, that even my father wouldn't strike, was a bloody, sticky mess. Here and there you could see white teeth sticking out. Her head was a lot wider than it should have been. The top of her head, from her forehead up, was completely broken up. Between the chunks of broken skull oozed dark, thick blood mixed with this other, lighter, grayer stuff that I guess was her smashed brains. You could hardly even tell it was her, except for her clothes, and here and there you could see a clump of her maroon hair where it wasn't matted in blood.

I knelt down next to my sister and held one of her bloody hands. For some reason, I couldn't make a goddam sound. I wanted to say something, make some noise, scream at God and that fucking perfect, unfeeling sky. I wanted to tell my sister I loved her, as if she could hear me. But I couldn't. I was purely speechless. I looked down at the hand I was holding and turned it over. The bones of her wrist had been shoved through her skin, and they were about even with the middle of her palm. I thought I saw some long fiber things that looked like tendons just sort of hanging out of the jagged opening. I don't know why, but that, her wrist coming out and all, was too much. Maybe it was because I was holding *on* to it, I don't know. Nothing made sense. I leaned over onto the ground and puked, still holding on to her wrist bone and her hand and those stupid tendons even, as if it would somehow help things, as if I could somehow comfort my sister.

Behind me I heard Billy calling my name, and Mandy's, as he came around the bend. He was only about ten feet away but it sounded like a mile, it really did. Everything was sounding very far away. When he saw Mandy he got real quiet suddenly, and didn't say anything for a while. When he finally did speak, it was to me. "Jimmy? What's going on, Jimmy? What's going on?" He kept asking me that, like I had some magical answer. I just wished he would shut up.

The sirens were right on top of us now. I heard voices, doors slamming.

"What's going on, Jimmy?"

I looked up at him. Philly was standing behind him. His face held no expression whatsoever. He had his hands on my brother's shoulders. I don't think he was holding Billy back, but if my brother had tried to get any closer, I think he would have. Billy was sobbing, clenching and unclenching his fists.

"I don't know, Billy," I said through my own tears, speaking slowly and stumbling over the words like I was learning to talk all over again. "I don't know."

"C'mon, Billy, you don't want to see this," Philly said, sort of pulling him away. "C'mon, go home, huh? You don't want to see this."

He meant well, he really did, but I couldn't see it then. "Good old Philly," I said, my voice gaining momentum. "Trying to protect everybody. Trying to save everyone." Philly was just standing there, looking at me like I was murdering him with my words. I didn't care. "Well, go ahead and try, Philly, but it won't work! You can't save her! You can't save anybody!"

"Go on home, Billy, okay? Go get your parents," was all he said, and it looked like even that was a great struggle. He turned Billy away then, and gave him a gentle shove. Billy didn't argue. He took off running. Running home. Philly was right about that. He needed to go home.

"Can you? You can't save her, can you?" I just kept on saying that, even after he knelt down next to me and put his arms around me.

Two paramedics showed up then, carrying a stretcher. Watching them slide my sister's body onto it, I quit throwing accusations at Philly, dying on the inside. As they picked her up a lot more brains and blood spilled out of the top of her head, and I bent over to puke again, but there was nothing left. I stood up slowly, my knees shaking, and started shouting my head off at the paramedics. "Where are you taking her? Where are you going? She's *dead,* can't you assholes see that?" They didn't look back. "Hey! That's my sister. You can't have her!" I tried to chase after them, but I fell down on my knees. "Hey, don't take her away, please? She's my sister, please don't take her away . . ."

Philly had stood up with me, his arms still circling my torso, and when my knees buckled and I collapsed it was into those arms, into his embrace. He didn't mind, though. Covered in blood and puke as I was, he held me anyway. He was holding me, and that's all there was. I was finished blaming him. I needed him. I was letting him hold me, and listening to him for dear life. He was whispering in my ear; I don't even remember what he was saying, just telling me it was going to be okay. He just kept whispering to me and rocking me for a very long time, and I got the feeling that if it took forever for me to be ready to stand up, then he would rock me forever.

He was holding me, and that's all there was.

21

We had the funeral a few days later. It was in a Methodist church, with all these picture windows and Jesus paintings and this terrifically high ceiling. That was the only thing Mandy would have gotten into. She was really into those kinds of ceilings that are like a mile off the floor, especially the really slanty ones. That was about the only way I could think that it was sort of okay that we had the funeral in a Christian church. I really don't think she would have wanted it that way, not at all. She used to tell me stories about some Indian tribes that didn't even bury their dead, who built these platforms and put the dead bodies way up in the trees. I mean, each body got its own tree and everything. She always said that's what she wanted done with her when she died. So it was awful to see her in a coffin; I mean, it was a closed casket but I still knew she was in there, you know, and it sort of pissed me off to know that her goddam body wasn't even going to be done away with the way she wanted. I barely even listened to the preacher all through the service. I just kept thinking about how I wished I could have put her body up in a tree.

I didn't cry at all. Leslie was there and she was crying, and my little brother was crying, and my mom was crying her *head* off, and Philly was crying, hell, even Jeremy was crying, a little. The only person except for me in the whole place that wasn't crying was my dad, and he never cried. Not that I saw, anyway. Everybody was crying. That's what you do at funerals. I didn't, though. I was finished crying. I didn't even remember how. I sort of felt like I *should* be crying, but I didn't really *feel* like it. I didn't feel that much of anything, to tell you the truth. Mostly I just felt numb.

I didn't even sit with anybody. I mean, Billy and my parents were sitting together, and Philly and Jeremy and Leslie were sitting together, and I could have sat with either of them, but I didn't. Actually I didn't really sit down at all. I just sort of hung out at the back of the room, near the door, and when everybody went up to pay their respects to the coffin, I didn't go up then, either. I figured I could just pay my respects in my head, and if she could hear them in the coffin, she could probably hear me just thinking them anyway.

And I didn't go to watch her get buried. I was actually supposed to be one of the pallbearers, but I ditched out on that job. If she was going to be buried against her wishes, somebody *else* could do it, not me. When everybody filed out to get in their cars to start the procession over to the cemetery, I just sort of slipped off. Philly came with me. He wasn't too hot on funerals, either. What we did was, we went off and got really loaded, knocking back about fifty ounces of Robitussin and smoking some marijuana I had scored a week ago, topping it off with a very serious bottle of whiskey. It sounds awful, and I feel pretty terrible about it now, but that's what we did.

OCTOBER 1991

22

The first six weeks or so after the funeral, I never really left my bed much at all. Just to eat or go to the bathroom, and even then only once a day or so. Once a night, I mean. I only got up at night. Those first six weeks, I hated the sun. I hated the blue sky. It made everybody so goddam bright-eyed and cheery, and every time someone laughed I felt like murdering them. The light was too harsh for me. Even today, I almost always wear dark sunglasses.

So I just lay there, in my bed. For weeks. Staring at the ceiling. Choking. I couldn't believe my own mind, my own memories, my own sanity. I couldn't believe she was gone.

School was out of the question. My mom just called me in sick every day, and when a secretary at the school finally got around to calling and asking about me, my mom said I had mono. Which was good of her, I guess. She was pretty understanding about the whole thing. Or maybe she just felt helpless. Either way, she left me alone.

My father was a different story. If anything, he drank more after Mandy died. And I had never been beaten so often in my life. I didn't even have to do anything. Just my being there and not saving Mandy's life was enough to earn a lifetime's supply of beatings from my dad. As if I didn't feel guilty enough. As if I didn't go over and over that day, those moments, questioning myself, interrogating myself, every day, every hour, about how I could have saved her, what I could have done. But it wasn't enough. Not for him. So he cursed me, he beat me, he gave me my own private inquisition.

Night after night, he would enter my room. The light from the living room would wake me as the door swung open and he stumbled over to my bed.

"Jim? Jimmy, are you awake?" he would say, whispering into my ear, his hot whiskey breath washing over my face.

I would say nothing, as always. And as always he knew I was awake.

"Why didn't you save her, Jimbo? Huh? Didn't you care? Did you even try to stop her? Or did you do it? Did you *push* her, Jim? Because that would be bad. You'd have to go to jail. They'd have to put you away. Would you like that? Would you like to go away?"

He would go on and on like that, and each minute was a year.

On the good nights, that would be it. I would say nothing, do nothing, lift not a finger, move not an eyelash. On the good nights, he would get tired of talking to a brick wall, and eventually he'd leave me be. If not in peace, at least in silence. But sometimes I would lash out at him. Sometimes the pain got to be too much, his tongue got too sharp, and something he'd say would hook me, gleaming shiny and silver in the darkness.

And I would talk back to him, or push him away, or even just turn my head from him.

And the hook would draw blood.

That's when the beatings started. I would try and cover my head with my hands, protecting at least my face. He would tear them away. Sometimes he even dragged me out of bed, pushing me up against the wall, holding me there with one hand while he tore away at me with the other.

I never hit him back.

My mother always told me never to hit anybody, that retaliating would only make you just as bad as the bully. On the nights when it got really bad, the noise woke up my mother and Billy, and they would stand in the doorway, silent witnesses. With her there, watching me watching her, I could not, would not let her down. Still, neither of them ever said a word. Every so often Billy would make a sound, or open his mouth to speak, and Mom would put her hand over his mouth, ensuring that no sound came from either of them. And it shouldn't have. There was no stopping him, and their words of protest would only have drawn his rage to them as well.

The only sound, aside from Dad's grunts and curses, was my own laughter. Always I laughed. A slap evoked a snicker. A punch, a giggle. Throw me to the ground, I laugh loudly. Kick me in the ribs, and I have never heard a funnier joke.

I would never cry in pain, but always I would laugh. It was my escape, my ticket out of there, my get-out-of-hell-free card. It was the only way I could bear it. And no matter how much he hated it, my father could not not keep me from it. It was the one thing he could not take away from me. And it marked the one thing he would never have. Hearing my laughter echoing in his ears as he beat me, he knew he would never, ever have my respect.

At first, Philly and Jeremy came to visit me every day. They were always trying to get me up, trying to convince me how much fun we'd have. Especially Philly. I mean, Jeremy, too, but he didn't try as hard. He was different after Mandy died. Colder. Angrier. He had once been so much softer, more affectionate. He never once offered me a hug after she died, and I didn't see him touch Philly, either. He was still my friend, and he still cared, but it was like he had taken his heart out of it. Like he had it tucked away, hidden, safe in the darkness behind his rib cage.

But they both tried. In the beginning I was worse off even than Jeremy, and we all knew it. I never volunteered anything to them, and barely answered when asked a question. Sometimes I even rolled over and stared at the wall, my back to them. After a while they didn't come over much anymore, and eventually not at all. It wasn't out of hurt feelings that they left, though. It was out of respect. Respect for the dead, and for the grieving. And though none of us ever said anything, even after we got together again; we all understood.

Leslie only came once. She told me everything would be okay, and I threw a beer bottle at her. I didn't hit her, but it shattered on the wall about a foot from her head. She didn't come again.

I wouldn't even talk to Billy.

All our hearts were broken, one way or another.

My only companion was a butcher knife. I got it from the kitchen one night and took it back to my room. I was planning on stabbing myself in the stomach and bleeding to death. But when I lifted up my shirt and pressed the point into my skin, I couldn't do it. After just a tiny prick, a little sliver of blood trickling down my stomach and pooling in my belly button, I pulled back. I wasn't afraid of the pain. I was afraid of the dark. I was afraid of the darkness I was sure would come after, the absolute not-being. I started thinking about my own funeral, and how it would most likely be just like Mandy's, and I wouldn't even be able to go. And I decided I didn't want a Christian burial, either. I told myself I wouldn't die until I could arrange to be put up in a tree, the way Mandy had wanted to be. That was my excuse for not carving my heart out.

Mostly, I just don't think I had the guts.

Still, I kept that knife in my bed. I slept with it, carried it with me to the bathroom, so that just in case I changed my mind, I'd be ready.

I was planning on going on like that forever, but after a month and a half I put my shoes on and went for a walk.

I hadn't been outside in weeks. A cool breeze greeted me as I stepped out of the house, seeping right through my sweatshirt and blue jeans, wrapping around my skin, caressing my bones, looking me up and down like an old relative. The ground was damp. It had rained that night, and I could see by the quiet glow of the street lamps that in places the pavement was still stained a darker shade of gray. Houses were dark, and there were no children crying or dogs jingling their tags or adults talking about their workday and the weather or brakes squealing or motors revving or horns honking. No birds sang. It must have been about two or three in the morning, and the world was asleep. And that was the way I needed it to be out there. I wasn't ready yet to shield myself from all the harshness of a live city. I needed to be soothed, rocked, gently sung a lullaby by the stillness of the night. Even the grass comforted me, soft and billowy under my feet. I took it up on its offer and pulled my shoes off, carrying them in my hand. I decided next time I went out, I wouldn't wear shoes to begin with. Actually, unless I had to, I never really wore shoes after that. Just to remind myself of the comfort the earth could give, that it gave me that night. I heard an Indian saying once that if you wear shoes, and your feet are just half an inch away from the earth, that is as far away as the earth from the sun. As far away from that comfort, that mother.

The next day, and over the following week, I started going out more and more, during the day even, until eventually I gave old Philly a call and the three of us, Philly and Jeremy and I, started hanging out again.

23

About noon, Philly and I were chucking a football around in the park behind his house, catching only about every twentieth pass because we were both stone drunk. We hadn't had anything to drink that morning, but we'd drowned ourselves in vodka the night before, and as soon as we woke up we each ate about five aspirins, which brings it all right back. It was a Saturday, Billy's birthday. We were waiting around for Jeremy to show up with a surprise he said he had for us, and then I was planning on heading home to visit my brother.

Eventually we got tired of the football and lay down spread-eagled in the center of the park, pointing out obscene cloud shapes and laughing. That was only so much entertainment, though, and quickly we were on our feet again, racing—"Last one there sucks cocks!"—to a great climbing tree at the edge of the park. It was our favorite tree and we both vaulted through its familiar branches deftly, easily, like dancing with an old partner. Once we got as high as we could manage without swinging around like crazy (a good fifty feet or so), we settled in on our perches. There were three good ones in that tree, perfect for Philly and Jeremy and me. Philly got the best one this time, highest up and shaped just like a chair. You could lean back against the main trunk and stare up at the sky or down at the little kids and their parents below. Even the adults looked like dwarfs from that high. Man, it was fantastic up there. A couple years before, during the later part of the summer, when the tree was covered in huge oak leaves, the three of us had dropped bucketfuls of acorns on unsuspecting passersby. The beauty of it was, if we were quiet, there was no way they could tell anybody was up there, and they were left thinking it was a freak accident that all those acorns had fallen at once, right on their head. The best time was when there were two lovers under the tree, just getting into some pretty heavy making out. Philly was in favor of leaving them alone, busying ourselves hoping to catch glimpses of the action. Jeremy and I, though, aspiring ruthless villains that we were, spared no quarter and let fly with two full buckets of acorns. You should have heard them scream. The best part was that the guy, probably seventeen or so, screamed exactly like the girl, high-pitched and squeaky. Boy, was he embarrassed. The only drawback to the whole thing being so hilarious was that we were all up there laughing our asses off, damn near falling out of the tree even, and that guy knew we were up there sure as his face was red. He started hollering every swearword he could think of, saying he was gonna come back with his BB gun and blow us out of the tree. Of course we cut out of there as soon as they were out of sight. Jeremy convinced us to return to the scene of the crime anyway, and we hid in some bushes while we watched him fire his air rifle off into the empty tree, hollering curses with every shot. We just about strangled ourselves to keep from laughing out loud that time.

We weren't up to any mischief this time, though. We were busy fantasizing about what Jeremy had in store for us. Philly hoped it was an inflatable girlfriend. He was moaning about how he hadn't gotten laid in a month.

I said I hoped it was a tent, so I would never have to stay at home again. For the past couple of weeks I'd been staying at Philly's house except for a few nights at Jeremy's. I didn't say much to either of them about the nights with my father, but they knew it was bad and had no problem letting me crash at their places. Jeremy knew enough not to ask me about it. Philly, however, was naive enough to miss the fact that I didn't want to talk about it, and he was real concerned, always asking, always probing.

"What's the deal, Jim? You gotta go back sometime, for God's sake. Whaddaya, never going home? You can't just *do* that, you know."

Maybe I should have known enough to quit bringing it up around him. "It's nothing, Philly. I'm just sick of it there."

"What, Jim? What are you sick of? It can't be just the usual bullshit. Not this, man. Not like this."

Or maybe I needed to talk about it. I said nothing though, staring at the sky, halfheartedly pretending to be concentrating on the clouds again.

"You can't just not say anything, Jim. This is me!"

For a moment, a heartbeat, I broke. I looked up at him as I spoke. "God, Philly, you're right. I gotta, it's just, there's nothing to even say that would—"

"Get outta the tree, ya fuckin' animals!" It was Jeremy's voice, screaming at us from across the park. We both grinned, glad to see him, and immediately I clammed up again. Philly looked at me as he started climbing down, one of those I'm-not-gonna-forget-this kind of looks. And he didn't. But I never spoke to him about it again.

24

Philly slid and scrambled down the tree quickly. I stayed up on my perch, frozen by the sight of who Jeremy was walking with.

I hadn't seen Leslie since she'd come to visit me after my sister's funeral. That was my own fault, though. It had been months. Not that I didn't miss her. It was just that even thinking about her hurt terribly, and I was sure that if I saw her, all I would be able to think about would be her red face, screaming and bawling over my sister's body.

I took my time climbing down. With every branch I wrapped my fists around, every twig I snapped, my breath got shorter. My heart beat faster the closer I got to the ground.

I had kept tabs on her through Jeremy, who saw her quite often, and he said she'd totally cut out drinking and getting high, and I was so into it, I thought I'd be embarrassed to see her. I don't know why, but that, too, had really kept me from seeing her.

The three of them were waiting for me. I extended my hand to Jeremy first. I had to leave it hanging there for a few seconds before he took hold of it and nodded. Even that was a lot for Jeremy in those days. In drunker moods, I would have given him a hard time about it. We'd seen this video at school about a prehistoric guy that gets dug out of the ice in the twentieth century, and everybody called him Ice Man, or just plain Ice. That's what we called Jeremy, when we were screwing around. He hated it, though, so we had to be kind of high on something before we were big enough insensitive jerks to say it to his face.

Next I said hello to Philly, even though I had just been with him a minute before.

That was it, though. I couldn't put it off any longer. I had to look at her.

It wasn't as hard as I thought it would be. She just looked like Leslie. No horrified looks, no angry words, no tears, no sweat. Just Leslie, the beautiful, darling girl I was in love with.

I lost my breath anyway. Just the normalness of her beauty, the realization that I was in love with her, still, not a drop less than I ever had been, knocked the wind right out of me. I had thought I'd left her behind. I thought she was gone, disappeared into the shadow of my sister's gravestone, buried with Mandy and my innocence.

Boy, did I have another think coming. She had a sort of wistful half smile on her face, her lips just barely parted. Her eyes were shy, hopeful, her eyebrows raised and her forehead all wrinkled up the way it always was when she was nervous. She was cracking her knuckles behind her back. We just sort of stared at each other for a while, silent, wanting to say a hundred things at once but not being able to stammer out even one. I watched her size me up the way I had her. She licked her lips, another thing she did when she wasn't sure what to say. It was irresistible, the way she did that. I remembered kissing her for the first time, and all the other wonderful moments that had followed between us, all the times we bumped into each other's noses, all the times I had wiped an eyelash off her face, all the times she had pretended to whisper something in my ear and then bit me, all the times our hands had sweated together.

For once, I was the first of us to speak. "Leslie?"

She giggled as she reached out for me. "Jim? Is it really you?"

From very far away, I heard the guys mumble something about leaving us alone and going to toss the football. Neither Leslie nor I responded. They disappeared. As if they weren't already invisible to the two of us the instant we laid eyes on each other.

We embraced. I held her weakly at first, stiffly, not even getting close to her. She pressed her heart against mine, though, and I melted against her. All these knots in my heart and my belly just dissipated, all at once. Like everything was suddenly okay, however briefly. The world was not going to end. For all the dark moments, there would always be sweet, radiant ones like this to keep me going.

And then suddenly, without warning, things turned bitter. Two things happened, one barreling down on top of the other like sucker punches. First, as I was holding my love so tightly, that picture I had been so afraid of seeing flashed before my closed eyes. Leslie, screaming, her face in terrible anguish, red as the remains of my sister's. It was only there a moment, but it was plenty long. The memory lasted. And in that moment, and in those after, my body tensed up and I pulled away slightly, split, severed.

The second thing that happened was that as I pulled away Leslie moved to kiss me. And just before her bright innocent lips touched mine, she smelled the vodka on my breath, still hanging around from the night before. This time *she* pulled away. The look painted on her face was one I didn't recognize. It took me a second to figure out what it was, but once I did, I almost fell over backward sure as if I really had taken a sucker punch in the face. It was something I'd seen on other people's faces, even toward me, but I had never seen Leslie exhibit it toward anybody. When I looked at her face, I saw disgust.

She spoke first. Which was a good thing, because I couldn't have. "You know this can't work between us with you ruining yourself doing those things, Jim."

My first reaction was to get pissed off. "What do you mean, those things? There's nothing wrong with getting drunk every now and then! You did it!"

"Not anymore, Jim."

"Well, you did, Leslie!"

"Not so much."

"I don't drink that much!" I was getting louder and louder. She was getting quieter and quieter, which was infuriating in itself. I felt bad just about yelling if she wasn't going to do it, too. I couldn't give up, though. I couldn't admit she was right. I wasn't even sure she was. I hadn't fallen far enough. You'd think I would have, but I hadn't. So I fought against her, my last remaining sweetness.

Jeremy and Philly stopped playing when they heard me shouting; they walked over toward us, standing silently by, watching the way people watch a building burning down, fascinated, upset, helpless, small.

"How much do you drink, Jim?" That one hurt. Maybe that's another reason she was so hard to be around. She could see me.

"Not too much," I said defiantly, looking to the guys for backup. "Not too much, huh Philly?"

He was silent.

"I don't drink that much, do I, Jeremy?"

Jeremy laughed. Not a nice laugh, though. "No more than me."

I should say something here, about the funny thing Jeremy and Leslie had with each other. They were bonded, in a way Leslie and I weren't. It wasn't better, or even closer, but they had an understanding. Jeremy could act like a total asshole, act totally beneath Leslie's standard of ethics, and she wouldn't give him a hard time about it. She would forgive him. Not that he came to her asking for forgiveness, but she gave it to him. Maybe it was because he was always honest with her, and he spent a lot of time with her. He was an asshole, a drunk, and a criminal, but he made no bones about it. And underneath all that, he had a good heart, and she knew it. She knew how much Mandy's death had warped him, even destroyed parts of him. But for me, that wasn't a good enough excuse. I had to be the perfect one. They were friends, and we were lovers. She needed me in a way that she never needed Jeremy.

Leslie asked Jeremy how often he drank.

"You mean, really stinking, shitfaced drunk, or just tipsy?"

Jeremy was having a great time, in an awful way. I was getting madder at him by the minute.

Leslie didn't crack a smile. She was smart enough to know his laughter wanted to be tears. Which was more than I knew, at the time. "Shitfaced."

Suddenly Jeremy was deadly serious, realizing the implications of his words. It was no longer a joke to him, if it ever had been. Still, he had no plans to change. To him, drinking, getting fucked up out of his mind was life. It was a makeshift cure. Not perfect, but it worked as well as anything we knew. It was all we had.

"Really shitfaced?"

Leslie nodded somberly.

He chose his words carefully, feeling their weight. "Every night."

Leslie looked over to me with the sad, knowing smile I knew so well by now. Only this time, it was almost apologetic. "I can't be with you like this, Jim. I can't. I can't watch you do this to yourself."

"Do what?" I asked, almost for lack of anything better to say, my lower lip trembling.

When she spoke again, it was a good-bye. I knew it would be even before she opened her mouth, and in the split second before she did, I prayed desperately that she wouldn't, that she walk away without saying anything at all, as long as it wasn't good-bye. I think I instinctively knew how much it would hurt, how much further I would fall as a reaction to it, how much it would backfire. She meant it to sober me up. She meant well. I don't blame her for what happened afterward. But I think if she knew how I would react, if she knew how many ways I would torture myself for that statement, I don't think she would have said it.

"Drinking killed Mandy, Jim. Her drinking, your dad's drinking, and yours. You could have been there for her. She needed you to be there. But you weren't. You weren't there. Next time you kiss a bottle, ask yourself where you were. Ask yourself who you're becoming.

"I'll see you around. I'll talk to you when it's really you again."

I could have protested, argued, begged, pleaded, cursed, promised. None of it would have done any good. I did say one thing, without meaning to. It just sort of bubbled out of me, against all my wishes and better judgment. "I need you."

"Like a drug?" she asked plaintively, but it was not a question.

I never should have opened my mouth. The damage was done. Like everything else, it could not be reversed. And like so many things, I desperately wanted it to be.

She walked off then, head bowed, taking each step away from me carefully and consciously.

25

We were quiet for a while, the three of us, friends, companions, brothers almost, watching her leave. It was me she was leaving then, but we all felt it. We all knew, in our own ways, how much her walking away meant.

Jeremy spoke first, and his voice carried far more than what he said. "You guys want to see the surprise I brought you?"

One at a time, Philly first, then me, said yeah, we would.

Jeremy reached inside his jacket and pulled out a new, unopened bottle of old-style 150-proof Russian vodka.

My eyes widened. I had never seen anybody drink liquor that strong, except maybe in the movies. I watched wordlessly as he broke the seal, slowly, deliberately unscrewing the cap. I watched wordlessly, instinctively knowing the heaviness of his actions as he touched the bottle to his lips and took the first sip.

With that, he had agreed. He would go along, wherever we went.

One at a time, Philly first, then me, kissed the bottle.

Normally, in other places, at other times, with other people, maybe none of this would have been such a big deal. But with the three of us in the park that day, standing in the shadow of Leslie's warning, Leslie's last stand, we had made our choice.

Don't get me wrong, I mean, we weren't exactly overjoyed about it. It wasn't like that. It was like pleading no contest. It was being too young, too weak, too naive to know we had another choice.

Jeremy looked pleased with himself as he put the cap back on the bottle.

"Where the hell'd you get that, Jeremy?" I asked, smacking my lips. It tasted abominable, but even a little sip was enough to make me shiver, feeling the familiar rush of liquid heat through my veins.

"I lifted it from Sunshine."

"Sunshine?" Philly asked, surprised as I was. Sunshine was the last place in the world one of us would have ripped off. But I guess it had come down to that, to going all the last places we would have gone, doing all the last things we would have done.

"It's just one fucking bottle, they're never gonna miss it. C'mon, let's drink this baby and you guys'll forget where it came from. Pretend it fell from the sky or something."

"All right, that's cool, man," I said, sort of trying to play it off like it was no big deal. No one bought it, I mean they never really did, when I tried to act like a tough guy or very cool or something. Philly or even Jeremy could pull it off no sweat, acting very smooth and all. I never could, though. I could never say the exact right thing, or make it sound the exact right way so as to come off like a hotshot. I don't know why I even tried. I was always trying to act like that, which was especially stupid around the two guys who knew me better than anybody else in the world. Anybody left, anyway.

"We can't drink it here . . . ," Philly said, looking around the park, checking for observers.

"Of course not," Jeremy said scornfully, leaking a sharp acidity I still wasn't used to. "I know a good place."

The place Jeremy wanted to go to was downtown. We hopped on a bus, Philly and I firing questions at Jeremy the whole way about how hard it was to steal from Sunshine. After we got over our initial moral objection, we were pretty curious about it. We were all thieves at heart, and having one of us break one of our unwritten rules made it somehow more acceptable for us to do the same.

Jeremy didn't respond. That was something else he'd started doing, about half the time you asked him something. It really got on my nerves sometimes. You ask the guy a question, the least he could do is say yes or no, right? Not Jeremy. Not in those days. Old friend or not, sometimes he wouldn't even look at you.

We got off the bus downtown, where all the taller buildings were. Not like in a big city where you're surrounded by skyscrapers or anything, but you knew you were downtown. The sky was darkening, but you could still see little glints and glares of the sunset in cracks between buildings and in reflections off the buildings themselves. I usually hated the way those mirror-plated buildings looked, but at dusk it was pretty impressive.

Jeremy led us into a little alley between two three-story buildings. I looked sidelong at Philly before going in to see what he thought about it, but he just nudged me forward. I didn't much like being downtown at night, especially not in dark alleys. The only reason I didn't beat it out of there was Philly and Jeremy didn't seem too worried, and I didn't want them to think I was chicken.

The alley was a dead end, but there was an old fire escape alongside one of the buildings. The bottom of it was raised up aways off the ground the way fire escapes usually are, so no one can reach them from the ground. Jeremy had been there before, though, and he had it all figured out. He climbed up on top of a Dumpster, and from the edge of it he jumped out and grabbed the last step of the fire escape, swinging it down noisily on its rusted old hinges. That way it only took a short jump and a pull-up onto the main staircase. From there he looked down at us, grinning. "C'mon, it's cool. Mandy showed me this place. Nobody lives here anymore."

Walking up the escape itself was pretty scary. It was old as hell; its coat of black paint was almost entirely peeled off and the whole thing was covered in rust. Every time you took a step you could feel it teetering. Its attachments to the wall looked like they would break off if you touched them. It probably hadn't been used in years, except for Jeremy and my sister. I was practically terrified, shaking more than the fire escape. Heights scare the daylights out of me even with something to stand on.

The steps went almost to the top of the building, and from there we just had to climb a short ladder to get to the roof. Philly went first this time, scrambling right up without a problem. When Jeremy was nearing the top of the ladder it made this high-pitched creaking straight out of a horror movie and leaned outward a little, pulling completely away from the wall a few inches, standing straight up in the air, with Jeremy still on it. It hovered that way for a second or two. Jeremy looked down at me frantically. After a moment of stillness, the ladder continued to fall backward over the ledge of the fire escape and down four stories. At the last possible moment, Jeremy leaped off sideways, landing almost on top of me, and together we fell hard onto the metal grate that was supporting us. Jeremy quickly slithered over to the edge so he could see the ladder finish its fall and go clattering onto the pavement.

When it was done with its racket he looked up at me, a huge grin replacing the sick fear that had possessed his face a moment before. "Did you see that, Jim? Did you *see that*? That was a close one, huh?"

He'd almost been killed, and he thought it was hilarious. At first I was shocked and then my face twisted up in anger. "Yeah, I saw that! And it's not funny, Jeremy! It's not fucking funny!"

"Chill out, Jim, I'm okay. Nothing happened, okay, buddy? I'm fine. I didn't get hurt. See?" He started waving his arms and legs around to show he wasn't paralyzed. He was still laughing, though. Looking back on it now, I'm not sure if he was really amused or just surprised and nervous because I was flipping out on him.

"You think this is funny? You almost die, and you laugh? Is death a joke to you, Jeremy?" I knew as soon as I said it that it was an awful thing to say. As soon as I said that, my anger fell away, dropping faster than the ladder had. Looking at Jeremy's face, all I felt was guilty.

His face blanched as if I'd just stabbed him. His lower lip was trembling like it does sometimes when someone's about to cry. He didn't cry, though. He just kept looking directly at me, right into my eyes, with the coldest stare I had ever seen him give anybody. "I can't believe you just said that to me."

I wish now that I hadn't, I wish that badly, because what I said to him that night changed things between us. After that, he acted sometimes like I was a stranger. Like he couldn't trust me. Like I might stab him in the back. And maybe he was right not to trust me. Maybe he couldn't have, and maybe he shouldn't have. Not if I was going to say things like that to him. Not if I was going to hurt him like that again.

"I'm sorry, Jeremy. I really am," I said, and we both dropped it, eager to shake the sheer awkwardness of the moment.

26

With a little extra resourcefulness Jeremy and I made it up on the roof anyway. Jeremy gave me a boost on his shoulders and I grabbed the ledge and pulled myself up. It was a gravel roof and holding on to it took most of the skin off my fingers, but I made it up. Jeremy, stronger and braver, or maybe just stupider, managed to get up by finding little handholds and ledges here and there. Only thing was, at one point he had to swing out over a four-story drop and pull himself up by his fingers, clenched white aganst the gravel. I wouldn't do that in a million years. Not sober, anyway. I can't even dive off a high dive, for God's sake.

Once we were all up, we sat in a triangle next to a heating vent (it was pretty drafty up there) and watched as Jeremy took out the bottle and slugged off it again, harder this time. For a second his eyes rolled back in his head, and he shuddered noticeably. Drinking alcohol had become like one of his natural functions as a human being. It wasn't, though. Not like sleeping and breathing and eating, anyway. Drinking is more like bleeding. Bleeding out all your peace, all your sanity, your love, even. You eventually bleed everything, until there's nothing left. Then you get hollow. That's when it gets really bad. Don't ever try living hollow.

Still smiling, he looked around at us. "Who's next?" he asked, as much a challenge as an invitation.

"Me," Philly said, almost without hesitation. I could hear the cocky overconfidence in his voice. Jeremy watched as Philly put the bottle to his lips. He didn't nod or anything in approval, but he didn't do anything negative, either. He just stared intently, half smiling and half serious. As Philly swallowed, hard, the way Jeremy had done seemingly effortlessly, his head jerked back violently and he coughed the vodka right out of his mouth, spraying it all over me and spilling about half the bottle onto the roof. I grinned nervously, the awareness that it was my turn next overriding any irritation at being soaked in half-drunk vodka. Jeremy didn't even blink. He just kept right on staring at Philly, never taking his eyes off him, like he was watching the best movie of his life. Philly was embarrassed as hell; he was sheepishly handing the bottle over to me when Jeremy spoke.

"No. Try again. You've got to learn it right." He said it like an order, and Philly listened. "Hold still this time. Let the burn pass through you. It only lasts a second."

Philly did hold still, swallowing the liquor and his obvious grimace with flying colors. He passed the bottle to me, woozily shaking back and forth like he was about to pass out.

I was prepared for the burn so I didn't jerk around or spill or anything. It was more like a sting, actually. It wasn't so bad, just a shock, a surprise. It was almost twice as powerful as anything we had been drinking previously, and it stung my throat almost twice as bad. Once that was over, though, I felt a surge of electric-like waves through my entire body as the alcohol raced through my veins, making me feel giddy, twice as alive. That only lasted a second also, but it didn't completely leave. I was really drunk out of my mind by the time we were done, seeing crazy things. I felt great, though, like I could do anything. I was a superhero. We all were. We were above everything.

For a long while me and Philly occupied ourselves in fantastic surreal play on the roof, Superman and Spider-Man, dancing, running, wrestling, jumping, rolling, experimenting with our alcohol-induced electric lives, stopping now and then to drink some more. Jeremy just stood quietly motionless in the center of the roof, staring up at the stars, looking like Batman silhouetted against the white glow of the capitol building behind him. For a while Philly was doing cartwheels on the edge of the roof, four stories off the ground. He didn't even look nervous. If I was him, I wouldn't have been, either. There was no way he was going to fall, or at least it sure didn't seem like it from where we were. It was a silliness, an elation, a drunken knowledge of absolute perfection. It was having no concerns, nothing significant anyway. And eventually it was being able to do nothing but collapse in a laughing heap, staring at the blurry stars and not even remembering how to count to ten.

It was sure something to see. It was a good place to visit, once. And I am not sorry I did it. Once. I am sorry I did it hundreds of times after that, night after delirious night, stumbling toward a light that wasn't there, stumbling toward the ultimate gutter.

But that night was the first for us, for Philly and me, at least. Our first time in that place, our first time being that fucking crazy drunk, and we all fell in love with it, in our own way. It gave something precious to each of us. A kind of redemption, a kind of absolution. We never wanted things to be another way.

Eventually Jeremy summoned us to go, in his own caustic way. He walked casually over to the edge of the roof, looked down for just a sliver of a moment, and jumped. I bolted to the edge, covering thirty feet in about three giant steps, and leaned over. He was standing on the fire escape a few feet below, where we had come up. I was surprised to see him alive. I had forgotten that's where the escape was.

He looked up at me calmly, lighting a cigarette.

"Where ya goin'?" I stammered, still spaced out, shocked. It was taking my hazy brain a while to figure out why he wasn't splattered on the pavement below.

"I don't know. I'm sick of it up here." He started walking down the steps.

I ran back and got Philly, who was puking over the edge of the rooftop onto somebody's car. We caught up with Jeremy just as he was making it out of the alleyway. Whether he would have left without us, I'm not sure. I think he probably would have. I'm glad he didn't, because I was still plenty wasted and didn't even have the foggiest idea where I was.

27

I was too drunk to go home right away, and besides, I wanted to get my brother a birthday present. We walked around aimlessly, looking for a good place to rob blind, eventually settling on a massive department store inside a mall on the west side of town. This was a stupid idea because those kind of places are always loaded with security, but we were pretty loaded ourselves and I guess not thinking too straight.

We got to the mall about ten o'clock, I guess, after a pretty sobering two-hour walk. Sobering enough that I could walk straight, anyway. We agreed to split up so we wouldn't look like a mob of hoodlums or anything. On the way there Philly had dodged into a gas station and lifted enough mints to last us a lifetime. We ate about twenty each, all at once, and it seemed to pretty well cover the rank vodka breath that was a sure ticket to getting busted. Learning to be inconspicuous is the key to a successful shoplifting career. Don't get noticed, and you won't get caught.

Once inside I wandered over to the toy section, figuring I could pick something up for Billy. Like that would somehow make me a good brother. I hadn't seen him in weeks. It wasn't that I didn't love him or anything. I mean, he was my brother. But I was just gone, man. I had no energy to talk to him. I was afraid he would ask me questions I knew I didn't have the answers to. I could barely keep myself going, you know?

Still I felt guilty about the way things were, and I wanted to at least bring him a birthday present. I know it sounds like bullshit and I don't expect anybody to believe me, but I really wanted to be good. I wanted to be a good son to my parents, a good brother to Billy, a good lover to Leslie. I was really trying. That just isn't how things ended up working out. Hard as I tried, I didn't know how to do anything but keep running.

I decided to get my brother a Game Boy. They were small enough to fit inside my jacket, and I'd seen one with a game about spaceships. Billy was still wild about spaceships. Before taking it I casually strolled around the rest of the toy section, making sure there was no one else around. It was close to closing time for the store and past most little kids' bedtimes, so I figured there wouldn't be anybody, but I had to make sure. I knew places like this had floorwalkers, security guards dressed like customers, so if anybody at all was around I was planning on hanging tight till they left.

There wasn't anybody in sight. I looked up and checked out all the mirrors within range of me. I could see a couple people but no one looking my way. The store had those curved mirrors up all over the place. I'd stolen plenty of stuff from places with mirrors like that, though, or even cameras. You just had to be pretty sure nobody was looking. Places with cameras especially, no one ever sees you. They figure with all their security measures nobody'd be stupid enough to steal from them and they forget all about it. Ha. They didn't count on me. James Evan Drake, Crack Shoplifter.

I made my way quickly but inconspicuously back to the video games. This was The Moment. I could feel the adrenaline coming on strong. Reach up, grab the game, and slip it inside my jacket, under my arm. That's right, one fluid motion. Glance up at a clock. Pretend it's past time to go, which gives the perfect excuse for zipping up my jacket right inside the store. Okay, that's it, done. Perfect. Now a purposeful walk out of the store, making sure not to make eye contact.

I was walking past the appliance aisle, everything going perfectly, when a hand reached out from behind me and pulled me into the aisle. I saw a shining silver glint of metal moving quickly, then felt what I was sure was a knife at my throat. For one very long moment, I was scared half out of my mind, so much that I let the video game fall out of my jacket onto the floor. Then I heard Philly's poorly concealed voice. "Gimme all your money, kid."

When I realized who it was, I got irritated as all hell. "Philly, put the fucking knife down. Are you outta your mind? Do you want us to get *busted*? Huh? Lemme go. Don't be an asshole."

He kept holding on to me, though, the knife still at my throat. I could hear him trying to stifle his laughter. "Shut up, kid. Gimme all your money."

I was really getting pissed off. I knew security could come around the corner any second, and if they did, we'd be in all kinds of shit. And even though I knew he was only kidding, I couldn't help wondering if Philly had suddenly gone psycho on me. Just the idea, even at the edge of my mind, of him slitting my throat right there, was really shaking me. I was afraid of what I might do if he didn't let me go, right away. *"Fuck you,* Philly. Put the knife down. We're gonna get busted."

He let me go then, laughing and giving me a shove. I didn't see it as so playful, though, and I almost tackled him before I remembered where I was. It took great effort to chill myself out enough to leave Philly alone. That's the thing about too much hard liquor. Sober, I never would have hit him. Drunk, I came very close.

I picked the video game up off the floor where I'd dropped it when Philly pulled the knife on me, wondering whether I should put it back on the shelf or pocket it again. Ordinarily there would have been no question. Something like that happens, any sane thief puts the merchandise back on the shelf and gets the hell out of there, marching off double-quick. I was overconfident that night, looking around for a second and stuffing it back up my jacket.

I looked over at Philly, still irritated but mainly just wanting to vacate the premises. "Let's go, man, security's gonna be all over us."

Philly didn't respond. He was admiring the knife he had held me up with. It was a butcher knife, long and fat and shiny as hell. He looked up at me. "You like it? I got it out of a package. S'posed to be the sharpest kind of knife you can get."

I couldn't believe him. "I'm gone, man. You can stick around all goddam night if you want. Not me."

"Okay, okay, I'm coming. Don't be so paranoid."

I didn't say anything else. I was concentrating on leaving. Once we were out of the store we were home free. Walk quickly, purposefully, like you got somewhere to be. Don't look at anybody.

Out of the corner of my eye I saw a man in dark blue coming toward us, his badge shining what seemed like extra brightly on his chest. Doesn't matter. Ignore him. *Don't* look at him. Just keep walking.

Two more coming from the other direction, from the entrance to the store, where I'm headed. Gonna have to walk past 'em. Don't think about 'em. If they smell your fear you're finished. Concentrate on walking. Keep walking. Keep—

"Freeze! Hey! Don't move!"

They grabbed Philly first, throwing him to the ground. I wondered for a moment if the knife had stabbed him when he fell. I hoped not. The others were coming toward me, two of them, coming at me from both sides, big guys. I should stop walking, just let them get me, I should stop, I should stop. I kept telling myself to stop; all I had was a goddam video game, no big deal, right? But that arrogant electric impulse was still going through me, spurring me on, and I didn't stop. I couldn't. I kept right on walking as if they weren't even talking to me, as if they weren't *yelling* at me to stop. I just kept walking, and when they got too close I broke out in a dead run, heading outside. Outside the store they'd never catch me.

I didn't even make it past the register. One second I was running and the next I felt a huge crushing weight on my back and I hit the floor face first. I connected with the floor at an angle, taking it in the teeth. My whole face was jarred, hard, and I heard my right front tooth shattering. The two security guards that had tackled me flipped me over roughly, unzipping my jacket and searching me. They found the video game. When they figured out that was all I had they stood up in disgust. The guy that had got Philly walked over and stood next to the two that got me, holding the knife Philly had swiped, turning it over in his hand. There was no blood on it, so at least I knew he hadn't accidentally stabbed himself on his way down.

"This is all he had," the one that held my video game said. "Just a game, Peter." He was talking to the one who held the knife, who I guessed was their boss, just by the way he carried himself, and the way the others looked at him.

"Yeah, well, the other kid had a knife. We didn't know what this one had. You were right to take him down," Peter said. "Pick 'em up, take 'em to the room. I'll be in in a minute."

As they stood us up, I watched Jeremy walking calmly out of the store, not looking in our direction. One of the guards, the heaviest one, ran over to him and grabbed him by the shoulder, demanding, "Are you with these guys?"

Jeremy looked at us for a moment and then back at the heavy, his face betraying no sign of recognition. "Never seen 'em before in my life," he said flatly. Christ, even I almost believed him.

He kept hold of Jeremy, though, looking back and forth between us, not knowing what to do. "You sure?" This guy was a pile of brains, let me tell you.

Jeremy looked straight into my eyes when he spoke. "Of course I'm sure. Now will ya lemme go? I gotta get home."

"Awright, get outta here, then," the heavy said roughly, giving Jeremy a little shove on the arm he'd been holding on to. Jeremy stumbled a little, caught his balance, and walked casually out of the store without even so much as a glance back at his best friends.

I wondered at the time if I would have done the same. Sure we had a pact not to rat on each other, but that was different. He wouldn't have been ratting on anybody but himself, and he probably wouldn't have gotten in too much trouble, if any at all. But to avoid the chance he cut himself off from us completely, denying our friendship. And in doing so, just for that moment, he denied all our memories, all our adventures, all our tragedies, everything we'd shared. Just to avoid the chance. I wondered if it was worth it. I wondered if I would have done it.

We were escorted to "the room," which turned out to be this tiny cell off the perfume section with a desk in one corner, a few basic chairs, and about twenty televisions, showing what was going on in just about every little corner of the store. Boy, had we picked the wrong place. It was like going up against the fucking Secret Service. The room was painted this awful shade of puke yellow. I wondered if they did that on purpose just to make people like me feel uncomfortable.

We sat in there for about an hour, waiting for Peter to come in. In the meantime we were instructed by the one guy that stayed in the room to just sit quiet while he put the merchandise, first the knife and then Billy's present, up on the table against the beautiful yellow wall and took Polaroid snapshots of each. That cracked me up. I mean, what the hell were they gonna do, use them as exhibits in our big upcoming jury trial? It wasn't like we'd just robbed a bank or anything. He'd have to take them home to his wife and brag about the big bust. Or maybe he could frame them and put them on a wall for dinner party conversation.

My tooth hurt like hell. I wondered how much of it was left. I'd have to go to the dentist for sure. I hated the goddam dentist. My whole life I'd had this one goddam dentist that my mom was convinced was the greatest guy in the world. Dr. Barton, his name was. He wasn't a great guy, though. As a matter of fact he was a real bastard, a real sadist. Every time he was torturing me with one of his evil power tools, he had this huge grin on his face like he was having a goddam ball, like he wasn't watching me in practically the worst pain of my life. I swear I'd walk around for months with a cavity in my mouth, sore as hell, without telling my parents, just to avoid that bastard Barton.

I was getting pretty depressed sitting there thinking about the dentist, so I distracted myself by watching the different screens, trying to catch some other hapless delinquent in the act of trying to rip this place off. No dice, though. Maybe nobody else was stupid enough. Every now and then I glanced at Philly. He was looking down at the floor. I don't think he looked up once. From what I could see of him, he looked like he was steaming mad.

When Peter—the main man from what I gathered—finally showed up, he asked us about a billion questions. Our names, birth dates, parents' names, height, weight, everything about us. Then he started in on the really stupid questions. Why did you do something like this? Did you think you'd get away with it? To top it off, he let all his words roll off his tongue with a real cowboy drawl, leaning back on two legs of his chair with his thumbs stuck in his waistband, probably like he'd seen in TV interrogations. It was like he thought he was an FBI agent putting the heat on the heads of a terrorist ring. You got the feeling he would have been smacking us around if he thought he could get away with it. The only upside to the whole thing was Philly answered him like a real smart-ass. Everything the guy said, Philly came up with a witty comeback. And if he couldn't think of an answer to the guy's question, he'd just tell him to go fuck himself. Me, I was the straight man, polite as hell. I figured I'd get off easier that way. I thought of doing something crazy, like start bawling my head off and moaning about peer pressure, and how I was really a good kid and all, but I didn't think I could actually pull it off. That's the kind of stuff I think about doing but never really have the guts to do. It's funny, I can be very gutsy, stealing all the time and everything, but if there's someone right there, watching me or pointing the finger at me like this guy Peter was, you'd swear I was the biggest wimp you ever saw. I just answered his questions until he didn't have any more, and then a while later a real cop showed up.

28

She looked us over a moment and then told us to stand up. She handcuffed us, separately. The cuffs were pretty tight, and I had to hold my hands a certain way to keep them from digging into my skin. She escorted us out of the mall, one hand on each of us. Everybody was standing around gaping at us. The older people, and the employees and all, were looking at us disapprovingly, disappointed in us, sort of shaking their heads back and forth, that kind of thing. The younger jerks, the loser kids who hung around in front of the mall twenty-four hours a day, smoking and trying to act tough, were snickering at us, pointing and laughing like a bunch of morons. I was uncomfortable, but I was also proud, in a way. I mean, at the time I thought it was even a little bit cool, having handcuffs on and getting escorted away by a police officer and everything. I liked the attention.

Outside the cop searched us carefully, taking everything out of our pockets and putting all our stuff into these big Ziploc bags. We rode in the back of her car over to the police station. She was a hell of a lot nicer than the security guards had been, chatting with us the whole way over, treating us like regular people. She wasn't even condescending to us the way most adults were. She wasn't at all attractive, really, except in a sweet homely kind of way, but she was nice, and that counted for a lot by me, especially after my experience with Pushy Peter. Philly didn't talk to her at all, but I loosened up pretty quickly and by the time we got to the station I was having a regular conversation with her. We were just talking about ordinary stuff, the weather turning into fall and how I liked school and how she liked being a cop. She even held the door open for us getting in and out of the car. I didn't know if she was required to do that or not, but I liked it anyhow.

Inside the station the cops weren't as friendly. Sarah, the one who'd taken us to the station, said good-bye to us and turned us over to two other cops. I was told to go with one, and Philly with the other. The cop I got was another woman, a lot older, like maybe fifty. Sarah had seemed like she was only thirty or so. The new one sat me down at a desk, in a room with all kinds of other cops sitting at desks and talking on the phone and typing away. No one was getting shoved around or yelled at, but otherwise it was just like you see in the movies when someone gets taken down to the station. I was pretty interested in the whole thing. I had never been in an actual police station before.

The new cop asked me all over again about what happened and why I was doing it and if I was planning to hurt anybody or anything. She wasn't nice like Sarah had been but she wasn't as much of a jerk as Peter, either. I don't even remember what she looked like. She kind of blended in with her uniform. I got the impression she didn't care much what my answers were; she was just doing her job. I said no, I wasn't planning on hurting anybody, and told her about how all I had was the one video game and I didn't even take it out of the store with me. I mean, I was going to, but I didn't make it out of the store. I was pretty honest with her. I did lie to her about one thing, though. I told her I wasn't on any drugs or alcohol, and that I never did any of that stuff. That was actually a pretty big whopper, and I think the only reason I was able to pull it off was that by then I was mostly sober, at least so I wasn't thinking too fuzzy anymore. I'm an awful liar anyway, so I was sort of surprised that she seemed to believe me. I don't even like lying. I hate it, actually. I feel like a real jerk when I don't tell the truth, to anyone. I guessed it would save me a lot of trouble if I lied about the drinking and stuff, though, so I did.

When she was done questioning me, she looked at me funny for a moment, confused, and then asked me to stay put for a minute. She went over to this other guy's desk across the room and talked back and forth with him for a minute, laughing about something. Then she came back over to me, still smiling.

"Well, Jim, looks like you're going home. Turns out you didn't actually break any laws. You didn't take anything out of the store, and there's no such thing as attempted shoplifting."

I smiled back then. That was good news. The main thing I had been worrying about was getting in trouble with my dad, and if this whole thing didn't go on record, he didn't have to find out.

The cop reached for the phone. "I'll just call your parents and have them come down and get you, and you'll be on your way."

"No!" I said, louder than I meant to.

She put the phone down and looked at me, looking concerned for the first time since I started talking to her. "What's the problem, Jim?"

I thought carefully about how to word it. If I told her my dad was doing anything illegal, like beating the shit out of me, he'd find out about it and beat the shit out of me again. Also, Philly had told me how before he moved here with his mom from Philadelphia, he'd tried to rat on his dad for pounding on him, and the cops wouldn't even believe him. His dad just said Philly fell down the stairs, and the cops actually believed his dad. Philly told me that's how it practically always was. So I figured there was no point in telling them, not unless I wanted an extra beating.

"My dad . . . it's nothing, really, I mean, he just drinks a lot sometimes is all, just now and then . . . what I mean is, he can't come get me tonight. He's probably drinking, I'm pretty sure."

"How about your mother? Could she come get you?"

That would be no good, either. Dad would find out for sure if Mom came and got me. "Umm . . . how about you just have an officer take me home? I think that would work out best."

She looked at me carefully, silent for a while. Finally she nodded. "Okay." Then, calling over to the guy she had talked to before, "Hey, John, can we get someone to take him home? Who's still around?" It was pretty late at night by now, probably close to three or so. "How about Coughlin? She took him in."

John shrugged his assent before going back to guzzling his coffee like it was the last cup on earth.

"Get her, wouldja?"

John looked irritated as he got up and left the room.

"She'll just be a minute. You can wait in here," the old lady cop said, escorting me to a room. It was the only time I was in an actual cell the whole time. It wasn't even a real cell, the way you normally think of one. I mean, there was no cement bench and heavy metal bars and all. It was just a big white room. That was it. There was one window high up in the door so that when I slouched down in the corner, which I did immediately, exhausted as all hell by that point, all I could see out of it was the wall in the hallway. More white. For a moment, I wondered what had become of Philly. I guessed his mom had come to pick him up. He was lucky. His dad, violent as he was, lived in Philadelphia, and his mom was an all right lady. Sure he'd be in hot water, but nothing like I would be if my folks caught wind of the night's goings-on. I also thought about Jeremy, deciding he must have gotten home fine. He'd walk if he had to. And there would be no way his parents would find out, not the way he had dealt with things at the store. As far as he was concerned, it had never even happened. And even if his parents did know, they wouldn't do anything. They never once punished him in any way that I know of. His mom had this idea about unconditionally accepting him no matter what, and his dad pretty much went along with it. Sounded good in theory, but really it was all talk, something they'd read about in *Reader's Digest*, just glazing over the stale cake inside; the truth is, the only way they knew to relate to him or show him love was to give him things. And they were rich enough to do plenty of that. They had their hands full trying to get through to Jeremy, though, you had to give them that. Lately, anyway. All through his childhood, he had really been a model kid, full of heart, smarter than a bull's-eye, always at the top of his class. By the time we met him he'd already given up on that, but it wasn't until Mandy died, until his first genuine love was ripped away from him, that he lost all his heart. And what was left was scary, in a way. He still had that razor-sharp intelligence, but it was all practical now. There was no compassion in him anymore. What had happened that night in the store, Jeremy would never have done that a year ago. He would have bragged about knowing us, telling the guards what fantastic chums we were, trying to cajole them into letting us off the hook. It might even have worked. But not anymore. Things had changed. We'd all changed. That didn't mean I was used to it, though. I didn't know if I'd ever be used to it.

Even with all that to think about, I was terrifically bored by the time Sarah showed up, her face filling the window. I jumped up and grinned like an idiot when I saw her. Even though I'd only met her that night, and only talked to her that once, I was glad as hell to see her.

She opened the door and smiled back. Not like she was all up in arms to see me or anything, just nicely. "You ready to go?" she asked. I was beginning to feel sort of foolish for acting like she was my long-lost cousin. I put my hands in my pockets trying to play it off.

"Sure, okay." Mr. Casual. Truth was, I was about ready to explode my claustrophobic guts all over the wall.

I followed her out of the station, going past about twenty "G'night Sarah's" and "Seeya tomorrah's." The funny thing was, just about every cop we walked by really did have donuts and coffee on their desks. I started cracking up after about the tenth Dunkin' Donuts bag I saw. Sarah must have thought I was a maniac, but Philly and I had been arguing about that for years. I'd always thought it was a like a myth started by the donut industry, but Philly always said they all really were donutatarians—he was right. It was amazing.

I got to sit up front 'cause I wasn't under arrest anymore. I bet most cops would have made me sit in back anyway. She was really a pretty cool lady. After giving her directions, I decided to take a chance. "So, do you guys have a contract with Dunkin' Donuts or something?"

Sarah burst out laughing. At least she wasn't angry. "What?"

"Well, I just noticed—I mean, I always thought it was just a big generali—a rumor, but I just couldn't help seeing . . . Everybody in that place had donuts!"

She looked over at me. "To tell you the truth, Jim, it's as big a mystery to me as it is to you. I hate donuts. I can only eat about half of one before I get sick."

A cop who hates donuts. I'd have to tell Philly about her. Even though he had obviously won the war, it was at least a small victory for me. An exception to his almighty rule.

The ride home was too short. It really was good talking to Sarah. I mean, yeah, we were just talking, but it was moments like that, spent with adults who had nice things to say to me, who really accepted me, cared for me even, that kept me going.

And sitting there talking to her, I got this funny idea inside my head. Crazy as it was, I began to think we might be friends. I mean, I knew I was doing all kinds of shit she wouldn't approve of, and I was just a kid and all, but it seemed possible. And I really wanted it, you know? I wanted to know someone wise, someone who'd gotten past the age of eighteen without losing it. I wanted to know her, a cop who gave half of a fuck.

I felt a little stupid asking, but I did it anyway, just as we were pulling into my driveway. It took me that long to work up the guts. "Say, do you think . . . I mean if you're not too busy and all . . ."

She looked at me again. Her brown eyes were kind. "Jim?"

"Yeah. It's nothing, really. I mean, I was thinking maybe we could . . . It's okay if you don't—"

"No, Jim, it's okay. I'd like to see you again."

"You would?" I asked, so hopeful, so young.

"Yes, I sure would. That's what you meant, wasn't it?"

"Yeah." I nodded. "It sure was."

We were both quiet for a minute, and there was only the steady sound of the motor running and the whirring buzz of the streetlights on the corner.

"Okay," she said, smiling thoughtfully. "I'll make sure to visit you some time soon."

"How?" I asked.

"Huh?"

"I mean, how'll you get ahold of me. See, you probably shouldn't call my house. It wouldn't go over too hot with my parents, having a cop calling for me and all."

"Okay."

"So how then?"

She was silent for a moment before speaking. "I'll find a way," she said, and I believe she meant it. She would have made good, too, if I was a normal kid, which she had no way of knowing how very much I wasn't. I never stopped running long enough for her to catch up with me. "I've got to go now, Jim," she said then, and I almost thought I heard reluctance in her voice.

I wanted to say good-bye somehow, I mean in a way that would really mean something, or at least take her hand or something. I didn't, though. I just blurted out, "Okay, bye!" and got out of the car and walked hurriedly into my house. I was embarrassed, in a way. I felt like a little kid running away from a girl he has a crush on.

I sometimes wonder what the world would be like if we all—everybody I mean—said what we really wanted to, what we really truly felt. I sometimes think that if everyone wasn't always going around swallowing their hearts, the world would be a hell of a lot nicer place.

After I was inside and I had watched Sarah Coughlin the cop drive around the corner and out of sight, I realized I hadn't even said thank you.

29

It was dark in the living room. Quiet. I leaned back against the front door and sank onto the carpet. In the stillness, I noticed the pain of my broken tooth again. I'd have to make up something to tell my parents. I'd tell them I got it playing ball. I'd feel like an idiot lying, even to them, but in this case I'd have to do it. We'd all be happier if I did.

I got up and went in the bathroom to take a look at it. I snarled at myself in the mirror. I looked like a pirate. Good for a few laughs, I guess, but I liked the full-set-of-teeth look better.

I tiptoed out of the bathroom, careful not to wake my parents, and was heading down the hall to sleep in my own room for the first time in weeks when I noticed the light was on in my brother's room. He wasn't usually up this late. I put my ear to the door to see if he was still awake. I heard nothing at first, then a faint sniffling. I knocked softly.

Immediately I heard my brother's voice. "Go away."

"C'mon Kid, it's Jim," I said, my face still pressed to the door.

"Beat it," he said, and something hard struck the other side of the door, hitting close to where my face was. I winced and put it together. In all the confusion it had slipped my mind. I had missed his fucking birthday.

"Let me in, Bill," I pressed.

"Forget it," he said. Then, "You're good at that."

"Ah, Christ, Billy!" I stormed in on him. A foot inside, I stopped short. He was sitting on the floor in his room, slouched against the wall opposite the door. Styrofoam popcorn was everywhere. In one corner of the room were about four maimed robotic action figures. Next to him lay the remnants of a radio control car. The antenna, bent in half, was stabbed into his bed. And at my feet was what he had thrown at me: a brand-new, very elaborate, very expensive model of the *Starship Enterprise*. Billy had been begging for that every day for a whole year. He had wanted nothing more. It was smashed. Its wings were broken off, and the little lights were shattered. Even the main disc was cracked. For one sick, terrible moment I was reminded of my sister, and it knocked the wind out of me.

He was looking at me, blinking. His eyes looked dry, but his cheeks were streaked with tears.

I looked back, trying to come up with something that wouldn't sound pathetic. I couldn't.

"Happy birthday," I said weakly.

"You missed it." His voice was flat, given-up sounding.

"I know."

"It's past midnight. It's over. You weren't here. Too late. It's not my birthday anymore. So don't say it." His dry eyes burned into mine. Not hotly, though. His eyes were freezing. So cold they burned. I tried hard to look away.

"I'm sorry, Bill."

"Yeah."

"No, I mean it. I am." God, even I thought I sounded insincere.

Finally it was he who looked away. He stood up and faced the wall, away from him. I heard him swallow loudly. "Are you, Jim? Are you gonna be here next time? Is that it? 'Next year I'll be there, Kid!' Huh?"

My eyes were stinging. "Yeah, I'll be there. We'll have a big party. Hell, I'll take you out, with me, anything—"

"See, Jim, the funny thing is, I don't think you will." God, he was a smart ten-year-old. "I don't think you will be here. You never are. You're never here. You think I like it here? I'm stuck here, you know. I'm always grounded, practically. Didja know that? Didja?"

I was choking back tears. "I'm sorry, Billy. I'm sorry." I stood, shakily, walking toward him. I stopped right behind him.

"They keep me here, Jim." His voice had lost its urgency, and suddenly he sounded like my little brother again. "For every little thing, they keep me here. It's like they don't want to lose me. They lost Mandy, and they lost you. They need me." He turned to face me then. His lips were quivering, as if he was afraid to speak. "I need *you*, Jim. And I think I've lost you, too." His mask cracked when he said that, and new tears rolled in old tracks down his face.

His words cut me to ribbons. We collapsed into each other, embracing each other as equals, as brothers. And I whispered in his ear, over and over, "I'm so so sorry. I'm so so sorry," even as I knew a million apologies could not heal his wounds.

We slept together that night. We talked for hours, swapping memories and dreams. We told jokes. We talked about Mandy. We were brothers. And when we were done talking, we crawled into his bed together. It wasn't even discussed. We just did it, the natural thing. And we slept, brothers, with only his teddy bear between us.

In the morning I woke before he did. I watched him sleep for a while. He had his teddy bear's ear in his mouth, the way he had slept all his life. His face was smooth, void of the wrinkles of pain. I got up quietly, slipping out of the bed and tiptoeing out of the room, careful not to wake him.

JANUARY 1992

30

Jeremy was holding the gun both times I've had one pointed in my face. The first time, he was kidding.

I was sprawled out on the floor in Philly's room where I had passed out the night before. I woke up to Philly and Jeremy trying to stifle their giggling. I didn't even think about opening my eyes. I had no idea what time it was, or even what day, but my head felt like it was being attacked by an army of vicious carpenters.

"W-wake up, Jim." Philly could barely contain himself.

I moaned.

"Time to get up, Jim." Jeremy kicked me in the ribs. It wasn't hard, but I wasn't ready for it, and I started coughing, spitting out gobs of phlegm and blood. I still had an aftertaste of whiskey in my mouth, and my throat was raw. It had been for days. I was pretty sure I had strep throat, but I couldn't remember the last time I'd been home, and I sure as hell couldn't afford a doctor. I hoped I wouldn't die from it. I had heard it could spread all over your body and eventually kill you. Jeremy and Philly were getting a kick out of it. I had had a bad coughing fit the night before, staining the inside of Philly's toilet red. Just for kicks Jeremy had called the emergency room while I was busy and told them his friend was dying of strep, and asked them what in the world he should do. He actually used those words, in this very uppity, nasal voice, very snooty and concerned. They told him to bring me in immediately and he hung up on them, laughing and telling me even the doctors thought I was going to die. Hilarious. I would have laughed my ass off if it wasn't me.

Another moan.

Then Jeremy knelt down and grabbed hold of my hair and turned my face upward. I was about to flip out on him when I felt something hard and metallic press against my forehead. I opened my eyes and *really* flipped out. There was a big fucking 9 mm gun in my face. One of those tough-looking L-shaped ones that just look made for blowing people's faces off. Not like all guns don't.

If I'd been thinking straight, I would have stayed completely still, and calmly, nicely asked Jeremy to put the gun down.

I wasn't thinking straight, though, and I followed my first instinct. My hands shot up and smashed into his wrist. He must not have been holding on to the gun too hard, or maybe he was just surprised, but the gun flew through the air sure as if he had thrown it like a fastball. It bounced off one corner and onto the wall opposite, and then dropped down onto the floor. None of us had time to move, or shout, or duck, or even blink, and when it went off as it hit the floor, it could easily have shot any of us.

Sometimes I think that when someone does something amazingly stupid—idiotically dangerous, I mean—then maybe God, or whoever, feels sorry for you and grants you a miracle. Sometimes, anyway. Maybe you only get one. Maybe we used up our one miracle that day. There were three of us in that tiny room, and that bullet could have hit any of us, but it went right into the wall.

Lucky, yeah, but it scared the living piss out of old Philly. I swear he went from his knees to standing in about half a second. He was hopping around holding his right ear and hollering, and at first I was sure he'd been shot. We were all yelling at once.

"What the—"

"Philly! You okay?"

"Yeah, I'm—"

"Wow!"

"Holy shit!"

"Did you see—"

"You okay?"

"I'm—"

"Oh my fucking God!"

"I'm fine, you fucking assholes! 'Cept I'm deaf in one ear! Jesus Christ that was loud!"

When we'd all calmed down enough so any one person could finish a sentence, Jeremy explained that he and Philly had found the gun in a Dumpster they landed in off a building after I passed out the night before. They were both laughing about it pretty quickly, but I was sore for a while. I could easily have had my brains blown out, with Jeremy pointing the gun at me the way he had. Still, I couldn't get more out of either of them than lame half-assed apologies, and after all, what the hell else was there to do? They both swore up and down they had no idea it was loaded, and by the time Jeremy had fed me breakfast and supplicated me with a bottle of penicillin he'd procured from his ma's dresser and we were on our way out the door, I had pretty much forgiven them.

This was a typical morning for us. I mean, the gun was a

new thing, but the air we breathed was not. The feeling was not. It was a closeness, a proximity, but it was not carefree. It was not the naive wildness that comes with being teenage boys. It was more a sickness, a shared disease. Waking up half drunk and smelling like puke and sweat and playing mean tricks on each other. I mean if you were an outsider, you wouldn't know we gave half of a fuck about each other. You wouldn't know we were the best of friends. Partners. We lived a wet dream. It would seem glamorous if you saw a movie about us, stealing booze and dancing on the edges of rooftops and lying to our parents and hiding from cops and only going to school when we felt like it. Real heroes.

But it wasn't a movie for me. I lived it. My life was slurred, a vodka-soaked dream. My knees were weak. My eyes hurt. I was in a constant state of wishing I could cry and not remembering how.

Still, I walked. I laughed. I watched bad television. I broke a lot of laws. I found things to do.

It was a Wednesday morning, and we were going to school. Philly and I were, anyway. Jeremy didn't bother anymore. He was going to walk us to the bus stop, though.

Stepping outside was like being teleported to the North Pole. It was nasty, biting cold out that morning, and the worst kind of snow coming down like tiny pinpricks. We had to walk two blocks through that to get to the bus stop. Knowing we were on our way to school didn't make the going any easier.

Thanks to a puritanical bus driver we ended up waiting about an hour at the bus stop, freezing our asses off, among other extremities. We wouldn't have waited half that long, but after a few minutes Jeremy passed out cigarettes and we all lit up while he explained that as soon as you pull out a cigarette at a bus stop, the bus shows up. Frustrating, but foolproof, he said.

He was right. Only thing was, the cocksucker driving our salvation caught sight of us smoking and passed right the fuck on by, looking back at us and wagging his finger self-righteously.

After futilely chasing the bus, screaming every swearword we'd ever even thought of, we set in on Jeremy.

"You asshole!"

"You and your damn cigarettes!"

"Hey, man, don't look at me, you smoked 'em!"

"Yeah, well . . ."

He had a point. Still, someone had to take the blame. Philly and I kept up ragging on him until he told us to fuck off, at which point we chilled out, not wanting things to get serious. Instead we started in on the bus driver, a target against whom we could all unite. "That ratfucker . . ."

"Great. He gets to be moralistic and we get to be frostbitten."

"Family values, my ass."

We developed a deep-seated hatred for the bus driver as we stood there in the snowstorm, killing a few minutes brainstorming up various ever-so-slow torturous deaths we could inflict upon him. But that got old pretty quickly, though; the cold burned away at us, eventually stripping us of our dreams of vengeance as we settled into a frigid sort of apathy.

"It's colder than hell out," I chattered after a long, shivering silence. We had decided it would be as much trouble to go back to Jeremy's house as it would be to just wait on the next bus, but now I wasn't so sure. It sure was taking its sweet time.

"Hell's hot, dumb-ass," Philly chattered back, breaking out a thermos filled with vodka and hitting off it. It was the Catholic in him talking. He was always chastising me like that, half-assedly correcting my blasphemy like a burned-out missionary.

"You'd know," I retorted, grabbing the thermos from him and swallowing a little heat. Thermoses were great for getting smashed at school. You could get drunk out of your mind in the middle of history class with nobody the wiser. Only thing was, half the time you ended up looking like a selfish asshole when you had to turn somebody down asking for a sip.

Jeremy was leaned against the bus stop pole, eyes closed. His fingers were turning blue, but he wasn't voicing any complaints. He didn't even have to be out there, actually. He had given up even pretending to go to school.

"You alive, Jeremy?" Philly took a playful swipe at him.

"Barely." He didn't open his eyes.

"Why the fuck are you even out here?" I asked him.

Now he did. Looking at me, he shrugged. "Where else would I go?"

"Huh." I was quiet for a while, thinking about that one. He really meant that. As much as he hung back, cold and withdrawn almost to the point of meditation, the Ice Man himself, the two of us were all he had.

"Yo, Jim! Bus! Jim! Get . . . on . . . the . . . bus!" Philly practically had to drag me on board. I'd completely zoned out, not even noticing Jeremy was gone until the doors folded shut behind me and I saw him disappearing through the glass, fading into the storm. It's funny, I thought about it often, but I never said a word about it. None of us did. There was so much that we held back, so much we kept hidden, secreted away in our innermost reaches, leaking out only very rarely in the quiet moments between jokes or murmured reluctantly in our sleep or in those moments in the early morning when we couldn't help it, sober enough to feel something and still buzzed enough to talk about it. But we knew about those moments and we learned to avoid them, constantly wisecracking and flat-out denying sleeptalking, and sleeping in past any possibility of honesty.

We spread out over the backseats, kicking our legs up onto the armrests of the seats in front of us until the bus driver got on the intercom and bitched at us. Philly muttered something about a stupid-ass rule and the intercom crackled at us, "What was that, son?"

"I said I was sorry I'm such a fool!" Philly hollered, not missing a beat.

The intercom grunted in approval.

"Gonna be a long-ass ride," Philly moaned, a little too loudly, probably on purpose.

"Huh?" The intercom demanded.

"Happy to oblige!" Philly hollered, as if the bus driver was about a mile away.

The intercom indignantly challenged Philly to repeat himself.

Philly took a deep breath. "I said—"

"Cut it out, Philly," I said.

"Why?" He looked hurt, in a puppy-dog kind of way.

"Because I don't want to get kicked off the fucking bus, that's why."

"Ah, ya spoilsport," Philly muttered grudgingly.

"What?"

"You're too fucking uptight these days, man. You never want to have any fun."

"Is that a fact?" I rolled my eyes at him.

"It is. And you know what? I know what you need."

He couldn't have been being more cocky, but I decided to play along. I didn't have anything better to do and there was another ten minutes worth of bus-riding time to kill. "Okay Dr. Watters, what exactly is it that I so desperately need? Enlighten me."

"Sex," he said matter-of-factly, as if it were obvious.

"Par*don?*"

"Jim, you need to get fucked. Tonight. I'll set it up." It wasn't a question. It was a sentence, passed down on me in that moment, riding a bus on a cold cold morning in the middle of the winter of my sixteenth year of life. And in a way, I had no choice. In a way, I couldn't refuse. Once, I had been saving my virginity for Leslie. It had been part of the plan, our plan, that we would one day make love in the quiet of the very late night or the very early morning, all alone and fully completely together, initiating each other into a new world. A nice thought. A romantic dream we'd shared without ever speaking of it. It was understood with the absolute certainty of two shy kids in love. There were no other avenues of possibility. Life was a long, straight highway stretching out as far as we could see, and we would go down it together.

Once, but that was before. Before Leslie left me, with an invitation to save myself and come back to her, and before I had turned down that invitation. Before I started drinking vodka like water. Before my sister kissed the lips of a moving freight train. Before a lot of things.

And now—now I didn't know. Leslie was a memory, a lost photograph, a fallen angel. I was a drunk teenager. Philly was my friend, my partner in quiet desperation. I hadn't masturbated in weeks. Being drunk half the time and depressed the other half didn't leave much room for sex drive. But right then, right there, sex, or the idea of sex, was like a filled shot glass Philly was holding out to me, telling me to drink, promising a cure. So what, I should turn him down? Leslie was gone. Cures were my life. In a way, the only way that counted, I couldn't refuse.

"Okay," I said.

"There's my man," Philly exclaimed, his eyes bright.

"I'll tell you what we'll do," he said, rubbing his hands together and practically jumping out of his seat. "I'll get three girls—"

"You know Jeremy won't go near 'em," I said.

He did know, or he should have, but there was no stopping him then. "Fuck it, he needs it bad as you. We'll hold the bastard down if we have to. Tell you what let's do . . ."

Philly's plan was this: he would work these three girls over during the school day, dropping a line at the end of the day about he and I and Jeremy partying with some fantastic dope over at Jeremy's house. He knew just the girls; they were pretty sexy and liked to sleep around, plus he'd heard one of them had a thing for me.

"Great plan," I said. "Where do we get the 'fantastic dope'?"

Philly looked at me casually as he got off the bus and merged into the mass of students. "That's your job," he said over his shoulder, tossing me the thermos filled with vodka, as if to say, "You'll need it."

I could swear I heard him snicker.

31

I could think of only one guy off the top of my head to get good drugs from at that lame-ass school. Tony, an eighteen-year-old sophomore, and that only because they felt sorry for him after three years as a freshman and figured he must have picked up enough from the three years put together to move on. Don't get me wrong, Tony had brains. He may not have been a math whiz, but he was sharp. As far as I was concerned, the guy was a walking nightmare. But he was always holding, and it was always the best.

Right away, I did the most useful thing I could think of to do. I went to class. At least it would get my mind off my fate for a while, and besides, Tony wasn't selling till lunchtime. But you could bet your sweet ass I wasn't going to buy from Tony. I'd find something. Somebody'd else'd turn up.

First hour. Algebra-trig. A source of constant torture. Lucky for all of us students, this teacher loved to make those awful screeching sounds with the chalk against the board, like she got a real kick out of screeching out uselessly intricate problems across our eardrums. What a fantastic way to start the day. At least it woke me up. The worst part was, it was a Talented and Gifted class, meaning I was in a room filled with all these overexcited, highly motivated bastards whose biggest joy in life was solving the extra credit Daily Challenge question the teacher gave us every day. I don't think I had looked at one once. My Daily Challenge was showing up. I remember once we had Any Questions day, where we were allowed to ask any question we wanted related to algebra-trig. About halfway through I stood up and asked our illustrious teacher how in the hell any of this was going to serve me in later life. She said I'd need it for pre-calculus next year. And pre-calculus was good for? Calculus, of course. I see, I said. How silly of me. Then I explained to her that I wasn't planning on needing anything beyond basic grocery store arithmetic, so could I please be excused for the rest of my mathematical career? She said I could excuse myself to the principal; he said he was sick of seeing me and I could excuse myself right back to the second half of Any Questions, which I certainly wouldn't want to miss. Of course not.

They gave us a four-minute break between classes. Which was ridiculous, considering it was practically a mile from one end of the school to the other. Forget about pissing, let alone talking or stopping at your locker to pick up a book. They gave you time for a dead run. The result was a four-minute marathon of a thousand teens dashing desperately through the halls, their backs straining under backpacks overloaded with all the textbooks and notebooks and folders and everything else they'd need for the day—forty pounds easy. The shit added up.

Me, I had the system beat. I had my own way of doing things. Mostly it just had to do with failing on purpose, but I was proud of it anyway. First, I couldn't give less of a fuck whether I got to class on time, eliminating the need for the mad dash. Then I'd located hidey-holes in every classroom where I could stash everything I needed, so I didn't have to carry it around with me. And homework? Forget about it. I threw my assignments in the trash can on the way out the door. This obviously didn't do wonders for my grades, but I usually managed to ace my tests anyway, so it about evened out. With these brilliant solutions to school's major challenges, the only problem I was left to deal with was dodging all the other maniacs who were playing human bumper cars, actually trying to get to their classes on time. Suckers.

Second hour. Western civilization. The torture continues. Actually, this was my favorite class. I mean, I hated all the stuff we were learning; I just couldn't manage to bring myself to give a flying fuck about Napoleon, aside from the interesting tidbit that he allegedly had a one-inch erection and some rich guy owns it. I mean it's in a glass case on some millionaire's mantel. But other than that, the whole class was bullshit, filled with maps and dates and dead kings who killed their wives. All that was deadly boring. Stuff to drink through. The reason it was my favorite class was the teacher. Mr. Rhodes was nearly deaf in both ears, and his favorite thing to do was tell you why. Back in World War II, after they ran out of regular soldiers, they started drafting all these idiots who would normally have been too stupid to qualify. Mr. Rhodes's job was to teach these morons to fight. I guess it was pretty ugly. I mean, if all the stories he told us were true, these guys were always having these terrible accidents that would have been hilarious if they weren't so bloody. Throwing grenades the wrong way and spraying each other with flamethrowers. The whole thing was a disaster. So one day one of these jokers is having trouble getting his missile launcher to work. Mr. Rhodes kneels right down behind it, saying he's going to fix it, but, "Whatever you do," he says, "do not touch this trigger." Just as he gets his eye up to the back of it, the guy goes, "What, this one?" and pulls the trigger. A missile launcher, Mr. Rhodes tells us, has a tremendous kick to it. Even though he wasn't in front of it, the force of the discharge sends him flying fifty feet, he spends two weeks unconscious, and when he wakes up he can barely hear a thing. Sounds like a goddam cartoon, I know, but he swears up and down the whole thing's true.

I drank my way through the second hour, still without any luck on the dope. After class I asked everyone even half likely if they knew who was holding. Then I asked everyone else. Nobody had nothing, and nobody knew anybody else who had anything. Not a single soul.

Except for Tony.

But I kept looking. I was even asking freshmen. I was ready to roll a joint filled with pubic hair and soap scum out of the urinal before I'd go buy from Tony.

Philly wasn't helping. I'd pass him in the hall between classes and he'd raise his eyebrows or mouth a question. "Ya got it?" "When?" "C'mon, Jim . . ." I'd shrug my shoulders and pretend not to know what he was saying, even though we'd been communicating that way for a year and a half, ever since we started high school, and I knew exactly what he was saying. We learned to talk to each other like that because Philly never wanted to be late for class, so there wasn't time for anything but lipreading and mimed gestures. Philly hated school as much as I did, don't get me wrong. But he actually cared about doing well. He wanted straight A's, and he got them. It went deeper than that, though. It went deeper than his A's and my D's and C's. I mean, we both knew I could do just as well as he did. I helped him with his homework, for God's sake. It went deeper than my general laziness and apathy. I mean, it was everything. It was Philly planning for the future. It was the light at the end of the tunnel that he was always looking at. I was blind to it. Maybe it was there, but I couldn't see it. I didn't plan for the future because I didn't think we had one. Philly saw all this shit we were going through as a phase, a teenage thing. He had optimism in his blood, like a sickness.

And then there was my chemistry class, which I hadn't been to in a month. The last day I had gone, I lit the ceiling on fire. We were doing this weird experiment where we had to fill these glycerine bubbles with a little bit of this flammable gas, butane, or something, and then have at the bubbles with matches and watch them go up in a puff of smoke. Only thing is, I guess I wasn't paying too close attention (surprise, surprise—actually, I think I was drunk as a skunk) when the teacher laid out the ground rules, so I ended up pumping a whole shitload of gas into this bubble, and then I was a little slow on the draw with the match and I ended up standing up on my lab table and setting fire to it right as it hit the ceiling. Boy, did that baby go. Because of all the extra gas, instead of a smoke bomb, it was a regular fireball. I managed to singe my eyelashes all to hell, and I had to put the ceiling tile out with my hand.

I wasn't much for science anyway. The year before I had managed to acquire the lowest grade ever in the history of Talented and Gifted biology. Not only did I miserably fail every test and not turn in a single homework assignment, I got points taken off for mouthing off to the teacher, who gave me a final grade of negative twelve percent.

I actually remember the day I hit zero. I was sitting in my usual spot on a stool at the very back of the room where I had been placed so I wouldn't distract my fellow classmates with the rampant day-to-day fucking off that served as my only means of entertainment in that rathole. After being planted out of sight and out of mind of the rest of the class, I generally wasted the minutes away staring at this goddam tarantula that never moved. All day long, every day, it sat stone still not once moving one iota. There was no lid on its aquarium and it could easily have bailed out, but it never even tried. So I just sat there, peering in at it, tapping and staring, staring and tapping, making funny faces, high-pitched noises, anything to stir it up. Nothing. Then one day, three days short of the end of the year, I was pretty much fed up with the catatonic fucker and I was occupying myself counting all the ceiling tiles in the room and then trying to calculate how many there were in the whole building. I did that pretty often, actually, giving myself tricky-as-hell math problems to figure out. It was a nice excursion for my mind, away from the here and now. I had heard there were whole religions based on existing in the here and now. Me, I thought they were whacked out of their fucking minds. That, or they had a lot better here and nows than I did.

This was really a complex problem with a lot of variables, and one of the rules was I had to do the whole thing in my head. It was basically taking the whole hour, ideal for this kind of situation. I had my eyes fixed to the front of the room, possibly even fooling my otherwise wily teacher into believing I was actually paying attention for once. I could just see the tarantula out of the corner of my eye, but I really wasn't paying any attention to him. I had a math problem to solve. Apparently, though, my friend the tarantula had other plans. Halfway through my calculations, right there, right out of the goddam blue, the little bastard jumped, right up onto the glass. I just about had a heart attack. I was actually terrified of tarantulas, regular moving ones anyway. I had gotten used to this one, basically considered it a benign lump, but as soon as he let me know he could move whenever he felt like it, we were back on enemy terms. At the sight of his menacing jump I let out a high-pitched holler and fell to the floor, taking my metal stool clanging down right along with me, all in all making one hell of a racket.

When the laughter of my peers died down and I'd picked myself and the stool up off the floor, my teacher looked down at me with a smirk on his face and said, sounding as if he had rehearsed these words over and over in his head, just waiting for this moment to come, "Congratulations, Mr. Drake, you have just received the great honor and distinction of a grade of zero percent. No one, in the twenty-year history of this Talented and Gifted biology program, has ever done that poorly. You have utterly and completely failed this class."

I could tell he got a real rise out of issuing that statement in front of the whole class. I decided to stick it to him and spent the last three days of class breaking every rule I could think of and then some, which won me the negative twelve. Three cheers for Jim the super-genius.

I guess I'm making it sound like a real blast. It wasn't, though. I mean, I could tell different stories and you'd feel so miserable you'd send me money. It wasn't any party. It's like I told you. It was drowning. But there were intermissions, you know? There were times when I had to laugh. I always imagined it was sort of like being in a war. Or at least like being in a war movie, which is about the extent of my knowledge about being in a war. Like the soldiers spend all this time being bombed and watching their friends get their heads shot off and missing their wives and crawling through the mud and blood-soaked fields dodging mines. They live in hell, their shirts soaked with sweat and terror and their pants filled with accidental shit they won't ever tell anybody about. But then, in between times, they go out. They play cards and listen to music and go to strip clubs and tell jokes and write letters reminiscing about better times. They dream. They hope. They wish on stars. And the hell is there, and their friends keep getting shot and they keep having nightmares, but they learn to live with it. Their lives are worse than they ever imagined life could get, but there's no use getting all wound up about it anymore.

32

Halfway through lunchtime, Philly finally pinned me down. Outside it had warmed up some since the morning. And the fresh air did me good. I was squatting on a bench in front of the school, slugging the last gulps of vodka and staring at a patch of evergreen bushes to avoid catching the eye of a patrolling security guard. They were all over the school, practically one per locker. Worse than real cops, really. I mean these were guys who for whatever reason, too stupid or too fat or too mean or whatever, weren't allowed to be real cops. So they became rent-a-cops and took out their repressed anger on us, high school students, victims of the system ourselves, rats in a trap. We had that in common, we were both getting fucked, but we hated each other. Even the goody-goodies hated the goddam rent-a-cops. It's hard to respect anyone who's got a badge but no gun. Maybe we all watched too many cop shows when we were kids, but we all understood that these guys were losers, and nobody gave them an ounce of respect. Not a day went by when one of the poor bastards didn't get hit with an unwanted bologna sandwich or a chocolate-milk grenade.

I just tried to stay out of their way. They technically weren't allowed to bother you if you weren't breaking some precious rule, but that was really no protection in a school with a rulebook bigger than the *Encyclopaedia Britannica*. If they didn't like the way you looked, they'd find something to give you a hard time about. And with that in mind, I was consuming some very hard liquor on school grounds, which could have developed into a serious problem if I caught the wrong eye. Thus did I keep my eyes nailed to the otherwise uninteresting bushes.

The thermos was empty by the time Philly pounced on me. I don't think I was showing it; when you get to the point where you're getting wasted at school you stop showing off and playing up how shitfaced you are and start practicing looking dead normal. It wasn't too hard, actually. It just takes a lot of tensing of muscles and careful, if not too cautious, movements. It sounds like that might defeat the whole purpose of drinking, but I wasn't drinking to get drunk anymore. I was drinking to keep breathing.

So I was fairly wasted when my best friend snuck up from behind and tackled me clear off the bench. I came very close to painting the evergreens with my half-digested lunch as I hit the ground. As it was, my stomach launched into my esophagus, which didn't exactly make me overjoyed to see Philly—not to mention that I'd been purposely avoiding him because I knew when he got ahold of me he was going to put a vise on my balls to go see Tony.

"What the fuck, man?" The drunker I got, the more articulate I was. Really.

"Haven't scored yet, have ya?" He was irritated.

"Naw, nobody's got nothin', man," I said, lying badly.

He was standing over me with his arms crossed. He always did that when he was pissed off. It was his I'm-more-stubborn-than-you-are-goddammit-so-don't-even-try-and-argue-with-me look. "Tony."

"Aw, c'mon, Philly—" I knew how pathetic I sounded, and how hopeless it was to disagree with him at this point, me drunk and out of breath on the ground and him angry and sober as he ever got, but I wanted to avoid Tony in the worst way.

Philly didn't budge. "Tony."

I stood up, slowly. I still had one eye on the security guards. They had both eyes on Philly and me. "Philly, would you not say it's better to stay out of that guy's way? I mean, I've heard shit that'll—"

"Rumors, man. Sure he's tough. He runs more drugs through this school than anybody else even thinks about. But it's not like he rips people off. He's never fucked up anybody that didn't ask for it."

This was Philly? He was blowing me away, just standing there. "Yeah, so what if he thinks I'm asking for it?"

"Don't. Just be cool, man."

"Philly, man, I'm your friend, remember? Friends don't send friends to trigger-happy drug dealers."

"Look, Jim." He put his hand on my shoulder, gripping tightly and holding my gaze just as tight, his blue eyes bloodshot as ever but deadly sure and serious mingled with a strange sort of earnestness that I didn't usually see in him. "I got three very sexy girls that are going to be very pissed if they don't get the dope I promised them. Now they are dumb sluts, but they're women, and you gotta admit we need them right now. Especially Jeremy. We all need to have a little fun. Just let loose and get fucked, just for one night. It'll give us a little peace of mind."

He was right. As sick as it sounded, getting peace of mind from "dumb sluts," we needed it. We were teenage boys. Having nothing else, we needed sex like it was water in the Sahara. So I understood. He was right. It wasn't good, not any of it was, but there it was. It was real, factual, hard as rocks.

"Tony?" I asked, knowing the answer.

"Tony." He answered me anyway, still gripping my shoulder. And for just the briefest second, at exactly the same moment, our faces flinched. His head shook backward, and I bit my lip. As if in that moment we knew, knew everything that was coming, and the knowing hurt us.

And then we broke, with the certainty of a football play. Not another word was exchanged. He was going to be a good student. I was going to buy drugs.

33

I had never been to see Tony before, but it wasn't hard to find out where he would be. He moved his operations every day so nobody would catch on. I just asked this guy Ryan Hertz, who bought from him all the time, where he would be that day at lunch. Turns out he was sitting on a bench inside a bus stop about two blocks from school. He was not tall, maybe five-six, with pretty dark skin and a completely shaved head. One of his cronies, a white guy I recognized named Kenny who was about six and a half feet tall and also very baldheaded, sat next to him. Both of them had biceps practically the size of my waist. Inside the bus shelter there was another kid, standing and talking something over with them. All three of them wore Starter jackets. The buyer, standing, was rocking nervously on his feet. At the entrance to the shelter stood another crony, this one black and just as tall and muscular as Kenny, acting as a sentry. These are guys that you would cross the street when you saw coming. On the curb in front of the sentry stood three other guys—in line, I guessed. I got behind them.

While I waited I watched, figuring out the system and working on staying upright. The liquor was hitting me pretty hard. There were no actual exchanges going on here. That was too risky with the amount of stuff they had going. All that changed hands here were notes. IOUs. They gave the buyer a note with the amount and type of drug they wanted. I didn't know what all they sold, but I had a feeling there wasn't a lot you couldn't get. The buyer gave them a note with the amount of money they promised to pay on it. The buyer signed both. Tony signed neither. Then they arranged a place and time to meet to do the real deal.

It took about fifteen minutes, but finally there was no one else in line. I wasn't shitting my pants, but that could have been the liquor talking. God knows I should have been.

Just as I stepped inside the bus shelter, Tony glanced down at his watch. He had a goatee. Call it a residual effect from middle school, or maybe it's just cause I can't grow one, but teenagers with real beards intimidate the hell out of me. And why is it that it's always the bullies that can? Must be a connection between a testosterone surplus and being an asshole.

Tony stood up. "Time to go, G." He looked at the kid next to him, who was practically at eye level with Tony even though he was still sitting down. "Got classes to attend." He walked out the other end of the bus shelter without even looking at me. His cronies moved to follow him.

"Wait!" I grabbed the elbow of the one who had been sitting down. Christ, I was drunk. This wasn't the kind of guy you grab and yell in his ear, not even a quiet yell. Not any kind of yell. He turned and looked down at me, exactly the way you'd look at a mosquito you were about to squash. I let go immediately. I wasn't *that* drunk. "I just need a little weed."

He sneered at me and turned away again, chuckling viciously. "Tomorrow's another day, punk."

I walked quickly—all but ran, actually—around the bus shelter to ask Tony directly. I couldn't help but feel a little like one of those disfigured children in India who tug at tourists' shirtsleeves and refuses to let go. "Tony," I said; using his name was awkward, but what else was I supposed to call him, sir? I mean, it's not like he was the president or something.

The way he looked at me, he might as well have been. His eyes were sunk deep into his head, and he had more wrinkles and creases in his face than I'd ever seen in an eighteen-year-old. He looked like an old man, with the body of a boxer. And, standing in front of him, I knew exactly why he was who he was, and why as many people listened to him as did. His face gave you nothing. He didn't seem to blink once while I looked at him. He breathed lightly through his nose and kept his lips shut, not tightly but just enough so you knew he would have some difficulty smiling. If he ever did. He was actually quite handsome. But what really grabbed my attention, grabbed it and held it, was the stillness. His face was completely still. He didn't swallow, his eyes didn't shift, his nose didn't twitch. And it's something you never notice until you see a face like his, but everybody's face is moving, some way, somehow, almost all the time. If it weren't for his eyes looking at me, he could have been asleep.

It must have only been a minute or two before he spoke, but it felt like an hour. It was like I could hear every second drag by, and I was acutely aware and embarrassed of every little move I made. And I made a lot of them: shuffling my feet, putting my hands in my pockets and taking them out again. I even sneezed. The whole thing put on me on edge. I did not feel one ounce the tough guy. "Whatchoo want, nigger?" he asked me.

"I . . . uh . . . I wanted . . . but maybe tomorrow . . ."

By that time his cronies had walked up behind him, flanking him. The black one spoke, reaching forward and poking me hard with his index finger as he did so. "He asked you a question, *nigga.*"

Tony brushed his hand away from my chest. "Back off, Leon." He didn't say anything to me, though, and it was clear that he was waiting for me to answer him.

Another minute passed again and I finally did, if only to break the heavy silence. "Okay, man. Okay," I said, picking up speed, "I want to buy an eighth."

"Of what?"

"Some good herb."

"Fifty," he said without hesitating.

"*Dollars*?" A stupid question, but twenty-five had been the going rate with the people I knew for a long time, so his price caught me by surprise.

This time Kenny spoke. "Yeah, dollars, motherfucker, who you think you're dealing with here, Santa Claus?"

Tony held his hand up, shutting him up. "Bitch," Kenny grumbled as he backed off.

"Fifty," Tony repeated. His eyes held a challenge. *Do you belong here?* they were saying. *Can you hack it, tough guy?*

And for what happened next, I have no good excuse. I accepted. "All right, man." I saw his challenge, and I took it. I didn't have fifty bucks. I didn't even have fifteen bucks. I was expecting Philly to front half of it. Half of twenty-five, anyway. There was no way he had even half of fifty. So why the hell'd I do it? I have no excuse. An explanation, maybe, but no excuse. See, with that look, that challenge, it was like he was questioning my right to be there. Not just to be there buying drugs from him, but my right to be buying drugs at all. My right to be drunk out of my mind at school. My right to be as far gone as I was. He was saying, *So what's your excuse, nigger?* So I answered. I puffed out my chest and bet fifty dollars on my right to be there, to be who I was.

The whole thing reminded me of being a little kid. When I was eight years old I was a lousy player on the lousiest team in the league. I mean, we were awful. We'd lose games like twenty to nothing, and that only because somebody's parents would feel bad and pull the ump aside and beg him to show some mercy and call the game. So one day in class—this is third grade—this loudmouth kid who's also the pitcher on the best team in the league is going on and on about how much we suck and how badly his team is going to whip our butts the next day. Well, there were pretty girls in that class, and I couldn't allow myself to be humiliated like that. I bet the kid five bucks that our team'd beat his the next day. This team regularly beats us *forty* to nothing. We didn't have a snowball's chance in hell of beating them. And I knew it. The pitcher was happy to take my bet, and the next day made good on it as his team whipped us forty-three to zip. That was one game that didn't get called early. Everyone wanted to, even the scary fanatical coach of the other team, who also happened to be the father of the pitcher. But I wouldn't let 'em. I refused to get off the field. I begged. I hollered. And we played the whole goddam nine innings, and didn't score a single run. After the game I was walking home and got surrounded by about half the other team. The pitcher'd told them all about the bet, and he wanted his five bucks. I told him I didn't have it, and when I did get it, I'd spend it on something better than his stupid ass. They beat the living shit out of me. I walked the rest of the way home with two black eyes and a bloody lip. I looked like Rocky, but I never told my parents what happened.

I went through the routine of exchanging notes like a robot, my mind on other things. Like getting killed. We agreed to meet behind Sunshine at four o'clock. Nobody was gonna call the game.

"Remember, fifty dollars, man, or we'll break your legs for starters," the white one called out as they walked away. "Bitch."

Tony said nothing. He didn't have to. I knew they weren't kidding around. I knew one guy who had paid Tony late—*paid* him even, just late—and they broke five of his ribs with a baseball bat. And they told him he was getting off easy 'cause they were feeling extra nice that day.

I walked back to school to see if Philly had any bright ideas that could save our lives.

34

"*Our* lives?"

"Well yeah, man, we gotta get outta this somehow," I said, trying to talk Philly into going along with me for the deal.

"Whoa, whoa, back up buddy. *Our* lives? *We?* Let me tell you something, man. *We* don't gotta get outta nothing. *We* didn't promise Tony money we didn't have. That's on you, man. I got the girls. The drugs were your end."

School was over and Philly and I were trudging through the snow along the tracks over to Sunshine. He actually was going along with me, but he refused to go do the deal itself. He was planning on waiting in the store and shooting the breeze with Charlie while I did the dirty work. Some bullshit about me picking up my end. "I know, it's just . . . I think we're—*I'm* in some serious shit here, man."

"It's not like you'll be alone, Jim. Jeremy's actually excited about going along on this thing. He's a smooth talker when he wants to be." We'd called Jeremy from school and filled him in about the party we had planned for the night, and our little afternoon difficulty we had to resolve first. He was about ten times more excited about the deal than about the girls, and promised to meet us at Sunshine at five minutes to four. "He'll get us out of this. He can sweet-talk his dad, he'll be able to talk some piddly-ass gangsters into holding their goddam horses."

I'd told Philly the story about the kid with the ribs, but he didn't buy it. Rumors, he said. He was sure Tony was just a regular guy. Tough, but not a psychopath or anything. "You haven't met this guy," I told him. He laughed it off. Rumors, man.

We got to Sunshine at half past three. We had a half hour to kill so I followed Philly inside. Charlie was up at the counter, along with his mother. I waved to them, but I was really too wound up to make small talk, so I started paging through a couple of magazines, trying to relax for a few minutes. I was looking for interviews with famous people that I considered at least halfway cool. I really liked reading what actors had to say. I mean even if it bored me to tears, it sort of fascinated me at the same time. These were people who actually made something of themselves, you know, who everybody else looked up to. I always wondered what it'd be like to have my picture up on thousands of teenage girls' walls, or have my face on the cover of one of those so-called hip culture magazines. I'd like it, I think. I'd feel redeemed, or something. And something else about it, too. You heard about a lot of those guys having really shitty childhoods or beating drug addictions, and I was almost proud of them. I sort of felt related to them, and it was nice to have somebody that made it out. I felt like bragging, even. *Say, you hear old Johnny finally kicked?* I'd say in my head, or in a quiet whisper. *He's in the movies now.* Gossiping with myself. Stupid, I know, but it almost helped sometimes.

Philly knew Charlie's mother, too. She was short, less than five feet tall, with huge breasts and smile wrinkles that went just about all the way out to her ears. She had a sweet face, just like Charlie's.

At twenty to four, I walked back outside, sipping absently on a Coke Charlie's mother had given me for free. She said I looked thirsty, and I said I was broke. A good woman. I felt pretty guilty about buying drugs behind her store. Like I was lying to her, you know, letting her think I was the real good kid she called me.

Unflappable Philly came out of the store at three forty-five, after chatting with old Charlie and his mom for a few minutes. I was beginning to hate my watch. I noticed every second tick by. Philly I wouldn't have even noticed, but the ringing of the bell on the door jolted me. I spilled the rest of my Coke on my jeans. I was edgy as hell. My stomach was in knots.

Philly lit a cigarette and offered me one. I took it. I looked at my watch again. Three forty-six. "T-minus fourteen minutes," I muttered under my breath.

"It'll be cool, man," Philly murmured thoughtfully, for the first time sensing how freaked out I was.

"Yeah," I said.

We smoked quietly. My fingers were pretty cold, but the rest of me was sweating. I was not hot.

Three forty-eight. "Wh-when's Jeremy coming?" I asked.

"Soon."

"Um." I shuddered.

Three forty-nine. I flicked my cigarette into the snow and watched it make its mark. I listened to the hiss of the snow melting, and thought about five ribs and getting off easy.

Three fifty. Tony and his hefty cronies walked around the corner and into my afternoon. They were looking directly at me.

"T-minus fuck," Philly breathed.

Fifteen seconds later, Tony was standing in front of me. He nodded toward the back of the building. "You're early," I said, almost apologetically.

"We're here," he said, quiet but forceful.

What was I gonna do, argue with him? In any case he didn't give me the chance. As soon as he spoke, he turned and walked around the building without looking back. Leon and Kenny followed him.

I looked at Philly. A bead of sweat made its way down his forehead, gaining momentum as it went and jumped off his nose. He put out his cigarette and licked his lips. It was a full minute before he met my eyes.

I didn't even have to say anything. "Of course I'm coming, man," he said. "I can't let you die alone." He grinned. I didn't.

We walked. "Let's hope Jeremy gets his smooth-talkin' ass over here."

"Yeah." I swallowed. "Let's hope."

There was a gravel lot in back of Sunshine, with a single tree sticking up in the middle of it. The tree, skinny and frail and hopeless-looking, had been dead for years. Tony and the other guys stood under it.

Philly and I walked toward them, taking our sweet time. The gravel crackled under our feet where we broke through the snow, marking our passage. Kenny spit on the ground at our feet as we faced them. He would have been funny if he wasn't so huge.

Tony was stone-faced, waiting. Always waiting, giving away nothing.

I stared and said nothing. I didn't know what else to do.

Don't do anything he doesn't do first. No sudden moves. No first moves.

And there it was. Nobody moved. I was starting to feel the cold, working its way into my bones. And suddenly, standing there in the bright sun, facing off with Tony, trying not to cave in and blurt out something stupid, I started giggling. It started with a smirk, and I tensed up my face something awful, but it wasn't long before it was just completely out of control, a full-blown, bona fide giggle. I couldn't help it. I couldn't help thinking this was just like one of those Wild West shoot-outs, and any second we'd turn from each other and take ten paces and spin around and blow the shit out of each other. The whole thing just struck me as so goddam funny, and I lost it. For once, even Tony didn't know what to do. He looked confused. He looked back and forth between Philly and me, and over at Leon and even Kenny—easily the dumbest of all of us—looking for anyone to give something away, something he could step off of, make a move. His cronies shrugged. Philly was as confused as Tony was, and shit-scared on top of it. There was only me, laughing at a drug deal with the most dangerous teenager in Madison.

I was in the Wild Fucking West. I was Billy the Kid, facing down Buffalo Bill on the outskirts of a ghost town. The dead, lonely tree cast the only shade in town. It was a shoot-out.

I turned around—I mean I actually, physically turned around—and went to work on my ten paces.

That didn't last too long. Leon reached forward and grabbed me roughly by the shoulder and spun me around. "Where you goin', man? We got a deal to execute."

"That's the thing," I said, rubbing my shoulder and stalling while I tried to think of something to say that would keep them from beating us to smithereens. I shot a desperate look sidelong at Philly. *Say something, man. Don't make me tell him.*

Philly shrugged helplessly. Where the hell was Jeremy? He was the talker. If anybody could get us out of this, it was him. Certainly not me. I was drunk, for God's sake.

"Here's the thing . . . ," I said again. I started rocking back and forth on my feet. Not a lot, but enough to notice. Enough to make Leon step toward me again.

The cold wrapped itself around me. It really couldn't have been less than thirty degrees, a warm day for January, but I was shivering violently. Shivering, rocking, and sweating. Philly stood motionless next to me. I knew he was panicking, too, but he was doing a lot better job hiding it than I was.

Tony reached into his pocket and threw a rolled-up plastic bag onto the ground. It hit a miniature snowdrift on the ground between us, sending up a little flurry of snowflakes. I watched, transfixed, as they danced their way through the air and onto my shoes. When they settled, quickly melting into tiny droplets and rolling off my shoes, I looked at the bag again, and then up at Tony. He didn't blink.

I reached down to pick up the bag. I didn't know what the hell else to do. I was waiting for Jeremy, praying for Jeremy, but he wasn't showing. I needed more time. I figured I could bullshit around a little, sniffing the dope. Lame, but not as lame as standing there like fuckin' Rain Man.

Just before my fingers embraced the bag, Tony put his foot out and stomped on it, hard enough to have broken some fingers if they'd been in the wrong place. They missed by less than an inch.

"The money," Tony said, sighing heavily. As if a decision had been made.

I was kneeling, my fingers still touching the edges of the bag. I looked up at him, almost pleadingly. His eyes met mine. As always, there was nothing there. Not even a flicker of recognition, as if I were about as significant as an ant. "See, we're gonna get it for you. We are. Tonight, or maybe tomorrow. We're *gonna* get it for you." His eyes, which I was still looking directly into, closed gently. And briefly, I thought he was thinking about it, letting us off the hook. I didn't get to finish my next sentence. "We don't have it, not just ye—" was as far as I got, before the rubber toe of his sneaker connected with my chin, shutting me up and sending me sprawling backward.

I landed hard on my back, knocking the wind out of me and giving me a cramp in my back the size of a bowling ball. I bit my tongue when he kicked me, and I could taste the blood rolling around in my mouth. I stumbled to my feet again, thinking about running. I looked at Philly just in time to see him lunge at Tony, fists flailing. He landed two hard punches, one just below his left eye and one directly into his teeth. I heard something crack. I wasn't sure if it was a tooth or a knuckle. Tony's face swung backward, but snapped back into place just as quickly. For the first time I saw expression in his zombielike face. It was twisted with rage. Tony threw himself at Philly, kicking and throwing his arms around, thudding into every part of Philly's body. Leon circled around behind Philly, pounding his fists into the back of his skull.

Kenny moved toward me, rubbing his hands deliberately. Coming at me like that, he looked taller than the Statue of Liberty. Without my even thinking about it, words started pouring out of my mouth like a river, like I was trying to sell him something. "C'mon, man, you don't have to do this, just chill for a minute, we can work this out, man, be cool, all right?"

It was hopeless. Kenny was too stupid to think about it even if he'd wanted to. Which he didn't. "You broke a contract," he snarled menacingly. "Bitch."

I didn't even try to hit him. I knew it wouldn't do any good. It might sound like an idiotic thing to do, but I just braced myself. Clenched my eyes shut and gritted my teeth, wrapping my arms around my head. I figured I'd just wait it out. I mean, how bad could it be? It had to end sometime, right? Worse came to worst, he'd just get tired after a while and lay off. Right?

It went on for-fucking-*ever*. I stayed standing for about two seconds, tensed up and waiting, like a little kid about to get spanked. He knocked me to the ground with the side of his fist against my head, and after that he mostly just kicked. Kicked everywhere. Kicked my knees, my thighs, my ass, my balls, my ribs, my spine, my chest, my skull, even my face when I left it uncovered to grasp at some other badly aching part of my battered body. I just rolled with it as best I could, and when I couldn't roll anymore I just lay there and took it. The whole time I kept thinking about how silent everything was. In the movies, big brawls are always accompanied by dramatic howls and grunts and smacking noises and tense music. In real life, it was almost peacefully quiet. The only noises at all were Philly's moans.

Philly was taking a different tack, which was probably why he was demanding the full attention of Tony and Leon, while Kenny got me all to himself. Me, I was just lying down and waiting for it to end. Philly wouldn't stay down. No matter how many times they kicked him, no matter how many times they spit in his face before punching it, no matter how much blood poured out of his nose, he wouldn't give up. He just kept standing up. Half the time he didn't even make it off his knees. Again, up. A kick in the stomach. Again, up. A kidney punch. Again, up. A knee in the jewels. Again, up. It was simple. He would not go down. He would not lie down for them. Stubborn Philly. And he was making it worse, for both of us. I was sure they would let us alone if he would just stay down. Just cry mercy. That's what it was too, a very serious game of mercy. What fight isn't, really? Once somebody cries mercy, it's over. That's all Tony was waiting for. Thing was, Philly wasn't playing. He wasn't fighting back, either, just exercising a kind of stubborn resistance. A fuck-you. He was saying it with his eyes, which he never took off Tony's. Between blows from Kenny, I watched them. Leon was a sideshow; I watched the two of them. I watched what was exchanged. *You're gonna have to kill me, motherfucker,* Philly's eyes told Tony's. *That's what it's gonna take?* Tony's responded. *Well, all right.*

The gun appeared in his hand as if by magic, it happened so fast. One second it was a fist, and then, with the same decisive, ruthless precision of that first kick, he drew a gun. It took one more instant to cock. One more to aim. And then I knew, knew as a cold, hard, uncaring, sure-as-shit fact, Philly had one second to live.

35

Except.

"Stop!"

Except Jeremy can shout his head off when he wants to, and when he does, every head turns, if only to see who the hell's rupturing their eardrums.

This time was no different. "Stop," he said, and everyone did. Kenny stopped kicking me, I stopped rolling, Leon stopped pounding his fists together, Tony stopped killing Philly, and Philly stopped dying. Every one of us looked at Jeremy, who had just stepped around the corner. There was a sort of bashfulness in the air, as if we were little kids who just got caught playing in the mud and were about to get punished.

Jeremy would have made one mean father figure. He stood twenty feet from us. As always, he wore all black. Black boots, black jeans, black leather jacket. His greasy blond locks hung down over his shoulders, framing his face. And Jesus, his face. His jaw was set hard against his teeth, his lips were stretched tight. His eyes were wild, fierce. And there was a coldness to him. Not a stone coldness, like Tony. More a sick coldness. It was his usual energy, his bitterness, his detachment, mixed with madness and one serious adrenaline rush. It was wickedness. And we all saw it, looking into his face. But more than that, we looked at his hands. See, a face like his, wickedness like that, would make anybody want to get the fuck out of the vicinity. But nobody moved, not a one of us, not an inch. All eyes were on his hands, his hands that kept us still. His hands held a gun.

The gun that had awakened me that morning, a hundred years ago. The gun Philly and Jeremy had found in a Dumpster, that had gone off in Jeremy's room, putting a hole the size of a softball in his wall. The gun now pointed at Tony's head. Fully capable of putting a hole the size of a softball in it, if the someone holding it was crazy enough to pull the trigger. Jeremy was. And every one of us knew it.

"Stop," he said again, quietly this time, but no less commandingly. He was looking at Tony. Tony, whose gun was still cocked and in Philly's face.

For a while nothing happened. People were thinking. We were behind Sunshine. It was a sunny winter day. Two guns were drawn. Philly and I were bleeding in the snow. We were all sweating like dogs, except for Jeremy, whose skin was dry. Two of us were facing death. The rest were watching. Things were quiet. We thought, we breathed, we bled.

Nothing happened, for a while. When the silence broke, it was Tony's voice that did it. "This your friend?" He never took his eyes off Jeremy.

"Yeah," Jeremy said hoarsely.

Neither gun shifted, not an inch.

"I could kill him," Tony said matter-of-factly.

"Yeah," Jeremy acknowledged, nodding. "And then I would blow your fucking head off."

Neither gun shifted, not an inch.

Jesus, I thought. This could turn into a bloodbath so fucking easy. "This is crazy," I whispered aloud.

Again, there was a pause. A silence. The red spot in the snow under my face widened a little. *Don't eat red snow,* I thought, and almost smiled. And thinking about that, a stupid pun, I got to thinking about the lightness in the world. Two guns were drawn. My best friend was on the brink of getting his face shot off. The other was seriously considering murder. It was a sunny winter day, and I was bleeding in the snow behind our favorite convenience store, remembering the jokes we used to tell about Eskimos—*Don't eat yellow snow*. It was all so bright, so harsh, so clear, and we, the six of us, enemies under the same blue sky, were wasting away together. No matter what we wanted, we were sharing the same air. What the hell was it all for? And what the hell was I supposed to do?

I didn't know. I really didn't, not anything, I mean. So I just sort of tuned out there for a while, and then I started to pray. Crazy as it was, that's what I did. I just put my face in the snow and hoped and wished and prayed as hard as I could, with as much faith as I could muster. First I prayed that there was a god, and then I prayed that wherever the hell God was, whatever the hell God was, that he or she or it help us out of this one. Have a little pity on our dumb asses and bail us out, somehow, give us another chance.

Tony considered his options. Jeremy stood his ground. No more words were exchanged. There was no need. All the cards were out. Tony had made a bet, Jeremy had called it. He wouldn't budge, no fucking way. It was up to Tony to make a decision. And for once, he balked. In a way, all our lives were in his hands, for those few moments. If he shot Philly, we would have our bloodbath. If he didn't, it would be Tony backing down for the first time I'd ever heard of, and I got the feeling for the first time, period.

It was a clear choice, really. Die or be humiliated. He knew what he had to do. I could see it in his eyes, his slouch, his trembling trigger finger. He knew, and he'd do it. But he was gonna choke on it on its way down.

For a moment longer, neither gun shifted, not an inch. And then, ever so slowly, gently, gracefully even, Tony dropped his gun. "Nigger's got a point," he said, and almost laughed, letting go of Philly and backing away.

I don't think it was my praying in the snow to a mysterious god that saved us that day. I think it was a little harsher than that. I think it had to do with Jeremy being willing to kill, willing to blow a softball-sized hole in Tony's head. But I don't know, maybe *that* was the answer to my prayer. Maybe my whole life, our whole lives, were all just answers to prayers, and everything just worked out the way it was meant to. It's a nice thought. I don't buy it, though. I guess in a way I'm too arrogant to. I have to hold on to the fact that it's all my fault, that I destroyed so much, because if I didn't, then Tony would have been right. I wouldn't belong. Not there, at a drug deal with two guns drawn and blood on the ground, not anywhere I had been. And I couldn't take that, even as a possibility.

There was an awkward moment then, after Tony dropped his gun. Progress had been made, but there we stood—or most of us anyway; two of us still off our feet—and it was like, what now?

Philly answered that one. One second there was nothing, just us all standing and kneeling there, and the next, Philly, who I expected would be passing out with fear and exhaustion right then, who gave no warning whatsoever, not even so much as a deep breath or a sigh, leaped to his feet in a flurry of lightning-fast movement, so quick he almost blurred. And then he was standing, Tony's dropped gun in hand, moving toward Tony. "All right, motherfucker," he said, coughing and swaying a little as he stepped, but ignoring his own poor condition, "what's it like now? What's it like now, nigger?" I'd never heard him use that word before. I'm pretty sure he was just mocking Tony, but I guess maybe what with being beaten all to hell and threatened with death and all, he'd developed a case of temporary racism. Either way the rage in his normally sweet, friendly voice shocked me. But you know, I just watched. I wasn't about to hold him back. I figured anything Tony got what he earned. I think at that point I could have just stood by while Philly shot a hole in every part of the guy's body.

Luckily, he didn't have that in mind. He was too good-hearted, too pure and innocent, even with everything he got himself involved in. He knew wrong and right, and he wasn't about to commit murder. Not then, anyway. He just wanted to humiliate Tony as badly as possible, if not in front of the whole world, then at least in front of Leon and Kenny, his now helpless right-hand boys.

He just wanted to rip him off.

"What do you want?" Tony asked him, hands in the air and still backing away. For every step he took Philly took one, matching strides and keeping the distance steady. Tony was not at all happy about it. He looked more nervous than he had the whole time Jeremy had had the gun on him. Jeremy had offered him a deal. Philly was just pissed off. He could snap. Tony knew he was in trouble.

"I want everything you got, asshole," he said, a vicious grin spreading across his bloodstained face.

Jeremy and I were starting to enjoy ourselves, now that the

tables were so very definitely turned. I stood myself up and moved to stand behind Philly, backing him up. Jeremy kept his gun trained on Leon and Kenny, just in case.

"Whatchoo mean, *every*thing?" Tony asked.

"You know," Philly replied nonchalantly, almost back to his old self. "Everything. All your drugs."

Tony did nothing for a moment, stalling uncomfortably. Then, "S'all I got, man," he said, gesturing at the bag of weed that still lay on the ground. It was a bad lie.

"All your *drugs*, man," Philly repeated, gesturing impatiently with his gun.

Tony's hand moved to his waistband, too quickly. Philly raised the gun and jabbed through the air at Tony with it. "Uh-uh. You feel like living today? Then gimme the other gun. And slowly. Like a goddam snail."

Tony scowled, losing his last ticket out of there as he ever so slowly took out his other gun.

"Drop it," Philly instructed him. He did. "Jimbo! Merry Christmas."

I reached down and picked it up. It was a revolver, not like the other two. A Russian roulette gun. I passed it from hand to hand, weighing it, testing the feel of having a stolen gun in my hands. It was a real rush, that was for sure. It almost felt good, but I knew something was very wrong. I was too uptight to own a gun. And more than that, what the fuck on earth were we doing? We were kids. Sixteen-year-olds. Our parents made us dinner, when we bothered to go home. My first kiss was a recent memory. I still had a teddy bear. Porn magazines were really exciting. I shoplifted. I paid the youth fare on the bus. I got wet dreams. I noticed new hair on my body just about every day. *We were kids.* And suddenly, so quickly I hardly noticed it happen until it was too late, we three kids had guns in our hands. Guns that we were not about to just put down.

We were robbing drug dealers. You do not rob drug dealers and then throw away your gun. You rob drug dealers and your life is not what it was. It is looking behind you every five paces. It is not going to school anymore, because that's where the dealers are. It's being afraid to go home, because they might find you there. It is precautions, countermeasures. Calculations of risk. It is you and your gun, where once, not so long ago, it was just you. Or you getting your first kiss. You sledding with your sister. You opening presents. You laughing with your buddies. You who hated hunters. You who never dreamed of holding a gun in your own hands, much less pointing it at somebody, another human being. It is now you making sure you live. It is you and your gun. And you can't go back to your teddy bear. The worst part is, you don't even really want to.

And it happened so fast I didn't even see it. We three kids were robbing drug dealers.

36

Jeremy and I watched, guns in hand, as Philly cleaned Tony out completely. And it was a sight to see. He took his gun, his drugs—which ended up being four more bags of the dope, some red pills that did God knew what, and what looked to my uneducated eyes like a bag of crack rocks.

At Philly's request, I collected all the various drug bags (I took the crack, too, just for kicks, even though we had no use for it and carrying around an unnecessary bag of crack cocaine was probably more trouble than the gag of actually having something like that in my own pocket was worth) and safely stowed them away in unlikely search spots throughout my body. Cops to my knowledge rarely searched crotches or boots, so that's where they went. We were gonna end up with some funkily scented drugs.

When I was done with that, Philly continued on his mind-boggling course of action. Just taking all the dealer's drugs wasn't enough for him. He had to take all Tony's *money* on top of it. Man, you shoulda seen Tony's face when Philly popped that one on him. His jaw just about hit his shoes. Which was maybe what gave Philly his next idea. After Jeremy received the great privilege of picking up off the ground the fifty or so dollars (now we've got it!) that Tony tossed there, old Philly really went flying off the deep end.

"Take your shoes off," he said, somehow managing to keep a straight face. Jeremy and I looked at each other, thinking the same thing. *Crazy son of a bitch has really lost it, hasn't he?*

"My *what*?" Tony asked disbelievingly.

"Your goddam shoes," Philly said insistently. "Give 'em here."

"You're outta your mind, motherfucker," Tony said.

"I'm the motherfucker that's pointing a gun in your face. Now don't piss me off," Philly said, in an already-quite-seriously-pissed-off tone of voice. His finger caressed the trigger on his gun, which was indeed still pointed directly in Tony's face.

We all watched as Tony took off his shoes, stepping onto the ice and snow-covered gravel in his flimsy white socks. And the whole time, all I could think was, *We are so dead.* If this guy ever catches us again, ever even *sees* us again, even hears one of our names, we are so fucking dead. My one comfort was that at least Philly seemed to be back to something like his old self, exercising his recklessly sick sense of humor again. Small comfort, though. Dead men don't tell tales, and they don't make wisecracks either.

Finally, the maniac got his fill and let them go. Kenny and Leon threatened and swore at us as they walked away, even drawing their fingers across their necks in menacing slicing motions. Not Tony. He didn't need to. He was deadly silent, saying not a word but keeping his eyes fixed on us right up until they rounded the corner. That was menacing enough, and it got the message out loud and clear. *Never let me see you again. Never.*

As soon as we were sure they were gone, we dropped the guns, as simultaneously as if it had been planned. We were quiet for a while, no one wanting to be the first to speak, for we knew it would do no good. There was so much to say, showing off of bruises and cuts, thanking Jeremy for showing up when he did, talking about how lucky that was, talking about the expressions on everybody's faces, especially Tony's when Philly asked for his shoes. Compliments to be handed out. Fears to be shared.

Then again, what good would it do? What good would it do to argue over the details, over who did what when, and to brag, and laugh, and shiver out loud? Things were understood. We had robbed some drug dealers. We couldn't go back to school, not with Tony there. Decisions had been made. We were in deeper. We were in real deep. So much for Philly's light at the end of the tunnel. We had so much to talk about, but at the same time, there was nothing any of us could say.

We didn't stand there for long. I think we all figured Tony could pretty easily re-stock up on weapons and come looking for us. And we were not exactly itching for a real shoot-out.

We had dropped our guns, and they lay in the snow at our feet like gravestones, markers for the parts of each of us that had died that afternoon behind Sunshine. "Do we take them?" I asked. It was the kind of thing where you know it doesn't need to be said, but you just go ahead and say it anyway.

"I think we better," Philly said, with a little uncertainty in his voice, so different from the way he had been with Tony.

"Yeah," Jeremy said. "We do."

It was an answer. We took it, and the guns, with us.

37

"Why the hell do you need those, anyway?" I asked Philly about the shoes as we walked away, making a halfhearted attempt at acknowledging his goof.

"I don't," Philly said flatly, tossing them one at a time into Sunshine's Dumpster as we passed it by. It was the closest we ever came to talking anything over. A single joke without a single smile.

In the silence that followed, where there could have been laughter, we all heard a door creak open. We turned, together, guns still in our hands, and saw Charlie standing in the doorway, clutching the waist of his raggedy red-and-black Harley shirt, as if for support. His mother was behind him, her hands on his shoulders. Her face was filled with grief. His was ashen, sober. The creaking door swung all the way open, and slammed loudly against the brick wall, pounding in the weight of the moment. We had been his heroes. We had been the good guys. All his older brothers were thugs. Now, so were we.

"Look, Charlie—"

"My name is Carlos," Charlie said listlessly.

"I'm sorry . . . Carlos," Philly said plaintively. But I could tell, even as he spoke, he knew it was useless. What was done was done. Charlie was looking at his heroes, the good guys, holding stolen guns. And there was nothing anybody could do to change that. Ever.

"Tell him, Carlos," his mother urged him. "And speak up about it."

Charlie gulped loudly and sentenced us. "Don't ever come here again."

Jeremy and I were still, and silent. Philly opened his mouth to speak, but no words came out. It was harder for him. Charlie had been like a little brother for him.

After a moment, Charlie's mother pulled her broken-hearted son back inside and then reached around and shut the door, never taking her eyes off us. And watching her, I realized that she, too, had cherished us as good boys her youngest son could look up to. She wasn't angry; she had seen too many of her own sons walk down the same road to be angry. But she knew where it led, and she looked very, very sad.

The door slammed shut, and we walked away.

It was not too long a walk to Philly's house, where he'd told the girls to meet us. He'd made our date for nine o'clock so we could get nice and spiffed up beforehand. After this mess, though, it was gonna be pretty hard to get spiffed up. We'd just have to cross our fingers and hope they were into guys with black eyes.

Philly's mother was home. We'd figured on that, but just planned on quick-timing it up to his bedroom, so she wouldn't catch sight of our battle scars. She foiled this plan, though, by greeting us at the door. Being on the old side for the mother of a son Philly's age, she was nearsighted something awful, so as we walked up the driveway she was smiling as wide as Texas.

As we hit the front step, though, we came into focus and she just about fainted. We must have looked awful. Neither Philly nor I was bleeding freely anymore, but there was no shortage of bruises and caked blood decorating our mugs. She went into immediate shock. Sweet as she was, up until that moment she had no idea Philly was in any kind of trouble. My parents had a pretty good idea I was headed down the tubes, but my dad didn't much care and I think my mother really had no idea what to do about it. Jeremy's parents had also wised up to his general condition, but he blew them off so hard and so often they'd just flat-out given up. Philly's mom really didn't know. He came home with good grades, and he was nice to her, and he'd never gotten in any trouble except for that little stealing episode at the mall, for which he'd been forced to do all those hours of community service—Look on the bright side, Ma, wasn't painting schools a good thing?—and which Philly had managed to convince his mother was just a onetime occurrence, a single bad mistake in an otherwise flawless life.

So seeing Philly like that, looking outwardly the way he'd actually been on the inside for quite some time, she almost checked out on us. Then she was all set to call 911. Philly started working on calming her down right off the bat, assuring her he was okay—it was just a fluke, we'd been jumped by some punks on the way home, no, no need to call the cops, the punks were wearing masks and it wouldn't do any good, the best thing for us was ice packs and relaxation. Watching them together, talking and hugging away, I almost got jealous. I hadn't been that close to my mother in years. I hadn't even seen her in a couple months. And worse, I didn't even really miss her. It'd been so long since I'd tasted that kind of proximity with her, I guess I'd forgotten what I was missing. I felt like the little matchstick girl, homeless and orphaned on Christmas Day, looking into picture windows at what she would never have.

Philly's mother did insist on administering us ice packs; then she cooked up some TV dinners, which we devoured like starving refugees. While we ate she drilled Philly for details—and details he gave her, not a word of truth included. According to him, we were walking home from school when six ski-masked punks jumped out of an alley with knives—no guns in this fairy tale—who proceeded to rob us blind and kick the living shit out of us. We knew they weren't kids from school; they were a lot older and bigger and we didn't recognize any of them. Jeremy and I backed up this story as if it were the God's truth, nodding and *yeah*ing our heads off. She ate it up, and by the end of dinner cops were the furthest thing from her mind.

After dinner Philly announced that we were going up to his room for some much-needed rest, and that we would be having a couple guests over later and she should please just send them right up. To this she agreed without a hint of protest, most likely just as glad as pie to have her son back in more or less one piece. Right then I think Philly could have told his mom he was taking the car to Costa Rica and she would have responded just about the same way.

Once firmly established in Philly's room, the padlock in place, our guns and drugs safely stowed in Philly's closet—sharing space with his wide assortment of porno magazines that for one night of our lives we would not be forced to break out—and Pink Floyd doing its very best to blow out the speakers on his chintzy boom box, we started getting ripped.

We broke out the booze first, saving the dope for later. As always, our man Philly had a couple of bottles of ridiculous-proof vodka on hand; over the next two hours we drained them completely, holding slugging contests to see who could slam the most at once, and, when we were done with that, holding walking contests. At one point Jeremy tucked a crack rock in each nostril, and he soon proclaimed they were completely numb. I didn't need crack for that. I already couldn't feel my body, every part of which had been killing me since Kenny had laid into me.

It occurred to me, quite a bit too late, that being sloshed out of our skulls was maybe not the most appealing way to present ourselves to our upcoming dates.

"Ah," Jeremy responded, more and more excited about the prospect of the girls' arrival with every passing mind-blowing blood-boiling throat-burning stomach-churning swig, "let's just hope they're into guys with black eyes *and* they like puke all over their tits."

In our vodka-induced stupor this was the funniest thing any of us had ever heard, and we came close to puking all over our own tits.

None of this was new for us. This was Happy Hour, our daily hour of near contentment, sandwiched between wanting a drink and being out of liquor and looking for a good place to puke. This was the intermission of our lives, our release, our pathetically futile attempt at grasping real, lasting peace. This was why we were who we were. This was why I hadn't seen Leslie or my brother for months. Because it worked. For a time, however short, once a night, it worked. One hour out of twenty-four, I was as close to happy as I thought I'd ever get.

Philly had set his alarm to alert us of the coming of the long-awaited and much-anticipated moment, but when the clock chimed nine there was still no sign of our promised girls. As revenge for their tardiness, Philly declared that we must take it upon ourselves to test the little red pills we had liberated from Tony. Not a glimmer of protest emerged from our wide-open mouths, waiting for Philly to feed us the pills like baby birds seeking the latest worm.

"What do these do anyways?" I asked after swallowing one, more to the air than to Philly or Jeremy.

"I haven't the fartiest idea," Philly shouted, downing four or five of the reds himself and simultaneous laying out a tremendously loud windbreaker. Jeremy and I clapped and cheered uproariously at our friend's wittily timed remark.

The pills kicked in a few minutes later, when the three of us, like clockwork in the order we'd ingested them, fell face first onto the floor. Luckily, Philly's room was graced with thick shag carpeting; hardwood would have been less forgiving. Apparently, our pills were downers. I thanked the good Lord I'd only eaten one. Likewise Jeremy. Philly, always given to excesses, was in real trouble. I'd be seriously surprised if he moved another muscle the whole night.

38

The girls finally put in an appearance at eleven, banging the shit out of Philly's padlocked door. Summoning all my reserves of willpower, I managed to let them in without pounding their faces in for sending the headache I'd acquired from the reds flying up and over the outer limits of my pain threshold.

The girls, who I guess were all relatively sexy, at least if you're into the dumb blond cheerleader type (I am, but up till then strictly in fantasy; I never imagined I'd actually associate with people like this in real life), seemed to possess a collective IQ of 150. Their names were Kate, Heidi, and Marie. Jeremy and I introduced ourselves. Luckily they already knew Philly, as he was by now totally nonfunctional and completely incapable of saying hello. He was lying half on and half off his bed, his head resting at an odd angle on the floor. His face was turning a handsome shade of purple, and an attractive pool of saliva was accumulating next to his open mouth. I would have thought him fully passed out, but every now and then his jaw opened and closed, forcing the saliva stream to start anew.

They surveyed the scene, obviously disgusted by the helpless Philly, but if I wasn't mistaken at least moderately turned on by me and Jeremy, who upon the girls' entrance had as discreetly as possible—which wasn't very—blown the crack rocks out of his nostrils and into his hand. I hoped the girls didn't notice.

They were at a clear point of indecision, not as yet budging from the doorway. There were three of them, and effectively two of us. Should they jump ship, leaving them all with a bad taste in their mouths from a wasted excursion, or stay, with only an unlucky one winding up disappointed?

They consulted each other with quick glances. I thought it best to mention the dope, perhaps adjust the sails a little bit. "Hey, you girls like to get high?"

"Sure," Marie said, breaking away from her girlfriends and sidling over to me, wearing a much brighter face than she had a couple seconds before. She had my sister's middle name. No point in telling her, though. "Sure we do. Why?"

"Why? Why?" I said, stuttering a little and grasping into thin air inside my sloshed brain for some choice words. "Umm, because we have some fine dope on our hands, that's why." There was certainly a shortage of eloquence in my brain right then, but there was no shortage of blood in my cock. I had a throbbing hard-on, which would have been embarrassing if I thought the girl in front of me minded, but it was obvious she didn't. Marie was right in my face then, her lips and hips just inches from my own. I could taste her breath. I closed my lips and looked away, hoping she couldn't smell mine. It was a lost cause, but she didn't seem to care. That, or she was willing to stomach it for the sake of an anticipated buzz. Her eyes were like rocks; I couldn't read her at all. Or there was nothing to read. Then again, I don't really believe anybody's like that. I mean I think everybody's got a deep-down. Still, I got the feeling that there was no way I was gonna get past the surface with them. But maybe that's how they wanted it. Maybe we were their party, their drugs, their sex, their night to brag about later. Maybe they were here to visit our world, use us up, and leave before the sun rose, going back to their shiny happy homes to sleep in their overstuffed beds under white lacy sheets they would never let us near, not with our dirty clothes and greasy hair and liquor breath. But why should they? And were we any better? We were the ones who invited them over, into our territory. And for what, if not a party, if not for drugs, for sex, for a night we could brag about later? For what, if not to use them? It was a fair trade, I guess. We could make each other feel good. And nobody was supposed to get uptight, or worry, or ask any questions. Of course I had to start fucking it up right off the bat, getting all personal and philosophical and even starting to care about these girls, trying to find some meaning in any of it.

"Well, whaddaya think about firing up a little of that fine dope you have on your hands, maybe having a little party?" Marie asked, so close I felt the words wash over my face.

"Well, I think that's a very terrific idea," I said robotically, playing the game out of a strange sense of obligation, but definitely not into it. My body was disagreeing with my heart, though; my cock was trembling, and even my thighs tingled. Marie really was a pretty girl. I mean, nothing like Leslie, but Leslie was gone. It was a different sort of thing anyway. With Leslie, given the time, under better circumstances, I would have made love. Marie and these other girls clearly just wanted to fuck.

"Well let's do it," Heidi said, stepping toward Jeremy and putting her hand on his chest. He gave her an awkward look but didn't push her away. Kate was left standing in the doorway, looking forlornly at my drooling friend.

I broke out the dope and rolled us up six skinny joints. I was a natural at it and it didn't take very long. I knew from experience to roll everything I wanted to smoke ahead of time. Try rolling one after you're high out of your mind and you'll know what I mean.

The five of us sat down on Philly's floor in a circle, piling up the joints like a funny little altar in the center, and lit the first one. It went quickly and easily, rolling down our throats and dispersing the initial giddy tingle that comes with good marijuana.

On to the second. We were all smiling by that point. No one was speaking. It was generally a silent ritual, this one. The noises came later.

After the third, things got a little loopy. Jeremy was having a hard time sitting up. The girls were all laughing hysterically, even lonely Kate. Marie abruptly put her head on my lap. It was anything but inconspicuous, and Kate and Heidi were seriously amused. As for me, I was freaking out a little bit. I mean, I hadn't lost my cool, but I was definitely uncomfortable. My lungs were having a hard time with the smoke. I had never had trouble like that before, but I was having big trouble that night, gasping for air in short little breaths and trying desperately to stay calm, not an easy thing with all that paranoid pot in me, whispering dreams of boiling lungs and a pulsating heart with a bad temper.

I beat the fear, though, at least for the moment, and kept smoking, hoping it would get better if I got higher. I made it through the fourth, which was as far as anybody got, and crawled away into a corner, holding my chest and clenching my eyes shut, and remembering how much I hated Philly's multicolored walls when I was wasted.

The smokers spread out across Philly's fairly large room, deliriously laughing their way into various resting points, abandoning the two remaining joints like orphans in the center of the carpet. Better than being burned alive, I thought to my stoned self. Actually, to be precise, I was drunk, stoned, and under the influence of an unknown tranquilizer. Quite hammered, in other words—more hammered than I ever remembered being. Of course, I said that every time, but this particular time it might have been a pretty accurate estimation.

My inflated lungs were still kicking my ass as Marie crawled over to keep me company. She didn't look quite as pretty anymore. It wasn't her fault, it's just that her head was alternating between fat and skinny and I kept on getting flashes of X-ray vision, vividly seeing her skull inside her rosy skin. I resolved to keep my eyes shut for the rest of my life, though that didn't help much, as my eyelids appeared to be coated with tiny movies of some very disturbing clowns.

"Hi," she said, giggling. The sounds coming out of her throat echoed inside my head, bouncing off the walls of my skull, back and forth and faster and faster until a stoned girl's giggle had become one solid high-pitched tone, like a tornado siren punching holes in my mind.

"Hi," she said again, petting my head sort of roughly.

I whimpered.

"You like to fuck?" she whispered in my ear, accompanying her own voice with that piercing giggle.

I said nothing. My lungs were exploding. I wanted it to be over. I wanted peace. I wanted air.

Marie squatted on my legs—a neat trick, seeing as how I was writhing and flopping around like a caught fish. "You like to fuck?" she whispered again, her fingers fumbling over my zipper.

I moaned softly. "Air," I said. Air, I wanted. I wanted a clear head and a milk shake. I wanted a sled. I wanted my sister.

Marie tore my pants open and pulled them off like the word *gentle* wasn't in her vocabulary. I didn't fight her but I didn't help, either. From very far away, I thought I could hear Jeremy and Heidi fucking. It sounded like they were hitting a wall.

Moan, moan, thump. Moan, moan, thump. I wondered if Jeremy was a virgin. He'd never told me whether or not he'd had sex with Mandy before she died. I never asked. I wondered then, though, if Jeremy was a virgin or if he was losing his virginity right then, practically right next to me. I hoped not. I hoped to God that he'd lost it to my sister, just so he wouldn't be doing something so pathetic as losing it to a cheerleader, wasted and fucking a girl he didn't even know on Philly's carpet. Because I knew that's what I was about to do, and I couldn't bear the thought of it happening to him, too. This moment, it could never happen again. You can't lose your virginity twice. But I was about to lose it in the most pathetic way I could think of, because I was too weak to do anything else. Because all I cared about right then was making my sorry desperate life somehow better.

I was wearing my boxers. Marie didn't bother to take them off. She just pulled my cock through the slot in the front. Even as high as I was, I was really hard. I'd never seen it that big before. Marie seemed impressed. "Nice," she said. Then, "What a nice big dick you have, mister."

"All the better to fuck you with, my dear," I murmured, without smiling at all. My eyes, my cheekbones, ached with impossible grief.

Marie laughed. "You're funny," she said. A compliment. Whoopee. Then, without warning, she knelt over and put my cock in her mouth. It felt amazing. She moved her lips up and down on me, and every now and then ran her tongue up and down the length, putting my balls in her mouth and then going back up and licking the head. I had never felt anything that good in my life. Below the waist, I was in heaven. Upstairs, I was wracked with pain. It was an odd mix, those two. Like sitting really close to a campfire in the middle of winter—your front is burning up but your back is freezing. And lying there, with that odd mix, I felt myself start to separate. I felt my bottom, pleasure-filled half start to float, up, up, and away, into space, into heaven. My top half stayed there on the floor, facing the fire. And of course it was the drugs talking, but it felt completely real. My cock went to heaven, and my heart went to hell. Jeepers, I thought, and it was the perfect word for the situation. I hadn't said that since I was seven or so, and that's about how old I felt then, lying there more gone than I had ever been, lying there getting a blow job, lying there with my lungs exploding.

Just before I came, Marie pulled away. "Hold on there, little fella," she said, standing up and stripping. "I want some of you down here." My cock was tingling ecstatically. She had stopped right at that excruciatingly tense moment of overpowering sweet limbo just before orgasm, and I just lay there and watched her through tear-stung eyes, my body taut with the memory of pleasure, my heart pounding with the ghost of real life. She pulled her T-shirt and bra off first and then went to work on her jeans. She had pretty small breasts. Her nipples were hard. She played with them with one hand as she tugged her jeans off. It wasn't easy getting them off. They were really tight. It was hard to imagine her voluntarily putting them on every day.

She pulled her black underwear off right along with the pants and stood naked before me. Her eyes were rocks. We were using each other. She was a high school cheerleader. I was a newly dropped-out drunk. I'd never met her before in my life. To her, I was just one more guy, and, wasted as I was, probably a pretty unimpressive one. She would forget me in a month. I would remember her for the rest of my life.

"Ready or not," Marie said as she knelt down on either side of my stomach and slid backward, slipping my cock inside of her. "Ahhhhhh," she said, a satisfied grin spreading across her face as she began to rock back and forth.

It was surprisingly easy. I fit right inside her. I mean, I guess that would be pretty obvious. I don't know what I was expecting. What it was was just warm, wet, prickly friction, and it felt better than I could ever have imagined.

I don't think she wanted to kiss me, and even if she did, she must have figured I wouldn't have been too into it. She stayed on top the whole time, sitting upright, quiet mostly but still giggling now and then, as if at some private joke only the two of us were in on. Except I wasn't laughing, not at all. Sobbing and twisting and moaning and coughing and thrusting and shaking, but not laughing. I was sort of dreaming of laughing, maybe. Wishing I felt like it. Wishing I would someday feel like it. I was dreaming of a lot of things, while Marie rocked back and forth on top of me. I wanted the old days. I wanted Mandy. I wanted Leslie. I wanted my mother. I even missed my dad, the way he had been when I was really small.

It took me a long time to come, actually. Philly had always said I'd come in a second if I ever got myself inside a pussy. And maybe I would have, in another place at another time. But not there, not that night. With my mind on so many other things, I barely remembered to thrust every now and then. Finally I did, though. It was an accident. I came right inside her, and my whole body rocked with halfhearted, almost involuntary pleasure.

When I was done, she rolled over and lay down next to me, putting her arm over my stomach. She was completely naked. I was still wearing my T-shirt and boxers, which were soaking wet now with each of our juices. I didn't feel split anymore.

"By the way," she said as we lay there together, "what's your name, kid?"

"Jim," I said, nearly choking up.

"Well, Jim," she whispered, and I could tell she was smiling, "you don't have nothing to worry about. I'm on the pill."

I had been too fucked up to even consider that it was a bad idea to come inside her. If she wasn't on the pill, I could have gotten her pregnant. Not to mention I had probably just caught about twenty diseases. And she hadn't even known my goddam name.

I cried myself to sleep.

39

I had the worst dream of my life that night. I was naked in a stone cell. Somebody was blasting that Def Leppard song "Pour Some Sugar on Me." There was a jailkeeper, some guy wearing a shroud so I couldn't see his face, and he kept unlocking the door and letting in visitors. Everybody came. Mandy, Leslie, Billy, my parents, Philly, Jeremy, Charlie from Sunshine, even my old journalism teacher Bore showed up. They were all deadly serious and nobody said anything to me. What they did was, they'd come in and look at me awhile, lying there naked on the floor, and then they'd rip open a bag of sugar and empty it out onto me, one after another, until I was completely doused in white crystal sugar. And when they all filed out, after they were gone and it was just me and the hooded jailkeeper, the ants came.

Thousands of them. Tiny, black, fast, and ferocious-looking. I've always hated ants. When I was little I was terrified of them. I used to stomp on them all the time, go out of my way to stomp on them, just to get rid of them, but even that scared me. I was always sure they were gonna get me back. I don't know what it was, really, that was so scary. It's just that they're so small, and sinister-looking, and they can get *any*where, you know?

So there it was. They were getting me back. They came from everywhere. Just through the cell door at first, but then from everywhere. They came out of the shadows of the room. They seeped in right through the concrete walls. They crawled out the cracks in the ceiling and dropped down on me. They were coming for me.

They seeped. They crawled. They scampered.

They were coming for me, and they were coming from everywhere.

At first I just lay where I was and watched them, fascinated. But when they got close, I sprang to my feet, and started trying to dodge them, but there was no place to dodge to. They were completely covering the walls, floor, bars, all racing toward me.

Then they hit. First it was just at my feet, and I felt little itches and tingles as they crawled around on my skin, and I just kept kicking them off, but pretty soon there were too many to fight off, and they were all over me, picking at the sugar that was coating my skin.

I started really flipping my lid, I mean *freaking out*. I was screaming, and running around the room like mad, trying to shake them off, and sticking my hands through the bars and begging the jailkeeper to let me out, who did not even look at me, who did nothing but somehow make the terribly relevant soundtrack about ten times louder.

Payback certainly is a bitch.

Mandy came back to the cell door. The jailkeeper let her in and slammed the door shut behind her. She had that same quiet, cold stare she'd worn before, and that all the other visitors had also had. I fell at her feet, my dead, dearly beloved sister, and sobbed. I told her I was sorry. I was sorry I'd killed the ants, I was sorry I hadn't saved her. I was sorry for everything. I pleaded with her to forgive me, to save me, let me out of the cell. Her expression never changed. Instead, out of nowhere, she held out another full bag of sugar. She tore it open slowly, deliberately. And with that same unfeeling stare, she began to pour.

I resisted. I screamed, and rolled away from her, and covered my head with my hands.

She got violent. My sister, who never in her life laid a hand on me to hurt, ripped my hands away from my face and pried my mouth open. Her nails dug into my face. She poured the sugar down my throat. I was too shocked, too weak to stop her. She left, and the ants got inside me.

They crawled in every hole you can think of. I gave up running and collapsed onto the floor, trembling. "Hey mister," I pleaded, shouting frantically at the jailkeeper. "Help me! Make it stop! How can I make it stop?!"

The jailkeeper turned and looked at me, for once responding. I still couldn't see his face. "Take off your skin," he said.

I could do nothing else. "Sorry," I kept saying, and I began to scrape.

40

I woke to Marie shaking my shoulder, whispering my name. "Jim! Jim! Hey, are you okay?"

I was facing away from her, pressed up against the wall. My forearms were wet. They stung badly.

"Hey, Jim, you were screaming in your sleep. It's four in the morning. You wanna quiet down if you're okay?" She kept shaking my shoulder like I was going to give her a medal or something. I still didn't say anything, and finally she gave me an extra-hard shake, a real prizewinner, and I rolled over.

I had my arms crossed tight over my chest like I was in a coffin, and when I rolled I hit her breasts with my stinging wet forearms.

"Hey, what—" She shifted her torso so it caught the moonlight that was shining through Philly's one window. My arms, and her breasts where I had touched them, were covered in blood. I had scraped half the skin off my arms. I could feel it built up under my fingernails. "Oh my fucking God," she said, standing up quickly and feeling around the floor for her clothes. "That is so sick!"

"Sorry," I said.

Just as that was happening, I heard Jeremy's voice mumble something I didn't catch from the other side of the room. He didn't sound good. He wasn't. The next thing I heard was him puking, immediately followed by a screech that easily could have emanated from the gates of hell, although more likely it was from Heidi, who I soon deduced Jeremy had just puked on.

Perfect timing. Heidi and Marie were dressed and ready to go at exactly the same time, and, almost as if they had planned it, they each took one of Kate's arms and dragged her out of the bed where she was crashed out next to Philly, yelling at her to get her clothes on. They practically dressed her, and I'm pretty sure she was still asleep as they walked out of the room. Marie went first, holding Kate's shoulder, saying nothing. Heidi went after Kate, holding her other shoulder and sort of shoving her along. I thought at first she would leave without saying good-bye, too, but just before she slammed the door she turned around. "*Don't* ask us out again," she said to no one in particular, a sneer on her face only someone who had practiced for long hours in the mirror could possibly call up on command.

Our one-night stand was over. The girl who took my virginity was gone. I didn't expect to see her again, and I never did.

I was bleeding, Jeremy was taking turns puking and wheezing, and Philly was zonked out. According to Philly's clock, it was four thirteen in the morning.

I decided it would be a good idea to bandage my arms. I took a deep breath, testing my lungs. I could breathe easily again. I smiled a little, barely noticeably. Maybe I should have been more relieved, but I really wasn't. So I wasn't going to explode. Hurray.

I got to my feet gingerly, wary of my unknown blood alcohol content. "Can he actually walk, folks? Can the Wasted Teenager known as Jim Drake actually put one foot in front of the other and support his own weight?" I whispered in the voice of an announcer at a freak show. I felt a little shaky, but otherwise okay. I gave myself the thumbs-up to proceed. "He's feeling confident . . . He walks . . ." I took a step, and crashed. My face broke my fall. "He falls." I finished off the announcer routine mumbling into the carpet. It lost some of its charm that way.

After careful consideration, I concluded that crawling would be my safest, if not quickest, mode of transportation to the bathroom. I maneuvered scot-free all the way to Philly's doorway, but traversing the hallway presented a new barrier. My bloody arms. Beautiful off-white carpet that was Philly's mother's pride and joy, scrubbed and primped by her on a daily basis. Crawling was a bad idea.

She didn't ever set foot or eye inside Philly's room, so it hadn't even crossed my mind that bleeding on his floor would be a problem. We'd done worse. But the hallway was a seriously different story. I spent a minute lying there, thoroughly stumped, frustrated, panting, and bleeding in the dark. I hated cuts, though, and the stinging motivated my thinking. I wanted nothing more than a bathroom sink and a box of Band-Aids. I rolled over on my back and started sort of slithering along, using my heels and my shoulders to propel myself forward, holding my arms over my chest, making sure any potentially offensive drops of blood landed on me and not the much more precious carpet. It reminded me of elementary school gym class, when me and thirty other little brats spent an hour moving around like that, knocking heads and chafing our backs on the linoleum. Our teacher called it the crab. I called it lame. Little did I know one day it would serve me so well.

Finally I made it to the bathroom. I didn't worry about spilling blood in there. It'd be easy to wipe off the porcelain and tile. I hit the light and for the first time got a good look at my arms. It was ugly. I had literally raked the flesh off in strips up and down both forearms. Band-Aids wouldn't do the job. After rifling through the various cabinets, I found a couple of Ace bandages and wrapped my arms in those. The blood soaked through immediately, but I had wrapped them pretty tight and I figured the pressure would stop the bleeding soon enough. I wandered back to Philly's room, returning the same way I had come. My arms didn't sting as badly anymore, at least. I've always heard that it's good to air out your cuts, but mine always feel a hell of a lot better bandaged up.

Jeremy was standing at the window when I got back to Philly's room. Philly was still passed out. I crabbed my way over to Jeremy. I was starting to really dig moving like that. I was considering just going around like that all the time, bloody arms or not.

"What are you doing?" Jeremy asked me without looking down. He was staring up at the sky, but I guess he'd caught me in his periphery.

"Crab," I said, smiling almost hopefully. "It's my new way of walking. You should try it. Puts a whole new perspective on . . ." I shut up when I realized Jeremy wasn't listening. Neither was I, really. I was just talking to fill in the cracks, and Jeremy didn't want them filled.

"What time is it?" Jeremy asked after a moment's quiet. His voice only made the quiet deeper, though. He wasn't just making conversation.

"Why?" I asked.

"I want to watch the sunrise."

"Four twenty," I said, glancing at the clock. "National pot-smoking time." Four twenty was the legal code of some marijuana violation in California, and somehow the fad of getting high at that time of day had really caught on.

"Think I'll skip it this time," Jeremy said.

"Me, too." Getting high filled in the cracks like nothing else, and that wasn't what we were doing, sitting there at Philly's window at four twenty in the morning. We were listening. We were listening to Philly's gentle, almost soothing snore, and to the occasional early-riser car that drove by, and to the wind in the trees, and to each other's breath. We were listening to the quiet. And we were smelling things, too. We were smelling sex, and sweat, and blood, and puke, and vodka, and smoke. We were smelling memories and dreams. For once, we were doing what we usually avoided like the plague. We were being still.

"Four twenty," Jeremy said, five minutes later, slumping down next to me. "Got two hours yet."

"Yeah," I said. "Gonna go back to sleep?"

"No."

"Good." I nodded. "Me, either."

He nodded then, too, as if in approval, and then I nodded again, and suddenly we were both just sitting there, side by side, nodding our heads off at each other like a couple of idiots, and we both burst out laughing.

We laughed long and hard. We laughed till our guts hurt. We needed to. And then we collapsed against each other. He laughed into my shoulder, and I laughed into his hair. We laughed so hard we cried.

He cried into my shoulder, and I cried into his hair. We cried till our guts hurt. And we needed that, too. Me and the Ice Man. Except I knew he wasn't an Ice Man, not then, not ever. He'd just been holding everything in. What else could he do? He'd seen the love of his life get hit by a train. What else could he do, to stay alive? He held things in. He drank. He never cried. And he avoided the quiet times, like the rest of us. Except for that morning, Thursday morning, in the middle of January. Right after National Pot Smoking Time. Right after having sex with a cheerleader named Heidi. Right after he pointed a gun in the face of a drug dealer. Things add up. And sometimes you just can't sleep, and the quiet catches up to you. And so one morning, that morning, out of some almost inevitable force of inertia, the ice cracked.

"That wasn't my first time, you know," Jeremy said.

"I kinda figured," I said.

"I'm sorry I never told you."

"It's okay."

"I mean, it wasn't long before she died, and I was gonna say something, I was, but then . . . it just didn't seem right."

"It's okay." He didn't need to explain things, because I already understood, but it helped him, I think. It was like a confession, almost. Just to clear the air. He was absolving himself with me, and it was important that he said what he needed to say, that each of us did, because we would never have another talk like that again, and I think we both sensed that. It was four thirty in the morning, and it was dark, and we were hurting, and nobody was watching, not even us, in a way, and we slipped through the cracks. It was a moment for the darkness. It was a rarity, in a time when we were running out of time. And without either of us saying so, we knew all that, we saw it for what it was, and grabbed it, and held it up in the moonlight.

"I really loved her," Jeremy said.

"I know," I said.

"No, I mean, I *loved* her, you know? I wasn't just in love with her. I fucking *cherished* her. I gave her my heart. I gave her my everything, and I'm scared it all got smashed with her on those train tracks. I'm scared I'll never get it back. I'm scared I'll never love again. Oh man, Jim, I'm really fucked up," Jeremy said.

"Yeah," I said.

"I mean, really, really *fucked*, you know?" He looked up at me. It was strange, seeing tears in eyes that were so often granite.

"Yeah, I know. I know." I was petting his head, running my hand over his hair almost maternally, in what I hoped was a soothing way. Look at me, actually trying to take care of somebody.

"I mean, I never knew things would get this bad."

"We didn't mean it . . ."

"No, man, I never meant it to be like this! I never wanted this, Jim."

"None of us did."

"And it's like, I don't know what to do, you know? I mean, it's funny, in a way, because even though we been through all this shit, I still don't know what the hell to do. No matter what happens to me, man, I still can't see nothin' comin'."

"Yeah, but that's kinda good, you know," I said, and saying it, I wasn't sure I meant it. I wanted to. I wanted to mean it, and I wanted Jeremy to think I meant it. I wanted to soothe him, offer some kind of comfort. "I mean, if we all knew everything that was gonna happen to us, who would bother? It's gotta be a mystery. That's part of living, man."

"So what if we die next week? What if all this is for nothing?"

Right at that moment, that was the closest I ever came to

just giving up. Quitting the fight. Quitting my life. And while I decided, there was only silence, there was only Philly's snoring and our intermingled breath, hesitant and thinking of quitting, and the memory of Jeremy's words hanging in the air.

And then I thought of Mandy. The silence, the question, the moment, reminded me of her. I was reminded of the night I met Leslie, a year before, after Mandy and I had gone home and taken a beating from Dad for being so late, and Mandy had put me to bed, and then later, she'd knocked on my window. I remembered how she asked me to take care of Billy. And I promised I would. I promised I wouldn't let Dad fuck him up. And maybe I wasn't doing the best job of it, maybe I barely saw him, but if I checked out on him completely, he'd really be fucked. His older sister and his older brother would be gone. He'd be left with two dead role models, left with the lesson that the only way to grow up was to die.

And in that instant, in the remembering, my mind was made up. "So what if we do?" I said to Jeremy. "So what if we do die next week? It's not for nothing, man. We gotta hope, is all. We just gotta hope."

I guess I wasn't exactly singing him a lullaby. But what could I do, promise him a white Christmas? We had burned the fairy tales a long time ago. We lived in the ashes.

"Yeah, I guess," Jeremy said. "Hope."

"Yeah," I echoed.

"You know what I been thinking?" Jeremy asked me after a long silence.

"Huh?"

"Just now, I mean just a minute ago, I realized how I could almost get back in the womb."

I laughed. It seemed out of place just then, but I was suddenly struck with this hilarious image in my head. "Whaddaya gonna do, stick your head up your mom's pussy?"

"Naw, man, I'm serious." He looked offended. He never had taken too kindly to mother jokes. It was his womb obsession. I always laughed at it, but I could tell he was really serious this time.

"Sorry," I said.

"For real, man, I just figured this out. I bet the ocean's the same thing."

"Huh?"

"I mean, not physically of course, it's probably colder than shit, but I'm talking conceptually here. Swimming in the ocean. Floating around in all that salt water, being held and rocked by the waves. I'm serious, man, it'd be the closest thing. I would love that right now."

"So let's go!" I said, suddenly excited at the thought of the adventure. More than that, though, I was thinking about it, and he was right. I had been there once, to the Atlantic Ocean, when I was two. It was my very first memory. Helping Mandy bury herself in the white sand, staring out at all that openness. And even though it's my first memory, it's very vivid. I felt something there I have never felt anywhere else, anytime else. I felt *home*. I will never forget it. And remembering, I knew Jeremy was right. If anything in the world is still pure, it's the ocean. If anywhere in the world you could find some semblance of real peace, it would be the ocean. In the ocean, everybody is anonymous. Everybody is seen, witnessed by the constant rising and falling of the waves. And there are no rules, not people rules anyway, not when you're alone on the beach. The ocean takes everybody, floats everybody, rocks everybody, bathes everybody. It's like a universal mother.

"Yeah," Jeremy said, "let's do it. Let's go to the ocean."

"How do we get there?" I asked, wanting to solidify the plans. I mean, we were mostly just fantasizing, but I think there was a little part of each of us that knew that maybe, just maybe, we could really do it.

"Bus," Jeremy said instantly.

"Where do we get the money?" I asked, and with each word we were convincing ourselves more and more that we should really go for it, that it was a good choice. Maybe our only choice..

"Rob a bank," Jeremy said, smiling quirkily, and I could tell that, just like the rest of this solidifying fantasy, he partly meant it.

"Why not?" I said, smiling right along with him. "We've got guns."

"And Philly?" Jeremy asked, even though we both knew the answer. It was more just thinking out loud.

"He goes," I said.

"But keep him out of the bank robbery," Jeremy stated. It was a fact. A rule.

"Yes," I agreed. "He wouldn't want in anyway. I mean, maybe for the excitement, but he's too much of a sweetheart to point a gun at anybody," I said.

"Except Tony," Jeremy said.

Jesus, I had forgotten all about that afternoon. It seemed like a decade ago. "Yes," I said, "except for Tony. That was different."

"Yeah it was," Jeremy said, and it was as if we were trying to convince ourselves of Philly's good heart. That he was different from us. We succeeded, I think mostly because we needed to. We needed to have an angel among us, real or imagined. And we stuck with that, right through everything. We still have.

"So let's do it," Jeremy said.

"Maybe," I said thoughtfully, turning the whole thing over in my mind, looking at it from all the angles. It looked good. A good choice. "Maybe."

Just then Philly, our angel, woke up, shooting upright in bed, rubbing his eyes for a moment, and then, seeing us sitting under the window, he launched off his bed and landed right on top of us.

"Oh man, you guys," he said, stretching his arms and smiling with reminiscent pleasure, "I got the best blow job ever in the middle of the night. My God, it was wonderful. Did you guys get any?"

41

"I could leave without you," Jeremy said coldly. He was speaking to me.

"I can't go yet," I said, repeating myself the way I had been for ten minutes now. We were talking about the ocean. Philly and Jeremy were all set to go right off the bat, but I wanted to wait.

"Wait?" Philly had exclaimed, a week after we started planning, when I first brought up my reservations. "Fucking *wait*? Why wait, man? What the hell for?"

"I don't know, man," I had said, "I don't know." I was still trying to convince my*self* I was making the right move. How could I explain it to Philly and Jeremy?

For a while, Jeremy had just stood by silently. He had been busy taking massive gulps of the fifth of vodka we were sharing for breakfast. Then he brought *this* up. I couldn't believe I heard him right.

"You could what?"

"We're not leaving without Jim, man." Philly immediately pounced on Jeremy's words, obviously angry and confirming that Jeremy had really said what I was afraid he said.

"You, too," Jeremy said, turning his once again ice-cold eyes on Philly.

"What?" Philly blurted out. He reacted the same way I had.

"You didn't just say that, Jeremy," I said, threatening.

"I did."

"Why, then? Why'd ya have to go and say a thing like that, man?" Philly demanded. He was as hurt as I was, if not more.

Jeremy saw that, in his eyes, in his trembling lip, and he softened up a little. At least enough to offer an explanation. "I mean, I've thought about it. That maybe the only way to patch things up, I mean make it all better, would be to get a new life. To just leave everybody I know—*everybody.*"

Philly and I were silent.

"It's not like I'm going to, guys. I've thought about it, and I'm not going to. Not now, anyway. You guys are my friends."

"For now," I said in a quietly angry voice.

"Yeah," he said. "And maybe forever."

"Maybe," Philly said, in a wounded voice as low as my own.

"Well, probably even," Jeremy offered, getting frustrated. "I mean, c'mon guys, things happen, you know? Who the hell knows?"

"Yeah," I mimicked him. "Who knows?" And from here, in retrospect, I can see where he was coming from, with the clarity that comes with grieving. But then, at the time, no way. Neither could Philly. All we saw was Jeremy ripping us apart. All we saw was somebody to blame.

"So we go together?" Philly asked suspiciously. And although I wouldn't ask the question myself, I waited anxiously for the answer.

"Or not at all," Jeremy said.

With that, we all relaxed a little. Not all the way, not even close, but a little, as if we had been holding our breath.

"Goddamn you, Jeremy," Philly said, but it could have come from either of us.

It was the first time, I mean the very first that I remember, that any of us brought up the possibility of a split. And even though we tried to forget about what Jeremy said that day, even as we buried it under plans and bottles and jokes and smoothed it over with renewed promises of friendship, we never forgot.

We were on the roof of an ancient, abandoned downtown movie theater. We went there most days, in lieu of school, where we couldn't go because Tony would kill us if he found us, and our homes, where we couldn't go because Philly's and my parents would practically kill us for dropping out of school, murderous drug dealer or not, and Jeremy's parents would rat on us to ours if we went there. So we were schoolless and homeless. Purely in terms of living conditions, it wasn't terrible. Philly had the hardest time adjusting. But after only seven days we were all getting pretty accustomed to it. That, or we were just too wasted most of the time to notice the difference. At night, we slept inside the theater. Daytimes, when we weren't out on the town or raiding a food pantry, we hung out on top of it. We went up there for a change of scenery, and to think, and talk. It was a good view. You could see the skyline in all four directions from up there, including the capitol. Plus you got to look down on all the pedestrians on their way to work and school and God knew where. We always used to spit on people and shout random names to see who would look up, and once Jeremy even took a leak on some poor bastard. One second he'd been walking arm in arm with his date and the next Jeremy was spraying piss on his head. Unfortunately, the guy took it personal. He turned out to be some kind of crazy samurai-type dude. He looked up and caught sight of Jeremy standing up there with his cock draped out and a bona fide shit-eating grin spread across his face. First he started shouting his head off, swearing like a madman, then he busted out with some high-class-looking karate chops, threw off his coat, and started climbing up the side of the fire escape. So much for his date. Some things are just more important than romance, I guess. Jeremy was laughing so hard the guy made it almost all the way up before he even started to run. He ended up leading the pissed-off (and pissed-on) samurai on a high-speed rooftop-jumping chase. Jeremy eventually escaped; turns out he was just a tiny bit crazier than the samurai guy.

We didn't do childish shit like that anymore. We didn't have the wild energy we used to have, I guess. Or maybe we were really growing up. Anyway, we weren't causing any trouble up there that day. We weren't even there to drink. That wasn't a scheduled activity anymore. It wasn't anything. We were a different kind of creature. We breathed air and liquor.

We were there purely for the view. And to talk about the ocean. Even though we'd decided, Philly and Jeremy were still trying to badger me into going right away, and I was still resisting. Things were tense. We were arguing as if we all knew that a lot was at stake. We were kids, shipwrecked orphans, swimming in parts of the ocean where we definitely should not have been swimming. And in those waters, we had different ideas about which direction to swim. So we argued about the ocean itself.

"Maybe I could go see Leslie . . ."

"Leslie said she didn't want to see you anymore," Jeremy said pointedly.

"She said she was waiting for me to sober *up*," I said defensively. "I could sober *up*, and then—"

"Oh fuck!" Jeremy scoffed, pitching the emptied bottle hard onto the gravel. It shattered, spraying shards of glass all over my legs.

"What the hell, man?" I jumped back, startled but also hurt. "What's 'Oh fuck'? I could fuckin' sober up, man!"

"Yeah." Jeremy rolled his eyes.

"Hey, guys . . . ," Philly said, trying to calm things down. It didn't work. Neither Jeremy nor I even glanced at him.

"Yeah," I said. "Listen, I can't go yet, all right? I can't leave Billy, for one thing—"

"Oh, you're doin' him a lot of fuckin' good here," Jeremy said. He'd been leaning against a concrete railing, but as he spoke he stood up straight, getting in my face.

He was pouring salt on all my sore spots. I tried to spit out a snappy comeback, but I just stood there sputtering uselessly, looking like a wounded puppy. The fact was, he was right. I wasn't any good to Billy. I was too scared to go home. I hadn't been there in months. My dad still scared the shit out of me. And I knew I was being a weakling and a lousy big brother, and even worse, a lousy *younger* brother; the one thing my dead sister had really asked me for in her life, I mean really *asked* me for, and I was too depressed, too weak, too scared, too drunk to do it. Not only was I a liar to my sister, I was a fucking wimp. Scared of so much. And you know what my biggest fear was? The one that kept me up every night, even when I was tired enough to sleep on everything else? That Mandy could've done it. Sobered up, faced Dad, taken care of Billy, quit stealing, loved Leslie, and had change left in her pockets. I *knew* she could've done it.

That was the great mystery of her short, sweet life—what was in her deal that wasn't in mine, that she couldn't make it? I knew she was stronger than I was. Hell, everybody knew that. It was common knowledge. What nobody knew, nobody I knew of anyway, was why she threw herself in front of that train.

And *that*, although at the time I didn't even fully grasp it, not the actual magnitude of it anyway, *that* was why, even with doubts and fears running around in my head that I knew were more than just inklings, even with all of us almost, almost knowing with a certain amount of psychic nagging and a certain amount of good old common sense just how much this wait would cost us, I had to wait. And thus, as we had just consummated with our agreement, we had to wait.

No matter what the cost.

MARCH 1992

42

It was two full months before we decided to actually go, before I was ready.

Two months full of sleepless nights at the theater and exhausted days on the street. Two months full of drunken rage. Two months full of broken glass, from empty bottles and storefront windows and sometimes both at once, as one shattered the other. Two months full of slipping into the shadows before the sirens got too loud. Two months full of nameless girls and fights with derelicts like us, only older. Two months full of perfecting the art of shoplifting groceries, which wasn't as hard as you might think. Two months full of eyes sore to the point of vision that was blurry even when I wasn't wasted, just from the pressure of the dammed-up rivers behind my eyes. Two full months.

It was a long wait, and every night I was reminded of it. Every night, as we lay down to try to sleep in the theater, curled up in an old seat (if you could find one without the springs sticking out of it) or sprawled out in the aisle or even for a change of pace lying toothpick-style on the narrow stage, they would ask me. Not both of them, not on the same night, but whoever asked me was speaking for both of them. "Can we go yet, Jim?" Philly would ask in a quiet, desperate choke, even after Jeremy had given up asking. "Not yet," I would say, just as desperately, wishing I could answer differently. He never asked me why not, and I was glad for that. Because I did not know why not, and I wouldn't have been able to answer. Philly sensed that and refrained from probing me, from forcing me to admit that all this was maybe for nothing, that I didn't even know why I wasn't ready to leave. I couldn't know. I was waiting *to* know. Philly knew that, though, and was gentle enough not to make me say it. And he knew, night after night, when he asked me if we could go yet, what my answer would be. That wasn't why he asked. He asked because without that question he had nothing. Without that question he severed completely his umbilical cord to hope. And so even though it hurt terribly to have to answer him night after sleepless, empty night, I never told him to stop.

On the night I finally answered differently, I didn't even let him ask the question. Even though I was finally ready to say yes, or maybe because of that, I couldn't bear to hear those words again.

It was four in the morning when I let myself into the theater. I stepped over Jeremy, who liked to sleep under the ladder in the projector room that led to the roof—the only way in or out of the building—and found Philly sprawled out in the middle aisle. His eyes were open, but watery. I thought maybe he was sleeping with his eyes open, but he greeted me as soon as I settled down next to him.

"Hi," he said, almost warmly.

"Let's go," I said, with no preamble. I wasn't aiming for drama. I was just ready.

"Where?" he asked, probably thinking I meant raiding the

display window of some liquor store, which we had taken to doing sometimes when we couldn't get to sleep and we had run out of booze. Both things happened to be true in this case, but that wasn't what I meant.

"Tomorrow," I said, answering not the question he had asked but the one that would follow.

He rubbed the water out of his eyes and bolted upright. "You mean it?" he asked.

"Yeah," I said solidly. "Yeah."

He was wide awake then. "Well . . . what happened, man?"

I told him.

He hadn't seen me since around noon the previous day, when I'd left the guys downtown at the homeless shelter where we usually scored a free lunch. I had said I wanted to be alone; they asked no questions. Philly had just nodded at me. Jeremy didn't even look up.

Actually, I sort of lied to them. I didn't really want to be alone, just away from them. Six weeks before, we'd made an agreement, if not a rock-solid pact, not to go home. Not any of us, not to anybody's home. If anybody did, it would cause trouble for all of us. At the least, it would mean beatings for me and truancy court all around. At worst we didn't know, but it wasn't anything good. So we all promised.

Yeah, well, sometimes promises are hard to keep. I needed to go home. I wanted to see Billy again. Besides, although the guys would never cop to this, it would be good for all of us. I was gonna loot the house for cash, and we could sure use some of that. And there was no chance of me getting caught. I was going in the middle of the day, on a Tuesday. Mom and Dad were at work, and Billy would just be getting home from school. The whole thing was foolproof. I mean, sure Philly and Jeremy would be pissed later when I told them, but I'd just stuff some money in their mouths and they would be cool. I hoped.

Truth was, I was homesick. I missed my bed. I missed the smell of home-cooked food. I missed my brother playing bad music at ungodly hours in the morning. I missed how my sister's window was right next to mine, and we could stick our bodies halfway out of the house and talk to each other over the bushes in the middle of the night, even though it was easier to just take the easy route through the hallway into each other's rooms. I missed my sister. God, did I. More than anything, I missed Mandy.

So I'd done it, that afternoon. I told a half lie to my friends, and then committed a much greater offense. I broke the one rule we had made for ourselves.

I caught a C bus back to my house. I walked slowly up the street from the bus stop, careful not to step on any cracks, an old habit I always slipped into when I got back in my childhood neighborhood. The sky was a cloudy gray, but it was warm for March. I unzipped my jacket. The noise of the zipper seemed strangely loud. I realized it was because I was back in the suburbs; everything makes more noise out there because everything else is so quiet. No sirens, no heavy traffic, no jackhammers. The weekly morning dump truck run is about as much commotion as we get out here.

Three children were starting a Big Wheel sidewalk race up the street, and they were heading straight for me. I just sort of stood there, watching them with a funny half smile on my face. Even as they neared me, ten feet away and less, I didn't get out of their way. Not that I was being an asshole. I wanted to move, I just more or less forgot to. I was fascinated, watching them, fascinated to the point of freezing. I forgot I was there. I was in a Big Wheel, taking my first ride ever. It was brand new, green and blue. I was insanely proud of it. A man's colors, green and blue, none of this sissy pink and yellow stuff for me. We were racing, on the sidewalk, down the street from our house.

Not too far, as I was deathly afraid of kidnappers when I was little. Especially Injun Joe, who snuck into Tom Sawyer's room. But I wasn't afraid that day, racing my first Big Wheel, its black wheels so shiny I almost didn't want to let them touch the sidewalk. I was next to my sister. I was four, she was six. We were laughing.

"Hey, mister, could you please move? We're tryin' ta race."

The bravest one was speaking to me. I was sixteen. He looked six. He had been leading the race before I blockaded them. He was standing in front of his Big Wheel. It was green and blue. The other kids were still sitting in theirs. They looked quietly terrified, and in awe of their buddy who had the nerve to speak to me.

"Hey," I said, excited as all get-out and kneeling down to talk to the brave one. "I used to have a green and blue one, too." I was smiling. He was not.

"Listen," he said, almost confidentially, "I'm not really supposed to talk to strangers."

"Oh," I said, straightening up, unreasonably disappointed. "Why are you talking to me, then? You coulda just gone around." I pointed out, gesturing to the street.

"We're not 'posed ta go in the road, *either*," he explained condescendingly. He might as well have rolled his eyes. "Now could you please *move*? We're *racing*."

"Yeah, sure," I said, stepping aside.

The talker scrambled back into his ride and they raced on by without another word. I kept walking.

There were two squirrels chasing each other around in my front yard. Or the front yard of the house I grew up in. I don't think I could call it mine anymore. I was a visitor.

I walked up the steps to the front door, scaring the squirrels away. Of course I knew those squirrels still would have bugged off even if I lived there, and I probably would have freaked out those little kids anyway, too, but some part of me, a big part of me, made believe that wasn't so. A big part of me felt like I was a stranger there, like everything was too fragile and my fingers had forgotten how to move delicately. Like I would break everything I touched.

43

The house was locked. We'd all thrown out our house keys as a sign of our agreement, but there was still one next to the front step inside a fake rocks which didn't look anything like a rock. It looked like a piece of plastic painted like a rock.

It was dark inside. All the curtains were drawn, as they always were when my parents were at work. I was sort of used to it, 'cause I spent quite a bit of time in the house like that when I got fed up with school halfway through the day and would come home early. I never opened the curtains or turned on any lights, just in case one of my parents came home. I never liked it, though. It was too much like being in a funeral home or something.

I headed straight for my dad's liquor cabinet. An old habit. It was locked also, but I knew where the key for this lock was, too. Lucky for me and any other burglars, my parents weren't too good at hiding things. I'd discovered it by accident when I was ten years old and when one of my action figures found it necessary to hide under the cabinet. Later that night, after my parents went to bed, I got my first taste of hard liquor. Of course I hated it, but I liked what it did to me, and I'd been hooked ever since. I once read somewhere that when you're twelve years old, it only takes two weeks of regular drinking to sign you up as a lifetime alcoholic. They didn't have any stats for ten-year-olds.

I felt around underneath the cabinet. Still in the same stupid hiding place six years later. I unlocked the cabinet after a few fumbled attempts. The key was much smaller than the house key, and I had the shakes a little bit 'cause I hadn't had anything to drink since the night before. I never got it real bad or anything. It was just hard to do things that required delicate motion sometimes.

I settled on a half-empty bottle of hundred-proof vodka. I felt like a bird: anything that's shiny, man. I tipped my head back and swallowed hard. Anything that burns.

After the half-empty bottle was three-quarters empty, I got up and walked around a little, walking off the rush. Without even thinking about it, I found myself at the door to my sister's room, one hand on the doorknob, the other still clutching the bottle like a lifeline. I considered not going in for a moment, conjuring up visions of what would lie on the other side. A black void, maybe. A hole in the ground. A gravestone. Actually, I figured it would just be empty, or maybe filled with knickknacks. A storage room. That's what I figured. But I went in just to make sure.

What I found was not what I figured I would find. What I found was the most obvious thing, but I hadn't even considered the possibility. Probably 'cause I knew I couldn't handle it. What I found was my sister's room, exactly as it was the day she died.

I stumbled back, then forward, then weaved side to side, moving like a drunken boxer, finally spinning around and landing on my back in Mandy's bed.

I lay that way for a long time, down for the count, not moving a single muscle except to close my eyes the moment I hit the bed. I was playing dead, hiding. I didn't know what else to do. If I can't see you, you can't see me. If I can't see this room, it's not here. I'm not here, I kept saying to myself over and over. This is not here. I don't know where I am, but I'm not here.

It was a worthless lie, though. I knew exactly where I was, and keeping my eyes shut didn't help, not one bit. I was seeing the room in my mind, every little detail. I could see the bed I was lying on, still unmade from the last time Mandy slept in it. I could see her dirty clothes strewn about the floor. I could see the magazine clippings, pictures and phrases Mandy had cut out and papered over her walls. NEVER CHANGE YOUR UNDERWEAR TWICE IN ONE DAY said one in monstrous, blocky letters. I LIVE ON TRIANGLES said another, in yellow italics. And then there were photographs, which took up even more space than the words. Some she had taken herself, of me and her friends, but most were cutouts from magazines. Not really famous people, or anything. Mandy said she was sick of looking at all those people. Except River Phoenix, who she insisted was a truly beautiful human being. He was the exception, though. All the other pictures were just weird images from ads and pictures of obscure (to me, anyway) dancers, stuff like that. Nobody I recognized. It would have been impossible, anyway, because most of the faces were collages of like five different people, even their two eyes were taken from different pictures.

I could see her old record player in the corner, and the five hundred and nine old records she had. She'd counted them twice.

I could see her bookcases, chock full of books crammed in every which way. Mandy would read anything. Famous literary stuff, sure, but other stuff, too. She loved hard-boiled detective novels, science fiction stories. She even read romance novels. The best part was, she really got into all of it. I mean, she was about the least critical reader in the world. It was like she really respected each writer's world, and trusted that they could tell it better than anybody else.

It was obvious nobody had set foot inside the room since Mandy died. I almost felt like I was trespassing. But then, if anybody had a right to come in, it was me. I got the feeling she would have wanted me to.

And I could see the bottom shelf of the bookcase at the foot of her bed. It was empty, except for two books. One was that old nineteenth-century diary our great-great-grandmother Frances had kept. Ever since she found it, Mandy had said it was her favorite book in the world. The other book was her own diary.

I got up then, opening my eyes hesitantly. Everything was as I had pictured it. My eyes were drawn irresistibly, as if by fate itself, to Mandy's bottom shelf. And on it, side by side, the two diaries. Frances's diary I had seen only once. I had never read a single word of Mandy's. Frances's book gave me the creeps, and Mandy and I had always promised not to keep any secrets from each other, so there would have been no point in looking at either one of them, even if I had ever wanted to. I never had. Until then. When I saw it that day, as sad and drunk and tired as I was, missing Mandy so much, I had no choice. Those two books were the closest things to being something left of my sister, who was dead and never coming back.

I stood up off the bed and walked to the diaries. My heart was burning. I was hopeful, for the first time in a long, long time. It wasn't a happy feeling, though. It was a sick sort of optimism, little kid waiting to find out if the chemo was working. I was making giddy wishes, but they were wishes I shouldn't have been making. I didn't expect to find any secrets. That wasn't what I was looking for. I just wanted to be close to Mandy, you know? I just wanted Mandy back, just for one fucking minute. I hoped Mandy, wherever she was, would understand. I hoped so, because I swear I had no choice.

Sick with my sad, desperate brand of hope, I sat down in front of the bookcase, and looked at the diaries. I put one hand on each of them, and decided to open Frances's first.

On that page, the first page I turned to, underlined over and over with a pencil until the lines were as dark as the type, were the words I had been running from since I first read them, when I was twelve years old. "That bastard beat me till I was black and blue, and then screwed me against my will, more times than I can recall. And so I strangled him in his sleep, and I don't feel no remorse about it neither."

Two words were handwritten in the margin. It was Mandy's handwriting, but written more clearly than usual for her, with a solid sort of deliberation to them. *"i wish."*

I read them again. *"i wish."*

Reading them, I could swear I heard Mandy's voice, saying them aloud. And, as it had always been between us, just as if she was right there with me, I knew exactly what she meant.

And knowing, I heard more of Mandy's words, only this time from a memory, and even more real. *"I was hoping maybe you would kill him."* The only time I ever heard my sister wish violence upon anyone, and she had been speaking of her father. Our father.

Without needing to, and with none of the optimism that I had approached it with, I opened Mandy's diary. The first entry on the first page was dated July 20, 1989. She had been keeping a diary longer than that, but that was when she'd used up the old one, and she had boxed it up and buried it somewhere. She made a map for it, and said she was going to dig it up when she was forty, but I think later she burned even that, saying she wanted to let the past drift away like ashes. I have no idea where she buried it, and I am glad. I don't want to know what's in it.

The first entry began the same as every entry, although I didn't yet know that. *"father fucked me again last night."*

My first reaction was to puke.

And puke.

And puke.

I doubled over as if I had been punched in the stomach, spraying half-digested beef stew and vodka all over Mandy's floor and her two most precious things. When that was gone, and my stomach was empty, I dry-heaved for what seemed like an hour.

The next thing I did, still hunched over almost fetally, was scream.

And scream.

And scream.

I screamed my fucking heart out. I screamed at the man who was my father. I screamed at the man who fucked my sister to death. I screamed at the world that had let this happen. I screamed at the reality I had been born into, that the most precious thing in it could be so ruined, so tortured, so wrecked. There could not have been a less deserving person, and I mean that with my life. I even screamed at my beloved sister with all my rage for not telling me. And that was when I began to cry. When I realized she *had* told me, in so many ways, and I had been too blind to see it.

With nothing else to do, nothing else I could do, I sobbed. My body was wracked with sobs, with the kind of pain you only get after you've given up on desperation.

Then it was my father's voice I heard echoing through my head, his whispered taunts to me as I tried to get to sleep on the nights after Mandy died. *"Why didn't you save her, Jimbo? Didn't you care? Didn't you care?"*

"I did care," I insisted out loud. "I *did* care. I just couldn't see . . ."

The voice didn't let up. Over and over it stabbed at me. My father's voice. My own father, who had beat her into submission and then fucked my sister to death. My family, who raped my family. *"Didn't you care?"*

"I DID CARE!" I shouted at the top of my lungs, louder than I had ever shouted anything my entire life. And then again, in almost a whisper. But with that merciless, relentless voice in my head, I had a hard time believing myself. He was my *father*. He said it was my fault. What was I supposed to believe? Even then, even now, some part of me wants my dad to be right, wants to be able to count on him. A drunken bully and a rapist, and I wanted him to hold me.

I sat there for another hour like that, hunched over and confused and lost and broken, rocking myself as if I could lull myself to sleep. But that was one thing I could not do.

Unable to sleep, I read. And rocked. And breathed. And drank. And read.

44

It was dark by the time my family came home. It hadn't been for long, though. I had watched the light changing and dying through the cracks in the blinds on the window of my sister's room. I pretended I was dying, too, right along with the sun, but eventually it was pitch dark and I was still wide awake, living despite myself.

I listened to them come in. I heard keys jingling and then one turn in the lock. They all had their own keys. The one in the phony rock was only for emergencies, and me. I heard the door open and the three of them walk in together, talking, laughing, and I heard the door shut heavily behind them.

Noisy. Everything seemed terribly noisy to me. I was shocked and mourning, and I wanted quiet. I wasn't ready for such rough, careless sounds.

They split up then. Somebody headed for the kitchen and started clanking dishes around. Probably my mother, making a late dinner. I heard my dad's heavy footsteps padding down the hallway to the bathroom, past Mandy's room where I was still huddled up on the floor. Luckily, I had fallen back against the door when I had first walked in. If it had been open, my dad would have known for sure something was up. The toilet flushed, and I heard his electric razor start buzzing away like a goddam lawn mower.

The TV turned on in the living room. That was the worst noise of all. Canned laughter. Sickeningly peppy commercials, with people you would never meet shouting at you about how much you needed a new pair of sneakers. I would have puked if I had anything left in me.

Instead I clapped my hands over my ears, and shivered. 'Course, the shivering was nothing new. I had done nothing *but* shiver for six hours. I was starting to think I would never stop. Everyone would think I had Parkinson's disease. Except that killed you. My kind of shivering would just be a lifelong torture. Drake's disease. Maybe I could get rich off discovering it.

I didn't start off shivering. I was rocking for a while, while I read Mandy's diary. Except for the last page, which I hadn't yet read at all, I read every page of it once. I read them once, those pages, her story, because I had to. I would never read any of them again. Any more than once seemed like blasphemy, a real sin. Whoring my sister's guts, that were spilled on every page.

I hadn't read the last page for a reason. Not just because I knew it would rip me apart. I could only read it once, and I wanted to make it count.

My father's razor shut off, and he walked back down the

hall into the kitchen and started talking to my mother. He sounded sober, or mostly so. My brother was still watching TV. I took my hands away from my ears. I needed them for other things, and I would just have to live with the noise. One hand picked up the now-empty bottle of vodka. The other picked up Mandy's diary, open to the last page, which was dated the day she died. I wondered briefly if she had chosen that day because it was the last page in the book, and she didn't think she could live to finish another one. I hoped not, but I thought so. Mandy was like that—a very all-or-nothing kind of person. What that really meant, though, if that was true, was not that she died early because she couldn't make it another two years, but that she had died late, staying alive longer than she wanted to so she could finish the diary she was working on. I hoped not, but I thought so. I was shivering.

And shivering, I stood. My pants were wet; I had pissed myself without even noticing. I walked slowly, purposefully, to the closed door of my sister's room, rested my head against it for a moment, listening. The TV was still on. I heard my mom call Billy into the kitchen, and then it sounded like the three of them were sitting down to eat at the kitchen table. Probably spaghetti leftovers, judging by the smell of things and how quickly it was ready after they got home. My stomach rumbled. I hadn't eaten since the morning, but the rumbling was more the sound of distant thunder before a storm than it was a sign of hunger. Or if it was hunger, it was deeper than your typical man-I-haven't-eaten-all-day variety. It was the deepest hunger I have ever felt. It was a hunger for wholeness. A hunger to set things right.

I opened the door and walked down the hallway into the living room, using the wall to support myself every couple steps. I was a little wobbly, feeling the liquor in my blood.

Drunk, yeah, but at the same time I had never been more sober in my life.

Again I walked to the liquor cabinet. Not to drink from, just to sit on. It was right in the doorway adjoining the living room and the kitchen, right where I wanted to be, and it made a perfect platform for my purposes. Plus it was sort of comforting, knowing all that booze was there beneath me. Holding me up.

Getting the first look at my family was a jolt: it was like having one of those guys that practically breaks all your fingers when you shake his hand grabbing hold of my heart and digging in, squeezing it like it was the last hand he'd ever shake. I sat quietly and watched them for a while, perfectly still. Partly hiding, partly mesmerized.

Billy was telling them about a science project he was working on at school, something about feeding plants water versus sugar water and seeing who grew faster. That's what he said, "who." He'd named them, Margaret and Tom. That made me cry. It didn't look like my parents were listening too closely, though. They were too busy shoving microwaved spaghetti into their mouths. I mean, every now and then they'd look up and nod or something, but that was it. That was the kind of thing Mandy would have raised hell about. They looked tired, all three of them. Still, though, there was a kind of peace among them. Maybe Dad wasn't drinking so much. Maybe Billy was doing well in school, doing what they told him to. Maybe they were letting the past be the past. Maybe they were starting to forget. For a moment I considered just leaving them be, just quietly slipping out the front door and never coming back. Maybe it would be better that way. Especially for Billy. Let them forget. Let them never know.

I still haven't figured out whether what I did next was the most heroic or the most vicious thing I have ever done. I guess it depends on why I did it, and that I don't know. I could say I did it in the name of truth, and I would be a hero. Or I could say it was for revenge, and I would be a drunk asshole, destroying a family for my own gratification. Or I could say, yes, I am a drunk asshole. And yes, I am a hero.

For whatever reason, I did do it. After watching the family scene a little longer, tears and dreams running freely down my face, I shattered it. Without planning it, as if it were slightly more than a muscle spasm, my left hand hurled the vodka bottle at the picture window in the living room. The window shattered. It made a hell of a racket. My whole family jumped. I didn't even flinch. My whole family stood up out of their chairs. I was still.

For a moment, we were, each of us, frozen. My family stared at me. I stared back.

"Hi," I said flatly.

"Hi," Billy said shyly, hesitantly, as if hoping it was okay.

"Oh, Jimmy," my mom said, her eyes welling up suddenly.

My dad said nothing. Only I think he might have sensed what was coming, and his eyes, if I'm not imagining it, were pleading.

I opened Mandy's diary to the last page. "August eighth," I said, looking up at them. Billy's chin dropped and he stared at his shoes. My father's eyes widened. My mother burst out sobbing.

"No, Jim," she said. "Please, *please*, no."

An uncomfortable, sick sort of chuckle bubbled up from my throat, but I continued to read.

"father fucked me again last night. the usual. the details aren't worth wasting my energy on. it's never any different. you know, it never will be. i can see myself in ten years, coming home for christmas with jeremy. we'd be married. jim and even billy'd be grown up and moved away, and that'd be the one time we all see each other. and i

would come to see mother, and even father, who i still love. doesn't that make me a good christian or something? and i would sleep in my old room, which would be a guest room by then, and in the night, father would come in, and try to fuck me, and i would let him. a good christian. a scared shitless dead girl inside a woman beyond her years. oh my god oh my god i need a drink. am i dead or on my way. bleeding out the cunt i split between my boyfriend and my father (god, even sweet Jeremy feels like rape when we try to make love and all i can think of is him*) he has fucked me senseless, my father has, till all i see i know i made up. i made up these screams and this haze and all these broken rainbows and old bandages, but it's all i have and i hold on to it like nothing else. these bandages, they hold me together, bind me to you, but even they are falling away from all of you that i still might love, leslie and my brothers—fill in the blanks for me okay? and jeremy, god i want nothing more than to lie in your arms again, but i know i never will. i have nothing to give you, and i can't sing any better than when i first met you, but at least now i'll be free, and i know where the angels are . . ."*

I closed the diary, my fingers trembling so badly I dropped the book at my feet. It wasn't withdrawal this time. It was murder. It was dancing on the brink of psychotic rage. A shadow fell across my lap. I looked up, for the first time since I had started to read. I expected it would be my father. It wasn't.

"When did you write that, Jim?" my mother asked. Her face was ashen.

"She wrote it," I said through gritted teeth. "Her last words, Ma."

"No," she said dangerously. I had never seen my mother look threatening in her life. Until that moment. Until I told her the truth.

"Yes," I said, just as dangerously.

"Jim," my father warned.

"*Steve,*" I said mockingly.

"No," my mother repeated.

"Father. Fucked me. *Again.*" I spoke the words like punches.

She hit back. My mother, who had never, ever hit me, slapped me in the face.

My fist was formed before her hand left my face. It was an immediate reaction, instantaneous. It was the worst thing I have ever done. I punched my mother. I did not think. I did not aim. I swung. My fist connected with her forehead above her right eye, taking her glasses with it.

My mother fell backward into Billy's arms. Blood was spurting out of her forehead. Her glasses, smashed and crooked, still hung on her face. One frame, the left side, was still intact. The other was embedded in the flesh above her eyebrow. I made my mother bleed.

My father lunged at me wordlessly. He grabbed me by the throat and whipped me around wildly, so quickly I couldn't see anything but a dizzy blur. I felt his nails puncture the skin on my throat and the blood drip down my shirt and onto my chest. He took one hand off my throat and I heard the sound of a door opening. It was the door in the kitchen that led to the basement. I got one good look at the steps descending into the darkness before he flung me down them.

I landed on the steps about halfway down and stumbled backward down the rest, slamming my foot through the plaster wall at the bottom. The steps were carpeted. They used to be concrete, but when I was little I kept falling and banging my head on them, so my parents had them carpeted. If I'd been thrown down like that before they were carpeted, it probably would have killed me.

As it was, I wasn't hurt too bad. The worst part was my heel hurt like hell from knocking a hole in the plaster, but that wasn't even close to enough to stop me then. I screamed in rage as I yanked my foot out of the wall and vaulted up the stairs, flying into the kitchen and landing heavily. My father was just backing away from the stairs as I reached the top. He put his arms up to shield his face. I must have looked absolutely fucking terrifying coming up out of the darkness like that. I wasn't trying to scare him, though. I was trying to kill him.

I may never know why I read that diary entry aloud, whether for truth or vengeance. But I know why I did this. It was pure.

He was still shielding his face as I tackled him to the floor. I was raining punches in on him even before we hit the floor. I landed with one knee between his legs, and I was kneeing his balls repeatedly with a vicious relentlessness the entire time I was on top of him. I wanted to destroy them. I wanted to erase them.

He tried to double over, but I wouldn't let him. I grabbed him by the hair and started smashing his head into the floor, over and over. He hardly tried to fight back at all. Maybe he was paralyzed with pain. Maybe he knew he had it coming.

It took me forever to let up. It seemed like I couldn't hurt him enough. No amount of hurt would make up for those nights he beat me so badly after Mandy died. No amount of hurt would give me my sister back. No amount of hurt would make up for me being driven to a place where I could make my mother bleed. I was crazy with rage. The entire time I was beating him, I was screaming. It was an exorcism. I was venting on him, venting a lifetime wracked with pain and confusion, in which I was afraid of my own father. A lifetime in which my best parent was vodka. A lifetime I'd have to finish on my own. And when I was finished venting my own, I vented Mandy's. I hit him once for every time she wished she could have. I kneed him once for every time he raped her. And still it wasn't enough. And, knowing it wasn't enough, something in me snapped. It was a quiet craziness, and as it overtook me, I stopped screaming. It spread throughout my body like a chill in the air, and it got me to the bone. I was gone.

I slipped off of him slowly, and knelt next to his head. He was wheezing and shaking. "How was it, Dad?" I hissed. "Was she good?" Not knowing what I was doing, too gone to try to stop myself, I unzipped my pants and took my cock out. It was limp and small. "Did you make her suck you off?" I whispered. He didn't look at me. I grabbed him by the hair and forced his head to turn in my direction. He struggled against me, but I held fast, fighting against his jaw to pry his mouth open and pulling on my cock, shoving it in his face. "You did, didn't you, you sick fuck?" I said, talking as much to myself as to him. I was, too. Very sick, and helpless to it. Until Billy spoke.

"Jimmy? Hey, Jim, stop it, huh? Please. Don't hurt him anymore."

The voice of my little brother's desperation penetrated the haze of my sickness, and I did stop. I looked up at him. His lower lip was trembling violently. He didn't like to cry. He looked lost. He looked the way he used to look when he was standing in my doorway and watching my father torture me. Only this time, everything was flipped. I had just demonstrated for everybody what a chip off the old block I had become. I'd beat the shit out of my father. I made my mother bleed.

Billy's arm was around my mother, and hers around him. With her other arm she was holding a wad of paper towels to her forehead; they were soaked through with blood. Her face was framed by the redness. The way she looked made me sorry I was alive.

Her eyes glanced downward, away from my face. I realized I still had my limp cock hanging out. I popped it back inside my pants, fumbling over my zipper. My mother's eyes were on my crotch the whole time. I realized then that she hadn't seen me down there since I was half as old as I was then. Without taking her eyes off me, my mother reached for the phone on the wall. She dialed 911.

"Hello. Yes. It's my son. He's hurt me. No, with his hands. Yes, I need an ambulance. Fifty-six sixteen Montana Road. Police? Yes, as soon as possible. I don't know. I don't think so. I'll try. Yes. Okay." She let the phone drop away from her shoulder. It smacked loudly against the wall, and then dangled and twisted a foot above the floor. She spoke to me then, in the same voice she had used with the dispatcher. "You know, Jim, for the first time in my life, I'm wondering if we should have had you."

I could only nod. I stood up then, shakily, and walked over to the entrance to the kitchen where my mother and Billy stood. Neither of them moved. My mother's eyes were cold. She looked almost regal standing there, drawn up to her full height, facing me, with one hand around her good son and the other pressed against the open wound in her head. I looked at Billy. I wanted to hug him. Instead, I bent over and picked up the diary, which was still lying on the floor where I dropped it.

"The police are coming, Jim," Billy said softly, looking up at me.

I nodded, accepting. Billy stepped backward out of the doorway, making room for me to get out. Watching him move, I was struck painfully with how much I loved him. He was a damn good brother.

Just before I left, I looked down at my father. He was looking up at me, his eyes meeting mine. What I saw there caught me off guard, and I almost jumped. There was no bloodshot rage there, no drunk fury. What I saw there, for the first time in my life, was tears.

45

The night air was a little chilly, but the jacket I was wearing was plenty warm. For my skin, at least. I didn't know if my insides would ever warm up.

I paused on the front step for just a minute, figuring out where to head. Catching any kind of bus was out: the cops would be looking for me there. And I didn't want to head back to the theater. I couldn't deal with the guys just yet. But I didn't want to be alone, either. Where the hell could I go? For a moment I felt utterly, completely lost in the world.

And then I knew. It seeped in quietly at first, through a crack in the back of my mind, but it was the best idea I'd had in as long as I could remember. Without a second thought, I took off walking. I was sick of second thoughts. I was going to see Leslie.

I took the back roads, walking in the shadows as much as possible. I was probably being overly paranoid, but I wasn't just hiding from cops. My life was too much for me, and I wanted out. So I hid. And walked.

It took a long time to get to Leslie's on foot. I had no idea what time it was when I got there, but I guessed around eleven. My legs felt like dead weight dragging behind me. My whole body was exhausted. I was too tired to yawn.

I stood in front of the brown-and-white rundown apartment house that had once reminded me of a castle. I could only hope she still lived there. I walked around the side and stood in the alley, looking up into the window of her room. I could see Leslie's silhouette in the window. She was writing. Seeing her up there, I remembered. She was more than an image of a screaming girl next to my sister's dead body. I remembered Leslie before my sister died. I remembered *me* before my sister died. I remembered us happy, and in love.

And standing there in the alley, I remembered the way Mandy and I used to sing Leslie's name to get her attention. I tried to do it again. I tried to bring it back. I tried to sing, but all that came out was a croaked whisper. "Lesleeee . . . ," I said, so quietly I barely heard it myself.

I remembered. We used to throw gravel rocks from the alley up at her window. Impulsively I bent over and scooped up a handful and hurled it up at her window. The little rocks rained against the glass, and her head snapped up instantly, staring out the window as if expecting to see somebody right there outside it. I waited. She stood, unlatched the window and slid it open, sticking her head out and looking down at me.

She didn't looked surprised or especially glad to see me. In fact her face didn't register much of anything at all. I got the feeling she had known I would come, but she wasn't sure if she wanted me to. "Hi," she said evenly, as if she had seen me just yesterday.

"Hi," I said quietly.

"I'll be right down," she said. I watched her press down hard on the window frame, latch it, and walk out of her room.

I went around to the front of the house and up the steps. I faced away from the door, tapping my foot nervously. I was nervous, in a funny way. Like I was on a first date or something.

I heard Leslie come padding down the steps and out the front door, which was still off its hinges. I heard her pick it up and set it aside. I felt her hand press tenderly against my back, between my shoulder blades, her touch welcome but almost unfamiliar. I turned to look at her, and saw real affection reflected in her pale blue eyes. I lifted my hand to touch her face but collapsed before reaching it.

She caught me gently and without a word helped me up the stairs, supporting most of my weight. I realized as she cradled me that I'd been carrying too much for too long, and I just couldn't do it anymore, not any of it. I was weak, and tired. I wanted to fall asleep in Leslie's arms, sleep for a couple years. Sleep for as long as I'd been wide awake, wrecking my life.

All the lights were off inside Leslie's apartment. It was late, and I figured everybody else was asleep. Leslie never went to sleep until after midnight. She used to tell me she liked to write poetry when all the ghosts were out.

Her home smelled really nice. She burned a lot of incense. It was relaxing, and comfortable, except that it made me realize how badly I must have stunk, soaked in vodka, sweat, blood, and piss. "Phew," Leslie said, smiling softly the way she always did. "You need a bath, honey."

I didn't argue. I was plenty happy letting Leslie hold me, guide me. If she thought I needed a bath, then by God, I'd have one.

She walked me into the bathroom and set me down on the toilet. I slumped back against the seat cover, watching her untie my shoes. Done with that, she undressed me completely, not even holding back when she got to my piss-soaked underwear. I didn't help too much, but I certainly didn't fight her. She was right. I needed to get clean.

Eventually I stood naked in front of her, not feeling the least bit sexy. I felt pathetic, and small. She looked me up and down anyway, just taking me in. "You're beautiful," she said.

I nodded thanks and stood, waiting, shivering while she ran the water, testing it with her elbow to make sure it was the right temperature. When it was ready she gestured for me to get in.

I got in warily, testing the water gingerly with my toes before stepping all the way in. It wasn't that I didn't trust Leslie:

if I trusted anybody it was her, but I hadn't taken a bath in years. It was foreign to me. It was plenty warm, though, and I settled all the way in, lying back so that only my head and knees were poking out of the water. Then, slowly, softly, privately, Leslie bathed me.

She was very thorough, and it took a long time. I needed it to. I needed that time with her, naked and open and letting her touch my body, the only sound being the little splashes the water made against the tub as I shifted around. I needed that time to last as long as it could, and I think Leslie knew that. So we stayed in there until the water cooled, and my teeth were chattering. Leslie handed me a towel and I dried myself off while she waited, looking openly at my entire body. That was one thing I had always liked about her. She didn't play stupid games or try to hide her desires. If she wanted to see something, she looked at it.

I didn't bother to get dressed again. My clothes were filthy, and besides, putting them on would have been more than just getting dressed. It would have been taking my old world back. We left the clothes strewn about on the bathroom floor. Leslie didn't say anything about it. She was being as quiet as I was, and I was thankful for that. One thing I really couldn't have handled right then was a lot of questions. I didn't want to tell stories, or make promises. I wanted to forget, and to rest. Leslie picked up on that completely, and she didn't make a single demand of me the whole night. She could smell the liquor on my breath, but she took me in anyway. I think she was past trying to change me.

I followed Leslie into her room. She didn't turn the lights on, but there was a giant green candle burning near the window, next to the notebook she had been writing in. It was enough to see by, dimly. Leslie stripped her own clothes off then. I had never seen her fully naked before, but there was no fanfare from either of us. She knelt, lay down in the little alcove where she always slept, underneath her raised bed. She slid up against the wall and made room for me. I lay down next to her. I didn't make any advances toward her. I lay on my back, my arms almost stiffly at my sides. My cock couldn't have been more limp. I wanted nothing more than to sleep, but I couldn't. Even as my eyes burned, I couldn't close them. I was next to Leslie, and, even as weak as I was, I wanted every moment, every memory I could get.

Leslie was nowhere near as passive as I was. We couldn't have been lying there more than a minute before she started kissing me. It was an awkward minute, and I could feel her indecision, and I thought she might just pass out. But then, in a graceful flurry of movement that seemed almost in slow motion, she was on top of me, and kissing me.

She kissed my face all over, except my lips. Leslie once told me that she wasn't sure, because she'd never had intercourse, but she thought kissing on the mouth was the most intimate thing of all. I think that if I had tried, she would have kissed me there, but without my reaching out for her, she avoided it. She did kiss the rest of me. After her lips and tongue danced over my hair, my open eyes, my ears, and my neck, she moved down onto my torso, playfully tugging on my nipples, then kissing harder when I didn't react. She wanted me to embrace her. It felt good to feel her hot breath and her wet lips on my skin, but it made me sad, too. I was reminded of Marie, and how much rougher she had been than Leslie ever was, and how sorry I was I ever let Marie touch me. Lying there prone, while Leslie painted my skin with kisses, I was sick with guilt. Here was the one person who'd always been good to me, the one person with whom things had always been pure, and she wanted me to hold her, and I couldn't, not without feeling like a liar and a cheat.

Leslie didn't give up, though. Not for a while. She kissed my cock, taking it gently into her mouth. It was the first time she had done that with me, but I never even got the least bit hard. Eventually she brought her head back up next to mine, propped up on her elbows and looked at me.

"I'm sorry," I said. That seemed like the only thing I ever said anymore. It sounded hollow, even though I wanted so much to mean it.

"It's okay," she said, sounding even hollower.

It was an awfully awkward moment, and neither of us knew what to do or say. I was still lying on my back with my arms at my sides. Leslie set her head down, facing away from me. That hurt. A minute later she rolled over and lay her arm over my chest, just the way Marie had done. That hurt even more. I turned my head sideways and watched her go to sleep.

46

I watched her for a good couple of hours before I got the shakes again. They came on pretty hard after a while.

Leslie was fast asleep, but I still hadn't even shut my eyes. I was okay for a while, sober even, but eventually, just as I knew it would, the disease kicked in, cloaked in its own inevitability.

It was a familiar feeling. The desire to drink. Nothing new. And at first, it was faint, sort of shy even, like the point of very slight hunger that comes right after you've digested everything you've got in your stomach. It didn't take long for it to get less than friendly, and soon after that it was screaming at me. It was tricky like that. Knocking at the door with a grin on its face a mile wide, but when you let it in—out of respect, maybe, if not downright nostalgia—it takes you by the throat and slams you against the wall.

And it becomes all that matters, all that ever mattered.

So while Leslie slept, and I lay there next to her, it consumed me. I fought it, of course, but the moment it began, I started to sweat, sure it was a losing battle.

I let it go further than I usually did. I waited it out, lying on my back with my arms at my sides, trying to keep my mind on other things, trying not to shake. It wasn't a question of what I wanted, not really. I knew that, without any kind of doubt. I wanted liquor. I wanted the bitter taste that was an investment, a promise of a sweetness to come. I wanted to feel the burn in my throat spread to every part of my body, speeding through my veins, rushing around to cure every part of me, wrapping its careless giddy euphoria around my aorta. It wasn't a question of what I wanted. It was what I wished I wanted, deep down. What I wished I had the guts to take. I wished I wanted Leslie, and sobriety, and homework, and a curfew.

But a headful of wishes gave me nothing but regrets. There were certainties that, as much as I wanted to, I could never forget. I knew why I would never see my sister again. I knew I couldn't go home, and that the cops were looking for me. I knew my weaknesses. I knew I needed another drink, and I would always need another drink. And I knew, with as much certainty as I had ever known anything, that I couldn't stay there with Leslie. I broke everything I touched. I needed to leave. I needed a drink.

I got up slowly, sliding out from under her arm as gently as I could. Which wasn't very, in my deprived, desperate state.

I didn't go for my clothes right away. My first concern was getting something to drink, anything. I searched around her living room and kitchen as quietly as I could, but I ended up making a real racket, knocking over a lamp and clattering dishes around like I was working on an impromptu orchestra. I crossed my fingers and prayed Leslie wouldn't wake.

I felt around in every nook and cranny of those two rooms, and found nothing. Not even cooking wine or rubbing alcohol. I didn't know if I would have actually gone ahead and chugged the latter even if I had gotten my hands on it, but it seemed like an okay idea at the time. The shaking and the burning were driving me nuts. I felt like screaming. The sun was starting to think about rising, and I hadn't had a drink since the afternoon. Twelve hours. That was the longest I'd gone without sleeping through it in as long as I could remember, and I was beginning to lose it. I rifled through the rooms again, angrily, even though I knew before I checked the first time that I wouldn't find a fucking drop. It was a matter of making sure, though, double sure. In a case like mine, with the possibility of available booze in the area, you couldn't be *too* sure.

After my second looting I gave up on the idea of scoring anything in the house. I was naked, my teeth were clenched, and my fists were pressed rigidly against the living room wall. It was all I could do not to put a hole through it. I *needed* something, anything, to drink. Why wasn't it there? It wasn't fair, goddammit. I needed it. What kind of cruel trick was this? I even spoke aloud, "It's not fair, goddammit. It's not fair."

I was naked, swearing at a god I wasn't even sure existed. Things were bad. I had to leave. I walked quickly down the hall to the bathroom, stumbling over a bowling ball that had no business being there.

"Fuck," I said under my breath, along with a slew of other profundities. Good thing Leslie's grandmother, who slept in the room right next to the bathroom, was half deaf.

I was bending over to pull on my clothes when the hinged

mirror over the medicine cabinet caught my eye. Worth a shot, man. I swung it open eagerly.

Cotton swabs, hydrogen peroxide, toothbrushes and paste—and, BINGO, one eight-ounce bottle of my dear old friend Robitussin. It wasn't vodka, but beggars can't be choosers. At least it wasn't Listerine.

I wrapped both hands around the bottle and removed it from its resting place on the red shelf. Nudging the mirror shut, I looked myself in the eyes and unscrewed the bottle. I had to break the safety seal. Perfect: a full bottle. Just what I needed. I dropped the cap on the floor and downed the whole thing. It was overpoweringly syrupy and disgusting, but I wasn't in a position to mind. I didn't waste any time throwing my clothes on after I was finished chugging. I didn't want to spend too much time looking in the mirror. It wasn't that I was afraid of what I might see. I knew what I'd see. I was busy trying to forget. I was pale, and tired, and my lips were chapped, and there were rebel outcroppings of peach fuzz sprouting up all over the face I had never shaved. All of that was ugly, and pathetic, but I could handle it. What I could not handle, what every night I wished away and every day it seemed I acquired more of, were the scars. And the bruises. And the scabs. If there was a square inch of my body without some kind of wound on it, I didn't know where it was. I felt like a cripple. I didn't even know where half of them came from. Some were left over from the beating I took from Kenny; my arms were taken care of by my activities during the nightmare I had had later that night; a few new ones were bestowed upon me by my father only hours before. But most of them came from the brutality of my everyday life. From climbing barbed-wire fences on the edges of rooftops, breaking glass with my bare hands, falling down drunk. And from God knew where, when I would spend days on end in a drunken stupor, out of my mind and remembering nothing. I was not just pale. I was pale in the spaces between the scars, and the lacerations, and the bruises, red and brown and pink and yellow and blue and purple and white. I was a colorful guy, and I hated it. I hated wearing all those marks like merit badges for a full-time fuckup, reminders of memories I wished I never had.

Putting my clothes on was a funny thing. It wasn't really like dressing anymore, not the way it used to be. It was more like hanging my clothes on a collection of clothes hangers. My flesh was failing, and my bones ached. I was not at home in my own body. It was a vehicle for the cycle I was trapped in, for recycling. I drank and cried and pissed and puked and sweated and bled. Eating and shitting happened only on special occasions, and were more like little holidays than anything else. No wonder I depended so much on liquor. It was the source for all my gifts to the world, meager as they were. It was all I had.

With my clothes hung on my ragged holey frame, with eight ounces of very welcome Robitussin winding its way from my belly to my brain and making everything soft and blurry, I walked down the hall, past Leslie's room without pausing, and out of her house.

I leapfrogged down the steps, holding on to the banister and swinging over four at a time. All at once I was excited. I knew where I was going again. I had a plan, and when I reached the front step I did not have to wait there and make up my mind as I had done at my parents' house. I was leaving, and I knew exactly where I was going, and who I was going with. It wasn't a matter of making up my mind. I had made up my mind two months ago. We all had, all three of us. I started to walk, briskly. They were waiting for me.

I did stop once, right after I skipped across the street in front of Leslie's house. I had this feeling I was being watched, this kind of burning hole in my back, and I was going to ignore it, but then I just couldn't. I stopped, turned, looked, and three stories up, at a window in a turret in a house shaped like a castle, I saw Leslie, wrapped in a blanket, looking down at me. And I couldn't see her that well, but I could have sworn she was crying. Instantly, so was I. Not a lot, on either of our parts, just a couple honorary tears. Regrets, painting lines into our faces. She waved, slowly. I didn't. I swallowed hard and walked away, still feeling that hole in my back and hoping I would get used to it. I had to. I was leaving Leslie, and she was watching, and it was almost too much to bear. But my mind was made up, and there wasn't any kind of going back. So that, Leslie watching as I walked away, was just one more mark, one more scar to wear. And I hoped, as I made my way to the theater where Philly and Jeremy had been waiting for two full months, that soon I would be able to wash that scar off, along with all the others. In the ocean.

"Okay," Philly said when I'd finally finished talking.

It was the first thing he had said since he asked me what happened. I told him the whole story, coming down off the Robitussin as I talked, so that when I was done all I had left was a hangover. As for Philly, he never took his eyes off me, and he never moved. And when I was done, and he said okay, we both stood, and went up to the projector booth to wake Jeremy, where we told him we were ready. He didn't ask me why, and neither Philly nor I ever told him. To this day, he does not know why my sister killed herself. There's never any way to know for sure, but I do think it's better that way.

"So how do we get there?" Jeremy asked.

"Take a bus," Philly offered immediately. "Wasn't that the plan?"

"How much money you guys got?" Jeremy asked, knowing the answer but checking his own pockets anyway.

I had a dollar bill and two more in change. The other guys had less.

I was the rich one. I spoke. "So what do you think, Jeremy? Still want to rob that bank? We're gonna need a good couple hundred dollars for three bus rides to the coast."

"Not a bank. Too risky," Jeremy responded.

I could have asked him what then, but I didn't think it was necessary. I got the feeling Jeremy had a very solid plan churning around in his head, something he'd been thinking about constantly for two months. He was just taking his time telling us. And for good reason, I would fully realize when he told us what he had in mind.

"Sunshine," he said, looking hard at Philly, maybe to gauge his response, although I'm sure he was already certain what it would be.

"No freaking fucking way," Philly said, agreeing without knowing it. To disagree he would have had to kill Jeremy or himself on the spot. Anything less, and he was going along. He had to. He was one of us.

"Yes," Jeremy said, nodding and standing up.

"No, man," I said, knowing, even as I resisted, what was sure to happen, and feeling sick for it.

"Fuck you, you asshole," I said to Jeremy as we climbed up the ladder and hit the roof. He grinned at me and handed me a half-full bottle of whiskey. I quit arguing and emptied it down my throat, sucking on the bottle almost sexually. I didn't speak against robbing Sunshine again. Jeremy knew my position. He also knew I was coming.

Why? How could we do such a thing? Because we were scared little kids. Because we were best friends, and where one of us went, we all went. Because Sunshine was familiar. Because we thought it was safe. I think we each had our own reasons. I wanted out, no matter how. Jeremy wanted proof, proof that there was nothing left of the children we had been. And Philly, well he went along because he couldn't kill Jeremy, and he couldn't kill himself. For each of us, it was a matter of weakness.

But you know, all these answers, all these guesses, are nothing more than exactly that. I've asked myself the same question a thousand times, so I have these answers. I make guesses. I can never know for sure. In the end, all I can say is I don't know. I don't know why. We were drunk teenagers. We did a lot of stupid crazy things. That just happened to be the stupidest and craziest.

I didn't take long to cave in. I knew my options. The cops were after me already. I was too sick to stay, and if I wasn't careful I'd be too sick to leave. It wasn't a big choice. I mean, it wasn't a choice at all, really. It was the course things took. From the moment the word *Sunshine* rolled off Jeremy's tongue, I knew our fate. And I would go along. I would steal money from a Mexican couple who had one little boy with no role models and four thugs to feed. On one condition.

"No Charlie."

"What?" Jeremy said.

I repeated myself. "We don't bring in Charlie. This only goes down if Charlie's not working."

"So what if he is?"

"Then we go someplace else."

He was silent for a moment, considering. We were walking together, Philly and Jeremy and I, down Suicide Hill, digging our feet into the snow with every stride to keep from slipping and tumbling all the way down. Maybe once we wouldn't have bothered, maybe once we would have rolled down the thing on purpose, but not anymore. It was too harsh, too bumpy for us to handle. We weren't kids anymore. Our bodies were ancient, and tired. And for me, it held too many memories. I was extra careful not to slip.

Suicide Hill was on the way from our theater over to Philly's house, where our guns were stashed. We wouldn't have been on it at all if it wasn't such a good shortcut. I was trying to get Jeremy to agree to lay off the whole thing if Charlie was there. We'd ruined enough of his life already. I figured we ought to quit while we were ahead, or at least not in so terribly deep. Jeremy was a smart guy; he saw my point. I just wasn't sure he cared. Philly was walking behind us, still shaking his head and wearing a nauseated look on his face, licking his lips and sweating his conscience out of every pore. He was really in a bad state. He looked feverish. He knew this was wrong, from the bottom of his being.

"Okay," Jeremy said.

"Okay?" I said.

"Okay, we back off if Charlie's there. We'll go someplace else."

With those words, I was in for good. With those words, we laid down the terms of the ending of everything we had together. And the speaking of those words is one thing for which I will never forgive Jeremy.

Sometimes, like a little kid, I wonder about what lying is, exactly, and what if you mean something when you say it, but then you go back on it anyway. When I *was* a little kid, my mom said that wasn't lying. It was called making a mistake. Well, maybe I'm childish, but I called it lying. Jeremy lied to us that night, lied to me, and it cost us everything.

But he did mean it when he said it, I think, and I believed him. I bought his lie, and so did he.

Not Philly, though. He didn't buy it, not any of it. Not our angel. He played the part perfectly, never once wavering. It was no wonder we thought of him as the good one of us, the purest by far. He fucking *was*. If any of us had a shot at living, at loving, at finding peace, it was him. And it was exactly that, that purity, that remaining sweetness, that fucked it up for him.

He didn't buy it, and he did *not* want to go along. He just kept on shaking his head, over and over and over, like that was the last thing he knew how to do. He shook his head all the way through the walk to his house, and he shook his head as he opened the door his mother never kept locked, and he was still shaking his head when he came back out and shut the door behind him, carrying a brown paper bag.

He looked at us then, and with his trembling hands he handed us each a gun, and spoke up for the first time since we were all in the projector room when Jeremy had first announced his plan. "This is bad, you guys. This is so freaking bad." He was close to tears. His eyes were wide, terrified, like a good little boy who's about to break a very serious rule. This was Philly, this was Terence Watters, going against everything he'd ever believed in. It was him going against his heart, his conscience, his mother, even his religion, however far away it seemed to us. I think it was actually pretty close to him, his Catholicism, though he never talked about it. In a funny kind of way, though, up till then, he *had* lived it. I mean he did some pretty shitty stuff, along with the rest of us, but in his heart, and when you got right down to it, even in his actions, he was some kind of good Christian. I mean, being like a big brother to Charlie and all. He was always doing stuff like that. One time, less than an hour after we got done stealing the hell out of a liquor store, he helped this old blind lady walk across the street. He was just a genuinely *good* guy. Up till then. But he was about to jump off that bridge, and it was Jeremy and I who brought him to the edge, who all but shoved him off.

Still, he never wanted to. He tried to talk us out of it, as we stood on the stoop of the house he used to live in, holding guns like half-welcome strangers in our hands. And he shook his head no. Had we asked him if he wanted to come, he would have said no without a second thought. But we didn't ask. We just went, and out of his loyalty to us, he came along. He never did stop shaking his head, though.

He shook his head all that night, which we stayed up through, and he shook his head as we watched the sun rise, huddled together and freezing our asses off anyway, wrapped in the cool breeze coming off a lake on the east side of town where we spent the entire morning, cupping our hands around our eyes and pretending it was the ocean.

We had decided to wait a day to hit Sunshine, to spend one last day together on the streets of our hometown, visiting all our old haunts and telling tales of the youth we had spent together. Sharing Dumpstered bread and expired soda and memories. It was a good day, in many ways. We were together, and getting along, and laughing, and being best friends, and having a good time. We didn't really even get drunk. I mean, we each had a couple beers to keep us going, but nothing serious. We stayed close to sober, and talked about the ocean, and it was good. It was empty, too, though. I mean, it was filled with emptiness, with places we didn't go, homes we didn't visit, a graveyard we didn't go to, times we didn't talk about. But we did the best we could with what we had. And we kept busy, moving around the holes in our lives and trying not to think or talk about the night ahead. Every now and then there would be an awkward silence, and Philly would start shaking his head again, but Jeremy or I would tell him to cool it, or point out some crazy bum walking by that we could laugh at, or bring up the time Jeremy jerked off in that Italian restaurant, or the time Philly took a piss in the library in ninth grade, or some other wild thing one of us had done, and we would all crack up as hard as we could, under the circumstances. And for a time, Philly would forget. That's what we wanted more than anything else. It was okay if Jeremy or I was thinking about it, because we weren't freaking out. But Philly, with that head shaking of his, it was unnerving as hell. He kept it up, on and off. He was still shaking his head no when we showed up at Sunshine.

But in between, we had a good day together. As good as we could, as good as could be expected of us. It was our last day together, and though we had no way of knowing that, it was in the air. The bittersweet tip-of-your-tongue nostalgic memories of better days enveloped us, and filled the spaces between us. And in our own ways, without knowing we had to, or even that we were doing it, we said our good-byes.

When it was getting dark, the planning begun. It was not an exciting thing, to plan a robbery. Not like you'd think it might be. Not the way it is when you're just bullshitting about it, when you're fantasizing about robbing a bank and flying to Costa Rica. It wasn't like that at all. It was a thing of desperation, but the planning wasn't desperate either. It was more like planning a funeral. Nobody has a good time, but it's what you have to do when somebody dies. And nobody was having a good time that night, planning a rip-off of the least deserving people we knew. But it's what you do when you're dying, and drunk. It's what we did.

We planned as the sun set. This consisted mostly of me listening to Jeremy spout ideas and then me agreeing or disagreeing, to which Jeremy paid little or no attention. Philly didn't even bother listening. He just sort of sat around off to the side of us, equally absorbed in staring off at the fading pink horizon and bouncing a little swirly-colored rubber ball on the ground between his legs. He'd found it earlier that day and had been fidgeting with it ever since. Maybe Philly should have been helping us plan, but if the sunset and the ball kept his mind off the night ahead, neither Jeremy nor I gave him a hard time about it.

We'd never seen a full-fledged robbery before, so the whole plan was based on a hodgepodge of common sense and what we'd seen in the movies. Here was what we ended up with: Jeremy would be the front gun and do all the major talking. He'd go in first, gun out. We didn't want to waste any time. I'd follow him and play backup gun and cover, plus assorted yelling and general pandemonium causing. We assigned Philly as lookout; we didn't think he'd mind missing out on the action. Our getaway plan was simple: get the money from the register and run like hell. Crude, maybe, but there was no reason it shouldn't work if all went well. The whole thing would go down at night, right before closing time at eleven. That way we had practically no chance of finding Charlie working, as he was usually only there in the afternoons. His father worked the night shift.

We also took a good look at our guns, for the first time since we'd acquired them. Jeremy the whiz kid figured out how to click off the safety switches, as well as how to open them up to check the bullets without blowing our heads off.

The first gun we'd found, the Dumpstered one, had one bullet left in it. The other two were fully loaded. It was terrifying, in a way, looking at the bullets as Jeremy unloaded them into his cupped hand and then popped them back in, one at a time. Even he seemed uncomfortable with it, handled them awkwardly. Like strangers. Gangsters we weren't. It was hard to really get a grip on the fact that the little metal cases he was holding could kill somebody. It was hard to get a grip on the fact that we were going to put those little metal cases in a little metal machine and point it at a person, threaten their life. Somebody who in no way deserved it, who had done nothing to ask for it. We were going to threaten an innocent human being's life, for money. For a trip to the ocean.

48

It was time.

It was 10:47 P.M. on March 12, 1992, when Jeremy and I walked up to the door and looked inside. We were looking for Charlie. We see Charlie, we walk. We don't, we rob. That was the deal.

There was one person inside, kneeling down in one of the aisles, stocking some canned soup onto the shelves. We could only see the person from behind and couldn't tell who it was. We pressed our faces against the window, peering intently through steamed glass, trying to find an angle we could catch a good look from. It was impossible. I thought it was a guy, but more than that, there was no way to tell. The guy was bent over, facing away from us.

"It can't be Charlie," Jeremy said.

"Yeah," I said. "But he's kind of small for his dad."

"Is it Charlie?"

"I don't *know*," I said frustratedly, still straining for a good look. And then, suddenly, I did know. The person knelt over in the aisle was wearing a bright blue T-shirt. Charlie, for the entire time any of us had known him, always wore the same red-and-black Harley-Davidson T-shirt. No shirt, no Charlie. "It's not him," I said.

That was all the permission Jeremy needed. He swung the

door open, pulling his gun out as he did so, and walked inside. The cold determination decorating the way he moved was an eerie sight to see. I shot one last look over my shoulder at Philly, who was doing his job playing lookout on the corner. He gave me one last shake of the head—a double shake, really, but a solitary gesture. His face was pure panic. Pure desperation. Philly was dying there on the corner, nothing but helpless, alone except for the orange glare of the street lamp, bathing him. Making him glow.

I sort of shrugged my shoulders at him, wishing I could do more but knowing I couldn't, and followed Jeremy inside, catching the door as it swung closed and sliding through. I had my own job to do. The can stocker heard the bells on the door jingling and looked up in time to see Jeremy level his gun at the stocker's head.

Charlie's eyes widened in terrified recognition. Jeremy's gun arm lowered ever so slightly, and trembled just as minutely. I sucked in about a gallon of air so suddenly I almost choked. There was a pause, deadly silent; decisions were made. Jeremy's was different from mine. I took my hand off the gun I had been pulling out of my jacket and clasped it against my other palm in a spontaneous gesture of prayer. A second chance, I wanted. A way out. Jeremy's lips tightened and he inhaled through his nose deeply, holding the air in. Maybe issuing a prayer of his own. If he was, though, it was a different sort of prayer. His was for forgiveness. Absolution. Outwardly, his gun arm rose again, and he cocked the hammer back with his thumb. In the space of an instant, Jeremy broke the one rule we had laid down under our whole plan. No Charlie.

"Hi, Charlie," Jeremy said, almost warmly.

"H-hi, Jeremy," Charlie stammered.

"Where's your Harley shirt?" Jeremy asked, as if he were making small talk.

"M-my mom made m-me throw it out," Charlie said.

"That's really too bad," Jeremy said, almost sadly, but then his voice got cold. Back to business. "Stand up," he commanded.

Charlie got to his feet. He still had a soup can in each hand. Chicken noodle. He was shaking all over. He was twelve years old, and he had a gun in his face.

"Drop the cans," Jeremy said.

He did. He just opened up his fingers and let them fall. The left one hit the floor a split second sooner than the right. Each made a loud bang as it hit. Like gunshots.

I flinched. Jeremy didn't waver for a moment. Charlie was getting paler by the second as the blood drained out of his head. He was sweating now, and shaking all over.

"Get back behind the counter. And slowly."

Charlie began moving backward, never taking his eyes off the barrel of the gun that was aimed at his head. He didn't blink once.

Jeremy followed him, always keeping steady the six-foot distance between the two of them. Always keeping the gun aimed directly at Charlie.

I was supposed to stay at the door, but I didn't. I moved forward, mirroring the pace of the other two but walking a couple of aisles down from Jeremy. When Charlie had gotten behind the counter and moved to the register, half instinctively and half just knowing what we wanted, the three of us formed a triangle.

And then I watched that little boy do the bravest thing I have ever seen anybody do. Jeremy told Charlie to hand over the money, and Charlie refused. He stood behind that register with a gun pointed in his face, and shook his head no. Wordlessly, he defied Jeremy. He defied a seventeen-year-old alcoholic who had lost his heart and was ready to kill.

"Gimme the money," Jeremy said harshly, his lip curled back into a vicious snarl.

Charlie shook his head again. "No." His voice was cold, too, and you could tell he was scared shitless, but by God he wasn't gonna admit it. And he wasn't gonna give Jeremy his family's money. Not for the world. Not on his life.

And seeing that, seeing that kind of bravery, that kind of purity, a little boy who was ready to give up his life for his family, I knew I couldn't let him. I couldn't let Jeremy hurt this boy any more than we already had. We'd already taken his dreams. There was no fucking way in the world we were gonna take more. For that, I was ready to give up *my* life. I put my hand back on my gun, my fingers finding the right grip and clicking the safety off. "Jeremy," I said quietly, cautiously.

He ignored me. He wasn't listening. All he heard was Charlie's no. He blew up at him. "GIMME THE FUCKING MONEY!" He screamed at the top of his lungs.

Charlie was still. He tried to speak, but no sound came forth from his moving lips. I think he tried to say, "No way." He was sweating buckets, and shaking like crazy. Shaking like a little boy with a gun in his face.

I wanted to step back, but I stepped forward. Closer to Jeremy. I gripped the gun tighter and slipped my index finger into its place on the trigger. I was sick, and getting sicker.

Jeremy's own trigger finger was poised, dancing on the edge of contracting.

"Jeremy," I said again, louder this time, with an urgency in my voice.

He didn't hear me. Where he had gone, he couldn't hear anybody. Jeremy had lost it, and he was going to do anything to get that money. To get to the ocean. For him, this had become the only way. I could see it in his face. And in a way, he was right. If we backed down on this, if we walked away, we'd never get to the ocean. The moment we walked through that door with guns in our hands, we had narrowed our options down to two. Get the money and go to the ocean, or back down, get caught, and go to jail. And for Jeremy, there was no cost too great. He had lost his heart, and in trying to get it back, he made sure he never would. He was ready to kill a twelve-year-old boy.

I wasn't. I mean, that night was filled with split-second decisions, and every one of them was based on a maybe, but I thought about it as much as I could in half a minute, and I was pretty sure Charlie's life was worth more then Jeremy's, more than my own. He was still pure. He still had a chance. We were walking dead. And even though that walking dead kid named Jeremy was one of my two best friends, I couldn't let him hurt Charlie.

I pointed my gun at Jeremy, and said his name again. Loudly. "JEREMEEEE!"

It was a torn and ragged scream from the depths of my torn and ragged soul. He turned his head to look at me, saying "What the—unnh!" His words were cut short with an awful grunt, as if he'd been punched in the stomach. As if he'd seen his friend pointing a gun at him and looking crazier than he did.

His gun was still trained on Charlie, who was frozen, but his eyes were on me. "You put that fucking gun down, Jim."

"You first," I said quietly, resolutely. My eyes stung. Much as I wanted to, much as I wished I could, I couldn't put the gun down. I didn't move.

Jeremy knew me, maybe better than anybody, and he knew I wouldn't back down. And he knew he couldn't, either. So, with tears in his eyes, in about the time it had taken him to be ready to kill Charlie if he had to, he turned his gun on me. In a breath, he was ready to kill me. "Don't make me do this, Jim," he said, warning me.

"No Charlie," I said. "Remember, Jeremy? You can't do this. *We* can't fucking go through with this." I was through pleading with him, through making deals. My voice was hard, and I meant what I said. I did not drop my gun. Instead, I cocked it.

"Goddammit, Jim," Jeremy began, raising his voice, but I cut him off.

"No, Jeremy, goddam *you, fucking goddam you*! You back the fuck off! You are not going through with this!"

"We are, Jim! There is no other goddam way! We are taking—I am taking this fucking money!"

"You better fucking shoot me then, old buddy, 'cause I'll kill you first!"

At that moment, the room exploded. There was a flurry of motion and noise on both edges of my periphery, from behind the counter and at the front door. Charlie, who had been frozen, moved like lightning, pulling out from behind the counter a huge revolver that looked almost ridiculous in his small hands. I had exactly half a second to notice that before I noticed it pointing at Jeremy. In the same half I heard the doorbells jingle and saw Philly, in a blur, pull his own gun. I did not see where he was pointing it. The three of us were clustered too close together. A shot rang out, deafening and terrifying. In the second that followed, I did not have time to hit the floor, which I might have done otherwise. Things were moving too quickly. In the first half of that second, I had time to realize, by looking at him, that it was Philly's gun that had gone off. And in the next half second, I had time to see that it was little Charlie who'd been hit. He was still alive, even standing up sort of, slumped against the back wall. I think he was knocked out, though. His face was pale. His chest was red. And for another full second, all was silent.

It was the most awkward silence I have ever heard in my life. At the same time, it was the most certain. There was absolutely nothing to say. At that moment, as we stood in an uneasy triangle and looked each other in the eyes, we knew, without a word exchanged, we knew it was over.

Everything that transpired between us from that point on was not dealings between friends. It was taking care of business. It was for old times' sake. We spoke as friends, but we were not. We spoke as if we still knew each other, but we did not. It was a wake, and it was conducted somberly, and with respect. You don't talk badly about dead people, and you don't talk badly about dead friendships, either. You try to pick up the pieces. And you grieve, and wonder.

Sirens wailed in the distance, breaking our silence.

Philly spoke first, beginning the ceremony, which took on a real sense of urgency with the crescendo of approaching sirens. "Oh shit," he said, looking at us, his eyes dilated with shock. "Oh shit you guys, we really fucked this up! We really fucked up," he said, switching from shouting to whispering in the space of an instant.

I swallowed hard, looking at Jeremy. "Yeah, we did. We really fucking did."

Jeremy looked back at me for a moment and then closed his eyes. It was his turn to speak, but he didn't. He moved. It gave me a jolt, actually, because I guess for a time I felt like we were all paralyzed, and we would never move again. He did, though. He opened his eyes and walked over to Philly, standing right up next to him. Then he extended his left hand, palm up. It was the hand not holding a gun. Philly flinched, as if he was afraid Jeremy was going to hit him. When he realized he wasn't, he said, "What?"

This time, Jeremy did speak. "Gimme your gun."

"What for?" Philly asked, a mistrust in his voice that had never been there before. Not with Jeremy. Not with me.

"Here." Jeremy sighed, handing Philly his own gun with his

other hand. Philly took it hesitantly, confused. He now held a gun in each hand. "Now gimme yours," Jeremy demanded again. This time, Philly handed it over. Jeremy took it and stuffed it into his jacket pocket.

"What's that for?" I asked, referring to the mysterious trade.

"Just in case," Jeremy responded, looking at neither of us, as if he knew he wouldn't be able to meet our eyes.

I didn't understand at the time, but when I finally did, half a year later, I understood Jeremy himself, as much as anybody could. He never wanted it, not any of it. Not the brilliance, not the love, not the sex, not the booze, not the violence, not the lies, not any of it. He never even wanted to get out of the womb.

At the time, though, I didn't see all that. All I could see was my ex-friend Jeremy trading guns with my ex-friend Philly, not explaining why, and walking away, heading for the door.

"Hey, where you goin'?" I called after him, like a little kid.

"I don't know," Jeremy said thoughtfully. "The ocean, I guess."

"Well . . ." My voice trailed off.

Jeremy pointed at the unconscious Charlie. "When he wakes up, the cops are gonna know who we are, and how many of us. We gotta split up."

"Yeah," I said. "Well, I guess I'll see you there, then."

"The ocean," Jeremy said.

"Yeah."

The conversation was empty. We were making plans, but they were vague, and hollow, and neither one of us expected to keep them.

Jeremy turned again to go. I stopped him again. "Don't you want the money?"

This time he didn't turn around. He spoke to the door. "No."

"I thought you said it was too late," I said.

"It is." He was still for a moment, his back to us, and then he left, without another word.

I turned to Philly, and he turned to me. The sirens were getting pretty loud. It was time to take off, past time to take off. If we hung around much longer we were sure to get busted. I told Philly as much.

"Yeah," he said, as if he didn't care.

"So what now, then?" I asked him, already knowing the answer but still feeling desperate, and small. I needed to hear it again.

"You heard Jeremy," Philly said. "He's right. We can't stay together."

"I know."

"So?"

"So I'll see you at the ocean." I wanted it more that time than when I had said it to Jeremy, but it was just as empty. There were no hard feelings, and we had an understanding, but we couldn't go on together. We had gone far enough already.

Charlie stirred then, and began to whimper. He'd been shot in the chest, and the blood had soaked his shirt through. He was twelve years old, and I was sure he was dying. Philly rushed over to him, leaping over the counter and catching him just as he started to sink to the floor. I stood where I was and watched.

"You okay, Charlie?" Philly asked him softly. A stupid question, but it had real love in it.

"Call me Carlos," the boy murmured weakly. There wasn't anger in his voice, though. He let Philly hold him, rested his head on Philly's shoulder.

"Sorry, Carlos," Philly said. "Sorry."

"It's okay. I understand," Charlie said. He did, too. Even though I had tried to save Charlie's life, and it was Philly who ended it, it was Philly who Charlie looked up to, and it was Philly who held him now, while he bled. You know, there's a little part of me that will always wish that I had shot Charlie, that I had stuck with my friends, no matter what. I mean, knowing every side of things, and knowing where it got Philly, I'm glad I did what I did, but sometimes I wish I could have been the angel, the one for whom things were so black and white. I think Jeremy probably does, too.

I stood and watched, listening to the sirens get louder. My heart beat faster the closer they came. "We really got to get out of here, Philly," I said.

Philly looked up at me, the hint of a smile spreading across his lips. It was a sad smile. His eyes were moist, and bitter. "My name's Terence," he said, holding Charlie tighter.

"Yeah, sure, Phil—"

"Terence," he reminded me.

"*Terence,*" I said. "We gotta split, man!"

"You split," he said. "I'm stayin' here with Carlos. I shot him, after all."

"What're you gonna do when *they* get here?" I asked, gesturing my thumb in the direction of the not-far-off sirens.

"I don't know," Philly shrugged. "I guess I'll tell 'em I walked in during the robbery and they went thataway." He grinned, sort of wistfully.

It felt wrong, way wrong, leaving Philly behind. I knew things were gonna blow up somehow. There was nothing I could do, though, to save my old friend. He was staying, and he was right to. Even if I had known what would happen, there was no way I could get him to come with me. It was over.

"Okay. Well I'll see you," I said, almost sure I wouldn't.

"At the ocean," Philly said.

"Uh-huh." I couldn't think of anything else to say. I turned to leave.

"Say, Jim?"

"Yeah?"

"Things sure do change, don't they?"

"Yeah," I said quietly. "They sure do." The sirens were practically right on top of us. I had to go. "Good-bye, Terence."

He didn't look up. I don't think he heard me say good-bye. He was rocking Charlie, who was bleeding to death at the ripe old age of twelve.

49

I walked across the street as quickly as I could without breaking into a run. I knew better than to run. If you walk away, most of the time they don't even notice you. You disappear. And that's exactly what I did, even though the cops were right around the corner. I made it across the street and out of range of the bright-ass street lamp just as three cop cars and an ambulance screeched into the Sunshine lot. My heart was just about pounding out of my chest. I could have kept walking. Maybe I should have. I didn't, though. I waited, hiding in the shadows of an alley, pressed as tightly as I could get against the wall of this red brick apartment building, and watched.

I watched the cops storm Sunshine. They drew their guns right away. I guess the gunshot had 'em freaked. Two went inside and one walked around the side to the back. A couple EMTs got out of the ambulance and sort of waited around at the front door, waiting for the cops to secure the area. From where I was standing I could see straight into the store. I had a perfect view of the counter where Philly was still cradling

Charlie. I watched a cop bend over the counter and look at the two of them, then talk to Philly for a minute. Philly stood up after that, propping Charlie up with his shoulder. Charlie's head was lolled over sideways, resting on Philly's neck. I hoped he wasn't dead, but I wouldn't have been surprised if he was. He had been bleeding pretty bad. I watched Philly point his free hand toward the back of the store. The opposite of the direction Jeremy and I had headed.

The cop who was talking turned around and signaled the waiting EMTs to go on in; then two more cop cars pulled up, and a moment later a third. Philly and Jeremy and I used to get a big kick out of how way more cops than you needed would always show up at the scene of a crime, and then half of them would just stand around looking useless and acting like assholes to the occasional passersby. I wasn't laughing then, though. I was sweating buckets. My stomach was in knots. I was practically beating my head against the brick wall for letting Philly stay behind. And even though there wasn't a thing in the world short of dragging him away kicking and screaming I could have done to get him out of there, I will always blame myself. I left him. I disappeared. And once I was gone, I watched. And what I saw, those two minutes I stood watching, I will keep on seeing, like a home movie I can't stop replaying in my head. Every slow motion second of it haunts me, makes me sweat. Because every time I watch it, it's my fault.

I saw the EMTs prop the door open and wheel the stretcher inside and up to the counter. They slid Charlie up onto it very slowly and gently. From the tilt of his head and his limp body, I was pretty sure he was at least knocked out again. Philly stood up, trying to help. One of the EMTs waved him off and a cop, taking the guy's cue, grabbed onto Philly's shoulder and pulled him backwards. Philly was oblivious: he stepped forward again, getting as close to Charlie as he could manage with the EMTs in the way. His face was blank. If I hadn't just seen him crying I wouldn't have known he was upset. I had, though, and inwardly, I knew the whole thing was tearing him apart.

One of the EMTs checked his pulse, then nodded. At first I wasn't sure what that meant, but at that moment, the EMTs kicked into high gear. Charlie was still alive. They wheeled him out of the store as quickly as they could. Philly was right on their heels, asking questions I couldn't hear. The cops were right behind him.

By the time the EMTs were sliding Charlie up into the ambulance all six cops were gathered around in a semicircle behind Philly who was behind the EMTs. Three of the six still had their guns drawn. All lined up together like that, they looked just like a firing squad.

A combination of things happened then—all in a very short space of time, maybe ten seconds. If any one of them hadn't happened, maybe I could still voice my apologies. But they all did. I watched them all, one after another. Halfway through, I knew what was going to happen next, and still I did nothing. I didn't even try to do anything. I was hiding, pressed as tightly as I could get against the red brick wall, wrapped in shadows and regrets.

This is what happened in the hardest ten seconds of my life:

Philly reached upward, maybe trying to touch Charlie's face as they loaded him onto the ambulance. One of the EMTs nudged Philly with his elbow, obviously irritated at the young punk getting in the way of his job. He must have been a real heartfelt motherfucker. He pushed Philly, whose arm was still stretched upward toward the boy he had shot, in such a way as to fling his unzipped jacket open. Out of Philly's flung-open jacket fell a gun. I watched it fall, and I stopped breathing. I didn't choke exactly; I just died for a moment. Long enough to see Philly reflexively bend down to pick up the gun before it had even hit the ground. Long enough to hear the closest cop yell, "Gun!" and another one instantly yell, "Drop it!" Long enough to wish Philly wasn't so freaked out at that moment that he wrapped his fingers around the gun anyway, and looked up at the cops and began to stand. It was an action born out of panic. I knew Philly as well as I knew anybody, and I goddam well know he wasn't planning on shooting anybody. He was about to turn over the gun. His first thought was to hide it, sure, but his second, an instant later, was to surrender it. It was a split-second decision. *Pick it up.* That's what he did. They told him to drop it, and he picked it up. He was gonna hand it over. He was standing up, and looking at the firing squad as he straightened. His mouth was open, as if to speak. He never made another sound. He was a sixteen-year-old alcoholic Catholic who had done everything he could to talk us out of doing what we did, and he was trying to surrender. I *know* that. But the cops, the firing squad, they didn't know that. They knew what they saw. They saw a young greasy punk, hanging around the scene of a near-fatal robbery, drop a gun and then try and pick it up.

They shot him dead. Six bullets from three guns, all at the same time, and then another one from another gun, almost as an afterthought or an accident, and every earsplitting heart-rending shot tore another hole in his body. I was screaming before his body hit the ground, which it did a half second later, jaw first, making another crack that, in an agonizing fucked-up distorted kind of way, I remember as being just as loud as the gunshots.

50

The firing squad turned their attention to me. All their guns were drawn now. One of them told me to freeze. I didn't.

"Freeze!" another one said, like an echo of the first.

I took off running.

I wasn't running toward Philly's body. I was mad, but I wasn't crazy. I didn't want to, anyway. I didn't want to lay my eyes on his ragged blood-soaked hole-ridden body. I had seen enough. I didn't need any more nightmares than I already had. I wished I was blind.

And I wasn't running home, or back to the theater. And I wasn't running toward the ocean. I wasn't running *toward* anything.

I ran back down the alley I was standing in, away from Sunshine. I could hear a couple of cops shouting and chasing me. I was rounding the corner at the end of the alley when I heard the shot that sliced off a chunk of my back. A second sooner and it would have been my heart. It wasn't a heavy thud, so I was pretty sure the bullet didn't actually get lodged inside me. It was more like it grazed me. Getting grazed isn't like they say in the movies, though. It hurt like fucking hell. But I kept running, stumbling over the train tracks behind the alley and then taking a hard right and running alongside the tracks. I didn't even slow down, not one bit. They could have shot me ten times and I wouldn't have slowed down. This wasn't an evening jog. It was a big fucking marathon, me and my life, my grief, my rage, my horror, my desperation, my empty heart, my gun, my gutlessness, my guilt, my scars, my memories, and my blackouts all running together. I was leading the pack, but I could feel them all behind me, sure-as-shit real. Man, was I running. I could have been in the Olympics.

The cops had given up chasing me on foot. They had all climbed back into their cars and they were driving along the roads fifty feet on either side of me. There were about a hundred cop cars chasing me. They all had their spotlights trained right on me, too, so I was lit up like I was onstage. *See Jim run.* They sure as hell weren't trying to knock me off anymore. There was no point, really. I guess they figured their cars would last longer than my lungs. They were right, too, but I didn't care. As I sprinted down the tracks and realized where I was headed, that there was only one place I could be headed, I wasn't running away from everything anymore. I was running into it, if anything. All I needed was to get to the bridge, and I knew I'd be all right. That was what I wanted, more than anything. To get to the bridge where my sister had died. Just to pay my respects. I had skipped out on the fucking funeral, for God's sake. The least I could do was go back to where she had died. It would be a good place to get caught, the place where me and Mandy and Leslie and the guys had all spent time together, back when we knew what innocence was. It would be paying respects to all of us. 'Cause in a way, we'd all died. And if anywhere was our mass grave, that was the place. And I was running like a madman for it. Maybe it was funny, and backward, but some instinctive part of me really believed that I might find some honest-to-goodness salvation there. That if I ran fast enough, I could get a little time to myself there. If I ditched the cops for a minute, I could hide out in the shadow of the railroad bridge my friends used to love, maybe wash my face for once, take a few gulps of dirty river water, maybe even cry a little, while my face was still soaked, so nobody but me would know the difference.

I could see the bridge up ahead a couple blocks before I actually got there. My lungs were about to burst. I had a cramp in just about every part of my body, and I was down one chunk of flesh off the middle of my back. The hole was bleeding like crazy. I could feel the blood wash down the small of my back and soak into the crack of my ass, gathering in a pool at my crotch and leaking down my legs with each fading stride. If I could have, I would have given it up right then and there. But the bridge, my bridge, was in sight. I could see it, up ahead, dark and huge and lonely, not quite lit up yet by the approaching spotlights. I clenched my eyes shut tight, took in a deep breath, and gave it my everything, this last hundred-meter dash.

The cops had their sirens going, and some bastard was shouting something at me through a megaphone, but I couldn't hear him. Loud as it was, I wasn't listening. I was looking. Those last hundred meters, sprinting as hard as I could in the spotlights of more cop cars than I had ever seen in one place before, I was looking at my life. I didn't need to look at the cops, or the bridge. I knew where they were. My eyes were shut, and it was March, the beginning of spring, and I was surrounded by cops, and Philly was dead, but at the same time, in the same place, it was winter, and Mandy and I were skipping across the tracks on the way to meet Leslie. And it was the end of spring, and Philly was alive, and I was fifteen, and we were smoking pot and daring each other to dive headfirst off the railroad bridge into the water. And it was summer, and I was watching Mandy's brains spill out onto the tracks as the paramedics took her away. And it was fall, and I was not at the bridge, I was home, and my father was beating the shit out of me, and my mother wasn't letting Billy make a sound. And it was winter, and I was losing my virginity on too many drugs and Philly's floor. And it was spring, and I was making my mother bleed. It was spring, and I was watching a twelve-year-old boy and a sixteen-year-old who had been my best friend get shot to death, and I couldn't stop either one. It was spring, and I was in the spotlights of more cops than I'd ever seen in my life. It was spring, and I was bleeding, and tired, and desperate, and I wanted nothing more than to lie once more under that bridge, singing my sister's name. It was spring, and Mandy and Philly were dead, and Jeremy was God knew where, and Leslie was brokenhearted, and Billy was alone, and I was praying for mercy, just one last fucking chance, God, just two seconds with my head submerged in dirty river water, just two seconds in a womb.

I was ten feet from the bridge when I twisted my ankle on a rotted-out railroad tie and fell flat-out, face first 'cause my arms were too tired to bother, and besides, somehow I felt like I deserved it. I didn't get up again. I gave in, and gave up. And in a stupid, childish way, I sort of thought that would be it. Like when Butch Cassidy and the Sundance Kid charge the cavalry, and you know they're gonna die, but the camera just freezes on them and cuts to the credits. That's what I was thinking, lying facedown on the tracks as I heard about fifty doors slamming as the cops got out of their cars and started moving toward me. I was waiting for the credits to roll. They didn't, though. There wasn't even a commercial break. Philly was dead, and I was shot in the back, and Jeremy was gone, but nothing stopped. The cops were getting closer. It sounded like a goddam stampede, and I could bet every one had their guns drawn. I wanted to jump up, and cry out, and speak to them, shout at them, show them my heart, tell them how I never wanted to hurt anybody, how it was all a terrible misunderstanding, how this world was too big and too cold and too dangerous for me, how somebody should have warned me, somebody should have held me. It was too late for any of that, though. I could blame anybody I wanted to, and maybe I was right, and maybe I wasn't, but there was no going back.

I heard the cops circle up around me, falling into formation. A brave one, or maybe just the one who had to, came up to touch me. Just before he rolled me over and cuffed me, I closed my eyes and pretended I was dead. Usually when I was playing dead I had to give it up after a few seconds because my dead face would leak a smile or otherwise give itself away, but not this time. They knew I wasn't dead, of course. My body gave me away. My heart rate was up, if anything, although on that evidence alone I might still have been able to pull off a coma. But from there they jumped right into the dirty trick of prying my eyelids open and shining one of those put-sunlight-to-shame Mag-Lites in my eyes. I caved in on that one. My eyes started tearing up like crazy, and I clenched them shut the moment the cop took his hands off me. Busted. I still refused to respond to anything, though. It wasn't like I was trying to come up with some kind of excuse or anything, reserving my right to remain silent. I just didn't want to deal with anybody right then. I couldn't. I didn't have it in me. I was tired, and empty. So what I did was, I kept on playing dead. Like when you're little and you think if you just close your eyes so you can't see anybody, nobody can see you. Pretty crude logic, I admit, for a teenager who's just been shot by a cop, but like I said, I didn't have it in me. That much, a plan that wasn't even a plan, based on a four-year-old's logic, was all I could handle.

Once they figured out that was all they were going to get out of me, the paramedics rolled in and slid me up onto a stretcher. Somebody said something about nonresponsive shock. Somebody checked my pulse again, and then told me all about how fine I was going to be, about how I'd be up and at 'em in no time. I wished he knew how wrong he was, and how much I wanted him to be right. I didn't tell him, though. I didn't do anything but play dead. I played dead while they slid me into the ambulance, and I played dead while they bandaged up my back, and I played dead all the way to the hospital. I didn't quit playing dead, in fact, until I was in a hospital room, and they had finally left me alone.

I opened my eyes hesitantly, expecting to have a hard time with the light. There wasn't much light, though, just a lamp in the corner. I stretched my arms gingerly, massaging my wrists. They were bruised from the handcuffs, which the cops had only finally taken off right before they left me alone. From what I gathered, they had a cop posted outside the room. They were going to have me spend the night, just to keep an eye on me. They were worried I might be more fucked up than they thought, since I wouldn't answer any questions about anything, including where I hurt. I almost had. I had almost said, "How do you mean, Doc?" when the guy who had examined me asked me if anything else hurt.

I was just sitting myself up when the door swung open. I considered faking dead again but decided to fuck it. I didn't even lie down again. I made sure my face was blank and looked up, just in time to watch Sarah Coughlin the cop walk in.

So much for a blank composure. I smiled outright, and spoke, breaking both the rules I'd been following for the past couple hours. Hell, it was *Sarah*. I know it sounds crazy, and we'd only met that one other time when she'd driven me home after Philly and I got arrested, but there was nobody else I would have rather seen right then. "Hi," I said, as brightly as I could manage. Even with Sarah, it was pretty hard to get very cheerful.

"Hi," she said, still standing in the doorway. Her hair was curly where it once had been straight, but other than that she looked pretty much the same. Still the same sweetly homely face. Still the same warm eyes. Still the same cop's blue suit.

"Come in," I said.

She did, sitting down on the chair next to my bed. We were both awkwardly silent for a moment, and then she looked up at me, grinning. It looked halfway forced, but under the circumstances, I understood. She had to know what kind of trouble I was in. "We gotta stop meeting like this," she said.

"Yeah," I said.

"You hungry?" she asked, and for the first time I noticed the Dunkin' Donuts bag she held in her hand.

"No," I said. I didn't know if I'd ever feel like eating again. Then, remembering the conversation that had first brought us together, I said, "I thought you hated donuts."

Sarah looked down, almost embarrassed. "Oh," she said. "I did. I mean, I used to. You get such a sweet tooth on the job. . . . Everybody likes donuts, don't they?"

"Yeah," I said.

"Oh, Christ, Jim!" she suddenly exploded, standing up and pacing all over the place. "What did you *do*?"

I didn't say anything. I knew she knew. Watching her, though, I started sort of squinting, trying not to cry, trying not to ask for what I wanted.

She stopped pacing and looked at me, her wide eyes piercing my squinted ones. I couldn't fool her. I might be able to play dead calm with a bunch of strangers, but Sarah knew me, somehow. "Oh, Jim," she said sadly, coming over to the bed and putting her arms around me. I was still sitting up, and she was standing, but I leaned against her a little bit, resting my head on her breast and tightening my face up even more, holding in the tears. She kept talking, holding me like she would never let go. "I know what happened. Your father packed his things and left last night, without saying a word to anyone. He was gone before we got there. He's gone, Jim. Nobody knows where, but he's gone. Your mom told me everything."

Hearing that, I couldn't hold back any longer. I burst out crying. First it was just a few tears running away from my eyes, but as she kept talking, it wasn't long before I was full-fledged sobbing into a cop's breast. I didn't know how to feel about what she told me. My dad was gone, and it was my fault. Was that good? I didn't know. It wasn't what I wanted. I didn't know what I wanted. Nothing seemed right anymore. I didn't know how to feel. I was crying, though, and Sarah was holding me, and that was something.

"I tried to find you, Jim. Not just today, while everybody was trying. I've been looking for months. I promised you I'd find you, and I couldn't. You disappeared. You weren't at home, or school, or anywhere, you know?"

"I know," I said softly between sobs, holding her tighter.

"No, Jim, that's the thing. *I* know. I see you. I know why you did what you did."

"That makes one of us," I said, cracking a joke but sobbing all the harder. She was giving me what I had always wanted.

"I'm sorry, Jim," Sarah said after a time, gently withdrawing her arms and letting me sit by myself. "Believe me, I'm sorry. I wish I could have stopped this somehow."

"You couldn't've, Sarah," I murmured, wrapping my arms around myself, trying to replace her. It wasn't the same. "You couldn't've."

She nodded at me. Her eyes were wet. Mine were soaked. I guess that was how it should have been. I was the one in all the trouble. "I just wanted . . . I wanted to save you, Jim. And I couldn't. I couldn't even *find* you. And now I have to watch them put you away."

Suddenly, as she said that, it hit me. *They were gonna lock me up.* And with that thought, that knowledge, a little spark of something else reared its fiery head. A little declaration. A little life, for once. A little *no*.

"They'll take you to the station in the morning," Sarah said as she walked out the door. "I'll see you then." If she'd known what was in my mind, she wouldn't have been so casual about saying good-bye. But it was good, the way it was. We'd already said what we needed to say, and anything else would have been worthless. Her giving me advice I couldn't hear, maybe. *Take care of yourself, Jim.* Or worse, trying to talk me out of it. Making her stand up for the system that was going to put me away, and I knew for a fact that was the last thing she wanted. But she would have, if she had to. No, it was good that she didn't know. Easier, for both of us. It was good that I nodded back at her on her way out, which was the biggest lie I could manage. I could say it wasn't even a lie, but it was.

"No you won't," I whispered, too quietly for her to hear. It didn't make up for the lie of the nod, but it was something.

The door slammed behind her. She hadn't meant it to, but the spring on the hinge was broken. Gentle as she was, she left me with a bang. And as gentle as I wanted to be, I was going to leave with a bang, too. It was the only way out.

I stood up off the bed a couple seconds after she left. It wasn't easy to stand, with the bullet wound and all, but it wasn't the hardest thing in the world, either. I felt kind of rickety—old—but I was moving.

I went over to the window then, looking out and down. I was only one story up, and the base of the building was lined with evergreen bushes. Not exactly a soft landing, but it wasn't cement, either. Next I checked out the window itself. It was screwed in pretty good. So much for removing it. Ah, well, there were other ways.

It took me about two seconds to come up with one. By that time the fire inside me was everywhere, and strong, engulfing even my fingertips. I needed to get out. I wasn't ready to be locked up. Even Sarah knew it. I was too scared, too wild. I needed time to sort things out. I knew this would all catch up to me someday, but I had things to do first. Places, or maybe just one place, to go. For Philly. For Jeremy. For all of us, for every kid that has ever gone crazy with the harshness of life.

The ocean wanted all of us.

With both hands, I grabbed the base of the metal chair Sarah had been sitting on and hurled it through the window.

The major problem with my plan to go out the window, I realized as I heard the chair clattering onto the cement below, was that the cops would know exactly where I had gone. It would take them less than a minute to nab me.

It had been about a second since the window had shattered. I figured I had three, maybe five more at the most before Sarah and some other cops came storming into the room. I could hear their voices and footsteps racing down the hall already.

I walked into the bathroom. That was two seconds down the drain. Then I looked at myself in the mirror, taking a deep breath, preparing to be busted once again. Two more. I could hear the door to the room opening, and in the last free second I had to my name, my eye caught the reflection in the mirror of the shadow behind the mostly open bathroom door, and instantly, in the same moment the cops entered the outer room, I stepped behind it, hiding.

From their voices, I could tell it was Sarah and some guy. They went to the broken window first. If I'd been out there, running across the hospital yard, they would have seen me for sure.

I heard the guy swear and dash out of the room, saying he was gonna go down and find my ass. Sarah was behind him. On her way out of the room, she glanced into the bathroom mirror. Straight into my reflection.

For a moment our eyes locked, and we both froze. Neither of us said a word. Our faces were blank. If our eyes weren't meeting, I would have been certain she hadn't seen me at all. Absolutely nothing went between us. And at the same time, without any kind of signal, everything did.

"Whatsamatter? You see somethin'?" I heard the other cop ask her.

And Sarah Coughlin lied for me. "No," she said. "Nothing."

In the last second before she disappeared around the corner, I unfroze and nodded at her, I guess thanking her.

She didn't nod back. She shook her head no at me, ever so slightly, almost imperceptibly. I couldn't tell what she meant. Maybe it wasn't for me that she had lied. Maybe it was for her. Or maybe she was already sorry. Maybe it was because she had started liking donuts. I'll never know, I guess. I never saw her again.

I grabbed my clothes then, pulling off my hospital gown and putting them on in record time. I was moving quickly, but I wasn't actually scared. It was funny; I mean, maybe my heart should have been pounding its way out of my chest and all, but I felt pretty calm. I was tired, too tired to have my heart racing all over the place. Too tired to sweat. Too tired to run.

So I didn't run. I pulled off a great escape that would have done Philly and Jeremy proud. I walked. I walked out of the room, down the stark white hospital hallway, down one flight of stark white hospital steps, and right the fuck out the stark white hospital lobby, nice and slow, real casual. I even sort of nodded at the secretary on the way out, thinking, "Man, you have no idea."

I walked my ass out of the hospital, and I kept on walking, taking the back roads the way I had when I was going to see Leslie the night before. Had that only been yesterday? It seemed like years ago.

I wasn't in much of a hurry. I just headed east, nice and easy. Easy east. I'd be long gone by the time the cops figured out what I'd done. At least if Sarah kept quiet. And I was pretty sure she would.

I was good and lost after a couple hours of hiking those back roads, but I didn't stop walking there. I kept walking, actually, walking and hitchhiking anyway, all the way to the coast. To the ocean.

AUGUST 1992

51

Between the hospital and the ocean is where it gets pretty hazy. I mean, I remember the first ride I got. I remember getting picked up by a trucker after waiting about an hour on the side of the highway. I remember him donating a nice pint of whiskey to my cause. I don't remember him dropping me off. I don't remember much. Flashes, here and there. Walking a lot. Hitching rides. I don't remember faces, really. I remember cars. I remember bottles. I remember alleys, although they all seem like the same one. I remember puking, and making wishes, trying to find a reliable star. I remember being gone a long time. And I remember the ocean.

I don't know how long I'd been in Point Pleasant, New Jersey, before I knew where I was. Maybe only a day, but maybe more. Maybe a month. I only remember the day I found out. I remember going for a walk to the edge of town, early in the morning, as it was getting light. I was drunk out of my mind, but I felt like moving anyway. So I walked toward the sunrise.

I could hear the waves crashing against the beach for a couple of blocks before I actually touched sand. I thought it was just the liquor, though. I didn't believe it was real. How could I? It had been so, so long since I'd even thought of the ocean. I was just going for a walk. East.

The closer I got, the louder they were, and I almost let myself believe. And almost believing, I let myself run, as fast as I could in my drunken stupor.

And running, stumbling, swaying, sweating, tripping in the sand and leaping to my feet with tears and grit in my eyes, I saw what I hadn't seen since I was two years old, helping Mandy bury herself in the white sand. For the first time in fourteen years, I saw the ocean.

And seeing, I dove in, tearing off my clothes after I was already halfway in, hurling them back toward the shore. I didn't know if I'd ever see them again, and I didn't care.

The water was shockingly cold, and it sobered me up like nothing else. Each wave crashing into my naked chest sobered me up that much more. And with each wave I screamed, as if to wake myself up, and laughed, at the ocean's joke that had no punch line. I jumped around and beat my chest like a madman. I was freezing. I had goose bumps the size of peas all over my body. I was in the Atlantic Ocean, off the coast of Point Pleasant, New Jersey. The names meant nothing, though. The waves meant something. The sand meant something. The sunrise, ever brighter on the horizon, peeling back the black of night, meant something. *I* meant something, for once.

I stayed there, at the ocean, for two days. I didn't leave once. I hardly even moved. I put my clothes back on after the sun rose, and I might have pissed a couple times, but mostly I sat. Huddled, more like, just close enough to the water that the real whopper waves would soak me somewhat, and all the others just teased my toes. I didn't eat. I didn't sleep, much. I didn't even drink. I watched. I watched couples walking and children building sand castles and teenagers arguing over volleyball rules and a fat man swimming with flotation wings, which seemed sort of odd to me. More than that, though, I watched the things that mattered. I watched the waves, and the seagulls, and the clouds, and the sun rising and setting, and at night I watched the Big Dipper, and the man in the moon.

The only thing I missed, really, the only thing I might have changed, would have been to have Philly and Jeremy there with me. But then, maybe even that was the way it had to be. They needed this, too, sure, as badly as I did, but it wouldn't have been the same thing if we had come together. We would have cracked too many jokes, and drank, and fought too much for a time like this. If Philly went where he believed he would, it was probably a nicer ocean even than the one I was at. And Jeremy, well . . . he'd get here when he got here, I guess.

It wasn't that I didn't care anymore, about the guys, I mean, don't get me wrong. It was just that I wasn't fighting so hard anymore. The tide kept rising and falling, and every day the seagulls came out to play. Nothing was gonna stop that. Not kids arguing about volleyball, not a fat man with flotation wings, not a sixteen-year-old withdrawing from alcohol who hadn't moved in two days, not his sister who offed herself, not a *hundred* convenience store holdups. Life keeps moving. Hope keeps moving. You keep breathing.

After two days, I was ready to leave. Before I did, I took Mandy's diary out of my bag and gave it to the ocean, burying it as deep as I could in the sand on the shore. I was sure she would have wanted that, if she had been with me. Then I called Leslie and asked her to send me enough money to catch a bus back to Madison. She did.

52

Leslie held me while I shuddered and cried my way through my history. I hadn't said a word to her in hours. I hadn't even opened my eyes. For a long time now, I hadn't even moved. I wasn't sleeping, though, and neither was Leslie. We were together, in love and memories. Our skin was touching, in places. I breathed when she did. Her heart beat when mine did. We were alone. Billy had headed back to the car an hour or two ago to crash out for the night. Some night, though: the sky was already getting light.

And some day ahead of me. I knew this morning what I had to do with a certainty I had not had the night before. I couldn't keep running anymore. Even if it meant getting locked up, I needed to settle down. It was time to let everything catch up to me, to finally let myself feel the full weight of it, so I could quit dragging it around behind me. So that one day I could let it all go. I didn't tell all that to Leslie, though. I didn't have to. She knew me. She knew my story. Or enough of it, anyway. When I did speak, it was not much and not loudly. "I'm going to turn myself in today." I said the words into her neck, where my lips had been resting for a while. Not kissing, exactly. Just touching.

I heard Leslie suck in her breath sharply and hold it there for a moment. When she exhaled a moment later, though, her breath was gentle. She put her hands on my cheeks and turned my face upward so my eyes met hers. If she'd had any tears left she probably would have been crying. Instead, she almost smiled. "You want a ride?" she said.

I kissed her then, and she kissed back. I didn't have anything in mind; I just loved her. We were lying side by side on the earth, resting our heads on the thick, woven roots of an ancient tree, its trunk towering above us. The stream was at my back, running and trickling and splashing its way on by. I have never felt so safe and protected as I did in that forest, and maybe that's why we did what we did. It was August, and the sun was shining through the trees, and even naked, we were plenty warm. We both knew this was our last chance, and we didn't want to leave anything undone, any kiss unkissed. Any touch untouched.

"Is this your first time?" I asked, my voice trembling. Not because it made so much of a difference, really. I just wanted to know.

She shook her head no. "You?" she asked.

"No," I said. "It isn't."

Neither of us was angry. Sad, sure, but not angry. We both understood. We had gotten older. Things had changed. It was not our first time, and could not be. But we could do it this time, and mean it, and that would be something. That would be a lot.

When we were done we held each other a while longer, and then we washed ourselves off in the stream, and we dressed, and then we stood and said good-bye to the place where we'd been. And in doing so, we said good-bye to everywhere we had been. We said good-bye to *who* we had been, together and apart. I was going to jail, and there were a lot of good-byes to be said.

It was a good place to let go. At the ocean, I had been content. Here, for a time, with Leslie, I was happy.

"Ready?" Leslie asked.

"As I'll ever be," I said.

We walked back through the woods then, to where Billy was sleeping and the car was parked. As often as we could, we held hands.

We were still holding hands when I walked into the police station. We held hands until they ripped our hands apart and put mine in cuffs. Leslie put her arms around Billy then, trying to comfort him. She had promised me she'd take care of him, the way I had once promised my sister the same thing. I knew she would.

He was crying as the cops took me away, escorting me to a cell. Leslie and I weren't crying, though. We were remembering, and hoping.

EPILOGUE

Jeremy turned himself in the day after I did. I guess he was waiting for me. Leslie brought me a letter he had given her for me. It explained things, briefly. It explained why he had switched guns with Philly. He wanted me to testify that he had shot Charlie, and that Philly had only come in to try to stop him. He wanted us to tell things like they should have been, instead of how they were. He wanted me to lie in court.

I did.

They threw the book at Jeremy. He was the oldest of the three of us anyway, and according to our story he carried the most guilt. He got remanded to adult court, where they gave him ten years.

I was there when the judge told him he'd be tried as an adult. He wasn't upset. He looked relieved. And watching him, I wasn't surprised.

We were escorted out of the courtroom that day at the same time, side by side. I hadn't talked to him directly in seven months.

He looked almost good. So did I, I guess. Our mothers had gone shopping together and we were wearing matching suits. What pathetic beards we could grow had been carefully shaved that morning, and Jeremy had even cut his locks off. He could have been his own lawyer.

I whistled as I came up behind him.

He turned his head for just a moment, just long enough to see that it was me in his periphery, before facing straight ahead again. He did not meet my eye.

"I'll visit you," I said, meaning it.

"Don't," he said, meaning it.

I never have.